AN UNLIKELY PROMISE

Fox felt her arms around his shoulders and her fingers kneading his neck as if to spur him on, and she moaned in his arms. His body was on fire for her. He came up, gasping for air, her face so near to his that he could see the fine soft hair on her cheeks. Her eyes opened, languid and drugged with pleasure one moment, then sparkling with laughter the next. Her breaths were little puffs on his face.

"Extraordinary." He gave a wry laugh. His ears burnt. "I had meant our first kiss to be a little less wild."

"No." Her lips curved mischievously. "I liked it exactly as it was." Her eyes dropped to his mouth. "*Exactly* as it was..." She purred and ran her tongue over the seam of his lips.

Helpless, his fingers spasmed. He groaned, making her chuckle with delight.

"Witch."

Her expression sobered. "Yes." Once again, she rubbed her hand over his cheek. He wished she would shed her gloves. "You can't have thought..." Her eyes seemed to glow when she looked at him. "Fox, I *love* you. Nothing will make this love go away. Nothing."

Other books by Sandra Schwab:

CASTLE OF THE WOLF
THE LILY BRAND

Sandra Schwab

Bewitched

LOVE SPELL   NEW YORK CITY

To
all past and present members
of the Team Reitz—
I hope you'll enjoy your adventures
as bold knights and fair maidens!

LOVE SPELL®

April 2008

Published by

Dorchester Publishing Co., Inc.
200 Madison Avenue
New York, NY 10016

ISBN 10: 0-505-52723-5
ISBN 13: 978-0-505-52723-3

10 9 8 7 6 5 4 3 2 1

Visit us on the web at www.dorchesterpub.com.

AUTHOR'S NOTE

My recollections of my years as a student in Mainz are, for the most part, a comfortable blur. One of the memories that sticks out is a scene from my first seminar in English Lit: while we were discussing the effects of the industrialization in Britain in general and the invention of canals in particular, our professor demonstrated how to work a lock. We were, of course, suitably impressed. Back then I didn't yet know that I would one day work as a student assistant for this professor, and eventually as a lecturer for his chair. By now, I've been part of the "Team Reitz" for eight years (Our office parties are the envy of the rest of the department!).

Bernhard Reitz is one of the leading critics in the field of British theatre—though he is known to have reacted adversely to the suggestion to stage a performance of in-yer-face theatre (which usually includes a certain amount of violence, rape, exploding trash cans and the like) in his sitting room; he likes ships (both big and small, hence his knowledge about locks); he is intimately acquainted with the dangers of climbing about apple trees; and he always serves *Feuerzangenbowle* at our annual Christmas party at his house. He has, to my knowledge, never been embroiled in a magical intrigue—until now. His appearance in this novel is a belated present for his sixtieth birthday.

No doubt he will be happy to discover that I didn't neglect my academic research while writing *Bewitched*. The *Horrible Histories of Mayence* might be a fictional book, yet the direct quotations are all taken from an 1824 edition of *The Seven Champions of Christendom*.

Other parts of this novel have been influenced by the fantasy fiction I read during my teenage years: I first encountered the concept of the Great Marriage in Diana L. Paxon's *The White Raven*. I have, however, considerably changed it in order to suit my needs in *Bewitched*.

[Continues on next page]

The circle ritual my heroine performs in the second part of the novel is loosely based on a ritual described in Zsuzsanna E. Budapest's *The Holy Book of Women's Mysteries*; and my characters' many strolls through the park and gardens of Rawdon Park have been inspired by the wonderful BBC series *The Victorian Kitchen Garden* with Peter Thoday and the lovely Harry Dodson. Watching it, I learnt more about gardening than ever before in my life, and I am happy to report that plants no longer automatically wither and die when I come near them.

For my research of Albany I found Sheila Birkenhead's *Peace in Piccadilly* and Harry Furniss's *Paradise in Piccadilly* particularly useful—and yes, there really were water closets in the dressing rooms of Albany even back in the Regency era!

Last but not least, my thanks go to Edward Storey: his book *The Winter Fens* helped me to envision the vast skies and the flat landscape of the Fen District, and many of my descriptions of the land and the people who live there owe their existence to him. You will be pleased to find out, though, that I did not use the fried mice, even if in days past they were thought to be the best cure for whooping cough!

Bewitched

Prologue

A lazy breeze stirred the late-summer air and played with the leaves of the trees along the canal that bisected the meadows and fields. It tousled the mane of the horse trailing the heavy barge filled with Black Country coal and tickled the cheek of the boatman. The breeze blew on, over sheep-dotted green, over the ruins of a castle that had once belonged to a favorite of the Virgin Queen, over an old battlefield where Roundheads and Cavaliers had met long ago; on and on it blew until it whistled around the pointy spire of a small parish church. From there it followed the slow rise of the hills and teased the branches of a grove of elm trees in the valley beyond. Here the air was filled with the chirping of birds and the hum of wild bees. The grove opened into lawns of lush green and flowerbeds blazing with color. Amidst the gardens nestled a small, stout manor house in the honeyed tones of the local sandstone. Bulky chimneys stretched heavenwards, emitted a trickle of smoke. Nearby, a lark rose jubilantly into the clear blue sky, and the breeze ruffled the bird's feathers.

One of the chimneys twitched. The breeze died away. The birds fell silent. Even the hum of the insects stopped.

A shudder ran through the chimney. A sliver of cobalt blue appeared at its top. It stretched, widened, forked like lightning, sparked more spots of blue. These spanned the roof, ran down the gables; one reached a window in the upper story.

The back door slammed open, and Cook came running out, then her kitchen maids, shortly followed by the housekeeper, the upstairs maids, the footmen, and the butler. The last drew a handkerchief from his pocket and dabbed his forehead while he watched the blue spread.

Inexorably, cobalt covered the house.

Another door was flung open. Boots clattered on the front steps as a horde of boys and young men rushed out into the forecourt. The sunlight glinted on their curly black hair as they craned their necks to look in dismay at the increasingly blue walls.

"Uh-oh," the youngest said and put his thumb into his mouth.

"Darn it," the eldest swore and rubbed his neck.

A petite young woman was the last to leave the house. Her golden brows knitted, her rosebud mouth pursed, she stomped down the stairs. A smudge of dirt clung to one rounded cheek, and under her arm she carried an enormous leather-bound tome.

"How bad is it?" she asked, without turning around.

Wordless, her black-haired cousins stared back at her.

She sniffed. "That bad?" She risked a look over her shoulder. Her eyes widened, and she swung fully around. "Blast it all! How in blazes did *that* happen?"

"Well. It could've been worse, you know," one of the boys offered. "Just think what would've happened if Mother hadn't gone to visit Lady Grisham today!"

"Or if Father weren't out on his daily ride just now."

"Indeed, with some luck it'll have vanished before he returns home."

They all eyed the house. Blue ran down the walls like icing from the top of a cake.

"Mmmhm."

"Yes."

"Exactly."

"Just think what—"

Stone groaned.

They took a step back.

And another.

"What? What is it? Why doesn't it stop?" The young woman started to leaf hectically through the book she was carrying. "That's not what was supposed to happen!"

"Uh-oh," her youngest cousin mumbled around the thumb in his mouth and pointed toward the grove.

A lone rider had appeared between the elm trees. Just then, he caught sight of the blue house. Abruptly, he reined in his horse, stared, . . . and fell out of the saddle.

The young woman visibly paled. "Oh blast, I'm in *so* much trouble," she whispered.

The walls shivered. The glass in the windows rattled as the house raised itself from its fundaments and, swaying gently to-and-fro, came to stand on two giant chicken legs.

Chapter One

London, autumn 1820

"I am"—Andrew Fermont flopped down on an armchair in the smoking room, closed his eyes, and heaved a blissful sigh—"in *love*."

Cyril Jerningham, Lord Stafford, exchanged a glance with Sebastian "Fox" Stapleton and rolled his eyes. "You don't say?" He blew a puff of smoke into Drew's face. "So, do enlighten us: Who is this week's lucky lady?"

Unperturbed, Drew waved the smoke away and gave another, even more blissful sigh. "Miss Amelia Bourne," he breathed, in a tone that suggested he had beheld a divine apparition. "I swear, she has captured my heart—no, my very *soul*—forevermore."

Fox raised his brows. "How . . . dramatic."

A loony smile appeared on Drew's face. "She is exquisite." His hands sketched the outline of a female form in the air. "The epitome of beauty."

"Tell us something new." Cy yawned and looked around for a place to leave the remains of his cheroot. "It seems that at least half the male guests at this oh-so-wondrous ball have declared themselves in love with Miss Amelia Bourne."

"Oh no." Dismayed, Drew stared at his friends. "What about Munty? Has he said anything? Is Munty after her, too? Oh dear, oh dear, if Munty's after her, what with him being not just an earl, but also filthy rich . . ." He tore at his hair. "Whatever shall I *do*?"

Cy leaned forward to pat his shoulder. "Do not despair, my friend," he said kindly. "By the end of the week you'll have fallen out of love with her anyway. You always fall out of love with them by the end of a week."

"I know." Drew studied the ceiling. "But what is a man to do with so many bewitching young ladies about?"

Fox took a sip of his wine. "And their numbers increase with each year," he added wryly.

"Indeed. Ah well . . ." Drew straightened and abandoned his dramatics. "But still, Miss Bourne *is* exquisite." He reached over and took Fox's glass. "Have you danced with her?" He regarded his friends over the rim of the glass while he took a deep gulp of the wine.

"Pansy-eyed, blond little chit, reaches up to about here?" Cyril indicated a spot in the middle of his chest. "Yes, I have." He shrugged. "A bit disconcerting, if you ask me, such a little bit. Makes you wonder how . . ." He frowned. "If . . . you know."

Drew grimaced in distaste. "Heavens, Cy, don't be vulgar! At least not while Miss Bourne still holds my heart."

"Soul," Fox corrected. "Give me my wine back."

"Did I say soul?"

"You did." He held out his hand. "My wine."

Drew drank the rest of the wine and handed the glass back. "I guess I must have. How many times did Munty dance with her? Did he say?"

Mournfully, Fox regarded his empty glass. "If you weren't my friend, I'd have to call you out now."

Cyril snorted and answered the question. "Twice."

"Two dances? Goodness!" Drew slumped back in the chair. "I am devastated! I had only *one*!"

"Serves you right. You drank my wine," Fox muttered darkly.

Drew gave his friend an exasperated look. "Ahh, damn it,

Foxy, do stop that annoying whinging and let me suffer in peace, will you?"

Fox looked up. His eyes narrowed. "I am"—he rudely poked his finger into the other's chest—"so going to break your heart, sir."

Drew batted his hand away. "Piffle."

Fox arched his brow. Leaning forward, he let his lips twist into an evil smile. "I am—"

"Ye-s-s-s?"

"Going to dance the *waltz* with your dear Miss Amelia Bourne."

"Indeed!" Grinning, Drew waved the threat aside. "I'm sure you won't. She's a debutante. As fresh as newly fallen snow. No way you'll get her to dance the waltz."

Fox showed him two rows of pearly white teeth. "Oh, I will." He waggled his eyebrows.

Cy clucked his tongue. "Children, children . . ."

Leaning his elbow onto the table, Drew put his chin on his hand and smiled. "No. You. Won't."

Fox stretched lazily, like a great cat before it goes on the prowl, and rose from his chair. "Oh yes, I will. And you will be so heartbroken."

"No, no."

Cyril rolled his eyes. "Lawk. *Infants*!"

Fox shot them a grin before, softly whistling, he strolled toward the ballroom.

"Puh." Clutching her glass of lemonade like a deadly weapon, Amy flopped down on a chair at the edge of the dance floor, where the gossiping matrons and unfortunate wallflowers had gathered.

Being a wallflower sounded awfully good at the moment. She grimaced and wriggled her aching toes. Every blasted man younger than seventy at this blasted ball had wanted to dance with her at least once. They had given her foolish smiles, had talked to her in avuncular tones while leering at her bosom, and—to make matters worse—some of them had actually stepped on her toes. One hundred and eighty pounds of solid male stepping on one's toes while they were sheathed in only the lightest satin slipper could by no means be regarded as amusing.

Amy took a sip of her lemonade and warily eyed the crowd. Egad! She gulped. There he was again! That horrid Lord Munthorpe. Who had talked about nothing but his family's sheep breeding in Scotland. Woolly baa-sheep. Ack!

Amy looked this way and that, and finally spied a giant potted plant in the corner. Hastily she stood and prepared for a strategic retreat, just when the orchestra struck the first notes of a new dance.

A waltz.

Her shoulders slumped with relief. Thank heavens! Immediately her mood brightened. She had, after all, not yet been given permission to dance the waltz. Even Munthorpe, the dolt, would know that! Smiling, she took another sip of her lemonade and watched how the dancers got in line. Another few beats—Amy's foot tapped the three-four rhythm—and then the couples started: a lovely whirling of colorful dresses around dark male evening clothes.

She leaned her shoulder against the wall.

The waltz certainly made for a beautiful sight.

"Miss Bourne."

She looked around. And up.

Mr. Stapleton, the man generally known as Fox, smiled down at her from his lofty height. His blue-gray eyes were crinkled at the corners, and the candlelight created fiery little sparks in his red hair. Well, "Fox" would probably be considered a more flattering name than "Carrot," she supposed. Or "Fish." For he was as cold as a fish, this one.

She gave him a bland smile. "Mr. Stapleton."

He bowed. "Would you do me the honor of another dance, Miss Bourne?" He held out his hand.

She looked first at his hand, then at his face. "This is a waltz."

He arched his carroty brows. "Indeed?"

Mindful that it wouldn't do to decline an invitation to dance, Amy held up her glass. "I still have my lemonade."

His brows shot up even higher. "Have you?" Then he simply took the glass from her hand and put it onto the windowsill. "And now?" he asked politely.

He had, Amy discovered, a sprinkle of freckles on his nose. She clasped her hands behind her back. "Sir—"

His eyes twinkling devilishly, he leaned forward and whispered, "You are not afraid, are you?"

She opened her mouth. "My . . ." Amy frowned. How to describe Mrs. Bentham? Not guardian, not chaperone—what then? "I haven't been given permission to—"

"Oh." He sighed. "So you *are* afraid." He drew back to regard her earnestly and, she thought, somewhat pityingly. "What an utter shame. I would have thought . . . I had suspected you—rather falsely, it now seems—in possession of some courage."

Amy narrowed her eyes at him. At her sides, her hands curled into fists. The oaf! He accused her of being a *coward*? This was surely too much! After an evening spent in the company of abhorrent people, she would not suffer such ludicrous accusations.

Mr. Carrot Stapleton turned as if ready to stride away.

Amy reached out and put her hand on his elbow. "Sir?"

He turned, eyed the hand on his arm—granted, the hand looked rather small there—before he slowly raised his gaze to meet hers. "Yes, Miss Bourne?"

She gave him a sweet smile. She would show him! Lacking in courage? Ha! "I believe this is your dance."

"Is it? Is it indeed?" He put his hand over hers and gently squeezed her fingers. Somehow his thumb came to rest on the small spot of skin above the button of her glove. His blue-gray eyes seemed to burn into hers as he drew a tiny circle with his thumb. A hot tingle shot up her arm. It was an effort to meet his gaze calmly.

"Your dance, Mr. Stapleton. Or do you prefer to just stand around until it is over?"

Abruptly, the gentle pressure on her fingers ceased. "Not at all, Miss Bourne." He winked at her. "After all, I wouldn't want to bore you. Shall we?"

And with that, he drew her onto the dance floor. His expert eye regarded the whirling couples, and when a gap opened, his arm came around her shoulders, his hand clasped hers, and with a quickness that made Amy gasp, they joined the dance.

There was, Amy quickly discovered, a subtle difference between dancing the waltz with one of her lanky cousins and dancing with a nicely built stranger. When she had danced with Coll, for example, she had never noticed how hard the hand was that held hers, or how strong the arm was that curved around her shoulder, or how gracefully his body moved with the music. And she most certainly had never noticed a tiny freckle, like a speck of cinnamon dust, on Coll's earlobe.

Entranced, she stared at that tiny spot of skin, while Mr. Stapleton whirled her around in three-four time.

She saw how the muscles of his neck moved just before she heard his voice above her. "So, do you find the waltz as scandalous as you've suspected?"

She looked up and found his eyes twinkling down at her, which seemed at odds with his coolly polite voice. Oddly, she found his dusting of freckles greatly destroyed his aloof facade. For how could you consider somebody a cold fish when his face was full of endearing little cinnamon spots? Thus, despite herself, her lips curved into a mischievous smile. "I daresay this might not be quite as scandalous as waltzing in a damp shift."

His eyes darkened until they were the color of the stormy sea. His arm around her shoulders tightened, and he subtly drew her closer to his body. For a moment he turned her without answering.

"Miss Bourne, I think I owe you an apology," he finally said, very quietly.

"Indeed, Mr. Stapleton?"

"Indeed, Miss Bourne." His hand on her back shifted; instead of just touching her with its side, he now held her with his flat palm, his fingers splayed wide. Her stomach fluttered, and her face felt hot.

He lowered his head toward her. "You are a woman of exceptional courage."

She blinked. A woman of exceptional courage? Her eyes widened and the flutters died. Because of a *waltz?*

She just about managed to turn her guffaw into a cough. Hastily, she turned her head to the side and, screening the lower part of her face with her free hand, she indulged in a series of little coughs. Finally, her merriment had sufficiently subsided to allow her to murmur a faint, "Pardon me." When she risked a look at Mr. Stapleton, she saw that his eyes had narrowed in suspicion as if he knew she had been covering up a fit of giggles. *Oh dear.*

"I hope you are not feeling unwell," he asked stiffly.

"Oh no. *No,*" Amy hurried to say. "After all, there is no traipsing around lonely hills after *belles dames sans merci* to be had in London, is there?"

Yet no spark of humor or even recognition lit his eyes. Instead, the look he threw her now suggested he assumed she had taken complete leave of her senses.

Uh-oh. A cold fish and a dolt!

"You don't like Keats?"

At the sound of the hapless poet's name, a grimace of distaste flickered over Mr. Stapleton's freckled face. Underneath her fingertips she could feel how his muscles stiffened.

"No 'O what can ail thee, wretched wight'?" she prodded.

His lips thinned. "Mr. Keats's poetry is too . . . *fanciful* for my liking."

Heavens! He made it sound as if it were something terribly improper! "Fanciful?" Amy echoed. Quite suddenly she was gripped by the urge to needle him and crack his slick, formal shell. "Ah, so fairy maidens and their dark enchantments are not for you?"

With a snort, he gripped her hand a little tighter and maneuvered them past another dancing couple. "My dear Miss Bourne," Mr. Stapleton said, and managed to sound like a stern tutor lecturing a riotous child. "You ought to know that fairies and magic and other such ludicrous things are nothing but figments of the imagination. The products of some poor fellow's overheated mind. It does not do for the improvement of rational thought to indulge in such flights of fancy."

Amy bit her lip. "Ah," she said. Her stomach muscles quivered with the strain of holding in her laughter.

"Indeed." Again, Mr. Carrothead gave a sage nod. "Such drivel should never be published. For who knows? It might even prove dangerous to the impressionable minds of young ladies!"

Did he really believe in the nonsense he sprouted?

This time, Amy couldn't help herself; she burst out laughing. If only he knew!

Across the ballroom, Miss Isabella Bentham's fan flicked open and fluttered agitatedly, thus screening the lower half of her face. Her eyes cast daggers at the scene enfolding on the dance floor. "The nerve!" Color came and went in her face. Should all her chances be ruined by that stupid chit? Wasn't it enough that all men sighed over Amy like a herd of dimwitted mooncalves? No, now she was even cantering around the room, dancing the waltz of all things! Apparently, the country bumpkin had never heard of modest reserve. Even worse: such behavior could only reflect poorly on Isabella. Whatever had her father been thinking to invite that girl into their home? Who cared whether she was the niece of an old friend or not!

Isabella's fan swished shut and she strode across the room to where her mother stood chatting with Lady Westerley. "Mama!" she hissed. "Look at that, over there."

"Whatever is the matter with you?" Mrs. Bentham turned—and stared. Her hand flew up to cover the base of her throat. She gasped. But then her face darkened dramatically, seemed to turn inward, shrinking into a mask of anger. "Your father must hear of this!"

In the refreshments room, Mr. Bentham poured himself another glass of punch. "Just another dram to warm these old bones," he murmured. Surreptitiously, he tugged at his cravat. These horrid tight knots!

Muttering, he shook his head and took a sip from his punch, and didn't notice the gentleman stepping up to him.

"Mr. Bentham. Good evening."

Caught by surprise, Bentham choked. Spluttering and coughing, he put his punch glass back on the table. Out of breath and patience, he narrowed his eyes at the stranger, a tall, smiling youth, exquisitely groomed. Why, the polished buttons of his coat shone like small suns. "Do I know you, sir?"

The man's smile deepened as he reached for a cup with slender, long fingers and poured himself a cup of tea. The smoky aroma of bergamot wafted up. A splash of lemon drew pale streaks in the reddish brown liquid. The man meticulously stirred, his small, silver spoon clinking against the china.

Bentham's furry brows met over his eyes in displeasure. He cleared his throat. "Sir?"

Unperturbed, the younger man raised the teacup to his lips.

"What—"

"We've got a mutual friend," the stranger said.

"A mutual—"

The young face turned toward him, a hint of cruelty visible in the twist of the lips. "Lady Margaret," he said. He

happen to have an unmarried daughter—if you catch my drift."

Bentham's mouth opened. "The . . . the . . . I . . ." Isabella? He was to sacrifice his only daughter?

The younger man turned his head a little and caught the expression on Bentham's face, and he laughed—a slick, smooth sound. "Ah, never fear. Your daughter, your *real* daughter, is quite safe. For by chance, haven't you happened to gain the responsibility for a young ward?" He cocked his head to the side, wordlessly inviting Bentham to follow his gaze, to look at the dancers.

Bentham's eyes widened.

"A most happy coincidence, don't you think?" the stranger asked softly. "Bourne's little brat. Pair her off with him. You will be given some . . . assistance."

"Assistance?" Bentham echoed. Yet when he turned, the stranger had already disappeared.

"She did *what*?" Drew burst out laughing. He fell sideways and rolled onto his back on the black leather seat of the carriage. One foot braced against the door, he crossed his hands behind his head and threw his friends a smug look. "Serves you right for attempting to break my heart."

They had left the ball and were now headed to other entertainment.

Fox rolled his eyes. "*Soul*," he corrected in a mutter.

Cy frowned. "I'll tell you which part of you's going to be broken: your neck, if you continue lazing around like this."

"Did I say 'soul'?"

Fox's eyebrow arched. "You did."

"Fiddle-faddle." Airly, Drew waved a hand. "You said you were going to break my heart. Don't you think a man would remember a threat like that?"

"Or," Cy continued with a sigh, "you might just bump your head and addle your brains."

Fox leaned close. "His brains are *already* addled," he disclosed to his friend in a stage whisper.

"Ha!" Drew struggled upright and pointed a finger at him. "Whom did Miss Bourne laugh at, hmm? You or me?" His smirk flashed a dimple in his cheek.

Fox couldn't help himself: He grinned. He had always found Drew's chubby cheeks highly amusing, given that the rest of the man most definitely did not incline toward chubbiness. Yet, with his curly blond hair and puppylike brown eyes, Drew generally resembled an oversized cherub.

"Touché." Still grinning, Fox raised both hands.

"Got you there, didn't I?" Drew's nose wrinkled. Looking like a big, fat tomcat that had just devoured a particularly tasty mouse, he tapped his fingernail against his teeth. "But did you not find her delectable?" A dreamy look came over his face. "A face like a French porcelain doll . . ."

"With a body as plump as a peach," Cy provided helpfully.

"Ah, no, Cy!" Drew grimaced. "That's crude."

"Don't tell me you didn't notice her body!" His friend shook his head.

Drew adopted a pious expression. "In matters of the heart, my dear Lord Stafford, a man tends to concentrate on the . . . um . . . *inner* values."

Fox and Cyril exchanged a glance before both burst out laughing. "Dear God, Drew!" Cy managed to gasp after a while. He wiped his eyes, which had overflowed with merriment. "These *tendres* of yours always turn you into a raving lunatic!"

"Quite true." Fox agreed with a chuckle. "You spout the most nonsensical notions that would do any March hare proud. Why, it puts a man quite off developing a *tendre* himself."

Drew cocked his head to the side. "Foxy, Foxy, Foxy." With an expression of utter sadness he shook his head. "Don't tell me the charms of Miss Bourne left you cool as a cucumber. This would be most shocking indeed!"

"Ah, Drew, you know how Fox is." Cy heaved a dramatic sigh. "While at Eton we all wallowed in calf love. Not even sweet Nettie at the baker's could wrench a sigh from the depths of Mr. Stapleton's chest."

A little self-consciously, Fox shrugged. "The little blonde? You know I prefer women of a more Italian hue." Though he never dabbled in matters of the heart. For those, he had on good authority, could bring a man to ruin in no time at all. He shrugged again, to dislodge the uneasiness which gripped him: the tickle of ice down his spine, the tightening of his guts.

The bland smile he gave his friends proved a bit difficult to fabricate.

They were silent for the moment, and the sounds of London intruded into the cozy space inside the Stafford carriage. A city like London never slept—not even in the darkest hours of the night when the Wild Hunt was said to haunt the land.

Not that such a thing as the Wild Hunt had ever existed, of course. It was nothing but an old wives' tale, the remains of a pagan past when Britain had been caught fast in the clutches of superstition. Luckily, science and progress had erased all such fancies and replaced them with rational thought. Yes, rational thought. It was something in which Fox believed above all else. Always had. Not for him the fanciful notion of love ever after.

He rolled his shoulders in an attempt to shake off his irrational worries once and for all. For what was there to feel uneasy about? After having witnessed what had happened to his brother, had he not sworn never to shackle himself to any woman, be it in love or—heaven forbid!—holy matrimony? Not that his friends would understand his rationale; certainly not Drew of the thousand *tendres*.

Besides, if Fox ever married, he would have to divulge the crude facts about his birth to his wife. How distasteful would that be? Certainly nothing he wanted to contemplate! There might be other men who were born in similar circumstances and who didn't seem to care a fig whether the world at large knew about it or not. Fox, by contrast, would never willingly consider making himself vulnerable to society gossip.

Cyril cleared his throat. "Ah well." He clapped Fox's shoulder. "There you've got your explanation, Drew, why our friend here wasn't as smitten with Miss Bourne as you were. Now, then . . ." He rubbed his hands. "All this talk about women and peaches is enough to make any man lusty, don't you think?"

Glad for the change of topic, Fox stretched his limbs and yawned. "Absolutely." While he might consider matters of the heart, and indeed marriage itself, a waste of time, matters of the flesh were an altogether different cup of tea. "What do you suggest?"

"Well . . ." Cy looked from one man to the other. "It all depends on whether you are in the mood for some sweet talking, or just some jaunty rut, doesn't it?" He looked at them inquiringly.

Fox glanced at Drew. "A jaunty rut," they said unison, and grinned.

"For of sweet talking," Drew pointed out, "today we most definitely have had enough."

"All right, then." Cy raised his walking stick to rasp against the front partition of the carriage. "In this case I'd suggest Madame Suzette's. Any objections, gentlemen?"

There were none.

Chapter Two

The next day, London woke to the news that a young gentleman named Henry Boothby had committed suicide. "His Braynes were Spleweth over the Walls of his Appartement," one newspaper put it, with a regrettable lack of delicacy and an even more regrettable grasp of orthography. Before he murdered himself, young Mr. Boothby had apparently written a note—printed in whole by the newspaper, of course—saying he could no longer endure the ennui of buttoning and unbuttoning. Sadly, even in death he had to follow the dictates of the fashionable world and sprinkle his sentences with French terms.

Turning the page, Amy grimaced and started nibbling on another biscuit while she digested other horrors London had to offer.

In the meantime, Mrs. Bentham's kitchen maid laid out to the cook her plan on how to stake a slug. "I lets it crawl over me skin 'ere. Look." She waved her hand in front of Mrs. Hodges's face. "'Ere. And then all I needs ta do's stick the slug onna thorn. And as soon as the slug's dead, the wart'll be gone!" she ended triumphantly.

"Now, now, girl, don't excite yourself thus," Mrs. Hodges growled. "Get on with peeling the potatoes instead."

"But Mrs. Hodges!" Ethel wailed.

"Sticking a wee beastie onto a thorn..." The cook

shook her head in agitation. Frills of gray hair escaped from under her enormous white bonnet.

Amy put her elbow onto the table and rested her chin on her hand. Dear heavens, the whole of London seemed a madhouse! Who would have thought it? She turned her attention to the servants. "And if you just let it crawl over your wart and don't stick it onto a thorn afterwards?" she suggested to the kitchen maid. "It seems to me that it might be just the slug slime that—"

"Oh, but Miss Amy, that's not how the charm works!" Ethel protested. "Ya needs t' let it crawl o'er your skin and then stick it onna thorn, and when the slug's dead the wart'll be gone."

The charm. Amy suppressed a sigh. Growing up in the country, she knew a lot about charms: a Shepherd's Crown placed on a window ledge outside would keep the devil away; the possession of a Fairy Loaf would ensure bread in plenty; a Hag Stone suspended at the entrance door would keep witches away; carrying a horse chestnut would work against rheumatism; and carrying around the forefeet of a mole, cut from the poor animal while still alive, would forever free their bearer from toothache.

Amy snorted. These were not magic. Not *real* magic.

Real magic made getting rid of warts easy. After all, they were just misbehaving bits of flesh. All you had to do was to persuade the warts to, well, drop off. That would leave a tiny scar, of course, but you couldn't just take things away from a body and not expect any consequences. Still, this was most certainly better than tormenting a hapless animal. For real magic you didn't need dried bat wings or glibbery toad eyes or things like that. Instead, it was all a matter of skills and talent. And concentration.

Of course, there was that accident with the portraits and, even worse, the accident with the frog. But that had been years ago, and Coll had been just thirteen and believed he could transform the frog into a prince. After all, you always heard about how it was done the other way around, didn't you? Amy's nine-year-old self had found it endlessly entertaining to wade through the ponds on the estate with her horde of cousins hunting frogs. However, the entertainment value of the experiment had rapidly sunk when they later were all covered with sticky blobs of frog remains. Transforming a frog into a prince had turned out to be slightly more complicated than they thought.

"You know, you really shouldn't be here, Miss Amy." Mrs. Hodges checked on the soup that was boiling over on the fire. She turned and pointed her ladle at Amy. "What if the mistress finds out about it?"

Amy clasped her hands in her lap and aimed for an innocent expression. "Does Mrs. Bentham ever venture downstairs, Mrs. Hodges?"

"Well, of course not."

"See?" Amy gave the cook a winning smile. "And I just can't help finding your kitchen so very cozy." Also, this was the only place in the house where a person could escape Isabella tormenting the fortepiano.

"But where shall I find a slug?" Ethel spoke up in a wail.

The poor slug. With real magic it could have been spared its slow and painful death; yet after the Blue Incident, Amy's uncle had put a spell on her that would prevent her from mouthing any sort of spell or making contact with her family in any way for the foreseeable future. Instead of weaving spells or being led astray by her cousins, she'd been packed off to London to search for a husband. And that was that.

Amy sighed.

All because of one regrettable slip of concentration, or rather miscalculation. Could it be helped that she enjoyed testing the scope of her magical talents and putting together new spells? The one that should have turned her room at Three Elms cobalt blue had been an ingenious idea if anybody asked her. And exciting, a cost-effective way of redecoration. By mere accident the spell had gotten slightly out of hand. *Careless*, Uncle Bourne had called it. Or rather, he had shouted. But really, her spell had done no serious harm; neither had any strangers seen the blue manor house, nor had the effect proved to be long-lasting. By the next morning all traces of blue had already vanished.

She pursed her lips.

The vexing thing was that even without the Blue Incident it would have been only a matter of time before she would have been sent off to some fashionable town or other to find a suitable husband. After all, she was of marriageable age, and she well knew it did not do to lose time over such important things as the husband hunt, otherwise one would be considered firmly on the shelf before too long.

"And I really wouldn't want to spend the rest of my life as a hedge witch in a quaint cottage at the edge of a good, old English village and be called Nanny Something-or-Other," Amy muttered to herself. Even though the slug population would have rejoiced over their escape from a horrid death.

She heaved another sigh.

Sometimes she wished she had been born a man: then she could have taken a respectable profession and would have neither had to trouble herself with problems of matrimony nor with keeping her magic secret from a doltish husband. Furthermore, she wouldn't have needed to grant this same doltish husband any liberties with her body, just to secure herself a place in society. To imagine that Mr. Polidori's hero let the horrid Lord Ruthven marry his sister just so the girl wouldn't face social ruin! Thus, what the poor thing faced instead was being sucked dry by a vampyre. Marvelous.

Making a face, Amy reached for a biscuit.

Sometimes, a quaint cottage sounded awfully appealing. Even if it came complete with an ill-tempered, scarred tomcat!

That afternoon, when Isabella's torment of the fortepiano had ceased and Amy had slipped back upstairs so her absence wouldn't be noted, the young ladies in the Bentham household received a call. From Lord Munthorpe, no less!

The beaming Mrs. Bentham sat enthroned in an armchair, while Amy and Isabella shared one of the butter-colored settees. The other was occupied by Lord Munthorpe. Isabella poured tea and the Scottish earl told them all about the sheep that merrily bounced about his lands up north. "We also have Scottish Blackfaces, of course."

"Blackfaces?" Amy took a sip of thin tea.

Lord Munthorpe beamed at her. "On account of them having black faces, Miss Bourne."

"Ah."

Isabella trilled a laugh. "I am astonished you don't know these things, my dear Amelia." She shot Amy a look that was supposedly full of honeyed sweetness. "After all, you must have lived in the country all your life, isn't that so?" The way she pronounced "country" made it sound like a contagious disease. Which, Amy thought, was a bit daft considering she wanted to impress Lord Munthorpe so badly.

"Yes, it is quite true," Mrs. Bentham chirped in, using what she probably thought a sympathetic voice. "Poor Amelia has whiled away her days in the depths of the country and has unfortunately not been blessed with a suitable Town education. I have found, my lord, that it is only in London that one finds the best tutors, drawing masters, and music masters. Don't you think so?"

"Er . . ." After a moment of perplexed contemplation, Lord Munthorpe made a dive for a plate of sandwiches. "I can't really say," he mumbled apologetically.

Mrs. Bentham nodded sagely just as there was a knock on the door. It was flung open with flourish, and the butler announced, "Mr. Fermont."

Amy vaguely remembered the man who entered the room from last night. With his curly blond hair and soulful brown eyes, he reminded her of an overlarge puppy dog.

Daylight did not dim this—if anything, it even strengthened this first impression.

"Mr. Fermont, what a lovely surprise!" Mrs. Bentham enthused in syrupy tones.

"Mrs. Bentham." The man inclined his head. "Miss Bentham. And"—he turned toward Amy, his face lighting up to compete with the autumn sun outside—"Miss Bourne. Enchanted." A dimple appeared in his cheek and he bowed to her. Then his gaze fell on the other gentleman who currently occupied the Benthams' drawing room. "Munthorpe." The smile dimmed; the dimple disappeared.

"Fermont."

The men eyed each other with similar expressions of glowering suspicion.

"Won't you take a seat, Mr. Fermont?" From her armchair throne, Mrs. Bentham gave him a kind smile. Or it would have been a kind smile if her eyes hadn't glittered like a mad ferret's—a mad ferret about to strike and drag its prey off to the wedding altar.

Amy allowed herself a momentary lapse to roll her eyes. Mrs. Bentham, she had garnered very quickly after her arrival in London, was hell-bent on securing a betrothal for her daughter before even Christmas, before the new year would begin and see Isabella turn twenty-five—almost an old maid. Thus, while Mr. Bentham had welcomed her as the niece of an old and dear friend, his wife and daughter had regarded her as very *un*welcome competition from the first. Hence their desperate efforts to belittle Amy in the eyes of eligible young men who were supposed to vie for Isabella's attention.

Mr. Fermont gingerly sat down on the settee next to Lord Munthorpe, but made sure to keep as much distance between them as possible. The harmless puppy dog all at once looked sullen and ready to bite off the good earl's nose.

Folding her hands in her lap, Amy twiddled her thumbs. Indeed, it seemed to her that all of London was filled with the strangest people. She had found it amusing at first, she had to admit. Amusing and exciting. The smells and sounds of the big city, the endless clatter of hooves out in the streets, walking through Hyde Park in the afternoon, when fashionable gentlemen and ladies bloomed there like exotic flowers. She had enjoyed the shopping tours, too. Indeed, she had been awed by the amount on display, so much more than could be found in Mr. Clarke's general store or at Miss Lettie's millinery and haberdashery back at home. Yes, she had it found all very exciting. But now, after nearly three weeks of hustle and bustle, she longed for the quietude of her uncle's library, craved burying her nose in his old books once more. And she would very much have liked to figure out why her last experiment had turned into the Blue Incident. But most of all she yearned for behaving like herself again and not being forced to act like a twittering dimwit just so she wouldn't frighten the gentlemen witless by any display of female intellect.

". . . just talked about the superiority of a Town education," Isabella warbled. "And we all agreed—didn't we, my lord—that the best tutors are to be had here in London."

"Ah." Mr. Fermont shifted on the settee and threw a quick look at Lord Munthorpe. The earl mumbled something and hastened to stuff the rest of his sandwich into his mouth. Fermont looked down at his own cup of tea, which a footman had brought in. He cleared his throat. "Tutors," he said, and raised his gaze back to Isabella. "For drawing, and dancing, and . . . and music . . ." His lips lifted a little in a somewhat desperate smile, but no dimple showed.

"Indeed." Isabella nodded.

Mrs. Bentham's frilly cap bobbed with pleasure. "And for French and needlework too, of course. With dear Isabella we were lucky enough to get a French governess. Now she speaks the language like a native and I swear, her stitches are the tiniest in all of London." She beamed at the two gentlemen, who appeared suitably impressed by such accomplishments.

Demurely, Isabella bowed her head. "Oh, Mother," she murmured in a pretense of protest. "Surely such praise is too much . . ."

"Surely *not*!" Mrs. Bentham insisted, and looked at the gentlemen on her settee as if giving them their cue.

"Ah," they said, almost in unison.

Just barely, Amy resisted the urge to slap her hands onto her face and groan. She wondered whether her uncle had thought up all of this as a rather devious punishment, magicking her into a third-rate farce instead of sending her to London proper.

A little frantically, Mr. Fermont's eyes swiveled to her. "And you, Miss Bourne? Do you paint and sing and dance? Well, obviously, I already know you can dance, but—"

"Amelia?" Mrs. Bentham cut in, her voice much less syrupy than before. "I am afraid the poor dear grew up in the most shocking wilderness, as I have already told Lord Munthorpe. It is rather sad, Mr. Fermont."

The tops of his ears turned a glowing pink. "Is that so? Oh, well . . . I didn't know . . ." His voice trailed away; he shot a helpless gaze at Lord Munthorpe, who reached for another sandwich.

Amy frowned. All right, so she had been sent in exile to London, was not allowed to speak any spells or to communicate with her cousins in any way, and was obliged to pretend she didn't know left from right, but she would be damned before she sat another minute listening quietly to Mrs. Bentham's veiled slights. She forced her lips to lift in a cheerful smile. "Actually, I grew up in the Midlands—not quite an absolute wilderness, I should say."

Mrs. Bentham's eyes narrowed a fraction. "A nest of disquiet and riot. Very shocking, if you ask me. Don't you think so too, my lord, Mr. Fermont?" The latter opened his mouth, yet was interrupted. "Of course," Mrs. Bentham continued, "I expect it is quite natural for a young girl to be attached to her home, wherever that is." She leaned slightly foward, which apparently worried Lord Munthorpe so much he grabbed yet another sandwich in defense. "But imagine our shock when we found out that the poor dear couldn't even paint a vase of flowers!"

"Er . . ." Mr. Fermont looked from Mrs. Bentham to Amy.

A third-rate farce indeed! Amy wondered how she was ever supposed to find a husband when Mrs. Bentham was so fond of listing her deficiencies to every man in the vicinity. "Yes, fruit bowls are quite beyond me, too," she muttered darkly.

"Our Amelia doesn't even find enjoyment in the fortepiano," Isabella fluted.

By now, the whole of Mr. Fermont's ears glowed rosily. "Er . . . don't you?"

Amy gave him a bland smile. "No." For how could she learn when Matthew was almost always glued to the keys and the fortepiano had the unfortunate habit of snapping at everybody else—one of Mattie's charming little tricks to ensure nobody would touch his beloved instrument. And her uncle had never found out, because all those years ago the music master had left the house in such a hurry and with squashed fingers, and had never been seen or heard from again.

Mrs. Bentham nodded sagely. "Yes, it is quite sad," she confided to the gentlemen. "But of course we will do our utmost to help little Amy brave the foreign seas of genteel society."

"Very laudable indeed," Lord Munthorpe mumbled, and gazed forlornly at the empty sandwich plate. "I . . . er . . . must go, I'm afraid. I . . . um . . ."

"But I hope you will you come to Lady Worthington's musicale on Friday night, my lord?" Mrs. Bentham pierced him with a look.

"Er . . . I . . . um . . ."

"Oh, you must come, my lord." Isabella clapped her

hands. "It will be the musical entertainment of the month, I am sure. You cannot want to miss that." She batted her lashes at him.

"Er . . ." He turned this way and that, but did not find much help in Mr. Fermont, who just stared at him glumly. "Well, I say . . . perhaps I should—"

"How very good of you, my lord." Mrs. Bentham beamed her approval. "I am certain it would give my daughter great pleasure to discuss the music with you."

Amy wrinkled her nose. No, this was not a third-rate farce. It was a fourth- or fifth-rate one: Grandchildren-Craving Woman Throws Daughter at Hapless Rich Nobleman.

"Er . . ."

"So, this is settled then. And you, Mr. Fermont?" Mrs. Bentham turned on her second unfortunate victim. "I hope we will see you there, too."

"I . . ." Mr. Fermont glanced at Amy, and something like pain flickered across his face. "I . . . well . . ."

"Oh, but you *must* come." Mrs. Bentham watched him intently. "Perhaps you could help to explain the music to our dear Amelia." After all, he wasn't an earl with land and sheep in abundance. *These* were plainly reserved for Isabella alone.

"I . . ."

"I absolutely insist, Mr. Fermont. Shouldn't we all help Amelia to settle into the genteel world?"

Mr. Fermont threw Amy another desperate look. Finally, he bowed his head. "Quite so, madam," the gentle swain said, resigning himself to his utterly ghastly fate. Amy nearly snorted, finding his lack of enthusiasm far from flattering.

Mrs. Bentham, though, had no such reservations. "How delightful!" she exclaimed. "And will your friends come, too?"

"My friends?" He raised his head. His blond eyebrows drew together in puzzlement. "They . . . Probably."

"Good, then." With a strange smile, Mrs. Bentham leaned back in her chair. Perhaps Amy would have noticed the peculiarity of it had she not been secretly amused by the two visitors, who both used the momentary pause for a hasty retreat. Characters in a fifth-rate farce indeed!

Two days later, Fox was just penning a letter to his nephew, Baron Bradenell, age nine, when there was a knock at the front door. Frowning, he glanced at the clock on the sideboard. Not yet ten in the morning: Whoever would want to call on him at such an unholy hour? Irritated, he rubbed his forehead. "Hobbes!"

"C-Coming, thur," came the lisping reply from the entryway of his apartment.

"The door!"

"Thur?" Hobbes shuffled into the study-cum-library. The trusty valet, his cheeks hollow, his tufty hair carefully combed across his balding head, looked as if he had been born at the dawn of the last century. The breath rattled in his chest, giving the impression he was about to perish on the spot. Fox had inherited him from his father—his real father—and had repeatedly tried to send Hobbes into retirement ever since. Yet whenever the subject was brought up, the old man would look at him like a wounded doe, and Fox just couldn't bring himself to settle a pension on Hobbes and send him packing.

At moments like these, though, the prospect was tempting. "The *door*!"

Hobbes blinked. "Sh-shall I shut it, thur?"

The knocks at the front door took on a frantic quality. Soon, the whole floor would be awake.

Fox stood. "Never mind." He sighed. "I'll get it myself." He pushed past the bewildered valet and stomped through the small entrance hall. Wrenching the door open, he snarled, "What?"

"Oh God, Foxy, I'm in such a jam!" A rumpled, bleary-eyed Drew swept inside, bringing with him the smell of cold smoke and a much-too-long night. "You've got to help me! Good day, Hobbes."

"M-Mithter Fermont."

Once again, Fox marveled how his valet could radiate disapproval even though his expression never changed. With a hand on Drew's shoulder, Fox steered his friend toward the study. "We'll need a pot of coffee, Hobbes. *Strong* coffee."

"Yeth, I quite underthtand, thur." And the old man was on the way to the kitchens downstairs.

With a moan, Drew sank down on one of the leather armchairs. "I thought about it the whole night," he said bleakly. "The *whole* blasted night . . ."

Leaning against the edge of his desk, Fox crossed his arms in front of his chest and arched his brow. "And where exactly did you conduct your ponderings?"

"What? Oh." Absentmindedly his friend waved a hand through the air. "Here and there. First at White's, then at Madame Suzette's, and then at seven or so when I couldn't sleep because the blasted girl kept snoring so loudly, I rolled out of that bed and just wandered through the streets."

Fox felt his eyes widen. He barely suppressed the urge to slap his forehead. "Wandered through the streets? At this hour? Heavens, Drew, have you lost your mind? You could have been robbed or worse."

"Piffle. Whoever would want to rob me?"

Fox rolled his eyes.

"Anyway . . ." Drew heaved a sigh. "It is such a ghastly affair. Yesterday I even had to hide behind a tree in Hyde Park!" His head sank back until he stared at the ceiling. "Oooooh, whatever shall I do now?"

Fox threw a regretful look at his half-finished letter. "Why ever did you have to hide behind a tree?" he asked, resigning himself to his fate.

"Mrs. Bentham!" Drew groaned at the ceiling.

"Mrs. Bentham?" Fox frowned. The name seemed to ring a bell, yet—

"Miss Bourne's guardian."

"Ah."

"She is . . ." Curiously, Drew seemed at a loss for words. "Oooh, Foxy, you don't know what kind of woman she is!"

One of Fox's eyebrows shot up. Indeed. And no wonder that, since he had never made the acquaintance of the lady in question.

The front door opened, and a little time later Hobbes shuffled into the study holding a tray with two cups and a pot of fresh coffee. "The coffee, thur."

"Thank you, Hobbes." Fox waited until the old man had poured the coffee and left the room before he asked, "So, what about Mrs. Bentham?"

Another groan of utter desperation reached the ceiling. "She is a Xanthippish, jabbering magpie."

Fox tapped his foot on the floor and hoped his friend would come to the point. "Yes . . . ?"

Drew closed his eyes, as apparently he could no longer bear the sight of this cruel world—or at least the sight of Fox's ceiling. His Adam's apple bobbed up and down. "Because of her, my love for the incomparable Miss Bourne has died and shriveled like a raisin," he whispered, as if disclosing a terrible secret.

At his look of utter dejection, Fox had to bite his lip, hard. Andrew Fermont, Esq. was truly incorrigible. Fox seemed to remember that when they were sixteen, Drew had threatened to jump from a bridge and seek a damp grave in the Thames if Miss Nettie at the baker's would not answer his lovelorn pleas. Even at that young age, Drew had already achieved a talent for the dramatic.

"I am sure you will eventually overcome this . . . pain," Fox remarked drily.

The other man straightened, surprise registering on his face. "But that's not the problem." His soulful brown eyes regarded Fox solemnly.

"What is it, then?"

Drew sighed, grimaced, and finally came out with it.

"I am engaged to meet them tonight." Another sigh. "At Lady Worthington's musicale. And . . ."

Egad! Energetically shaking his head, Fox raised his hands. "Oh no. No no no. You cannot possibly—"

"Foxy, *please!*" his friend wheedled. "I can't possibly go! And you wouldn't want to leave me in the lurch, would you? And I'm sure you've got an invitation, too. Please!"

"Lady Worthington's musicale?" Indignant, Fox put his hands on his hips. "Are you mad? That's a musical purgatory!" He glowered at his friend in what he hoped was a suitably frightful expression. Unfortunately, it wasn't frightful enough. Not for Andrew Fermont.

"*Pleeease!*"

"No no no. Go and ask Cyril if you must!"

Drew's bottom lip trembled. "I've already asked him. I went to him an hour or so ago, and he sent me to you." He blinked. "Foxy, he actually threw me out! Can you imagine that?"

"Oh yes, I can."

"Foxy!" Drew stared at him with an utterly crestfallen expression. "We've always been such good friends—"

Fox raked his hand through his hair. "Yes, I was stupid enough to drag you from that blasted bridge," he muttered darkly.

His friend blinked, momentary confusion replacing dejection. "A bridge? Which bridge?"

Fox narrowed his eyes at him. "At Eton," he said testily. "Or has there been more than one?"

"Er . . ."

He groaned. "Venice! You wanted to jump into the Grand Canal!"

Drew gave him a sheepish smile. "Exactly."

Fox exhaled noisily.

His friend raised his brows.

"Drew—"

"Sebastian?"

Fox scowled at him. "You wily little—"

The other man batted his lashes.

Fox sighed. "All right. You win. I will go in your stead. But I swear, when I next meet our dear Lord Stafford, I'm going to call him out. Or better, even: run him through with the nearest pointy object at hand!"

Chapter Three

Lady Worthington lived in a picturesque cottage just outside of Kensington, three tollgates down the Bath Road. Earlier that day, Mr. Bentham's footman had been sent to the stables to secure a pair of horses for the evening's journey. The interior of the Bentham carriage was small, and Mrs. Bentham's overpowering perfume made it seem even more cramped. All the way to Hyde Park Corner, Amy felt as if she might perish on the spot, smothered by the scent of roses and surely a hundred other flowers besides. *Mors florea*—a cruel fate indeed, her uncle had bestowed on her. Amy sighed. And all because of a little bit of cobalt blue.

The elegant houses of Mayfair rushed past, accompanied by the walls of Green Park on the other side. Yet when the carriage rolled through the tollgate that marked the beginning of the great Bath Road, the scenery abruptly changed from that of city to village in the blink of an eye.

Mrs. Bentham pursed her lips. "How inconsiderate of Lady Worthington to live so far outside town. If only we aren't held up and robbed . . ."

Amy looked out of the carriage window and rolled her eyes. Truly, there was no need for Mrs. Bentham to worry: as soon as any highwayman harebrained enough to stop the Bentham coach opened the carriage door, a cloud of perfume would overpower the poor man and he would be dead to the world for at least a day.

The light of faint lanterns glinted on the signs above the inns at the side of the road. Trees flourished in front of them, their branches beginning to show golden leaves, slipping out of their gay, green summer dresses. A sparkle of water on the other side, and for one moment the ghostly reflections of the village pond skittered through the interior of the carriage. Soon after, the houses fell away on each side and left darkness in their wake—the darkness of greenery, of meadows and gardens—while the din of the town died away.

A sharp shard of pain sliced Amy's heart. This was what she missed most: the hurly-burly freedom of country air, the whisperings of the elms in the grove, the sweet, musty scent of rain-saturated earth, the raucous sounds of boyish laughter.

Her heart grew heavier when the carriage rolled through another tollgate and entered Kensington. Mrs. Bentham and her daughter gossiped about the illustrious personages who met at Kensington Palace. Even more fodder for talk offered the gates of Holland House past the third and last tollgate.. ". . . not a house any genteel lady should ever enter!" Mrs. Bentham concluded with satisfied self-righteousness.

Amy threw a longing look back at the gates. Perhaps she could bolt from the carriage and seek asylum at the home of the unconventional Lady Holland?

The coach left the turnpike and turned right onto a pot-holed side street. And then, illuminated by a myriad of tiny fairy lights, Worthington Cottage rose from the ground in front of them. With a low, thatched roof and gothic windows, it huddled among a few trees on a small hill, like a faithful little dog waiting for the return of its master.

Through the bushes, light from the conservatory streamed onto the driveway and fell upon the statue that graced the green round in front of the entrance—a young man of creamy white stone, standing a little bashfully on a low pillar, with long, flowing limbs, a ripple of muscle in arm, belly, and thigh. The light showed the expanse of his stony white skin in loving detail. His sensuous lips turned upward, as if in secret mirth over the spectator. A naughty, naked youth guarding the entrance to the home of an old, sharp-nosed, and sharp-eyed woman. Yet, curiously, he seemed a fit companion for Lady Worthington, who greeted them dressed in gay pink silk—Aurora, Goddess of the Dawn—at her dowager house.

They were led into the conservatory, which already buzzed with numerous voices. Two blazing candelabra flanked a midnight black grand piano. The light of the candles was reflected in the panes of glass, which the night had transformed into shimmering dark mirrors. The potted plants had been pushed to the walls in order to make room for the rows of chairs set up in front of the grand piano for the eager audience

Lord Munthorpe approached the Bentham party, his fair Celtic skin flushed below his dark hair—if from the heat of too many people in the conservatory or from the excitement of meeting them again, Amy couldn't say. Isabella put a proprietary hand on his arm and, with little persuasion, made him talk about sheep. They drifted away, soon followed by Mr. Bentham, who disappeared to God knows where, so Amy remained behind with Mrs. Bentham.

Like a sturdy flagship, Mrs. Bentham parted the crowd in search of some acquaintance or other. Soon she had spotted Lady Westerley, and the two women proceeded to exchange the news of the past few days. In hushed tones they talked about Henry Boothby, whom Lady Westerley declared to have been already stubborn and ill-mannered as a child. It left Amy to wonder what stubbornness had to do with "splewing" one's brains all over a wall. "Ill-mannered," though, she perfectly agreed with: After all, *he* didn't have to clean up the mess he had created. Though surely, people of her own class usually never cleaned up after their own messes. But of course some messes cleaned up all by themselves. Like houses covered in cobalt blue.

Amy scratched her nose.

"Don't tell me you're bored, Miss Bourne?"

Her head snapped around. Blue-gray eyes regarded her intently beneath arched cinnamon brows.

Her own eyebrows shot up in surprise. "Mr."—*Carrot*—"Stapleton."

"Miss Bourne." He inclined his head, and the candlelight ran a fiery path over his hair. When he straightened, she noticed how his dark brown coat accentuated the breadth of his shoulders. A golden floral pattern gleamed on the black waistcoat beneath. Very stylish.

Apparently disinterested, he gazed over the crowd while his fingers drummed a noiseless tattoo against his thigh.

Stylish, but sadly as cold and as odious as an old fish.

"A nice crowd tonight, is it not?" she remarked pointedly.

He turned his attention back on her, frowning. "I understand you were to meet Mr. Fermont. May I offer you his apologies? Unfortunately, he is . . . indisposed tonight." His lips curved into a charming smile. Charming, but careless. A smile one might bestow on a small child.

Amy's nostrils flared. Under the hem of her long dress her satin slipper tapped the floor. If he meant to impress her with all of his freckled, carroty glory, he'd failed miserably.

"He asked me to come in his stead. To make up for the loss. So . . ." He gestured with his hand. "Shall we take a seat?"

"Why not?" Other than the fact that, while his waltzing technique might be divine, he was as cold as a fish and apparently also a stiff bore.

They chose a pair of plush-covered chairs and sat down. Leaning his arm on the back of the chair in front of her, he turned toward her. "I understand I am to explain the music to you."

"Indeed." She clasped her hands in her lap and valiantly suppressed the urge to twiddle her thumbs.

"You don't normally like music?" His was a polite, bland voice. They might have been talking about the weather.

"The opposite is the case, I assure you."

"Ah." He nodded knowingly.

Oh yes. How could she have forgotten? Carroty hair, cold as a fish, a stiff bore, and on top of that he was a Mr. Know-It-All-Magic-Doesn't-Exist. Splendid.

Once again Amy was left to wonder what exactly she had done to deserve this. True, turning Three Elms blue was a serious offense—what if somebody had paid a visit that afternoon? Or what if one of the villagers had happened to pass by the house? Cobalt blue manor houses were rather difficult to explain away. But still, being forced to mingle with obnoxious people in a city that reeked with dirt seemed too harsh a sentence. The quaint cottage and the ill-tempered, scarred tomcat all at once appeared very appealing indeed.

"But you don't play the fortepiano yourself?" The voice of the horrid Mr. Carrothead cut into her reveries.

Now she did twiddle her thumbs. "No, I'm afraid not. I never had the opportunity."

The buzz around them increased as people chose seats, and chairs scraped over the floor.

"What a pity." He moved on his seat. "Then your family does not own a fortepiano?" When he leaned back, the sleeve of his coat slipped up and revealed a small strip of skin above the white glove.

He had, Amy discovered, freckles even on his forearms. Spots of cinnamon between coppery hair. Again it intrigued her, this contrast between attributes of maleness and the cheeky splatter of cinnamon dust. As if there were mischievous depths to that stiff, formal, probably even slightly bored man.

She shook her head and forcefully dragged her attention back to the conversation. "A fortepiano? No, it's not that. The instrument was just always"—*snapping at everybody besides my cousin*—"otherwise occupied."

Once more, her companion gave a sage nod of his head.

Cinnamon splatter or not, he was certainly most irritating! "I quite understand."

Amy gave him an arch look. "I seriously doubt that, Mr. Stapleton."

In a discreet corner of the room, Mr. Bentham clutched his glass of brandy more tightly as he saw Mr. Stapleton, like a ripe apple falling into his lap, step up to Miss Bourne. Bentham's hand shook, and quickly he downed the contents of his glass. He welcomed the burn of alcohol in his belly, the explosion of soothing heat.

Yes, the Fox was stepping up to the bait in the trap. But, he reminded himself, the bait was the niece of an old friend, and his responsibility for the time being. Was all of this right? Bourne had trusted him to look after her, to introduce her into London society, to secure a husband, and thus, happiness for her—which Bentham would do, he supposed, in a manner of speaking. Though of course, with Lady Margaret involved, there could be no happy ending for the girl.

But it couldn't be helped. Should he sacrifice his own daughter? Sacrifice Isabella's happiness? Impossible!

"Ah, Mr. Bentham."

A mere whisper only, yet the sound of the eerily familiar voice made Bentham start. His insides quaked. Too late now for a retreat.

"I see the fish has caught the worm," the stranger said in his smooth, pleasant voice.

"I didn't . . ." Bentham desperately wished for another glass of brandy. He wiped his hand over his upper lip. "It wasn't . . . wasn't *planned*. It's an accident, really," he mumbled.

A smile curved the other man's mouth. "An accident? Surely not! I would rather call it a twist of fate." He turned toward Bentham, his movements fluid and graceful. Over a rapier he would be a lethal opponent. Indeed, Bentham suspected the man would thrust his weapon into another's heart with a smile on his lips. "And since Fortuna seems well-disposed toward us," the hateful, smooth voice continued, "we should make sure the fish is truly hooked ere the evening is over." He produced a small phial filled with white powder. "Put a bit of this in their drinks, and the game will run its appropriate course."

The phial nearly slipped through Bentham's damp fingers. "I—"

But again, the stranger had already disappeared.

Helplessly, Bentham stared at the white powder. It wasn't poison, he was sure of it. Lady Margaret's mind worked differently. When she administered a death blow, literally or not, she would want to see recognition flare in the eyes of her enemy.

Bentham shivered. Not poison then, but what else? Whatever it was . . .

He slipped the phial inside his coat, where it seemed to burn through cloth and skin. Sweat formed on his forehead, trickled down his back. He still could recognize the fire of a bad conscience. And yet, what were his alternatives?

He closed his eyes as the first notes of the fortepiano drifted through the room. No, it couldn't be helped.

Though music was the food of love, Lady Worthington's musicale was poison to every finer sentiment.

A faint, niggling headache had started to build behind Fox's temples while the old lady gave her recitations. But, of course, a gentleman would not rub his temple, even if ever so discreetly. No, a gentleman sat and suffered in silence.

Not even Miss Bourne's loveliness could outshine this musical fiasco. And she was lovely, he admitted grudgingly, in the way of a plump, golden partridge. Twice now, however, he had received the impression that she was silently laughing at him, mocking him.

Impertinent chit. Who did she think she was? A little nobody dragged from the depths of the country and without any polish or style. Why, she couldn't even play the fortepiano! The most basic of female accomplishments! He shuddered to think what would have happened if poor, deluded Drew had decided to marry the chit. Not only would she have pecked the poor chap to death with her sharp retorts, no, she also would have been a disaster as a hostess. Surely she would have turned Drew's dinner parties into scandalous, ridiculous affairs, and thus become fodder for the gossipmongers. In all likelihood, she would have ordered her guests around like servants in the manner of that horrid dragon Lady Holland. How fortunate that Drew had seen the light of reason in time!

No, Fox would not be sorry to see this evening wind down. Perhaps, if he were lucky, the damp, crisp autumn night would dispel his headache and he could sojourn on to merrier grounds, escape to chase away all lingering memories of this ghastly event.

Fox half closed his eyes in sweet contemplation. He had enjoyed his time at Madame Suzette's. The doxy into whose bed he had tumbled was much to his liking: dark and mysterious, with lush, honeyed curves that looked as if they had ripened under a hot southern sun. For a few pleasant hours a man could thoroughly lose himself in the arms of such a woman, revel in the feel of dewy soft flesh pressed intimately against his own. Not the gates to paradise, perhaps—which mortal ever found heavenly pleasures during his time on earth?—but infinitely better than listening to Lady Worthington's shrill voice, or exchanging inane pleasantries with a friend's bygone infatuation.

Impossible to say how much time passed until the recess. To Fox it seemed like an eternity, all spent in musical purgatory. Wryly he remembered his words to Drew. How sad they had proven all too true. To exact revenge from Andrew Fermont, Esq. would be necessary.

Beside him, Drew's angelic Miss Bourne sat as if petrified.

"Miss Bourne?"

"That was—"

"Rather abhorrent, I know." And because of her, because of his promise to Andrew, the pea-goose, he wouldn't be able to extricate himself early from this glorious musicale. "Would you care for some refreshments?"

She turned toward him, her eyes flashing with pansy blue annoyance. "*Interesting*, was what I wanted to say."

Gracious, what was wrong with this girl? Snapping and yapping like a rat terrier!

"I stand corrected." Did he mean it? No, of course not. Platitudes spilled easily from his lips, platitudes and flirtation he had perfected during all those years among the bon ton.

Her blond brows arched. "But faith, sir, you still sit."

The musical, mocking lilt of her voice grated on his nerves just as had the unmusical experience of Lady Worthington's songs. He inclined his head. "Then I *sit* corrected, Miss Bourne. Now, will you allow me to accompany you to the refreshments room?" He would let Drew buy him a bottle of old, old port for this. A *barrel* of the stuff.

"Else we should sit stupidly like two hens on a perch?" She stood, small and graceful, a quail rather than a hen. "By all means, let us proceed toward the punch."

He offered her his arm, and her gloved fingers slipped into the crook of his elbow so he could lead her away from this scene of musical criminality.

"I assume you enjoyed the performance then?" he asked lightly, even though only the deaf could have.

She gave him a look which made him think she probably regarded him as the greatest nidget of all mankind. "As I said, it was interesting. It's not something you get to hear every day."

"And thank God for that!" he mumbled.

Around them, the hum of voices rose and fell as if the guests had turned into a swarm of bees. "A veritable crush, is it not?" Miss Bourne purred, her voice sweeter than sticky molasses. "It makes one wish for the green hills and meadows, where one might meet a fairy's child—oh I *am* sorry." Her free hand rose to cover her mouth, while she trilled a laugh. Fox swore he could see a devilish glint in her eyes as she goaded him. "You don't read Keats."

"Indeed I do not," he forced out between gritted teeth. By Jove, he had never felt the urge to strangle a woman, but this one—oh, he would happily put his hands around her white throat! But because he could not follow these urges in such a public setting, he needed a drink. Fast.

The refreshments room, however, Fox saw with dismay, was packed: The battered audience sought fortification before the second part of the musicale began. Properly sloshed, a man might even find its entertainment value increase. Yet before a man could become chirping merry in this house, he apparently had to hack his way through the masses. With even the comforts of alcohol be denied to him tonight, he'd be *deuced*—

"Ah, there is Mr. Bentham," Miss Bourne murmured, her catty tone suddenly gone as if it had never been. Ah, well, she probably knew it would not do if her guardian caught her at playing Miss Hoyden.

Fox followed the direction of the subtle rise of her chin and found a middle-aged, potbellied gentleman coming toward them and carrying two glasses of red liquid. The candlelight transformed the sweat forming on the man's forehead into a shimmering ooze that seemed to grow out of his skin.

What a decidedly distasteful image! Fox frowned. Make that two barrels of port his friend owed him.

"Mr. Bentham," Fox's fair but rather unpleasant companion murmured as the man reached them, sweating and out of breath. "Mr. Stapleton, may I introduce you to my present guardian, Mr. Bentham? Mr. Bentham, Mr. Stapleton."

Fox made his lips twist into a polite smile, while his gaze was inexorably drawn to the small drops that rolled down from Bentham's temples to soak his collar.

The older man cleared his throat. "Ah, yes. Yes. Stapleton. P-Pleasure, sir." He had to clear his throat once more. "Are you enjoying yourself, my dear?" he asked Miss Bourne, but then continued without waiting to hear her answer. "Saw you f-from the refreshments room and I thought . . . and I thought . . ." He lifted the two glasses. He blinked rapidly as sweat fell into his eyes. "Thought I'd better bring you some of the punch, so you w-won't have to dive into the cr—" He breathed heavily.

"Mr. Bentham?" Miss Bourne's fingers dropped from Fox's arm when she took a step forward. "Are you quite all right? Do you feel unwell?" Fox looked down on the golden crown of her head, which was crooked to the side in apparent concern. My, my, who would have thought it? There was a feminine heart beating in that Amazonian chest after all.

Bentham's lips trembled a little, before he managed a smile. "Not at all, my dear. F-Fit as a fiddle. But just couldn't let you walk into the crush." Again, he lifted the two glasses he carried.

Fox narrowed his eyes. The man appeared sloshed. Too much punch, probably.

"Oh, you shouldn't have," the fair Miss Bourne protested.

"My pleasure, my dear, my pleasure. Do take a glass." Bentham pressed a glass into her hand. "You, too, Mr. Stapleton."

Fox found himself holding a slippery glass of warm punch. The spicy aroma drifted up to tickle his nose with hints of cinnamon and cloves.

Bentham looked at him. "Consider it a thank-you for entertaining my ward tonight," he said in a surprisingly clear voice before, blinking rapidly, he walked past. His only farewell was a murmured, "Need fresh air. Yes, some fresh air . . ."

Deucedly odd, that fellow. Yet he had spared Fox the fate of being crushed to death in the refreshments room. A man had to appreciate that. With a shrug, Fox turned back to his lady for the evening. "So, what shall we drink to, Miss Bourne?"

She started, as if she had been miles away, then raised her pansy blue gaze to his. For a moment the curves of her face looked soft and vulnerable, but almost immediately the effect was destroyed. "What do *you* propose, Mr. Stapleton?" she asked in mocking tones.

So the yapping terrier was back. Her insolence annoyed him. Oh, how it annoyed him, especially coming from such a fresh chit. Yet he would be damned before he betrayed himself in any way. He inclined his head as if flattered by her question. "This is your first stay in London, is it not? Then I drink to a pleasant and unforgettable time in our fair city." He raised his glass high in salute.

"Well, thank you." She mimicked him, and they both drank.

A wave of red rolled toward him. Cinnamon and clove enveloped him in their mingled scent as the punch flowed into his mouth and exploded on his tongue. Wine and cinnamon and clove and a dreadful bitterness. And salty like tears. He grimaced and put his glass down.

He saw how Miss Bourne wrinkled her small nose. "Do you think there's something wrong with this punch?" she asked, a little breathless. "That's not how it's supposed to taste, is it?"

"I should hope not!" He took another cautious sip. The bitterness was still there, if somehow muted. In fact, it tasted better now. "It grows on you, I say."

That made her raise her brows again, those two semicircles of burnished gold. "Indeed?" She raised her glass to her lips. "An acquired taste, you mean?" She drank.

Over the rim of his glass, Fox watched how her lashes came to rest on her rounded cheeks when she closed her eyes. The muscles of her throat moved as the liquid ran down her throat. More punch flowed over his own tongue, sweetly this time. Her lashes fluttered, and her eyes looked directly into his. Blue as wide as the sky, as wide as the ocean. And then her lips curved into the most charming smile he had ever seen.

Perhaps it was due to the punch, for just like it, Lady Worthington's musicale seemed to grow on a man, and Fox liked the second part much better than the first. So much did he enjoy himself that he drove home whistling madly, as if to compete with the now-absent sparrows on the rooftops. A myriad of stars glittered in the night sky, a diamond-besprinkled coat for the new moon. Pale like a maiden's breast, her thin crescent peeked shyly out from behind a flock of clouds.

But then Fox's hired carriage reached the outskirts of town, the noise and rumble and lights of Mayfair, and her light seemed to dim. Never mind; the hackney rumbled down Piccadilly, past slowly aging mansions on one side and the bare trees of Green Park on the other, until it came to a halt in front of a red-brick house. Still flushed with delight, Fox alighted from the carriage, paid the driver, and walked across the courtyard and finally through the gates of dignified Albany.

His steps echoed hollowly on the marble floors of what once had been Lord Melbourne's town house before he had exchanged houses with His Grace the Duke of York and Albany. In 1802 debts had finally forced the duke to sell the estate, thus opening the way for York House to be transformed into this quiet paradise of bachelorhood.

Fox slipped out through the back door and from the brightly lit hallways of the mansion, he stepped into the subdued twilight of Rope Walk. The mellow glow of lanterns enveloped him as he strolled down the roofed pathway. In the long-stretched houses to his left and right, candlelight flickered in the windows as if welcoming and urging him home. Ah yes, it was for *this* that he preferred entering Albany from the south instead of choosing the shorter way to his apartment through the gates in Viggo Street. This was home: a safe haven amidst the teeming life of the city he so loved. Indeed, a most suitable den for a fox.

He grinned.

After the stuffiness of Lady Worthington's conservatory, the crisp night air stung pleasantly in his lungs. Truly, this was an enchanted night!

Energized, he stepped through the entrance of block F and walked up the stairs to his set of chambers. Yet when he unlocked his front door, he found the entrance hall strangely dark and deserted, with no Hobbes in sight. Frowning, he slipped out of his coat and left it with his hat on a chair in the hall. A splinter of light came from his study and, when he pushed the door open, he found Andrew Fermont sprawled in an armchair and obviously engrossed in a book. "Drew."

The man looked up, and his face broke into a delighted smile. "Foxy! There you are!" He gestured to the glass on the table. "I took the liberty and helped myself to some of your brandy. Hope you don't mind."

"Not at all." Perplexed, Fox started tugging at his tight gloves and walked to the other armchair. "But what are you doing here? And where's Hobbes?" The gloves fell onto the table and he sank down into the comfortable leather seat.

Drew shrugged. "I sent him off to bed. Figured the old chap could need some sleep."

Fox scowled. "And who's going to see after my clothes tonight?" he asked ungraciously.

"Lawk, Foxy!" His friend rolled his eyes. "A strapping big lad like you should be able to see after his clothes himself for once!" He leaned forward to add in a mocking murmur, "It seems that your cosseted upbringing has made you a bit soft, Mr. Stapleton."

"Not at all, Mr. Fermont." With deft fingers, Fox opened the buttons of his jacket. "If you remember, I nearly gave you a lovely facer at Gentleman Jackson's last week."

"While I nearly ran you through with my épée at

Maestro Angelo's at the beginning of this week." Drew grinned. He leaned back and crossed his legs. "But do tell: How did you like Lady Worthington's musicale?"

"Surprisingly entertaining." Fox shrugged out of his jacket and flung it aside.

Drew looked surprised. "*Entertaining?*" he echoed, as if he could hardly believe his ears. "You do shock me, Foxy. Didn't I hear you speak of musical purgatory only this morning?"

Fox reached up to loosen his neck cloth. "Ah well, it is all a question of circumstances, is it not?"

"Circumstances?" If possible, Drew's brows climbed even higher. "I gather you enjoyed the company, then? How deliciously unexpected!" His eyes twinkled. "I had got the impression the company of Miss Bourne left you somewhat . . . bored."

"*Bored!*" With the indignant outburst, the snowy folds of Fox's cravat fell open. "Who could ever be bored in Miss Bourne's company?" Memories of the evening rose in front of his inner eye and brought a smile to his face. "Miss Bourne is surely one of the most charming ladies of my acquaintance. An utterly delightful creature, I should say. In fact"—with a blissful sigh, Fox leaned his head back and closed his eyes—"in fact, she is the woman I'm going to marry."

Chapter Four

The ton dubbed it a whirlwind romance. After Lady Worthington's musicale, the Honorable Mr. Stapleton was a daily visitor of the Benthams, or more specifically, of their young ward, Miss Amelia Bourne. He was captivated by her beauty, her charm and wit. At night he dreamt of her sweet, dear face, of the gentle swell of her breasts, of the delicious shadow in between—which he longed to explore, to caress with fingers and lips. It might be exceedingly improper to harbour such thoughts about a gently bred young lady, but what man could help his dreams? And so he dreamt of her small but appealingly lush figure at night, and during the day despaired that heavy winter dresses did not grant him a glimpse of her legs. Surely that would have been heaven, to glimpse the outline of her legs. They would be firm but beautifully rounded. And short.

Fox smiled. Everything about her was short, petite. It made him want to tug her under his arm, shelter her from the world so no harm would ever come to her. He lived for a smile from her, which would set her blue eyes sparkling. Pansy blue, summer-sky blue, as wide as the ocean. He yearned for the day he could touch her bare hand and link their fingers, skin to skin. And for the day—oh, the day!—when he could press his lips to hers, when they would open under his and he would be granted his first taste of her. It would be sweeter than honey, for sure.

For now he accompanied Miss Bourne and Miss Bentham on their outings in the park, met the whole family at soirees or at the theater. And afterward he couldn't wait to hear Miss Bourne's opinion on the play they had seen.

The days raced by and he lived only for the precious moments he spent in her company. His spirits soared when he walked beside her, and his heart thudded in his chest whenever her laughter trilled in his ears.

His friends declared him mad. "You, my dear boy," Cyril said, "act like a man possessed."

Possessed?

If he were, it was a sweet possession indeed, a madness he didn't want to be cured of. Amelia Bourne was bewitching and beautiful; she was all he had ever dreamt of. Now that he had found her, he wouldn't be able to bear it should he lose her again. Her regard seemed to him the most precious gift. The mere thought that he might forfeit it because of his birth made him break into cold sweat. But he wouldn't: if he never told her, he would never lose her and thus she would be with him forever.

Forever.

Surely nothing could be any sweeter than that.

An empty glass in his hand, Bentham sat in an armchair at his club and stared into space. Brooding. These days his acquaintances gave him a wide berth, yet he hardly noticed. A vise constricted his chest, squeezed his lungs, and he felt trapped, so horribly trapped. Hell, he felt as if he had sold his soul to Beelzebub himself.

Sweet heavens, what had he gotten himself into? If only he had never taken Lady Margaret's cursed money! True, at the time—was it ten years now?—he had had no other options; the moneylenders, the greedy bastards, had started to regard him with suspicion. Therefore, when he had heard about the mysterious Lady Margaret it had seemed a godsend. *I will give you the money, and you will pay it back when you can.* An unusual arrangement, to be sure, yet it had seemed so simple, so astonishingly easy. *Pay it back when you can*. Something he had always put off, until it slowly but surely slipped his mind. The right time for paying his debts had never come; he always needed more money—and more—and more—and more. Truly, he had tried to stop for a while, but how could he withstand the lure of the cards? The thrill? The excitement?

And now . . .

He shuddered, and a snap of his fingers produced a footman, who poured him more brandy. With a trembling hand he raised the glass to his mouth and downed its contents. Liquid fire burned down his gullet and into his stomach. Closing his eyes, Bentham waited for the explosion of heat that would relax his tense muscles.

"Ah, Mr. Bentham."

His eyes snapped open. Disbelieving, he ogled the stranger who slipped into the empty armchair facing him.

"So, our Sicilian Dragon has been successful, I've heard." His voice smooth and pleasant, the man crossed his legs.

"How the devil did you get in here?" Bentham snapped, while the alcohol rolled sickeningly through his stomach.

One dark blond eyebrow arched. "I get admission everywhere, my dear Mr. Bentham. I thought you would have guessed by now."

And what was that supposed to mean?

Sweat trickled down Bentham's temple as, with apparent interest, the other man looked around the room. "Such a nice, cultivated place, a gentleman's club. Prestigious, you might call it. Does it not just ooze wealth and distinction?" He turned back to Bentham, his lips curved. "What a lucky man to belong to such an institution. You have been . . . successful?"

At the man's sneer, Bentham felt his insides quake. He felt like a rabbit at first sight of a snake. "Yes." He fumbled for his handkerchief to wipe his forehead. "Yes. I have . . . they have . . . drunk . . ."

"And now they are violently in love. Beautiful, is it not? I have no doubt he will ask for her hand in marriage, soon. You will consent, of course."

"Of course," Bentham muttered, twisting the handkerchief between his hands. In a way, wasn't this what his old friend Bourne had asked him to do? Help his niece find a husband? And so he had, Bentham thought defiantly. So he had. Surely Bourne would understand his predicament—indeed, he had been a deucedly good friend back in their days at university, hadn't he? Of course, Bentham had never told him about the gambling and the debts he had run up even back then. A gentleman didn't talk about such base things as money. Besides, Bourne had always been such a stickler to the highest moral ground; he probably wouldn't have understood.

Sweat dampened his temples as Bentham realized that in all likelihood Bourne wouldn't see the reason for Bentham's present actions, either. How could he? He lived in the country, far away from the pressures of Town. No, it was better if Bourne didn't know, didn't know *anything*.

"Very good. I see we understand each other." The stranger regarded Bentham indulgently, as one would a favorite lapdog. "With the festive season approaching, Stapleton will want to go and visit his family soon. Rather disgustingly dependable, the Stapletons are in that respect. Yet thanks to our little intervention, he won't be able to stand even the *thought* of being apart from the object of his lovesickness for too long. So, naturally . . ." He paused, as if wanting to draw out the moment and prolong the tension.

Bentham gripped his handkerchief so tightly that his knuckles shone white against the skin. God, how he hated this bastard with his smooth voice! But no, no, he was trapped by his debts, by his obligation to his family. It could not be helped . . .

"Naturally, he will want to take her with him. You should make sure your daughter accompanies them."

Isabella? The thought was a painful stab to his heart that made the breath catch in his throat. "My daughter?" he echoed.

Those blond brows rose mockingly. "Indeed, your daughter. Surely that won't be a problem?" Light blue eyes bored into his.

Bentham dabbed at the sweat on his upper lip. "No."

"Very good. For just think how unfortunate it would be should our alliance no longer work."

Bentham swallowed, hard. "That won't happen," he assured the man tightly.

"That's what I assumed." Another hateful lift of lips. "Her presence at Rawdon Park is crucial, for she will be given little . . . *presents* for the family." The fingertips of his hands pressed together, the stranger leaned back, sultry satisfaction saturating his voice. "And then we shall make our Sicilian Dragon breathe fire."

Bentham looked at him blandly. "Dragon?" he asked.

The man looked him up and down. "Not a player of chess then." His thin lip curled. "Well, I would have been surprised if you were."

Amy put on her bonnet and eyed herself critically in the mirror. She turned her head a little to the left, then a little to the right. "Not bad," she murmured. She had spent last afternoon trimming the bonnet so she would have lovely new headwear for the outing today. It now perfectly suited her dark blue pelisse—a color that always made her eyes seem to sparkle with extra intensity.

Not that her eyes would have needed any more sparkle.

Amy smiled at her image in the mirror as she tied her bonnet under her chin. Did not the eyes of those in love sparkle like the stars in the night sky?

In love.

She pressed her hands against her chest. Yes, yes—she was in love, passionately and completely. In a few short weeks Mr. Stapleton had become more precious to her than the air she breathed, had become her endless joy, her reason for being. She could spend hours studying the patterns of the cinnamon marks on his face. She wanted to memorize each and every one of them, starting with the sweetest of them all, the one on his earlobe. With a blissful sigh, she closed her eyes.

In the next moment, a sharp knock at the door interrupted her reverie. "Will you come downstairs?" Slightly muffled, Isabella's voice reached her through the door. "The carriage is already waiting."

"Oh." Amy's eyes snapped open. "Oh!" All at once, her heart thudded in her chest; her cheeks heated. Soon, soon she would . . . She snatched her gloves from the table and hurried out of the room. Wriggling her fingers into them, she followed Isabella downstairs. And there, there he was.

Her breath caught. At the small sound, he looked up and their gazes locked. Surely she must have flown down the remaining steps, for the next moment she was at his side, gazing up at him.

The corners of his eyes crinkled with a smile. "Miss Bourne." He inclined his head.

"Mr. Stapleton." Breathless, she curtsied.

"So very lovely to see you again," he murmured, his voice softer than velvet.

Amy felt her cheeks flame with mingled pleasure and shyness, and lowered her gaze. "And you," she breathed. It seemed to her they were enveloped by a rosy glow, sealing them together, making their hearts beat as one, and—

"Surely we must be on our way." Isabella's sharp voice dimmed the glow considerably. "I don't suppose they will wait for us at the museum."

Amy sighed. When she looked up, she caught Stapleton's rueful expression. Wordless, but with a small smile hovering around his lips, he took her hand and placed it on his arm to escort her out into the street.

Soon they were all bundled into Lord Munthorpe's landau, its hood pulled down so they could bask in the rays of the golden October sun. The sun sparkled on the windows of the houses they passed and made the trees in the squares and parks glitter like flitter-gold. They joined the flow of carriages in Oxford Street, most of them no doubt traveling toward Hyde Park. Lord Munthorpe's landau, however, turned east toward Tottenham Court Road. They passed the old School of Arms and the once-proud Pantheon, now deserted and stripped of its fittings. On they drove, past the boundary stone and into Bloomsbury.

It was not too long before Lord Munthorpe, sounding extraordinarily pleased with himself, said, "Here we are," just as the landau rumbled through an open gate into a wide forecourt, where a few other carriages had already been parked.

The landau halted in front of the stairs leading up to the entrance of the museum. Munthorpe opened the door, stepped out, and turned to help Isabella and Amy down. Mr. Stapleton was the last to alight from the carriage. The sunlight made his hair glint like molten copper—a sight that distracted Amy from admiring the stately building. She just couldn't help smiling at him. Oh, he was so dear to her!

His lips curving, he came and offered her his arm. Amy slipped her hand into the crook of his elbow and shivered a little when her arm brushed his side. "What a beautiful house," she said quickly.

"Oh yes, enormous, isn't it?" Stapleton cast a look around the forecourt before he looked down at her, one eyebrow raised. "Just as enormous as the debts Montagu incurred when he had it rebuilt after a fire. How desperate must a man be to marry a madwoman?"

"A madwoman?" Amy held her breath, enchanted as always with his stories.

The corners of his eyes crinkled, and she wished she could reach up and put her finger there. Or even her lips. A blush warmed her face. She was turning into a terrible wanton.

"He had to pretend to be the Emperor of China before she would agree to marry him. It's said the servants had to serve her on bended knee."

"Really?" Amy imagined a stately matron adorned with fantastical dresses—for surely the Empress of China had to wear fantastical dresses—and sitting enthroned on a chair in the drawing room, while the poor servants had to slither around on their knees. She giggled.

As he searched her face, the smile disappeared and his expression turned solemn. "And would you need your future husband to be a crowned head, too, Miss Bourne?" he asked softly.

The breath caught in her throat, which suddenly seemed to be filled with the thudding of her heart. "What?" she croaked, rather unladylike.

Yet that special moment had already fled. He looked past her. "It seems that Miss Bentham is impatient to explore the wonders of the British Museum. So, shall we?" He cocked his head to the side.

Amy bit her lip. "Of course," she murmured. For one moment she had thought he meant to ask something she'd been hoping with all her heart to hear.

He led her up the stairs to where Isabella and Lord Munthorpe were already waiting for them. Isabella scowled at Amy. "We don't want to be too late for our guide," she said, her nose pinched with displeasure. "After all, we wouldn't want to miss the barometz." She turned and managed to switch from an expression of annoyance to a simpering smile in a heartbeat. "Isn't that so, my lord?"

Lord Munthorpe's chest swelled. "Quite so." He beamed at her.

"Er . . ." Sometimes, Amy thought, it took heroic effort to stay polite in Miss Isabella Bentham's company, especially when she was playing the sweet, coy girl for Lord Munthorpe's benefit. Worst of all: the poor man seemed to fall for her tricks! "I'm sure we wouldn't want to miss the . . . er . . ."

"Barometz," Mr. Stapleton cut in quickly.

She cast him a grateful look and, smiling, he pressed her arm a little tighter to his side in answer.

Isabella sniffed. "Shall we proceed inside?"

"Of course." Lord Munthorpe hurried to lead her gallantly through the entrance of the museum.

"Hm." Amy stared after them. Isabella, she was sure, would have relished the role of Empress of China. As it was, she seemed hell-bent on becoming at least a countess. "So, what exactly is a barometz?"

Beside her, Mr. Stapleton shrugged. "I haven't even the foggiest." His blue-gray eyes danced with merriment as he laughed down at her. "Yet knowing Munty, I would almost bet it has something to do with sheep. Shall we find out?"

Laughter bubbled in her throat. "Oh, I absolutely insist, Mr. Stapleton."

He sketched her a comical half bow. "As Your Majesty wishes." And grinning, he swept her through the door.

In the front hall, overshadowed by solemn-looking marble statues, he produced their tickets for the porter. The portly man showed them to a room where a small group of people was already waiting for the tour to start. A few minutes later their guide, a pale young man, appeared, and they were finally led into the hallowed hallways and galleries of that venerable institution, the British Museum.

They admired sculptures from Persepolis; a marble bust of Hercules with curly hair and beard; a twelfth-century reliquary, said to have contained some remains of Thomas à Becket at one time; Sir Hans Sloane's *materia medica*, a pharmaceutical cabinet full of seeds, dried fruit, bark, roots, ground mummies' fingers for treating bruises, and rhinoceros horn, an antidote to poison. One room was filled with fossils, petrified teeth, and bones of enormous animals dug up from the earth—Devil's Toenails and snakestones.

"Once collected by our superstitious forebearers as

charms against bad luck," their young guide intoned in the slightly bored voice of one who had repeated the same words a thousand times, "we now believe these fossilized items to be the remains of extinct plants and animals." Dutifully, the group looked at the teeth.

Charms and magic . . .

Amy could not help lightly resting her fingertips on the glass of the display case, which held the smaller teeth and bones. Her hands tingled with remembered power. She had to bite her lip to smother a gasp. Oh, how it hurt in such moments, the loss of her magic, of the joy and the power.

A hand touched her shoulder. Unwilling for someone else to witness her yearning, she jerked away. Her head whipped around and up, and she looked straight into Stapleton's worried face.

"Are you all right, my dear?" he asked.

His gentle concern touched her heart and made the pain ebb away. "Yes. Yes, of course." Stepping away from the display case, she forced a smile to her lips. "It's just . . ." She turned and, with her head crooked to the side, pretended to study an enormous jawbone with teeth as big as her fists. "It's amazing, is it not, to imagine that such large animals once roamed the earth." Oh, how she yearned to tell him about the magic and the wonder of it! But she couldn't, for had she not been taught from an early age never to share her family's secret with an outsider? And never ever to perform magic where other people might watch. Still, she felt she could tell Mr. Stapleton *anything*. Dear Sebastian . . .

"Heroic ages when men could still fight dragons and monsters to prove their worth to the women they loved." Amusement tinged his voice.

Following the pull of a new magic altogether, Amy turned her head to meet his gaze. As she watched, amusement left his blue-gray eyes and was replaced by a strange, compelling intensity.

The memory of loss and pain fled her thoughts. Just as

in the courtyard, Amy's breath caught and her heartbeat thudded in her ears. Dust particles danced around Mr. Stapleton, glittered in the sunlight that fell through the windows. His hair glowed like embers when he lowered his head toward her.

"It would have been an honor to put the head of the largest dragon at your feet," he said.

"You would have done that?" she whispered, drowning in his eyes.

"Yes." He took her hand. His thumb brushed over her wrist as if he wanted to feel the pulse that fluttered there like a little bird. "But would you have accepted it?"

Another brush of his thumb, and—though he didn't even touch her skin—Amy felt her insides melt. "Oh yes. *Yes*."

"Will you all please step this way?" the voice of their guide came from the other end of the room.

A slow smile curved Stapleton's lips as he raised Amy's hand to his mouth to bestow a quick kiss on her gloved knuckles. Then he tucked it into the crook of his elbow and led her back to the hallway.

Another room held treasures from the New World: a shaman's drum, a lidded casket of dyed cane, and— something that made the ladies gasp and the gentlemen shudder—a human scalp stretched on a wooden hoop. From there they went into the curiosity cabinet and beheld petrified fish, a bottle of stag's tears, a little silver box containing the stones taken out of Lord Belcarre's heart, the skin of an antelope that had died in St. James's Park, and . . . the barometz: a faintly shriveled something in tones of light brown that bore a faint resemblance to a sheep. Obviously deeply moved, Lord Munthorpe stopped in front of it.

"Rooted in earth, each cloven foot descends," he intoned, and his voice trembled with reverence.

"And round and round her flexile neck she bends,
Crops the gray coral moss, and hoary thyme,
Or laps with rosy tongue the melting rime;

Eyes with mute tenderness her distant dam,
And seems to bleat . . ." He sighed. "A *vegetable lamb.*"

Amy bit her lip to prevent herself from bursting out in laughter. It didn't help that Stapleton's breath tickled her ear as he bent to whisper, "See? I told you: *sheep.*"

"Ah, I see you've found our Vegetable Lamb of Tartary." Their guide joined them.

Lord Munthorpe heaved another sigh. "The barometz." His hand touched the display case as if he yearned to reach through the glass and cradle the miniscule lamb in his hand.

Dutifully, Isabella stepped closer to the case to admire the lamb as well. "Oh, it's *exquisite!*" she breathed. "Surely it's the prettiest thing I've ever seen!"

"It is a hoax, of course," the young guide said. Naturally, he had no idea he was crushing another man's dreams.

Lord Munthorpe's face fell. "But . . ."

"It's only the root of an exotic plant. The Royal Society found it out even before it was presented to us as part of their Museum of Curiosities some forty years ago. Excuse me, I have to assemble the group. We need to continue."

With a woebegone expression, Lort Munthorpe gazed after the young man. Isabella merely blinked, obviously struck speechless that she had just admired nothing but an old root.

Stapleton left Amy's side to clasp Munthorpe's shoulder. "Don't take it to heart, Munty. After all, this doesn't prove your barometz doesn't live somewhere in some faraway country. Who knows what is possible when dragons did indeed once roam our land?"

Indeed, even in this day and age there was still ample opportunity for a man to perform chivalric deeds—as became clear when they entered the room where the spoils of Lord Elgin's Greek expedition were displayed.

"Oh la, what a wonderful frieze of riders," Isabella exclaimed, then half turned to flutter her lashes at her companion. "What do you make of them, Lord Munthorpe?"

At being granted another dose of Isabella's attention despite the sheep disaster, he perked up a little. His chest swelled. "Rather splendid specimens," he pronounced.

"Oh yes, and look at these. . . ." Isabella's gaze was drawn to a group of headless and thinly clad women of stone. Faced with the sheerness of their garments, she wrinkled her nose. "I say! How shocking."

Stony fabric clung to the women's breasts and outlined them in loving detail. In fact, the imaginary fabric was so delicate that even the women's marble nipples could be seen clearly.

"Hm," Mr. Stapleton mumured beside Amy. "I find these rather splendid." When she glanced up at him, his eyes twinkled with silent laughter—and another emotion that made her cheeks flush.

As she watched, one corner of his mouth lifted into a provocative smile before he turned his attention back to the stone women in front of them, subjecting each to a thorough perusal. Shockingly, Amy imagined herself in place of the statues, his gaze traveling over her.

As if her fantasy had suddenly become reality, Amy could feel her breasts swelling against her stays, and her face grew even hotter than before. Heavens! The things he was doing to her! Never before had she entertained such wanton thoughts. But then, she mused, she had never been in love before, either.

Dreamily, her gaze wandered to the next exhibit, the head of a stone horse, nostrils flared, and the next—Isabella gave a shriek and fainted artfully into Lord Munthorpe's strong arms—a stark naked man. And while his hands, feet, and half of his nose were missing, his other appendage most certainly was not.

"Oooh," Isabella moaned.

A hectic flush blooming on his face, Lord Munthorpe fanned air at her with his free hand. Other ladies of their group were quite overcome by the sight too, and had to be escorted from the room. Angry murmurs could be heard.

"Shocking!"

"Most indecent . . ."

"—should be forbidden!"

"Heavens, man!" one of the gentlemen barked at their guide. "How can you allow ladies to enter this room without giving fair warning beforehand?"

The young museum attendant paled even more. His Adam's apple bobbed up and down and he gulped. "I-I apologize m-most profoundly," he stuttered. "If you would like to step into the next room . . ."

Amy couldn't help chuckling at the whole brouhaha—all because of a little bit of stone. Quickly, she raised her hand to her mouth to stifle the sound, but obviously not before Mr. Stapleton heard.

"Miss Bourne!" he said.

She looked up at him, still trying to subdue her merriment. A cinnamon-colored eyebrow arched.

"Why, how shocking, Miss Bourne: you appear to be not shocked at all!"

A gurgling laugh escaped her lips, which made his eyebrow rise even higher. "I can assure you, Mr. Stapleton, that having grown up with seven male cousins I am well acquainted with the male form." A new, unfamiliar thrill coursed through her veins as she teased him. Feeling naughty and daring, she cocked her head to the side.

He promptly took her up on her silent invitation. "Now you shock *me*, Miss Bourne."

Delighted with their game, Amy gave another laugh. "We are like brothers and sister—nothing terribly shocking. I came to live with my Aunt and Uncle Bourne when I was only three years old." Her smile dimmed and fleeting sadness passed through her as she thought of her parents, who had died in a carriage accident on icy roads. Her mother had been the one who had been seriously injured. And while her life had ebbed away, Amy's father had tried to save her with magic—yet it had been all in vain: the effort to save her had drained all his powers and he had died along with her.

But the shadow of the past quickly dissolved. It had all happened so long ago! And her aunt and uncle loved her as if she were their own child. Indeed, hadn't Aunt Bourne often told her how happy she was to have a little girl among the horde of her sons?

"My cousins," Amy took up the thread of their conversation, her lips curving. "During the summer they all go bathing nude in one of my uncle's ponds. And they apparently like to compare the sizes of their . . . appendages on this occasion." She lifted her shoulders. "You men can be quite vain, it would seem."

Chuckling, he offered her his arm again. "Oh, you wound me, Miss Bourne. Shall we follow our group ere I fall at your feet, bleeding from the wounds you've inflicted?"

"By all means, Mr. Stapleton. Though I have to say you appear much sturdier than you let on."

"Self-defense, Miss Bourne. Pure self-defense."

Grinning like fools and both slightly out of breath with merriment, they caught up with their museum guide and tour group in the next room, which was filled with more—though less scandalous—artifacts from Greece. Indeed, Isabella appeared almost recovered, even though she was still leaning heavily on Lord Munthorpe's arm. Not that he seemed to object too terribly: judging from his expression, he felt exactly the same as any worthy knight who had killed a dastardly dragon.

Amy's lips curled. Quickly, she averted her gaze before another bout of hilarity could overwhelm her, and she concentrated her attention on their guide instead. His voice had taken on a higher pitch than before, undoubtedly due to frayed nerves. *Poor man*, she thought.

". . . red-figured *hydria* . . . er . . . water jar. Signed by the artist." He gulped. "Meidias. One of the objects of the collection Sir William Hamilton s-sold to the museum and ... and ..."

"And this one?" boomed one of the gentlemen of their group. "Charming bull's head."

The guide ran his tongue over his lips. "Another water jar, decorated using the black-figure technique," he said desperately. "With a bull's head flanked by two swans. It was actually used as ... as ..."

Everybody stared at him expectantly.

He blinked several times. "An urn," he whispered. "For a man called Dorotheus. His name is incised above the bull's head, here." He pointed. "And the next object"—he made a sweeping gesture—"the so-called Portland Vase, property of Lord Portland. The fourth duke was kind enough to lend it to the museum. A most wonderful example of a cameo glass vessel, depicting a mythological scene on the subject of love and marriage. As you can see—"

"Ooooh," Isabella moaned.

Lord Munthorpe's nostrils flared. Like an irate bull, he turned on the hapless museum attendant. "More people in the nude? How can you leave such indecent objects standing around for all to see?" And, in a gentler tone while turning to Isabella, "Come, Miss Bentham, allow me to lead you out into the hallway."

Isabella's eyelashes fluttered. "Oh, Lord Munthorpe, whatever would I do without you?" she choked out.

Amy rolled her eyes. Heavens! Isabella should take to the stage instead of trying to grab a husband. Surely, she would be able to earn a fortune in drama!

Once more, Amy and Mr. Stapleton lagged behind as everyone else hastily left the room. It allowed them to step up to the vase and admire the intricate white carvings on the otherwise black glass: a woman sitting between two men, with a small Amor overhead. From beneath the woman's arm a bearded snake wriggled forth and raised its head.

"How very curious," Amy said softly.

"A strange ménage à trois indeed for a depiction of marriage," Mr. Stapleton agreed.

"Perhaps the older man is her father."

"They certainly all look at the other chap. A strapping young lad, that."

From the corner of her eyes, she saw his lips quirk. Oh, so he was thinking of turning the tables and was now teasing her? How utterly delightful! "Hmm."

"Rather fetching."

"Well, *she* certainly thinks so!" With a cheeky smile, Amy turned her head to look up at him.

She found his gaze resting warmly on her. As their eyes connected, the teasing glint disappeared from his, and his expression turned serious—even intense. "My dear Miss Bourne." He took her hand and, very slowly, very gently, unfastened the buttons of her glove and drew it off. She should remind him how improper such behavior was; truly she should. Yet as his thumb whispered over her palm, Amy felt her stomach give a funny lurch and all she could do was stare at him as if mesmerized. "My dear Miss Bourne," he repeated, and then bent his head and his lips touched her skin, making her nerve ends sizzle. When he looked up, a strand of hair fell into his face and gave him a sweetly boyish appearance.

How she yearned to reach up and stroke it out of his face, to cup his cheek in her hand! Amy bit her lip. No, she mustn't, *mustn't*.

"Dearest, loveliest Miss Bourne. Amelia . . ." Again, his thumb whispered over her palm and sent thrill after thrill through her body.

"Yes?"

His lips curved, and she mused on how dear his smile had already become to her. So very dear.

"Will you do me the honor of becoming my wife?"

Then she did reach up to cup his face in her hand. "Oh yes," she murmured. And louder, laughing as joy exploded in her veins, "Oh, yes!"

His smile widened and seemed to fill her whole field of vision. She felt his free hand snake around her waist. He drew her against his body, their joined hands clasped to his heart. "My dear Miss Bourne . . ." And then the joy of it all caught up with her and, laughing aloud, she flung her arms around his neck to hold him to her and never ever let go.

Chapter Five

For the rest of the afternoon Amy walked about on a cloud of pure bliss. As soon as the gentlemen had accompanied the two young ladies back home, Stapleton requested a private talk with her temporary guardian. Meanwhile Amy, Isabella, and Mrs. Bentham awaited the outcome of the talk in the drawing room over a cup of restoring tea. Mrs. Bentham had forced poor Lord Munthorpe to stay with them, perhaps under the assumption that the evidence of so much premarital happiness would somehow induce him to rush to Mr. Bentham's study too, in order to make an offer for Isabella.

"You will have the most illustrious connections, my dear," she informed Amy. "Just imagine: sister-in-law to an earl!"

Delicately, Isabella wrinkled her nose while seeming to concentrate on choosing a cream tart. "But married to a *younger brother* of the earl." She picked up a tart, then turned to Lord Munthorpe, a radiant smile on her face. "Tell me, my lord, does Mr. Stapleton not live in rented rooms in Albany?"

He flushed a little under her gaze, but manfully squared his shoulders. "Indeed he does, Miss Bentham. A most worthy institution, Albany is." At this, Isabella's smile turned into a dark glower, which clearly disconcerted the poor man. "B-Byron had rooms there," he mumbled. "And Mr. Angelo—"

Mrs. Bentham's brows rose. "The fencing man? How utterly ghastly, my lord!"

At a loss, Lord Munthorpe looked from one lady to the other. The inhabitants of Albany had probably considered it splendid to have the famous fencing academy on the premises. It was, after all, a legend in its own right. Hadn't one of the Angelos even taught the present king himself?

"What I am *saying* is," Isabella continued scornfully, "how very uncomfortable arrangements are going to be with Mr. Stapleton having no estate of his own. Is that not so, my lord?" She gave Munthorpe a sharp look.

He gulped. "Yes, Miss Bentham." Though it came out more as a question than a statement, it obviously satisfied Isabella, who nodded.

"Indeed." She shot Amy a pitying look. "Wherever are you going to live, my dear? You must be dreadfully worried!"

How very typical of Isabella to try and dim Amy's happiness! But, truly, *nothing* could dim it, nothing at all! For was she not engaged to the most handsome man, with the most adorable sprinkle of freckles on his nose? A man who felt most wonderful in her arms—though it was probably improper that she knew of these things, even if they were now engaged. Yet . . . oh, how could she not think of that divine moment when his arm had closed around her, pressing her against his body, so she had been able to breathe in his scent. No, she hadn't yet identified its components, but given further opportunity, she had no doubt she could. And would! Just as she would count those freckles on his nose one day. Soon! And kiss that most precious speck of cinnamon on his earlobe.

She felt her cheeks heat a little at her thoughts. However, before anybody could notice how flustered she was, the door opened and Mr. Stapleton—Sebastian—came striding through, wearing the most blissful expression imaginable. "All is settled," he announced. He walked to Amy, took her hands, and drew her to her feet. "I am delighted to inform you, Miss Bourne, that your guardian has graciously agreed to let me have your hand in marriage." His smile widened, and it seemed to Amy his freckles glowed with joy. "I hope you are quite overcome by happiness, because I most certainly am." And with that he raised her hands—her ungloved hands—to his mouth and pressed tiny little kisses all over her knuckles.

Mrs. Bentham pointedly cleared her throat. "What delightful news, Mr. Stapleton," she said, her face as sour as any lemon. "Congratulations."

He turned to her, still smiling, still holding Amy's hands. "I thank you most sincerely, Mrs. Bentham. Your husband has furthermore agreed to accept an invitation for Amelia to Rawdon Park, my brother's country estate, for the weeks before Christmas."

"Ohh," Amy breathed.

He shot her quick glance and pressed her fingers more tightly. "I hope this is not going to inconvenience you and your plans for the season." He turned back to Mrs. Bentham. "Especially as the invitation is extended to your daughter." He gave Isabella a smile, which however seemed to leave the girl utterly cold, judging by her stern frown. Perhaps she regretted that she would have to leave Lord Munthorpe behind if she accompanied them to Rawdon Park. Fleetingly, Amy wondered whether Isabella felt any real affection for Munthorpe, or whether her regard was all for his earldom. In the face of her own happiness, however, such practical, commonsensical notions were quickly brushed aside. Who cared about a title and a vast estate when one could have Sebastian instead? Was he not all she had ever dreamt of? Perfect in every way?

"Lord Rawdon thought Miss Bentham's presence might

make my Amelia feel more comfortable among the hordes of Stapletons," he continued.

Now it was Amy's turn to press his fingers, for how could she ever have felt uncomfortable in the presence of his family? He gave her a warm smile, one of the sort that made his blue-gray eyes light up with tenderness.

"How very kind of you, Mr. Stapleton," Isabella said frostily.

From the corner of her eye, Amy caught Mrs. Bentham prodding her daughter rather urgently.

"I will of course gladly accept your invitation," Isabella continued, though it sounded as if she had gritted her teeth. "And congratulations on your engagement to our dear Amelia."

Her well-wishes, however ill-meant, acted as the cue for Lord Munthorpe, who jumped up, clapped Sebastian's shoulder, and pumped his arm. "Congratulations, my dear fellow. Congratulations. I am most glad I had the opportunity to share this happy day with you. Miss Bourne." He let go of Sebastian's hand and sketched her a bow. "My best wishes for your upcoming nuptials."

Amy curtsied. "Thank you so much, my lord. I am sure we will be most happy." She looked up at Sebastian, *her* Sebastian, and smiled.

No, nothing could disturb these moments of bliss. Not Isabella's jealousy, nor her ungracious well-wishes, nor either woman's sour expression. Not even the fact that when Amy later was alone in her room and tried to pen a letter to her aunt and uncle, the spell was still intact: everything she wrote vanished on the spot; the ink bled out of the paper until it was white and pure once more.

It was vexing, and she had to ask Mr. Bentham to write a letter to her uncle in her stead. Not that Mr. Bentham knew of the spell, or of *any* spells. She told him it would be more proper if the letter came from him, her temporary guardian. It would lend the happy news more weight, to be sure.

She wrinkled her nose.

Yes, it was vexing. One might have expected the spell to end with her forming a permanent attachment. After all, had this not been the reason for the exercise, that she should find a husband?

Oooh, and what a husband she had found for herself! Charming and witty and utterly, utterly gorgeous to behold.

And thus, all gray clouds completely fled her mind.

Once again Bentham sat in his club, drinking and brooding, as he did so often these days, hoping the brandy would silence his conscience.

With trembling fingers, he raised his glass to his lips. Yet even though the alcohol rolled down his throat and exploded hotly in his stomach, his thoughts would not quiet. He sat and brooded and wondered.

"Ah, Mr. Bentham."

He gave a violent start and his glass slipped from his nerveless fingers.

"Tut-tut, not so careless, dear Mr. Bentham." Thin lips curved into a cruel smile, the stranger held out the glass he had caught—and not one drop was spilled. "Surely you don't wish to create a scene."

By now Bentham's hands were trembling so violently that he had to take the offered glass with both, even though he wanted nothing more than to hurl it away like a poisonous snake. But—oh, God—he was the rabbit caught by the snake. A snake that could swallow him whole, if it so wished.

He shuddered.

The stranger pursed his lips, as if amused by his discomfort. "But I forgot: It is impossible to create a scene in a venerable institution like an English gentlemen's club, no? Has it ever struck you how much they resemble a Catholic confessional? Most curious."

Sweat formed on Bentham's forehead. "What do you

want now?" he snapped—and flinched as he heard his own words. Careless, careless.

The stranger obviously thought the same; he raised dark blond brows and cocked his head to one side to study Bentham more closely. Yes, as a snake would study a rabbit.

Stupid, stupid rabbit.

Bentham searched his pockets for his handkerchief, yet could not find it. Had the stranger made it disappear to watch him squirm? The notion seemed fantastic, but had he not seen effects of that strange powder? It had changed Miss Bourne completely: Gone was the rebellious gleam that had so often lit her eyes. Indeed, she had been transformed into a model of feminine sweetness. Could a normal drug effect such a thing? Bentham doubted it. Hell, if he only had more brandy! But his glass was almost empty, so terribly empty again, and once more he could not suppress the shudder that wracked his body.

The stranger leaned back in his armchair. "So, he has proposed."

"Yes." Bentham forced the answer out even though the previous words had been more of a statement than a question.

"How very wonderful." The stranger put the fingertips of his hands together and regarded him with obvious amusement.

Bentham wiped his hands against his breeches. The dampness of his palms left smudges on the chamois-yellow fabric.

"And has your ward also received an invitation to accompany the fox to his den?"

"Quite . . . so."

"Ahh, I see. Excellent. And how delicious that it is Bourne's niece of all people who will become our cuckoo child!"

Bentham started. "Y-you know Bourne?"

Yet, instead of answering, the stranger only stared at him until Bentham squirmed in his seat.

"More brandy, Mr. Bentham?" he finally enquired with mock solicitude. Before Bentham could answer, the man had snapped his fingers at a nearby footman, who hurried to follow his commands. "One last glass, eh, Mr. Bentham? But you must drink up—*fast*. Quite fast, dear Mr. Bentham."

Against his own wishes, Bentham raised the now-full glass to his lips and tilted it so fast that the brandy nearly drowned him. He coughed, spluttered . . . and the stranger threw back his head and laughed. "How utterly charming you are, Mr. Bentham!"

Bentham's blood ran cold. What sort of devilish powers did this fellow command? "Why?" he finally managed.

"Why?" The other arched his brow. "What questions you ask! Because we must hasten to return to your house, of course!"

"My—"

"Have you forgotten the . . . shall we say "presents" your daughter will be required to bring to Rawdon Park? Ah, surely not, when our timing is most fortunate."

"Fortu—"

A malicious gleam lit the hateful, light blue eyes. "Indeed, fortunate. With the ladies of your household gone out shopping for the girls' stay in the country, we will be quite alone, will we not?"

Bentham nodded weakly. What other choice did he have? None. The answer echoed in his head in the most dreadful manner, and his very bones quaked with fright. There was no way out.

Those thin lips curled. "I see we quite agree in this matter." And in a tone of mock surprise, "Ah, you have finished your brandy. Then let us go." The stranger rose lithely and quietly. He hardly waited for Bentham to stumble to his feet before striding toward the door.

His spirits sinking even more with each step he took, Bentham tried to keep up. He barely had time to demand his coat at the front door, and nearly ran into his would-be companion when he lurched down the front stairs, struggling with his coat.

"Wha—?"

"My coach," the stranger said, as he slipped on snow white gloves. *Blanc d'innocence virginale.* But what a misnomer in this case! There was nothing innocent about this man. "Ah, here it is."

It came around the corner like the devil's own carriage: all in gleaming black, complete with a pitch black team. The tall, bony coachman looked positively ancient. As soon as he had halted the vehicle at the curb in front of them, the carriage door slid soundlessly open. The fine hairs on Bentham's neck rose.

The stranger's lips curved as he gestured toward the door. "After you, Mr. Bentham."

Sweating and trembling, Bentham climbed into the hellish coach, and when the door clicked shut behind the stranger, he could not help thinking of the lid of a coffin closing. Heavens, why had he fallen into Lady Maragaret's clutches in the first place? he asked himself, not for the first time. If only he had known then what a terrible price he would have to pay now! But too late, too late. All was in vain now. He drew his hand over his forehead, not caring what damage he did to his gloves.

All in vain.

The stranger lounged in his corner of the carriage and watched him silently, with one of these terrible smiles hovering about his lips. Bentham shuddered.

The other's smile widened. "Come, come, Mr. Bentham. Surely you can't be cold? With the winter not yet arrived?"

Bentham pressed his lips together and huddled deeper into the folds of his coat. What would that beast give Isabella to carry to Rawdon Park? Poor, poor child—if only his path had never crossed Lady Margaret's!

But all regrets were in vain, and Bentham hung his head. The drive from the club to his house seemed to pass faster than ever before, and in no time at all, the godfor-saken carriage came to a smooth halt. "Here we are," the stranger said as the door swung open. "After you, dear Mr. Bentham."

He stumbled out into the street, Lady Margaret's odious messenger following hard on his heels, now carrying a small leather case Bentham had not noticed before. They stepped up the front stairs and the butler opened the door for them.

"Good afternoon, sir."

Bentham gave him his coat and gloves. "We will be in the study and don't want to be disturbed under any circum-stances."

"Very well, sir."

The stranger stepped over the threshold, shrugged out of his coat, and gave it to the butler. An icy shiver ran down Bentham's spine, just as if he had let the devil itself into his home. He felt drops of sweat rolling down the side of his face. "I gather my wife and the girls are still out?"

"Indeed, they are, sir."

"Excellent," he mumbled.

The stranger gestured. "Shall we?" The hateful smooth voice was tinged with a trace of impatience now. Not a good sign. Not a good sign at all.

Bentham hurried ahead toward the study. Oh, if only this were all a bad dream! Yet no, he heard the man's steps behind him. The stranger was here, in Bentham's own house. *Dear God . . . dear God . . .*

Bentham pushed the study door open. He tried to infuse his voice with determination and failed miserably. "H-here we are."

The stranger brushed past him into the room. "Close the door, will you?" he said coldly, and put his case down on Bentham's desk.

Obediently—for what choice did he have?—Bentham shut the door, then ventured to the side table. "Drinks?"

The man shot him a withering glance. "I should think you've already had enough of those, Mr. Bentham. What use would you be with your wits all addled? Sit."

Heat surged into Bentham's face. So it had come to this? He was to be ordered around like a servant in his own home? At the thought, Bentham rallied. "Now look here—"

"*Sit.*"

Commanded in a such a dreadful voice, Bentham felt his legs fold all by themselves. Shaken, he sank down on a chair.

A thin smile lifted the stranger's lips. "That's better." He turned. With a flip of his fingers, he flicked the clasps of his case open and took out a small wooden box, which he opened as well. It was laid out in what looked like black velvet, and three small apothecary's glasses rested in three depressions. "Your daughter will bring these items to Rawdon Park. It is of the utmost importance that she plant them in the correct places, so you had better instruct her well. And make sure that the lids are not opened until she reaches the Stapleton place!"

"The first"—the man turned with a glass in his hand, and Bentham wrinkled his nose as he caught sight of the contents: a wrinkled brown blob with spiky things sticking out of it—"is a bullock's heart pierced with nails and thorns." Almost lovingly, the stranger trailed a finger down the glass. "A simple country charm, but add to it a little spell . . ." His eyes widened. "Most wonderfully effective."

Spell? Bentham thought, his wits scattering like a flock of birds before a sparrow hawk. Surely this could not be true! Who had ever heard of such a thing?

Vague memories stirred, of half-formed rumors at university—about Bourne, of all people! Of course, Bentham hadn't given a fig's end to such tales. Preposterous!

But this . . . *this* . . .

And yet, didn't the stranger seem to know Bourne? Dear heavens, in what wickedness had he become embroiled?

"It will have to be hidden somewhere among the stairs in the house," the other continued. "Rawdon Park is an old building, or so I've heard, and it should not be difficult to find a dark spot, a nook or cranny on the stairs." He threw Bentham a look, who hurried to nod.

"On . . . on the stairs."

"Exactly." Carefully, the glass was put back and the second brought forth for Bentham's inspection. Murky water swirled inside, and amidst the water swam a fat, black worm that looked almost like a leech. "This . . ." The stranger tapped the glass and immediately the worm swam toward him. As it reached the glass, it opened its eyes.

Bentham shrank back in his chair. They were enormous, these eyes, and they seemed to grow until they looked almost human.

The stranger chuckled softly. "Such a beauty. Tell your daughter to let it loose in the lake." He looked into the glass and his voice rose and fell in a hypnotic singsong. "Such a beautiful, beautiful lake Rawdon Park has. With ducks and water lilies and golden fish. Such a lovely, lovely place for our little beauty here. So much space to grow large and strong."

"It will grow?" Bentham asked in horrid fascination.

"Oh yes." The stranger turned to him. "Quite large. It would be better if your daughter stayed away from the lake after she has planted our little present there." He shook the glass slightly, and the thing inside closed its eyes and became a small, innocent-looking worm again. "Now to the third . . ." The glass was put back and then the last one was presented to Bentham.

"A shriveled plant?" Bentham frowned.

"It looks like it, does it not? It has to be planted in the gardens, in a dark forgotten corner, where it can grow roots undetected."

Chapter Six

It was, Amy mused, quite amazing how quickly time passed when one was having fun. She thoroughly enjoyed choosing presents for the members of Sebastian's family and she never tired of having him tell her about them. There was his brother Richard, the current Earl of Rawdon: "Truly, you'll have never met anybody so suited to country life than good old Richard," Sebastian said with a crooked grin. "There's nothing he likes better than roaming the Rawdon lands with his dogs all tumbling around his heels. I daresay, I can't even remember the last time I saw his boots not caked in mud. Can you imagine?" He glanced down at his own polished boots and gave an exaggerated shudder.

Laughing, Amy gave him a sharp nudge with her elbow. "Oh, stop it, Mr. Stapleton! I swear if you continue in this fashion you will make me believe you are the vainest peacock."

"And you can't stand vain peacocks?"

"Oh, I absolutely *detest* them," she said blithely. "If you continue, I fear I will have to break our engagement *immediately* and create a dreadful scene in poor Mr. Williams's shop." She bestowed a beaming smile on the tobacconist, who did his best to hide his amusement over their banter. "You would be terribly scandalized, Mr. Williams, would you not?"

"Oh, dreadfully so, miss." He even managed to keep a straight face.

"See?" Amy turned and batted her lashes at Sebastian, who gave a rueful sigh.

"Pity. We will take the *tabac de neroli*, Mr. Williams." Turning his attention back to Amy, he tugged at the frills of her bonnet and smiled. "You will be most glad, my dear, to hear that I have never polished my boots with champagne. Does that not appease you?"

"I will have to think about it." And with that she turned her back on him and took the package the tobacconist held out. "Thank you, Mr. Williams. Do you approve of Mr. Stapleton's choice? Is this good snuff?"

"One of the most esteemed French snuffs," he assured her.

"Marvelous." And what Amy considered even more important: it had a nice brownish color and didn't sport any of the strange hues she had seen this past half hour while the shopkeeper had opened box after box of tobacco for them. How anybody could stand to put violet or even yellow snuff up their noses was truly beyond her. "Thank you, Mr. Williams." She paid him and marched out of the shop.

Sebastian easily caught up with her. "Now who has scandalized the poor chap?" he whispered into her ear. His breath stirred the hairs that curled around it and delicately tickled her neck. A frisson of excitement made her spine arch, and she gasped.

"Oh."

The next moment, she felt her cheeks flame and hardly dared to look at him.

He had become very still. " 'Oh,' indeed," he finally said. When she glanced at him, she caught the most curious expression on his face before his lips curved into a smile. A rather worrisome smile. "What a delightful discovery." A bit of teeth showed.

Oh yes, definitely a dangerous smile, she thought. She would have liked to take a step back, but somehow he had taken hold of her elbow. And judging from his firm grip, she would have to wrestle it from him, and wouldn't that look most decidedly odd? So she only stared at him, wide eyed, as anxiety warred with excitement within her.

As if he sensed the turmoil, his smile gentled. "Truly delightful," he repeated, and trailed a finger down her cheek. "What do you say—shall we repeat the experiment?"

"I . . ."

But he was already bending down and, instinctively, she laid her head to the side. Rather as if he were a vampyre like the horrible Lord Ruthven! The thought made her giggle.

"I'm glad you find this amusing." She heard his voice above her and then—oh, the most extraordinary feeling!—he softly blew against her neck.

"Oh!" She shivered.

His head came a little closer. "You like this," he whispered. "Don't you?"

This time she actually moaned. Mortified, she clasped her hand to her mouth. Her cheeks burned. Heck, her whole body burned with embarrassment.

Immediately, Sebastian straightened. "Oh my dear . . ." He peered into her face and a rueful expression flitted across his features. His grip on her elbow eased, and his hand slid down her arm to catch her fingers. "I am so very sorry," he murmured. "I simply couldn't resist, but I swear I've never wanted to embarrass you." He pressed her hand. In a droll voice he added, "In your divine beauty you are too enchanting for this mere mortal."

At this she burst out laughing, as he had probably intended.

In a gesture that was by now dearly familiar, he tucked her hand into the crook of his elbow. "Shall we proceed? How do you fancy going to Gray's on Sackville Street? There we might find a more delightful snuffbox than the paper maché one from the tobacconist."

At Thomas Gray's they didn't only find a snuffbox for

the Earl of Rawdon—Amy persuaded Sebastian to buy a box whose lid was lavishly decorated with a scene from Shakespeare's *A Midsummer Night's Dream*—but also pearl earrings for the earl's wife, Mirabella. "Belle," Sebastian told Amy, while he bought the matching necklace for the earrings, "comes from an Irish family—and she looks it! All black hair, pale Celtic skin, and green eyes."

"But I thought . . . Aren't all Irish red-haired? Like you?" Amy batted her lashes at him. Yet just as she looked up, a shadow seemed to pass across his face. Surprised, she turned fully toward him. "Sebastian?"

His expression cleared so fast that she wondered whether the darkness she had spotted had existed only in her imagination in the first place. He wrinkled his nose at her. "Bah, Miss Bourne, how shocking. I daresay, you have never been to Ireland in your life."

"Indeed I have not."

He took their purchases and opened the door for her. "A toy shop now?" he suggested. "So my brother's offspring will love us forever and ever. And . . . a book for Sybilla, I think."

"Your mother?"

"The dowager countess," he confirmed.

She had raised her sons to appreciate the finer things in life: books and music.

"Though Richard must have driven her to bouts of madness," Sebastian told Amy. "He took after the old earl in loving to frolic and rollick across the outdoors—much to the old man's delight. Can you imagine? Even in the depths of winter, when the air was so chilling it gnawed to the marrow of your bones, the two would sojourn across the estate." For a moment he stared into the distance, as if he could glimpse ghosts of the past.

Amy saw his eyes darken and wondered what it might mean. "And you?"

He started a little. "I . . ." He threw her a glance, then shrugged, one corner of his mouth lifting in a lopsided smile. "Why, I had sense enough to stay inside. Have you ever visited the Fens?" When she shook her head, he went on, "There is nowhere such an expanse of sky as in the Fens. A giant dome of blue or gray, it crushes a mere human." He gave a little shudder. "Truly, you feel as small as a fly. Rather disconcerting, if you must know."

"So you stayed inside," she said.

"And so I stayed inside while Richard, much to mother's dismay, always managed to get mud on his books." Grinning, he winked at her. "Same as his boots."

Amy raised her brows. "You, of course, were always a model of good behavior, I assume?"

"Oh, absolutely!" His eyes twinkled merrily. "Though I freely admit to not sharing my mother's admiration for the current crop of poets."

"Foh, Mr. Stapleton!" Amy exclaimed in mock dismay. "How can one *not* like the verses of Keats, or Shelley, or Wordsworth? 'I wandered lonely as a cloud,'" she began in dramatic tones. Yet as the magic of the poem and her yearning for the fields and meadows of Warwickshire quickly caught up with her, her voice softened:

> "'That floats on high o'er vales and hills,
> When all at once I saw a crowd,
> A host, of golden daffodils;
> Beside the lake, beneath the trees,
> Fluttering and dancing in the breeze.'"

Amy sighed. A light touch on her hand made her look up. Sebastian searched her face, and once more he trailed a gentle finger down her cheek.

"Ah, Miss Bourne, I must admit the words of the current crop of poets sound much sweeter coming from your lovely lips." His own lips quirked.

Homesickness forgotten, Amy chuckled and thumped his arm. "That was a truly terrible attempt at flattery!"

"My rusty skills only need a little exercise," he replied drolly.

"Exercise, what fudge! Now it's time to exercise your feet, Mr. Stapleton, so we can walk to that toy shop you've mentioned." She took his arm. "And while we proceed you may tell me more about your family," she said grandly.

Sebastian laughed. "My dear, you are a true nonesuch." And readily he complied with her request by telling her more about his mother.

Widowed these past seven years, the dowager countess still lived at Rawdon Park, the house to which she had come as a young bride of seventeen. As part of her eldest son's household, she enjoyed being surrounded by her grandchildren. "Dickie—Lord Bradenell—is Richard's heir. We all hope he will reach maturity without breaking his neck first. He likes to climb things."

"Don't all little boys?" Amy cut in.

Sebastian grimaced. "I can't remember that *I* ever liked climbing anything higher than a footstool."

"You suffer from vertigo then?"

"I most assuredly do not!" He sounded indignant. "Really, Miss Bourne, your head is filled with the most extraordinary notions!" Ignoring her giggles, he added in a mock-serious tone, "I am just not a climber. Whereas Dickie certainly is."

Amy patted his arm. "I wouldn't worry too much about young Dickie's neck, though. All of my cousins were vastly fond of tree climbing. Some of them still are, to be more precise, and so far, their necks have not suffered from it in the least."

"I'm glad to hear it." He threw her a suspicious sideways look. "How many of them are there again, exactly?"

Amy pressed his arm and laughed. "Seven at the last count. Two are older than myself, the rest are younger."

"Dear God!"

"Mmhm." She gave him a cheeky smile. "And if you don't treat me well, they will hound you to the ends of the earth," she warned cheerfully, though she almost pitied him: The poor man looked dumbstruck. To distract him from the unpleasant image of seven angry, strapping young men coming after him—although most of the strapping young men weren't out of the schoolroom yet—she coaxed, "Tell me more about your nephews."

"And niece," he muttered, then glanced at her. "You are enjoying seeing me squirm. I swear, I *will* fall flat on my face at your feet in no time at all, bleeding from all those wounds to my heart."

"Then pray make sure not to bleed on the hem of my dress." Amy bit her lip so she wouldn't grin, and gave him a look of wide-eyed innocence. "Bloodstains are *so* difficult to remove."

"Minx." He tweaked her nose, obviously not caring that they were standing in one of the busiest streets of London. "I am incredulously glad to hear you care so much for me."

"Always. So . . . your nephews and niece?"

They walked on to the toy shop, and Sebastian told her more about Dick, the climber, and Pip—Philip—who loved doing finicky things, and about the princess of the family, little Annalea. Amy couldn't wait to meet them all, to get to know the family of the man she loved—oh, and how she loved him!

Finally the day came that saw her in the Earl of Rawdon's chaise-and-four, sent for by Sebastian. The middle seat had been drawn out to seat three—one of the Benthams' maids was to accompany the girls—while Sebastian himself rode alongside the coach, and a smaller carriage followed with his valet and the bulk of their luggage. Amy sat huddled between Isabella's writing desk and several small and large parcels that somehow had found their way into the chaise at the very last minute. Unperturbed by the tight squeeze, Amy pressed her nose against the glass to admire the landscape outside, while Isabella sat, looking sour.

They stopped for the night at an inn in Cambridge. Not even the fact that Amy had to share a bed with Isabella, who was probably pining after Lord Munthorpe and his sheep, could dim her excitement about the following day. For after they had left the inn the next morning, they turned onto the turnpike to King's Lynn, thus entering the marshes and moors of the Fens. Mist hovered over the flat land, clung to the clusters of trees and bushes, and enshrouded the windmills, which pumped the drainage from the land into larger canals.

"Dear heavens, what sort of place is this?" Isabella muttered. "I swear it all looks the same. Haven't we passed this spot before? I daresay, we wouldn't even know when we were lost!"

"Nonsense," Amy, who was enjoying the wide open spaces after the cramped nature of the city, said briskly. "Mr. Stapleton and Lord Rawdon's driver must know the way perfectly. I am sure we will reach Rawdon Park in no time at all." And really, how could one get lost on a turnpike anyway, even on a gray and foggy day?

So shortly after midday, they passed through a gate, rattled down a driveway, and behind a gently curving hill, redbricked Rawdon Park rose out of the mist. Dozens of chimneys emitted puffs of smoke, and several windows glowed with a mellow light and offered a warm welcome.

Amy clapped her hands together. "How extraordinarily lovely!" As soon as the chaise halted in the forecourt, she scrambled out, almost knocking over the footman who held out his hand to assist her onto the ground. In front of them stood the main building, a clock tower rising over the middle wing like a confectioner's sugary creation. To the right and left of the forecourt stretched two lower wings—the serving quarters, perhaps.

"Do you like it?" Sebastian's breath tickled Amy's ear.

With a smile, she turned. "I adore—" Yet before she had the chance to finish her sentence, the front door opened and:

"U N N N C L E STA A A P L E T O N!"

Two blurred, brown shapes hurled themselves at Sebastian and clung to his waist and his arms. Two small boys beamed up at him adoringly, their faces aglow with both joy and cold.

"We have been waiting for you!"

"The whole day!"

"We missed you!"

"Terribly!"

A burly, broad-shouldered man appeared in the doorway, holding the hand of a black- and curly-haired little girl. When she caught sight of the boys clinging to Sebastian, her small face darkened dramatically and her lips pursed into a pout. "Unco Shtapton." And, more insistently, "Unco Shtapton!" She stomped her little foot. "My unco." Then she let go of the man's hand and ran toward Sebastian as fast as her short legs allowed. "*Unco Shtapton!*"

Sebastian smiled down at her and managed to free one of his arms to ruffle her curls. "Hello, Annie."

With a happy sigh, she expertly shouldered the smaller of the boys aside to grab hold of Sebastian's leg. "*My* unco."

His eyes dancing, Sebastian turned to look at Amy. "Miss Bourne, may I introduce my hopeful young nephews and niece?"

The little girl glanced over her shoulder and glowered at Amy. "*My* unco," she repeated.

One of the boy's pinched her side. "*Our* uncle."

"*My,*" the girl insisted. "My, my, my!" She emphasized her point by stomping her foot once more. "My!"

The little one's grouchy behavior might be irregular, but it was still adorable. The girl reminded Amy of a furious kitten, hissing and spitting to no great effect. "How do you do?" she said, suppressing a smile. "You must be Annie— and Richard and Philip."

The girl eyed her suspiciously, while the boys stared with frank curiosity. "How do you do," they finally muttered.

"I hope you will excuse the appalling manners of my brood, Miss Bourne," a deep, male voice said from behind her.

Amy glanced around and up into the smiling face of the man who had come with the little girl, his brown hair tousled, his boots—she took a quick peek—muddied. She fully turned in order to drop him a curtsy. "How do you do, my lord?"

"How do you do." His voice was warm and welcoming, and Amy liked the earl instantly. He bowed his head. "I hope you will enjoy your stay at Rawdon Park, Miss Bourne."

"I'm sure I will." She answered his smile with one of her own.

"Shall I do the introductions?" Sebastian cut in, his voice laced with irony.

With a laugh, his brother clapped his shoulder. "And thus the prodigal son returns. You wish to stand on ceremony? With three monkeys clinging to you?" With his free hand, he removed one of his sons from Sebastian's arm. "Off you go. You must let him move if you don't want him to freeze on the doorstep." Sighing and muttering, the boys complied. "You, too, brat." With firm insistence, he caught hold of the little girl and set her down a few feet away. "And now," he said to Sebastian, "you can do the introductions proper."

Afterwards, they were whisked into the entrance hall, decorated in warm, buttery colors, where the two young women were given into the care of the housekeeper, Mrs. Dibbler. She showed them up a wooden staircase, past golden-framed portraits of men in wigs and down a gallery filled with more portraits and bookcases. Persian carpets swallowed the sound of their steps, while to their left and right, upholstered chairs invited them to sit down with a book. Next to bowls with budding cherry tree twigs, more books were piled high on sturdy tables. "This is the Long Gallery," the housekeeper told Amy and Isabella. "The grandfather of the present earl converted it into a library. And here's *his* son, the father of the present earl, standing beside the big oak tree down in the gardens."

The portrait had been painted when the late earl had been in the prime of his life. It showed a stocky, broad-shouldered man in the casual clothes of a country gentleman, his hair pulled back and laid in the then-fashionable curls above his ears. Yet it was not powdered, and its dark tones were reflected in the colors of the bark of the tree next to him, as if in this way the artist had wanted to show the earl's love for his lands. At his feet sat a monstrously big black dog, its eyes raised adoringly to gaze at its master, who in turn gazed across the gardens and the hint of a large lake at the house in the distance.

"Oh," said Isabella in the most curious voice. "There's the lake."

"Indeed, miss." Mrs. Dibbler beamed at her. "Right behind the house. Some say that the lake of Rawdon Park is the largest and nicest in all the gardens of England. Of course, there's not much to see now in late autumn. But you'll have a right lovely view of it from the South Drawing Room. Will you come this way, now?"

She led them up another flight of stairs and down a corridor, and showed them to their rooms where they could refresh themselves. This time, Amy was glad to find out, she would not have to share a room with Isabella. Instead, Mrs. Dibbler first opened the door to the room that had been set aside for Mr. Bentham's daughter. "I hope it will be to your liking, miss." Then she walked a little farther down the hallway and opened another door. "And this, Miss Bourne, will be your room." She smiled at Amy. "The countess specifically ordered to have this prepared for you. The Rose Bedroom is the prettiest guest room in Rawdon Park."

And pretty it was! It was papered in patterns of rose and darker red, and furnished with delicate cherrywood furniture. Cream-colored drapes framed the window, and the whiteness of the chimneypiece and brass bed lent the room a fresh, friendly note.

The housekeeper showed Amy the door to the adjoining dressing room, where two maids were busy unpacking her trunks. "Rosie"—one of the girls curtsied—"will be assisting you during your stay. If you tell her which dress you wish to wear for dinner tonight, she will have it ready for you at the end of the afternoon."

Amy chose a dress, then went back into the bedroom, where she left her pelisse and bonnet lying on a chair. On the washstand a jug of warm water stood already waiting, and she filled the china bowl to quickly wash her face and hands.

She brushed over her dress, deemed herself presentable, and went to Isabella's room. From there a footman took the two young women to the South Drawing Room in the back wing of Rawdon Park, where the family had assembled. The sun fell through the large, high windows and lent the room, done in shades of peach and cream, a warm glow. It sparked a fiery gleam in Sebastian's hair, who sat on one of the large sofas, his lap a throne for his little niece. Yet as he caught sight of Amy, he stood.

"Here they are." A smile lit his face as he spoke, and Amy felt an answering smile lift the corners of her mouth. He held out a hand and, reaching for it, she let him draw her to his side. "My dear." Tenderness softened the sharp angles of his face as he raised her hand to press a kiss onto her knuckles.

His warm breath whispering over her skin made her toes curl. Amy lost herself in the stormy blue-gray of his eyes. Her heart was beating madly, so loud he must surely hear it, so strong he must feel it pulsing in her fingertips. Would it always be like this? One look, and she was quivering inside. One touch, and her bones were melting.

The sound of somebody clearing his throat—noisily— brought her back to her senses. Her cheeks flamed. Heavens! What must his family think? For the first time Amy regretted her unconventional upbringing. She really must remember that she was now staying at the home of an earl, and hence behave with proper decorum! Hastily, she stepped back from Sebastian, but didn't get very far because he was still holding fast to her hand.

"Sebastian!" she whispered urgently.

"*My* unco!" a little-girlish voice growled beside her, and the next moment the tiny Lady Annalea Stapleton stepped in a rather unladylike manner on Amy's foot. Hard.

"Ouch!" Amy winced.

The little girl glared at her. "My unco!"

"Annie!" The tender expression was wiped off Sebastian's face. He glowered at his niece.

"Annalea!" A slender woman hastened to their side and took the little girl's hand. "You will apologize to Miss Bourne immediately."

Mutinously, Annie pressed her lips together and shook her head.

"Annie!"

"*My* unco," the girl muttered darkly.

The newcomer raised her head to give Amy an apologetic look. "I am appalled at my daughter's behavior. I hope you will forgive this atrocious lack of manners." Her curly black hair was done in a simple but beautiful Greek style. Her dress was equally simple but elegant, and the green of the material perfectly matched the green of her eyes. The Countess of Rawdon was indeed a striking woman.

Amy wriggled her foot and tried to ignore the painful throbbing. "It is quite all right." She forced a smile, then made the mistake of looking down at the belligerent Lady Annalea. The little girl regarded her as if Amy were the spawn of evil.

Behind Amy, Isabella gave one of her trilling little laughs. "What a . . . lively child!"

Annie directed her scowl at Isabella and stuck out her tongue at her.

Her mother clapped her shoulders in admonishment. "I have seen that, young lady. Barry, would you please escort Lady Annalea back to the nursery?"

"Nooooooo!"

"Of course, my lady." A footman stepped forward to take Lady Annalea out of the room. In the end, though, he had to tuck her under his arm, because not only was she screaming blue murder, but she also tried to wriggle away. The two boys were sent out with her, presumably to take their luncheon in the nursery.

"Heavens." Lady Rawdon sighed as the door closed behind the footman and her noisy offspring. She turned to

Amy. "I am so terribly sorry, Miss Bourne. I hope Annalea did not cause you great harm."

"Not at all, my lady." Amy opted for a cheerful note, since poor Lady Rawdon was clearly mortified. "I have grown up with seven cousins, so I am quite . . . sturdy, I assure you."

Isabella sniffed. Which was only to be expected, of course. Why the Benthams had insisted on sending their daughter to accompany her, or why Sebastian had invited her in the first place, was really quite beyond Amy. He couldn't possibly think they were fast friends, could he?

Sebastian touched her arm. "Are you sure you are all right?"

He looked adoring when he was worried, she found, the sprinkle of freckles on his nose a sweet contrast to his earnest expression. To forgive his lapse of judgment in inviting Isabella was a simple thing, and this time she didn't have to force the smile that curved her lips. "Quite."

He frowned. "I have never seen Annie behave in quite such a fashion."

"That, my dear son, is because you have never brought home a fiancée before," said a dry female voice behind them. "Now, will somebody be so good as to do the introductions?"

"Of course." Sebastian took Amy's hand and led her to the second sofa, where an older woman and man sat side by side. "Mother, may I introduce Miss Amelia Bourne? Miss Bourne, my mother, the Dowager Countess of Rawdon."

The older Lady Rawdon was surely in her early sixties, yet only few lines showed in her face. Instead of a lacy mob cap or coronet, she wore her dark hair dressed high, with a fillet of twisted satin and pearls wound around her head.

"How do you do?" Amy made a small curtsy. It was rather intriguing, she mused, that Sebastian should be the only red-head in his family. How could that be? Or had his mother's hair once been red and she was dying it dark only now? But no, her complexion was much rosier than one was wont to see in red-haired people. A most curious puzzle indeed!

A smile played around the dowager countess's lips as she said, "So, this is the young woman who managed to catch my elusive younger son. What a pleasure to meet you at last, my child." Her eyes sparkled. "We were intrigued, to say the least, when we heard of your engagement." Her smile became a grin. "You did well, Sebastian."

"*Mother!*" he groaned.

"Fiddle-faddle, 'Mother.' I am only telling the truth." She looked past Amy. "And who might this young woman be?"

Sebastian hurried to introduce Isabella, then properly introduced them both to the Countess of Rawdon, and finally to the tall, lean gentleman who had sat next to the dowager countess and had risen upon their entry. A short white fuzz covered his head and his light eyes disappeared behind sparkling silver spectacles. His short, grayish blond mustache and dark suit lent him a faint resemblance to a sea lion—an uncommonly lean sea lion. One who wore a white and green striped shirt.

"Admiral Reitz delighted in terrorizing Bony's fleet," Sebastian said. "However, he retired after the war and found himself a snug little house in Brighton, did you not, Admiral?"

"Indeed, I did." The other man's eyes crinkled at the corners as he smiled. "After having spent most of my life *on* the water, I now want to spend the rest of it at least *at* the water. And enjoying the theatrical performances of the London companies on tour."

Sebastian's lips twitched. "Not to forget Rhinelandish wine. Have you brought a box for Christmas?"

The admiral chuckled. "I hear they call you the Fox in London."

Oh yes, that lovely nickname of his she had heard mentioned in the ballrooms and drawing rooms of the *bon ton*. Though of course, Amy had never heard anybody calling him that to his face. Whom did he consider a close enough acquaintance to allow them such an intimacy? she wondered. How extraordinary vexing when she yearned to know him inside out, to learn all his secrets, great and small, be his confidante, his best friend. After all, he was her fiancé.

Fiancé . . . At the mere thought, a warm glow filled Amy. *Mine. Mine to love and cherish.* How utterly wonderful it would be to finally bear his name, be his wife and companion!

Sebastian's shoulders lifted in a small shrug. "Some do indeed."

"I wonder why, eh?" the Admiral said mildly.

At this Sebastian laughed out loud. "I haven't got the foggiest."

"My dear Miss Bourne." Admiral Reitz turned to Amy. "You have to keep an eye on this gentleman. He is a rather sly young fellow indeed."

"Indeed. And one who may tell Ramtop that we are now ready for the luncheon," the dowager countess cut in.

Sebastian grinned. "Yes, Mother." Softly whistling, he went to ring for the butler.

His mother stared after him, shaking her head. "Insolent cub," she muttered before she turned to Amy, smiling. "Miss Bourne, you must sit with me during the meal. I want to know *everything* about this young woman who has so enchanted my son."

"It would be my pleasure, my lady." Yet dismay sliced through Amy as she replied. *She can't want to know everything*, Amy thought. No, surely not everything.

Her gaze was drawn to Sebastian, and her stomach lurched. What would he say, what would his family say when they finally found out about the magic? She had been so happy these past few weeks, that for the most part she had simply forgotten—

The butler arrived. Sebastian spoke to him, then a smile creased his face. Oh, dear heavens, he was the most handsome of men when he smiled! Her moment of apprehension passed. All would be fine. How could it not when she was incandescently in love with him?

He turned and announced, "It seems that we can proceed to the dining room if we so wish."

As luncheon was a much less formal affair than dinner, they went to the dining room in a hurly-burly fashion as a cheerful, chattering cluster. It allowed Amy to sidle up to Sebastian.

His eyes lit, and he offered her his arm. "How do you like the Stapleton brood so far?" he whispered. "Have they already frightened you witless?"

Amy had to bite her lip to smother a giggle. "Have you just called your family a brood? Admiral Reitz was right: you *are* a sly fellow." She couldn't believe that only moments ago she had been pestered by worries. Worries? What fudge!

He arched a brow. "You mean, you didn't know about my slyness before?"

"I had an inkling." Her heart light, she pressed his arm a little closer against her. The brush of it against the side of her breast sent a secret thrill through her. A little breathless, she looked up at him. "Tell me about that nickname of yours."

"Fox?"

"Who calls you that?" *Bergamot*, she thought inconsequentially. *He smells of bergamot.* The realization momentarily distracted her.

He shrugged. "My friends do."

A speck of cinnamon dust . . . Her eyes flicked back to his. *Fox* . . . With such vibrantly colored hair, the name fitted him most perfectly. *Better Fox than . . . what?* A memory teased. Amy shook her head. She really must ask him about being the only redhead in the family, but that would wait for later. Her lips curved. "The name suits you," she said softly. And, "May . . . may I call you that, too?"

"You?" The tender expression that came over his face was almost too much to bear. "Oh, sweetheart, don't you know? You may call me anything you like."

Her breath caught, and her glance slid from his, while

she valiantly tried to swallow the sudden lump in her throat. Oh, how much she loved him! So much that it pierced her heart.

She pressed Sebastian's—Fox's—arm. Blinking rapidly, she fought against the tears that welled up in her eyes. Happy tears.

Oh yes, she thought. All would be fine. For how could it not be? They would share their secrets and laugh about them together. Only—she couldn't yet tell him of the magic. Not just now. How strange this would be, to reveal the secret of her family to an outsider when it had been so well guarded as long as she could remember. But soon, soon she would tell him. He would be intrigued, and she would be so extraordinarily pleased to show him all the wonders and marvels of the magic. Explain to him everything about this special talent, how the magic flowed inside you and you had to learn how to harness it in order to use it. Learn spells and perfect rituals—and duck your head if a spell went awry. The thought made her smile. Yes, all would be fine. Better than fine, even: a dream come true.

Later in the afternoon, the mist lifted and Fox took Amy on a walk in the park. Autumn had rendered the gardens a world of brown and gray. Gray, the sky. Gray, the gravel that crunched under their feet. Shades of brownish gray, the bare branches of trees whispering softly among themselves. And in between, the graceful, stony curves of statues—lion and griffin, the head of a unicorn in a maiden's lap, and the chubby charm of putti peeking through the bushes or frolicking around on small pedestals.

He wanted to show her all of it, all the places of his boyhood and youth. How strange it was: as a boy he had never seemed to fit. It was Richard who had been born with an understanding of the land—and small wonder: he had been born and bred to it. *Blood will always show*, Fox heard the voice of the old earl. In contrast to his brother, Fox had never felt comfortable under the wide, wide arch of the Fenland sky, which would turn into a dense expanse of blackness in winter nights, so heavy you feared it might crush you while you slept. And the fog—oh, that was surely the most awful thing about the Fens. Slithering across the land, the fog turned everything insubstantial. Even the sturdiest buildings became as ephemeral as shadows. It settled on the land like a shroud, oppressing all living things, weighing down a man's mind.

In all the years Fox had lived in Town, the yellow London fog had never felt as menacing. But then it didn't have such vast spaces to fill as the fog in the Fens. Here it seemed to swallow up the dark ground, while the distant gurgle of water served as a sharp reminder of the times when the sea and the rivers conspired to flood the land. They had drowned plant and animal and man before, and would do so again, despite all efforts to tame the waters.

No, Fox had always felt like an intruder here, whereas Richard—heavens, sometimes Fox believed Richard must surely have the legendary webbed feet of the Fenmen. Indeed, at times it almost seemed as if he could see all the seasons, weathers, the very land itself reflected in Richard's eyes. It was most disconcerting, and made Fox feel insufficient. And wasn't this what the old earl had called him often enough? *Insufficient in more ways than one. Bad blood will always show.* But now that the old man was dead, it did not seem such a hardship to return to Rawdon Park from time to time. Especially not this year when his Amelia accompanied him!

Sweet, sweet Amy. He darted a look at her and pressed her arm. How he hoped she would enjoy her stay at Rawdon Park and find the house and gardens to her liking! He surely wouldn't be able to bear it should anything mar her happiness! Therefore he would never burden her with dark memories, would never mar her loveliness with . . . with things she needn't know. But so far, she appeared to enjoy herself. And his family clearly loved her; there could be no doubt about it. The acceptance had been there in the satisfied smile of his mother and in the glances Richard had exchanged with his wife. For years it had been their secret wish that he would settle down, find a place to put down permanent roots. However, he had never had the faintest inkling to do so—until now. It seemed to him he had waited for Amy all his life.

Fox took a deep breath, smelled the scent of the damp leaves and the perfume of the woman walking beside him— just the barest hint of lily of the valley.

He glanced down at her. The crown of her head hardly reached his shoulder. As always, her smallness and vulnerability fascinated him and made him want to protect her from the world forevermore. He swallowed.

She didn't wear a bonnet, and it seemed to him that her pale hair gleamed like spun gold. "Does Rawdon Park appeal to you?" he asked, eager to hear her voice once more. Riding next to the carriage for one and a half days, so near to her and yet so far away, had been torture.

She raised her face to his, her cheeks rosy, her pansy blue eyes sparkling. "Oh, I adore it! Despite its size Rawdon Park is as comfortable as a family home can be. And the park and gardens are lovely—even now." She cast a look around. Her lips curved. "I love the little putti. They lend the gardens such a gay appearance."

"I am glad." All at once his tongue seemed tied in knots while his feelings for her expanded his chest until he felt he would simply burst with the joy of it.

But Amy glanced at him and looked away, biting her lips. "I've been thinking."

"What about?" It came out harsher than he had intended. Suddenly his heart thundered in his ears, and something like fear constricted his throat. She stopped walking, and her hand slipped from his arm as she turned fully toward him. How he would have liked to snatch her hand back! The loss of contact seemed horribly significant.

Her face serious, she studied him. "I was thinking about your family."

Pain flared in his chest. Fox closed his eyes. Now, *now* she would ask the question he feared, the question that might make him lose her because surely somebody as pure and innocent as her would find it abhorrent that—A fine tremor passed through his body.

"Fox—Sebastian?"

Heavens, only a few short hours ago she had inquired about the nickname, and how he had loved the sound of it on her lips! But now it was back to Sebastian, and soon, soon, it might be back to Mr. Stapleton.

"Sebastian?"

"Yes?" He forced himself to open his eyes and look at her. *Take it like a man.*

She regarded him solemnly, her head cocked to the side. The crisp air made her cheeks glow. God, how much he wanted to take her into his arms and make sure nothing would ever take her away from him. However, he also knew he would not be able to lie to her. His heart hammered almost painfully against his ribs.

"Yes?"

Get it over and done with. He would have to learn how to live with it.

Without her.

It did not seem possible.

He forced his lips to lift into a smile.

"I have wondered . . . ," she said, her voice sweet.

"Yes?"

Her clear blue gaze drew him in. If only he could drown in that blue.

"Everybody in your family is dark-haired—"

"Yes." Sweat tickled down his back and dampened his armpits. "The Earls of Rawdon—all brown as nuts."

"Except you."

"Except me." He took a deep breath, wanting to tell her, but his tongue seemed paralyzed.

Take it like a man.

Her gaze did not waver, though a little frown appeared to mar the smoothness of her forehead and the clear line of her eyebrows. "Why? It's curious, isn't it?"

Surely it felt like this to be stretched on the rack. "Not at all." Another deep breath. *Let me get through this . . .* "I resemble my father."

Surprise registered in her eyes. Her brows rose. "But on the way upstairs, the housekeeper showed us his portrait—"

"My *real* father." The thuds of his heart were tolling doom as he watched her face and saw understanding dawn.

Everything in her seemed to still.

"Ah." Such a soft sound.

It pierced his heart.

He swallowed hard. "The earl accepted me as his own, but in truth I'm another man's by-blow." And the old earl had never let him forget it, either.

A breeze picked up and played with her hair. "Your mother—"

"Yes." He turned his head, not wanting to wait for the condemnation to appear on her face. "It's none too bad, really." He talked rapidly, so the sounds would fill the awful silence. "He left me a small fortune of my own, enough to let me live in comfort. Why, it's even enough that I can buy a small estate somewhere, later, when . . ." He swallowed. "If . . ." *I marry. If you still want me.*

"I understand."

More darts to his heart. He bowed his head, defeated. "I was sure you would," he murmured. *Bad blood will always show.*

Something touched his cheek. His head jerked back. He stared at her. God, when had she come so near?

When she reached up to put her gloved hand against his cheek once more, his knees nearly buckled. "It must have been hard to grow up with this knowledge," she whispered.

"No. I . . . I . . ." Her thumb rubbed against his skin in tiny, shy circles. He couldn't believe what he saw in her eyes. "I . . ." He put his hand over hers, held it still against his face. "You don't . . . mind?"

Her eyes widened. "Mind?" An expression of extraordinary tenderness washed over her face and dumbfounded him. "Mind? Oh, Fox. Surely you didn't think—"

"I did," he said, rawly. His voice was so hoarse it sounded like a stranger's even to his own ears.

Her eyes softened. "Then let me show you how much I mind." And with that she rose on tiptoe, her free hand sneaking around his neck to draw his head down. Her lips touched his, sweetly, innocently.

It was a spark that ignited a fire. His arms closed around her, hauled her against him, tighter, tighter, so tightly their bodies would melt and become one. His hand buried in her hair, he opened his mouth and, not so sweetly, not so innocently, deepened the kiss, tasted her, devoured her.

And she—

—let him.

He felt her arms around his shoulders and her fingers kneading his neck as if to spur him on. On and on, until she moaned in his arms and his body was on fire for her.

He came up gasping for air, her face so near to his that he could see the fine, soft hair on her cheeks. Her eyes opened, languid and drugged with pleasure one moment, then sparkling with laughter the next. Her breaths were little puffs on his face.

"Extraordinary."

He gave a wry laugh. His ears burned. "I had meant our first kiss to be a little less wild."

"No." Her lips curved mischievously. "I liked it exactly as it was." Her eyes dropped to his mouth. "*Exactly* as it was . . ." she purred and ran her tongue over the seam of his lips.

Helpless, his fingers spasmed. He groaned, making her chuckle with delight.

"Witch."

Her expression sobered. "Yes." Once again, she rubbed her hand over his cheek. He wished she would shed her gloves. "You can't have thought . . ." Her eyes seemed to glow when she looked at him. "Fox, I *love* you. Nothing will make this love go away."

And with that, the last constrictions around his heart fell

away. He had not lost her. She knew his deepest, darkest secret and still he had not lost her. Warmth filled his whole being, made his chest swell and his eyes burn. He kissed her again, so she wouldn't see the tears in his eyes.

"I love you," he whispered against her lips. "I always will—whatever may happen."

Chapter Seven

By morning the mists had returned to smother Rawdon Park in thick layers of grayish white. From the breakfast parlor the trees beyond the pleasure green appeared as blurred, bulky, dark shapes. The gloomy weather made the room with its fuchsia curtains and the Chinese wallpaper, where exotic birds disported themselves among stalks of green grass, doubly cheerful. The tones of red were repeated in the chimneypiece, which had been contracted to fit a Rumford grate. As a result, the fire filled the room with comfortable warmth instead of acrid smoke. After the draft in the hallways this was very welcome, indeed.

When Amy entered the room, she found only Lady Rawdon present. "Good morning, Miss Bourne. I see you are an early riser, too? Excellent." The countess bestowed upon her a sparkling smile. "Let John give you some tea or coffee." Her brow wrinkled. "Or would you prefer hot chocolate?" She sounded a little worried. "I am sure our cook must have a block of cocoa somewhere in her pantry."

Touched and slightly embarrassed by this obvious eagerness to please her, Amy hastily assured the woman that tea was perfectly fine, so the footman hurried to fill a cup of tea for her under the critical eye of the butler.

"Thank you." Amy smiled at the lanky young man, who promptly blushed to the tips of his ears. A discreet cough from the butler made his color deepen until it competed with the curtains in brilliancy. Hastily he reached for a plate, which he handed her instead of the cup.

"Thank you," Amy said again, trying not to smile. In all likelihood this was the first time the poor man was serving at the table, and for his faux pas the butler would later box his ears for sure.

She continued to walk along the sideboard, where the breakfast dishes had been set up. Amy chose some toast, black butter, and a pastry, let the downcast footman hand over her cup of tea, and then went to the table, where she took the seat opposite the countess.

"Did you sleep well?" Lady Rawdon asked.

"How could I not? I have the loveliest room." Stirring her tea, Amy was distracted by the sight of even more exotic birds on the delicate, gold- and fuchsia-rimmed cup. Inadvertently, her gaze was drawn to the curtains and wallpaper, then back.

At her flabbergasted look, the countess laughed. "My mother-in-law so wished for a room that matched the china that we couldn't help choosing this decor when we redecorated the breakfast parlor a few years ago."

"Oh," Amy said faintly. To think of it: that somebody would choose their wallpaper to go with the china, of all things! She chuckled. "Will the dowager countess join us for breakfast?" she asked as she started spreading the black butter on her toast.

"No, she usually has a tray sent up to her rooms. And the earl is already around and about on the estate, I'm afraid."

"With his dogs," Amy blurted. The next moment, her face warmed. Yet when she looked up, the countess was chuckling.

"So, Sebastian has been talking, has he?" Her eyes twinkled. "Yes, indeed, Richard is bumbling through the fields and meadows with his dogs. I understand that he took the poor admiral, too. At an *unearthly* early hour, as your fiancé would say."

Amy grinned. "But then, he would be used to town hours." She bit into the toast, found that the black butter had obviously been made of black currants and gooseberries, and chewed happily.

"That he is. And he always has a devilish time getting used to country hours when he stays with us. You don't seem to be similarly afflicted."

Amy gave a little shrug. "I have lived in the country for most of my life." She didn't add that she was quite used to being woken in the early hours of the morning, when her family's fortepiano was acting up again or one of the boys had managed to blow up a secret experiment.

"And your friend?"

"Miss Bentham?" Not that Amy thought of Isabella as her friend. "Her family lives in Town, so naturally she isn't used to country hours either."

"Oh dear." For a moment, the countess looked disconcerted, before her expression lit up again. "Then perhaps you'd like to inspect our library after breakfast? I need to meet with our cook about dinner."

"I'd love to. I believe your housekeeper showed us through it when we arrived yesterday."

Relief registered on Lady Rawdon's face. "I hate to leave you all on your own, but—"

"Dinner." Amy smiled. "I understand." Even in the Bourne household, much smaller as it was, her aunt would meet up with the cook each morning to discuss the dishes for their luncheon and, more importantly, for dinner. And inevitably Cook would complain about her diminishing stocks in the pantry thanks to the healthy appetites of Amy's cousins. "They're worse than locusts! Worse than locusts!" Cook would wail.

To which Aunt Maria would reply, quite sternly, "Then you should stop baking all those treats, which you give them between the meals."

And Cook would stare at her full of hurt and disbelief, as

if her mistress had just suggested she should drown some hapless puppy dogs.

The memory made Amy smile fondly, but also with a pang of homesickness.

Lady Rawdon leaned forward. "Do you enjoy penny books, Miss Bourne?" Her eyes sparkled.

Amy thought of the many small books she and her cousins had devoured. Homesickness forgotten, she leaned forward, too. "I love them extraordinarily well."

The countess raised one dark brow. "Even more than gothic novels?"

"Oh, yes." She preferred knights and giants to skeletons in closets.

"Wonderful!" Lady Rawdon clapped her hands. "Then you simply must read *The Horrible Histories of the Rhine*! We've got it new; it was in the mail only a fortnight ago. It is a great joy to read. It has all the ingredients of an enchanting story: fencing, fighting, poison, true love. Some evil giants, beautiful women, beasts of all natures and descriptions. And, of course, the brave men who fight against them."

Exactly Amy's kind of story! "It sounds vastly entertaining," she said. And wasn't a cold, misty day the perfect time to sit down and enjoy a book?

Obviously satisfied, Lady Rawdon nodded. "Then I will have somebody fetch it for you. John? Please tell my maid to fetch me the book from my salon. *The Horrible Histories*."

While the footman was on his errand, Amy finished her pastry, which turned out to be a delicious apple puff. She had just picked up the last crumbs on her plate when John arrived with the book. "The fire in the drawing room has been lit. If Miss Bourne would prefer to read there—"

"Wonderful," the countess said. "Much less drafty than the library and much more comfortable seating. Will you be all right, my dear?"

"Perfectly so," Amy said with a smile.

After they had taken leave, she ambled to the drawing

room, chose one of the sofas, and sat down to study the book. The covers were of dark red leather, soft and smooth to the touch. On the spine she found gilt ornaments and the title, *Histories of the Rhine*.

She opened the book and grinned when she saw the title page:

THE HORRIBLE HISTORIES
OF THE RHINE
Being the True Story
of Seven Brave Knights
of Mayence
& what Befell them

The frontispiece showed a strapping young man in the dark robe of a scholar, with a book raised high over his head. With this he apparently intended to slay the—Amy squinted—three-headed black sheep with a rather unsheep-like tail?

"Lord Munthorpe would have a field day with this," she muttered, then grinned as she remembered the sight of His Lordship reciting his poem in the British Museum.

Her eyes dropped to the description of the illustration. "Worthy Markander and the three-headed monster poodle," it read.

A monster poodle?

A three-headed one on top of that?

Amy giggled. "I say!"

She turned the pages, skipped over the table of contents and the dedications, and settled back to read Chapter I:

After the angry gods had ruined the capital city of Florin, and turned King Burkardis's glorious buildings to a waste and desolate wilderness, Duke Cyrensius, driven from his native habitation, with many of his distressed countrymen, wandered about the world, like pilgrims, to find some happy region . . .

She read on about how they traveled all the way to old Germania, where they settled at the large river that was named Renos, or Rhine.

There Duke Cyrensius first laid the foundations of New Florin, which he called Florinouvant, but, in process of time, it came to be called Mayence.

Thus began Rhinelandia to flourish, not only in magnificent and sumptuous buildings, but in courageous and valiant knights, whose most noble and adventurous attempts in the truly heroic feats of chivalry, Fame shall draw forth, and rescue from the dark and gloomy mansions of oblivion.

But the most famous knights of all, Amy learned, lived during the reign of King Bernardius, in the Year of Our Lord 1410.

An hour later, Fox found her still engrossed in the book. "There you are!" He gave her a rueful smile. "You must think me a most dastardly fellow to leave you all deserted in my brother's house."

At the sight of him, the sound of his voice, a secret thrill coursed through her. It was probably terribly improper, but also rather delicious. "Not at all." She was pleased how calm her voice sounded. She shut the book, marking the page with her forefinger. "I had breakfast with Lady Rawdon." She watched him slowly approaching the sofa where she sat.

A reddish eyebrow rose. "I surmise you did not miss me then."

"Miss you?" she asked innocently, her eyes wide and inquiring. "Not at all. Should I have?" Oh, how she enjoyed teasing him! She bit her lip so she wouldn't smile and ruin the whole game.

"So you did not miss me?" A devilish light glinted in his eyes.

"No, indeed not."

By now he had almost reached the sofa. "Are you sure?"

"Oh, *yes*." She waved her free hand about.

"Absolutely . . . perfectly . . . sure?"

She had to lean her head back, for now he stood beside her, towering over her in mock menace. "Oh yes," she said blithely. "Absolutely, perfect—"

The rest of the word was lost as he swooped down. She had a short glimpse of the endearing sprinkle of freckles on his nose, before his mouth closed over hers and her eyes fell shut.

Instantly, heat rose between them, and excitement prickled in her veins like sparkling wine. "Mmmm . . ."

But he had already raised his head.

"Nice," she murmured, and when he didn't return, "More!" She opened her eyes, found him laughing down at her. "More!"

"No, absolutely not. I would only embarrass myself— and in my brother's drawing room at that! No, it's simply not done, I'm afraid." He offered her his hand. "But perhaps I can persuade you to have a cup of tea with me?"

Disgruntled, she took his hand and let him raise her to her feet. "Ah well," she sighed. "I suppose it would be terribly scandalous if we were to be found kissing."

"Terribly," Fox said straight-faced. "And we would be doing more than just kissing."

Her eyes widened.

He laughed again and kissed the tip of her nose. "Much more," he added in a whisper.

She couldn't help it: warm color crept up to her cheeks. "Hmph." It seemed she wasn't the only one who enjoyed a little teasing. Though perhaps—she eyed him speculatively— he wasn't teasing at all.

"Hmph," she repeated, but was in fact rather pleased with herself. And with him. Always with him. And how could it not be, when she loved him so? Even though it was wicked to enjoy his kisses when they weren't even yet married. But with each passing day she found it more difficult to care about conventions and propriety.

She held up the book. "If I shall keep you company during your breakfast, I'll need something to mark the page. Could a footman bring me my basket with needlework?"

"Of course." Fox rang for a servant and sent him off to fetch the basket, before they strolled arm-in-arm to the breakfast parlor. There they found Isabella, as well as Lord Rawdon and Admiral Reitz, who had just come back from their early-morning walk.

"Heavens, Richard!" Fox gave an artificial shudder. "You look disgustingly fresh and ruddy. Don't tell me you've already been outside!" His gaze dropped to his brother's boots. He grinned. "You *have*."

"Whereas you, my dear chap"—walking past them, the earl slapped Fox's back hard enough to make him stumble— "look disgustingly bleary-eyed." Chuckling, he stepped to the sideboard. "Ramtop, can you bring us anything heartier than toast? Are there any chicken baskets left from last night, per chance?"

"I shall ask the cook, my lord." The butler left the room.

The earl rubbed his hands. "What's better than a second breakfast after an outing in the morning? Coffee, Admiral?"

"Pitch black," was the answer.

Young John hurried to comply and filled cups with the steaming dark liquid. Amy took another cup of tea before she ambled to the table and, feeling she ought to be social, sat down facing Isabella.

"Did you sleep well?" she inquired politely.

Isabella sniffed. "How could I?" In a confidential manner, she leaned forward to whisper, "These beds are horribly lumpy, don't you think?" She grimaced and threw a look at the men who were still standing at the sideboard and were now inspecting the plate Ramtop had just brought in. "Well, I suppose, being in the country and all that, one can't expect the best of mattresses." With an expression of slight distaste, she looked down on her toast. "Nor the best of preserves."

With difficulty Amy suppressed the urge to roll her eyes. Why had she bothered to ask in the first place? "I was quite satisfied with both mattress and preserves," she said.

"Of course, you would be. After all you, poor dear, have lived in the wilderness of the Black Country all of your life." Isabella shuddered a little. Indeed, she made it sound as if Amy had crawled out from under a stone.

Amy wondered if there were a way to fling the contents of her teacup into Isabella Bentham's face and make it look like an accident. Speculatively, she eyed Isabella's cup. If only . . .

Her fingers twitched.

With a little bit of magic she wouldn't even have to use her own cup.

But alas, it was not to be.

Isabella smiled at her in a way that was probably supposed to be reassuring. "Nobody expects *you* to have developed a refined taste, Amelia."

Drat, it was also too late in the year to find some poor frog or snake to put into Isabella's bed.

"Refined taste?" The admiral, coming to the table with his cup and plate, had obviously heard parts of Isabella's last dig. "Which reminds me—have you heard of the latest theatrical scandal, Rawdon?" He sat down next to Isabella.

The earl joined them and took the seat next to Amy and opposite the admiral. "Ah, you know that I am more likely to read books and articles on husbandry and horticulture. But do tell—did that chap Kemble assault yet another of his female colleagues?"

Grinning, the admiral took a gulp of his coffee. "Not at all. Quite worse, in fact. It has come to my ears that a certain nobleman, who shall remain unnamed, chose to have a production staged in his private theater—"

"Nothing immoral about this," Fox commented, and sat down on the other side of Amy.

She took a peek at his plate and raised her eyebrows. It

seemed he had a fondness for apple puffs, given that he had taken not one, but four of them. Could it be that he had a sweet tooth? Amy smiled to herself, secretly thrilled at this new discovery about her beloved.

Admiral Reitz chuckled. "A sly one, just as I said. Now, what if I tell you that the aforementioned production involved some . . . um . . ." He coughed delicately. "Flinging off of clothes?"

At this, Lord Rawdon emitted a choking sound as if he had swallowed his coffee the wrong way. "Good God!"

Underneath his mustache, the admiral's lips twitched. "And not only that. There were also some monkeys involved, or so I've heard. To top it all, a rubbish can was blown up onstage. Followed by a potted apple tree."

"Followed by the stage." Fox's eyes twinkled with amusement. "Yes, I remember now. No, no, don't worry, Richard." He leaned forward to look past Amy and grin at his brother. "It was none of your acquaintances, so you wouldn't want to hear names."

"No, indeed not." Shaking his head, Lord Rawdon took a fortifying sip of coffee. "I must say, this sounds quite in-yer-face."

"Distasteful." Isabella turned up her nose.

Grinning, Fox bit into one of his apple puffs. He chewed, swallowed, then said, "The play sounds like the perfect drawing room entertainment, does it not?" For which he earned a scowl from his brother.

"Gracious." The admiral grimaced. "Not in my living room!"

Amy, thinking of all the things she and her cousins had blown up in her uncle's house, only grinned.

"Once again you surprise me, Miss Bourne," Fox murmured.

"Yes?" She turned her head to look at him and unexpectedly found his face rather near to hers. Mesmerized, she gazed into his eyes, admiring the startling contrast between pale cinnamon lashes and dark blue-gray eyes.

"Oh yes." His gaze caressed her face, lingered on her mouth.

The tip of her tongue darted out to wet her lips. All at once, she remembered the kiss they had shared the day before. Her cheeks warmed. That searing, wonderful, terrifying kiss. Not at all as short as today's kiss had been. Indeed, today's kiss had been rather disappointing by comparison.

Her cheeks warmed.

As if he had been reading her thoughts, Fox smiled. "Oh yes," he murmured. "Once again, you don't seem to be shocked at all."

"Oh?" What had they been talking about? The only thing she could think of was the feeling of his lips moving over hers, of his taste on her tongue . . .

Her blush deepened.

Fortunately, the footman chose this moment to enter the room and bring her the basket with her needlework. "Thank you." She took it from him, willing her blush to recede.

Even though the earl and the admiral pretended great interest in their breakfast, she was sure they must have followed the little exchange. And Fox, that big oaf, just sat beside her, drinking his tea and smiling like the cat that had got the cream. Beast!

With a "hmph," she opened the basket, took out her needlebook, and used it to mark the page in *The Horrible Histories*, before she rummaged around for some pieces of colorful thread. Quickly she knotted together a narrow ribbon to use as a bookmark. As she looked to the side, she caught Fox watching her. In silent inquiry, she raised her brow, but he only smiled at her and continued to munch his apple puffs.

When her new bookmark was in place and the last crumbs of apple puffs gone, Fox stretched his back and glanced out of the window. "Marvelous morning."

His brother snorted into his coffee cup. "Midday more likely, by now."

Unperturbed, Fox turned to Amy, "How do you fancy another walk in the gardens?" He looked up to include Isabella. "Perhaps you would like to accompany us, Miss Bentham?"

She made a face as if he had just suggested an expedition to Siberia. "I don't think this vaporous air would be advantageous to my constitution," she said primly. "It's different for dear Amelia, of course." Her lips curved into a saccharine smile. "After having lived in the country for all her life, her constitution is bound to be much sturdier than mine."

And now she has managed to make me sound like a cow, Amy thought wryly. "I'd love another walk in the park," she said. A pity about the magic. She would have loved to see Isabella's face dunked in tea! But alas, it was not to be.

Half an hour later Fox and Amy, now outfitted with boots, gloves, hat, pelisse, and coat, met in the entrance hall. They walked through the pleasure green around the house before they turned toward the lake. The worst of the mists had lifted by now, but a veil of haze still hung over the country and made all colors appear washed out. The bluish gray of the sky was reflected by the still vastness of the lake.

In short, it was the perfect day to go for a walk with a tall, handsome man and snuggle up to his side, Amy mused, and just because she could, she pressed his arm a little. In answer he put his free hand over hers and squeezed her fingers. Delicious, even with gloves!

She peeked up at him and was granted a view of his earlobe with that darling freckle and a few unruly strands of hair falling around his ear from underneath his hat. Heavens! In the dull light, his hair had a decidedly carroty tinge.

Carroty?

Her brows wrinkled. And where had she heard *that* before? Thoughtfully, she gnawed on her lower lip.

But the next moment Fox chuckled, distracting her from her thoughts. "When I was still a boy," he said, "I used to believe a monster lived in our lake."

"A monster? Like the one in Loch Ness?"

"Bigger. Fiercer." He laughed. "Whenever I could, I snatched one of the boats to row out on the lake and drop Cook's chicken baskets into the water."

"Whatever for?"

He threw her a mock patronizing glance. "Well," he said, his tone as grave as if he were divulging a great secret, "bread worked with the ducks . . ."

"And so it follows that something meaty must work with monsters?" Amy dissolved into giggles. "But what if it was a vegetarian monster?"

"A vegetarian . . . ? Oh!" He made a face. "Fiddlesticks. No wonder I never caught the tiniest glimpse of it!"

"Oh, you!" Laughing, she poked her elbow into his side.

He looked down at her and, with a smile, tugged at the ostrich feather that adorned her fetching little hat. "Yes, *me*."

They shared a long, loving glance and all their laughter fled. Their eyes roamed each other's faces, drank in the smallest nuances. Amy reached up and with her forefinger touched the corner of his mouth. His lips curved. His hand rose and cupped hers so he could press a kiss into her gloved palm.

The look he threw her was scorching.

Amy shivered.

Keeping his gaze locked with hers, he let go of her arm and slowly, carefully started to undo the row of tiny buttons at her wrist. His fingers tickled over her sensitive skin. When he was done, he raised her hand to his mouth once more, only now . . . only now . . .

Her breath caught.

A gleam lit his eyes, and he—

"UNCO SHTAPTON!"

Amy closed her eyes. *No!*

"Dash it!" she heard him mutter; then he sighed. Amy opened her eyes again, and he gave her a wry smile. "Another time," he whispered, before he turned to give his attention to his little niece, who came hurtling down the garden path.

When she reached them, she threw her arms around Fox's leg. "Unco Shtapton!" She scowled at Amy.

He put an arm around the child. "What is it, sweetheart?"

"You muss come," she informed him, took his hand and tugged. "Come!"

He threw Amy a look, shrugged, and obediently let Annie drag him down the path toward the lake.

A disconcerted young woman in the uniform of a nursery maid came toward them. "Lady Annalea!"

The girl shot the servant a dark look and continued to drag her uncle along.

"Mr. Stapleton, I am terribly sorry," the young woman said. "She must have heard you and—"

"It is all right," Fox said soothingly. "No harm done."

"Unco Shtapton!"

"Yes, I'm coming, sweetheart."

Now the sounds of boyish laughter reached them, and there on the banks of the lake they saw the earl's two sons skipping stones across the water. At their approach, the children turned.

"Uncle Stapleton!"

"What are you doing out here?"

"Look, look! We're skipping stones!"

"Just like you taught us!"

Annie stomped her foot. "My unco!"

Here we go again, Amy thought, and decided she had better stay well away from the little girl and her stomping feet. After all, one bruised foot was more than enough!

"Shh, sweetheart." Fox patted Annie's shoulder. To the boys he said, "Shouldn't you be with your tutor at your lessons?"

Philip grinned, displaying his splendid tooth gap. "Nah. Mr. Ford needed to go away to Scotland to look after his mother."

Richard nodded. "She has fallen ill, or something. Ergo—"

"No real lessons for us." Pip's grin widened. "Is it true that father used to be better at skipping stones than you?"

"Ha!" Fox put his free hand on his waist. "Did Lord Rawdon say that? The devil!"

His nephews giggled. Annie scowled. "I dun't wanna skip stones!"

Her oldest brother smirked. "That's because you're a girl. And girls can't do things like skipping stones."

Annie's little face turned dark as a thundercloud. "Can!"

"You can*not!*" Dick said.

Amy pursed her lips. No wonder the girl was so grumpy. Picked on by two older brothers? That was enough to make any girl ornery!

Dick turned to his uncle. "We showed it to her, Uncle Stapleton," he said earnestly. "But, you know, *girls* . . . One skip, and her stone sinks like a lead duck!"

"Now, now," Fox said just as earnestly. "You know that you have to make allowances for ladies, Richard."

Amy's brows rose. *Indeed?*

"Given that they're so much more fragile than us gentlemen."

His nephews hung on his every word. "Yes, Uncle Stapleton." They nodded.

Amy had to bite her lip so she wouldn't laugh aloud. "Oh. Is that so?"

"Naturally." Fox turned to give her a brilliant smile. "It is how nature made you—much to our delight. Now"—he focused his attention on his nephews once more—"how many skips did you manage?"

Abruptly Dick's face became somewhat glum. "Eight. And Pip nine."

Bested by one's little brother wasn't too much fun either, Amy supposed. Especially if you had to tell your favorite uncle about it.

"And how many skips can you do?" Pip gazed adoringly at Fox. His cheeks glowed with eagerness.

Fox straightened. From the way he drew back his shoulders, Amy assumed he was puffing out his chest. He was a vain peacock after all, she thought, snorting with silent mirth.

"Well now," he said, then leaned down to his niece. "Sweetheart, why don't you go and stand with Miss Bourne?" He gave her a gentle shove in Amy's direction.

"Unco Shtapton!" the little girl protested.

"Now go, Annie." Another gentle shove, but more insistent this time.

With an inward sigh, Amy held out her hand. It appeared she would have to brave the stomping feet after all. "Yes, come here, sweetie, and let us *delicate ladies* stand together."

Fox's eyebrows drew together and he threw her a questioning look. But she only gave him a sweet smile and put her arm around Annie's shoulder as the girl reached her side.

"Well now," he repeated and focused his attention on his nephews once more. "Have you got a stone for me?"

Eagerly, Dick squatted down to choose a stone for his uncle from the small battery the boys had collected earlier. He handed him a nice flat, round stone.

Fox cleared his throat, then threw a glance over his shoulder at Amy and winked.

Oh yes, definitely a peacock. She waved gaily and watched him strutting down to the very edge of the lake, where he took a while posing for dramatic effect.

Amy rolled her eyes.

But he handled the stone rather expertly, she had to admit. He threw it from his hip and with a nice splash it hit the water. One, two, three . . .

"Thirteen times!" young Richard crowed and jumped up and down with excitement.

His brother beamed up at Fox. "Spiffing."

Even little Annie laughed and clapped her hands. "Hooray, Unco Shtapton!"

Fox turned and made an exaggeratedly low bow. "Thank you. Thank you."

"Wonderful, Mr. Stapleton!" the young nursery maid gushed.

Grinning, Fox straightened and looked at Amy.

She raised her brow. "Not too bad. Now let us see what the delicate young lady can do, shall we?"

Swinging her hips from side to side, she marched toward him. "Stone?" she said to the boys.

Philip gaped at her. "You're a lady!" he spluttered.

And his brother added, "Ladies don't skip stones!"

"No?" she asked, then squatted down to pick a stone herself. She straightened then walked on, brushing past Fox. The look on his face nearly made her laugh aloud. Gosh, it reminded her of that time at Lady Worthington's musicale, when—

She frowned. When what had happened?

But the next moment she had reached the edge of the lake, and she shook her head. It didn't matter anyway. The only thing that mattered right now—a slow smile spread over her face—was to throw a stone and make it dance on the water.

And dance it did!

By the time the stone finally sank, the group behind her had fallen dead silent.

She turned.

"Seventeen skips," Pip muttered. His brother only blinked, as if in a daze.

"Not too bad for a 'delicate lady,' is it?" Smugly, she stepped back onto the path.

The nursery maid started chuckling, and little Annie beamed like a German Christmas tree.

"Dash it!" Fox groaned. "Those cousins again!"

"It *was* your cousins, wasn't it?" he asked when they continued their walk sometime later.

She threw him a mischievous smile. "Of course. What did you expect?"

"I should have seen that one coming." He shook his head. "You must think me the world's biggest fool."

"Don't take it so hard." Deciding she could afford to be magnanimous after besting the poor man, she patted his arm. "It was an understandable enough mistake—given the delicacy of young ladies and such," she simply couldn't resist adding.

He groaned. "I'll never live this down. But at least my niece is now wholly and utterly smitten with you after you've shown her how to do the skipping." His eyes twinkled.

"Just as well. I certainly wouldn't wish her to stomp on my foot again!"

In an instant his teasing gave way to concern. "Oh yes, your foot. Is it very bad?"

She lifted one shoulder. "It's a bit bruised."

"Oh, I must look at it!"

"What?" She laughed. "You're impossible!"

"No, no. I must kiss it better." He drew her along the path. "Come on, there must be a bench somewhere around here."

Still laughing she complied. "If you think I'll let you talk me into shedding my boot and stocking, you belong in Bedlam!"

"Hush. This is serious. Oh, look here! There's the small pavilion. Even better than a mere bench."

"There are pineapples on top of it."

"Stone pineapples." He urged her to sit down onto one of the benches in the pavilion.

"Why are there pineapples on top of it?" It struck her as absurd.

He shrugged. "Because grandfather liked pineapples?" he suggested. "I really don't know. Now show me your foot."

She laughed. "You're mad."

He went down on one knee in front of her, which brought their faces nearly on one level. With an impatient gesture, he whipped his hat off his head and put it on the other bench. A few strands of coppery hair tumbled into his face.

Oh my, she thought. *He looks delicious.* Her stomach lurched. This time, her laugh sounded more like a squeak. "You *are* mad."

Putting his hands on the bench on each side of her, he leaned forward until they were nearly nose to nose. "Mad with love," he whispered.

This time her stomach didn't only lurch, it somersaulted. *Oh my. Ohmyohmyohmy.*

He drew back and reached for her foot. "Now, let me do proper penance for my sins. Right foot?"

Amy opened her mouth and drew in a deep breath. "Really, this is not—"

"Right foot?"

They stared at each other. Those playful freckles across his nose were terribly deceptive, she thought. He might be playful, but first and foremost he was as stubborn as a mule!

He raised a brow. "Right foot?"

She heaved a sigh. "If you need to know—yes," she grumbled.

"Fine." With deft fingers he started unbuttoning her half boots, while she peered down to watch his progress.

"You will ruin your breeches and stockings," she told him.

"So Hobbes will have my head." He flashed her a roguish smile. "The things I do for my lady . . ." One of his big hands curved around her heel. With a slight tug, her boot came off. Fox put her stockinged foot onto his thigh.

Amy scowled down at his bent head. "This is most improper!"

"Umhm. Nice stockings."

She blushed—actually blushed. Then was mortified. "You cannot comment on my stockings!" she blurted.

He raised his head, and when he noted the heightened color in her cheeks, started chuckling. "Oh, my sweet." He leaned in to buss her cheek, not caring that her foot slid forward and bumped against his . . . belly.

"Gracious!" she groaned. She put her hands against his chest and felt his chuckles turn to rumbling laughter.

His warm breath caressed her ear. "Don't tell me that the same young woman who didn't bat an eye at the sight of Lord Elgin's very nude marbles, now quakes at the thought of showing me her unstockinged foot?" he murmured.

Ineffectively, Amy tried to push him back. "This is different." She gritted her teeth when he wouldn't budge. "Those were statues. This is me!"

He pulled back, his brow knitted in a frown. "Did I just say 'Lord Elgin's nude marbles'?" His lips twitched; then he threw his head back and roared with laughter.

Amy dropped her forehead into her palm. Why was it that males seemed to take so much delight in racy jokes?

Still chuckling, Fox wiped his eyes. "Uh . . . I . . . uh . . ." He gulped and made an obvious effort at bringing his hilarity under control.

Amy folded her hands in her lap and regarded him, her brows raised.

"Uh . . ." He coughed. Grinned. Coughed again. "I apologize," he finally managed, his expression suitably serious.

For a heartbeat or two.

The next moment his face split into a wide grin. "Still. Very pretty stockings." He pointed to her foot, which still rested on his thigh. Gently he cupped her foot in his hand, rubbed his thumb over the forget-me-nots embroidered on the white stocking. "Sweet."

Delightful tingles spread up her leg, but not wanting to let him see how much this simple touch affected her, Amy said primly, "I take much pride in my stockings, I must inform you."

"Pride, eh?" His hand crept up her calf and made her grip the edge of the bench because she suddenly felt rather weak.

And warm.

Definitely warm.

His eyes twinkled mischievously as he met her gaze. "So you admit to harboring peacockish feelings? How very shocking, Miss Bourne!"

She opened her mouth for a reply, but he chose that moment to brush his finger in a feather-light caress across the hollow of her knee. "Oooh," she breathed.

His expression softened. "Yes, 'oh,'" he murmured, and leaned in to drink her sigh from her lips. "Sweet." He drew back to smile at her. "Very sweet." With swift fingers he opened the bow at the top of the stocking and slid it down in a smooth stroke, all the while not breaking eye contact. Only when the stocking was off did he look down. His lips curved. "And sweet feet, too." He tapped against her pink toes, ahhed and oohed over the bruise on the back of her foot. When he bowed his head to actually kiss it better, Amy closed her eyes and decided she was way beyond blushes, beyond mortification.

However, Fox soon proved her wrong. He started scattering kisses on her ankle and from there moved upward, bunching her pelisse and dress in one hand.

"What—?" Amy's eyes shot open. "Fox!" Instead of an answer, he tickled her instep. "Stop it!" she gasped between giggles.

They engaged in a short, laughter-filled tussle over whether her dress would go up or not, and ended up kissing. Not short pecks this time, oh no! Hot, open-mouthed kisses that made her head swim and her heart sing. Somehow her fetching hat came to land on the ground behind the bench, and somehow his cravat became rumpled and halfway undone.

By the time they finally walked back to the house, Amy felt terribly tousled: her lips still tingled from his kisses, she could feel her hairdo hanging askew, and her hat would need a new ostrich feather. Yet Fox hadn't fared better: cravat no longer immaculate nor snowy white, mud stains on his stockings and breeches, and his hat—she really wondered what had happened to his hat. One of them must have inadvertently leaned upon it.

"Heavens!" she groaned. "We must slip in through a side door. And creep up the back stairs!"

He laughed and pressed her hand. "Relax."

"There is a backdoor, isn't there? Oh, what would your family think if they caught us like this?" They would think her a wanton, that was for sure!

"Don't fret." He pressed a quick kiss onto her temple. "They will think we are very much in love."

"But it is unseemly!" she wailed. She might have blown up any number of things in the past, why, she had even turned a whole manor house blue, but that didn't mean she hadn't been taught about proper conduct and decorum. What *was* wrong with her?

His eyes widened in mock horror. "That we're very much in love?"

She sent him a glare. "No, you great oaf. That we're behaving like . . . like . . ."

"People very much in love?" he asked helpfully.

She swatted at his arm. "Like barbarians! Savages!"

"Savages, eh?" he mused. "I like the sound of that!"

"Fox!"

"Amy!"

With his eyes all shiny and sparkling, how could she possibly be mad at him? She sighed. The next moment, however, her head jerked around. "Did you hear that? There's somebody coming! Quick, what shall we do?"

Manfully, he tried to hold back his laughter. "J-jump into the bushes?" he teased.

She cast wild looks here and there. "A statue? We could hide behind a statue," she whispered urgently. "Where's a statue?"

Fox pointed toward a small cherub. "This one?" He cocked his head to the side and eyed it thoughtfully. "On second thought, I hardly think both of us would fit behind it, do you?" He quivered with suppressed laughter. The sheephead! She gritted her teeth and kept walking.

But then they reached the crossways, where they met—

"Isabella!" Amy exclaimed in surprise.

The other young woman visibly started, then colored. However, she quickly caught herself. "Amelia." She raised her chin. "And Mr. Stapleton."

Amy goggled at her. "Whatever are you doing out here? Didn't you say the vaporous air—"

Isabella sniffed. "I took my watercolors." She held up the rumpled bag she was carrying. Glass clicked against glass. At the sound, her blush returned. Hastily she dropped the bag and let it dangle down her side once more. "Well," she said, "I must be going. All that wet weather . . ." And she marched off.

Perplexed, Amy stared after her. "Whatever has gotten into her?" She looked up at Fox, but he only shrugged.

"Oh, I don't know. Well, on the other hand"—he flashed her another of those devilish grins—"we might simply have shocked her witless."

Amy narrowed her eyes at him. "How so?"

"Well,"—he cleared his throat, then leaned down to whisper confidentially—"given that you look utterly ravished . . ." He burst out laughing as she punched his arm. Still laughing, he slung an arm around her shoulder and pressed her to his side, so her mortified groan was muffled against the sleeve of his coat.

Chapter Eight

In the afternoon, Lady Rawdon showed Amy and Isabella around the house. "The original structure of the house is Jacobean," she told them. "Before that Rawdon was a simple, small manor house, but when Sir Henry Stapleton bought the property in the early decades of the seventeenth century, he was determined to convert it into the most magnificent aristocratic house of his time—never mind that he was only a newly created baronet!"

They entered a long room lined by portraits all set in polished black frames. These formed an intriguing contrast to the walls done in terra-cotta red.

"The Red Picture Gallery," the countess explained, "where all members of the Rawdon family are neatly lined up."

"Like hens on a perch." Amy grinned. Allegedly, her uncle's house, Three Elms, had once sported such a picture gallery too, until a spell gone wrong had bounced through the gallery and the paintings had come alive—in a manner of speaking. Afterwards the people in the paintings and portraits had developed the uncanny habit of ogling everybody who walked past. As if this weren't bad enough, one from the sixteenth century, showing a seedy fellow with a moth-eaten beard and an eye patch, had whistled after the maids, while another, Uncle Bourne's great-great-something-aunt, had screeched, "My kittens! My kittens!" whenever it spotted somebody coming its way. It had been enough, Aunt

Maria used to say whenever the conversation turned to the Bourne portrait gallery, to unnerve the bravest soul. In the end, she had banished all of the portraits to one of the rooms in the attic and had conveniently lost the key.

Amy had always suspected the story was concocted by her aunt in order to get rid of portraits that she had never liked in the first place.

Lady Rawdon chuckled. "*Exactly* like hens on a perch."

At the repetition of her words, Amy's amusement momentarily abated. Why did this phrase sound so eerily familiar? Almost as if . . .

She frowned.

Almost as if she had said it once before.

She shook her head, annoyed. Gracious, one could be led to assume that her head was full of cobwebs! And so she smiled wryly and stepped up to Lady Rawdon and Isabella, who had stopped in front of a small, dark portrait.

"And here he is: Sir Henry." The countess grimaced. "He looks a rather disagreeable little man, doesn't he? The conversion of Rawdon Park ruined him. He simply didn't have enough funds to see it all through."

No wonder then that Sir Henry made such a sour face in his portrait!

"However, he did hire one of the best architects of his time, Robert Lyminge, who also built Hatfield House for the Earl of Salisbury and later converted Blickling Hall. Indeed, Rawdon Park looks remarkably like Blickling." The countess heaved a small sigh. "Unfortunately, Sir Henry died before everything was finished."

"And then?" Isabella asked as they continued walking.

"His son"—the countess pointed to the next portrait in line—"had the building work stopped at once. I assume the family regarded Rawdon Park as a burden. But because it was the only estate they had, they couldn't very well sell it. In subsequent years the family kept a low profile."

"Good for them during the Civil War, I assume." Amy looked at the portraits that followed: men with large, ruffled collars and women with voluminous, glittering dresses with lace at the necklines and sleeves. Many of them were depicted with their favorite dogs and their small children, the sex of the latter made undistinguishable by infant skirts and caps.

"Quite so. The family came through the Civil War and the Protectorate mostly unscathed." The countess contemplated the next two portraits. "In those days the Fens were still undrained for large parts and quite unnavigable if you didn't know the land. So the Stapletons ducked their heads and"—a mischievous smile played around Lady Rawdon's lips—"stayed put."

"But how did they become the Earls of Rawdon?" Isabella asked, and for the first time she seemed genuinely interested.

Lady Rawdon stopped in front of the next picture, a larger-than-life portrait of a beautiful woman clad in splendid silks and muslin, with skin as pale as milk, a full rosebud mouth, and ebony dark hair laid in tight ringlets. Next to her stood a young black girl who offered her a large shell full of pearls. "That was all due to her, Henrietta, the sister of the fifth baronet, and mistress of George II."

Isabella looked scandalized. "You mean—?" she spluttered.

Lady Rawdon sighed. "I'm afraid so."

"Oh dear." Amy bit her lip to suppress a giggle. From baronet to earl—all on account of one lusty sister! "Who is the black girl?"

"Flavia, her serving maid." Thoughtfully the countess regarded the young maid. "It is said that the king bought her for Henrietta from the captain of a slave ship."

A shudder ran down Amy's spine. She was more than glad to leave the picture gallery behind and to be shown through the salons and the formal Brown Drawing Room.

The main house of Rawdon Park was built around a courtyard, with towers on all four corners and an additional clock tower rising over the main entrance at the front. The heart of the latter consisted of a wooden construction that seemed alarmingly fragile as they climbed the narrow staircase to the small platform underneath the bell in order to enjoy the view.

Yet what met them at the top were two small boys with guilty faces.

"Mother!"

"I say!" The countess put her hands on her hips. "Were you not told to stay with your sister's nursery maid as long as Mr. Ford is away?"

Not meeting her eye, her sons looked down and scraped their feet over the floor. "Mmhm."

Lady Rawdon sighed. "Well come then, you two rascals."

Shamefaced, Dick and Pip trotted after their mother as she marched down the stairs of the clock tower. Isabella grimaced and followed, but not without muttering something about unruly brats under her breath.

Amy rolled her eyes. Trust Isabella to find fault even with children! For a moment she allowed herself to enjoy the view from the clock tower before she hurried after them.

When they reached the Long Gallery, the countess stopped and turned to her sons. "And what can you tell our guests about our library?"

Her eldest threw Amy and Isabella a skeptical look as if he could hardly believe anybody might be interested in an old library. He took a deep breath. "Great-grandfather had the bookcases installed. He liked books."

"But the ceiling was there long before great-grandfather." Pip craned his neck. "There are allegories of the five senses—look, there's the sense of smell." He pointed.

Amy looked up to admire the intricate stucco work. "I see."

Pip skipped a few paces ahead. "And here's the fireplace. Grandfather had all fireplaces converted to fit Rumford grates." He beamed at them, which prominently displayed his gap-teeth. The pride he took in the new, modern grates was endearing.

"Much to our delight." Lady Rawdon smiled. "If you like reading, Miss Bentham, Miss Bourne, do feel free to help yourselves to the books in our library." She winked at them. "We also have a very nice selection of gothic novels and Minerva Press books."

"And chapbooks, of course," Amy said cheerfully.

"Of course." Lady Rawdon laughed. "How do you like *The Horrible Histories*, Miss Bourne?" They continued walking down the gallery.

"Exceedingly well," Amy responded. "I've just reached the episode in which Markander slays the horrible three-headed monster poodle by hitting it over the head with *The Historie of Britannia* and is granted knighthood as a result of it." She chuckled. "The question of course is whether he hit the poodle only over one head or over all three of them!"

The countess's lips twitched. "A grave and serious question indeed!" She turned to Isabella. "Do you also enjoy chapbooks, Miss Bentham?"

"Chapbooks!" The young woman's horrified face was almost comical. She made it sound as if reading chapbooks were akin to running naked through the streets. "Indeed I do not!" she said.

Lady Rawdon seemed taken aback. "Oh."

There was an awkward pause.

Amy cleared her throat. "Speaking of slaying beasts by hitting them over the head with a book, didn't an Oxonian kill a boar that way?"

Pip, who was skipping alongside her, crowed, "Uncle Stapleton went to Oxford!"

"Did he?" Amy couldn't help that a broad smile spread across her face. How extraordinarily pleasing to learn new things about her beloved! So pleasing in fact, that she wanted to hug herself with joy.

Dick made a face at his brother. "Father went to Cambridge. And grandfather, too! And great-grandfather—"

"Went to Cambridge as well," Lady Rawdon finished as

they walked past the staircase that led to the guestrooms on the floor above. "No doubt, in ten years' time you will be the next generation of Stapletons at Cambridge."

It made Amy wonder why Fox had chosen to go to Oxford instead. Had his real father attended university there, perhaps?

They entered the next room—The King's Salon, the countess called it. Done in pale greens, the chamber was dominated by a large portrait of an aging Charles II. The coal black curls of a wig framed his face and formed an intriguing contrast to the lines age had burrowed into his skin.

Pip stopped in front of the portrait and peered up at the larger-than-life man, then threw a look back over his shoulder. "When the king visited Norfolk, a wheel of his carriage broke and Rawdon Park was the nearest house. And so he spent the night here."

"He liked the food here so exceedingly well that he stayed a fortnight," the countess added, a little wryly. "He sent this portrait as a thank-you present."

"There's a naked lady, too." With a mischievous grin Dick pointed at a portrait in the portrait.

Isabella gasped, and for a moment Amy feared she was going to faint again. But Isabella must have thought better of it given that there was no Lord Munthorpe present to catch her. Shaking her head, Amy stepped next to the boys and gamely inspected the naked lady in the small oval portrait that leaned against a wall and was half hidden behind the king's left leg. At the saucy, provocative look on said lady's face, Amy couldn't help chuckling.

"Charming."

"We think it might be Nell Gwynne, the actress," Lady Rawdon said. "Or perhaps the fashionable Barbara Castlemaine. Did you know that she was his favorite mistress by the time he married? Makes you feel pity for poor Queen Catherine, doesn't it? Even though she was Catholic, of course. Now, if you will come through here?"

They walked through two more rooms before they reached the spiral staircase of one of the towers. In contrast to the beautiful and elegant trappings of the rooms they had seen so far, the walls here were only whitewashed, with the brickwork still shining through. "This used to be one of the back stairways," Lady Rawdon explained, "but we decided to put the nursery and the schoolroom up in the second floor because these are among the sunniest rooms in Rawdon Park."

They left young Richard and Philip upstairs with the nursemaid and little Annie, who waved and shot a beaming smile at Amy. "Another hour of Latin vocabulary," the countess instructed cheerfully. "Your father will test you this evening. Huh," she added as she closed the door on the children, "I will be glad when Mr. Ford comes back. He has a firm hand and has so far managed to rein in my sons' more unruly moods."

The rest of the tour passed without interruption, and they concluded it an hour later in the South Drawing Room, where tea and light sandwiches already awaited them.

And Fox.

Amy's face lit up, and she thought she must surely have floated to his side. Smiling down at her, he pressed her hand. "Missed me?" he whispered.

"Always," she whispered back. How could she not?

Over the next few days they settled in a comfortable routine as all house parties are wont to do. Fox got used to country hours again, and in the mornings he and Amy always took a stroll around the park and gardens. They briefly talked about their wedding plans—a spring wedding it should be—but it all seemed part of a too distant future. The present proved a much greater lure: they lost themselves in the moment, in each other—and made good use of the small pavilion. Fox had not tried to kiss Amy's foot again; instead he had shown her the delight to be found in kisses strewn across her neck and throat and the curve of her shoulder. Once he had even talked her into wearing a rather low-cut dress—much too low-cut for taking a walk at this time of the year. Still, her pelisse had kept her warm until they had reached their pavilion and he . . .

And he . . .

And he had unbuttoned the pelisse, torturously slowly. Was it any wonder then that by the time the garment had fallen open, her breath had been coming in short, sharp puffs? With infinite tenderness he had trailed the backs of his fingers across her upper chest, raising goose bumps and making her shiver. Finally, his forefinger had slipped into the valley between her breasts to tickle her there. Laughter and lust had melted into one, and their mouths had fused with hungry passion.

At the back of her mind a voice clamored that she was behaving in the most improper fashion, but the delight Amy found in Fox's arms quickly quieted that annoyance. Perhaps it might be considered strange how effortlessly she cast off her inhibitions when she was with Fox, but then she loved him—oh, *how* she loved him! Propriety and common sense might dictate that she should not grant him any liberties until they were husband and wife so as not to court possible ruin. Yet this was *Fox*. So why wait when love, the most sacred emotion of all, already bound them together forevermore? Nothing could ever part them.

And so they kissed and caressed, and deep in her bones she knew that soon mere kisses and caresses wouldn't be enough. For day after day, her hunger for him increased like a burning fever in her blood. Thus, day after day, propriety and common sense became less and less important. Amy sometimes wondered that none of the others seemed to see. It appeared to her that all her love and passion must be a flame that lit her from the inside out.

But no, to all appearances none of the others noticed anything unusual. The world around Amy and Fox revolved in a comfortable country house routine.

In the afternoon they usually all came together in the South Drawing Room and played cards or read. Isabella found a fortepiano and chose to brutalize Beethoven. In the late afternoon the children were sent in, and while Fox taught Dick to play chess, Pip played hare and hounds with Amy. Annie, doll clutched to her side, sat next to them and watched the proceedings with wide eyes.

One evening Sir Richard Bedingfield and his wife were dinner guests at Rawdon Park, and a few days later he returned the compliment and invited them all to Oxburgh Hall. He also had invited other guests, so there was a big enough party for impromptu dancing after dinner. Footmen rolled up the carpet in the drawing room, and one of the ladies sat down at the piano. Because it was such an informal affair, nobody appeared scandalized when Fox stayed glued to Amy's side through most of the evening. Daringly, they even danced the waltz together. While they swirled through the room in three-four time, Amy had ample opportunity to feast her eyes on his face, on the sprinkle of freckles, on his blue-gray eyes, which shimmered softly in the candlelight. At that moment it seemed to her that she must have done this once before. Indeed, she was almost certain she had, yet the memory remained hazy.

She frowned.

Why, she almost thought she had been put out that first time! How extraordinarily strange!

She shook her head to clear the cobwebs from her brain, but then the waltz ended and Lord Rawdon laughingly stepped up to them and demanded the next dance with his future sister-in-law. Afterwards she danced with the admiral, then with Sir Richard, before Fox came to reclaim her with obvious—and rather satisfying—impatience.

On another day Lady Rawdon, Amy, and Isabella went out in an open carriage in order to enjoy a turn about the flat countryside. Unfortunately, it soon started to drizzle and they were forced to turn back. They had more luck on the day they visited the Roman ruins. The wide arch of the sky remained bright and clear while they admired the architecture of bygone ages.

A few days later, however, the drizzle turned into fat snowflakes that dusted the land like glittering flour.

"Oh dear," Amy sighed as they took their walk in the gardens that morning. "I'm afraid we will have to do without our pavilion today."

"Miss Bourne!" Fox breathed in tones of deep shock. "You surprise me. That a respectable young lady like you would—"

Amy thumped his arm, which only resulted in making him grin.

"Would contemplate—"

"Fox!"

"Would contemplate to—"

"Fox!"

"Oh, all right," he conceded. "I shall be magnanimous. Just this once, mind you!"

"You're too kind, sir."

He nodded smugly. "That I am."

Amy did her best to hide her smile. "And way too full of yourself as well."

"What?"

With a squeal she darted away and let him chase her down the garden path.

"And much faster than such a flighty little thing like you!" Fox laughed as he caught her from behind, one hand slung around her waist so he could draw her snugly back against his body. "I'm afraid I will have to exact revenge, madam," he muttered, just before he closed his mouth over hers in a deep, drugging kiss.

Hilarity, the excitement of the chase, and passion all mingled and made her heart slam against her ribs. She moaned a little when Fox started to unbutton her pelisse. "You can't possibly—"

"Shhh." His lips covered hers once more. While his tongue swirled through her mouth, he fingered the neckline of her dress.

"Drat!" He sounded so put out that Amy couldn't help giggling. "You're wearing one of these blasted high-necked dresses again!" He frowned down at her. "Will you stop laughing?" And kissed her again.

She leaned against him, but—

"No," he muttered and held her back. "Let me . . ." The rest was lost as she finally managed to snatch yet another kiss.

She loved how his mouth moved over hers, the way he nibbled and chewed on her lips, how he tasted on her tongue. She loved running her tongue over his lips, over the satin-soft skin inside his mouth. With satisfaction she heard his deep, heartfelt groan and redoubled her efforts. She wanted to enslave him as he had enslaved her, she wanted to—

"Oh, thank God, it's only held together by a ribbon!"

All at once a cold breeze wafted over her upper chest. With a sharply indrawn breath, she tried to pull back.

"Oh, no you don't," he murmured against her lips. "Stay!"

"Fox!" she protested. "You can't . . ." She looked down and her eyes widened: the upper part of her dress gaped wide open, wide enough to reveal the top of her stays.

An appreciative smile curved his mouth. "Beautiful." He reached out to touch her breast, but this time she managed to evade him.

Hastily, she drew the edges of her dress back together. "We can't possibly!"

"Can't we?" He took a large step toward her, forcing her to step back.

"We're in the middle of your brother's garden, for heaven's sake!" Another step back.

"We've already done all of this in my brother's garden, if you remember." His smile had taken on a decidedly wicked quality.

"Ha!" She took a step back. "But not in the middle of the garden path!"

He raised his brow. "No?"

Step back. "No. *Fox!*" And she bumped into one of the dratted statues.

"I like it how my name sounds on your lips when you're a little annoyed," he purred. "And just a little . . ." He stepped even closer until they stood knee to knee.

Or rather, knee to shin, Amy thought somewhat desperately as she arched away from him, curving her back over the cold stone of the statue.

"Just a little . . ." He leaned over her.

At that point Amy considered it best to close her eyes so as not to yield to the temptation of his mouth once more.

"Just a little . . ." His breath feathered over her face. A shiver ran through her body and, dear heavens, her breasts ached. ". . . *aroused.*" His lips covered the pulse point at the base of her throat. A heartbeat later she felt the sting of teeth. It was delicious.

"Oh dear," she panted. "Oh, sweet . . . oh . . ."

"All right, this will *not* do," Fox groaned. The next moment he had hauled her upright.

Her eyes snapped open. "What are you doing?"

His hand firmly closed around her wrist, he strode down the path.

"What . . ." She stumbled after him. "Fox?"

"Shh. Or else I'll ravish you here and now."

Her mouth hang open. He couldn't mean—could he?

"I swear, you're driving me deranged," he continued in an urgent tone. "But you're right, of course, there's no privacy on these paths. Anybody could walk by. I wouldn't want my brother's head gardener to box my ears for ravishing a young lady in his gardens."

"Ravish?" It came out as a squeak.

Fox threw her a crooked smile over his shoulder. "Of course, ravish. What else have I been doing just now? What else did I do all these past days and weeks? Gracious, if my family ever finds out about this . . ." He shuddered. "Seducing a gently bred lady under their very roof, even if she *is* my fiancée! Richard would flay me alive!" He turned his attention back on the path. "So you have to promise never to tell them," he said drolly. "This way." He turned right. "I have to say this is all quite uncharacteristic behavior for me." He threw her a somewhat worried glance. "I wouldn't want you to think I make a habit of ravishing young ladies in gardens."

"Oh, don't you?" Amy murmured weakly.

He shook his head. "Indeed, not. You must know I'm renowned for my cool and serious demeanor in London."

Oh yes. Cold as a—what?

"But not when I'm with you." Fox beamed at her, and the memory teasing at the back of Amy's mind evaporated. "I've discovered a fondness for such clandestine affairs. And even better: I know exactly the right place for this kind of thing."

"Oh. Do you?" Amy mumbled.

The smile he flashed her this time could only be called triumphant. "Oh yes! The Muses' Coffeehouse!"

"The what?" She nearly stumbled and fell, but effortlessly he drew her to his side.

"It's a temple, really. My great- or great-great-grandfather had it built on the other side of the park. Temple of the Muses. Nicely tucked out of the way."

"Oh," Amy said and walked a little faster.

He threw her a hot, sideways look. "It's perfect."

"Huh."

"You will like it." His voice had become hoarse. He lengthened his strides.

"Mmhm." Amy hurried to keep up.

"There's also a little bench inside."

"How"—she caught her breath—"fortunate."

They hastened across the whole park, and almost ran the

last part of the way, gasping and laughing as they reached the Temple of the Muses. Amy had only a glimpse of unadorned, classical pillars before Fox drew her inside a miniscule room, the walls decorated with faded pictures of the Muses—all naked, with rounded limbs and pink skin.

"Oh, Lord!" Laughter bubbled up in Amy's throat.

"I know, I know." Fox spread fervent kisses on her cheeks, nose, eyelids. "It's decadent."

"And freezing," she murmured, just before their lips met and clung. And a short time later: "Fox, you can't really mean to—it's colder than in an icehouse!"

He groaned. "Yes, yes, I know." He drew the edges of her dress apart and buried his face in the curve of her shoulder. "Blasted Muses."

Goosebumps broke out on her skin, and she wasn't able to tell whether it was from the cold or from Fox's attentions.

"I have to say scandalizing my family seems like a minor inconvenience right now." His breath felt hot against her flesh.

"Hmhm." Nodding eagerly, Amy tunneled her fingers through his hair.

All too soon he drew back to shrug out of his coat and spread it over the stone bench in the corner. Then he urged her to sit down, so he could ruin another pair of stockings and breeches by kneeling in the dirt in front of her. No doubt Hobbes, his valet, would have his head. Again.

But for now they kissed . . .

. . . and kissed . . .

. . . and kissed. . . .

After a few minutes Amy had forgotten all about the coldness and the hard bench, and if only the dratted thing had been a bit larger, she would have laid back on it and invited Fox to move over her. Would have *forced* him to move over her, common sense be hanged.

Her whole body trembled as one of his hands caressed the inside of her thigh. Skin slid smoothly over skin—dear heavens, when had he shed his gloves? His other hand spanned the back of her head and held her still while he kissed her. As if she would want to evade him!

His hand moved upwards. She moaned.

"Fox . . ."

"Just one touch," he muttered against her skin, and his hand underneath her skirts inched further up her thigh. His lips trailed a fiery path down the side of her neck to her shoulder.

Amy's back arched, her legs fell open.

"Yes." Fox sucked a bit of her skin between his teeth. "Mmmm." And then his thumb brushed lightly over the curls at the apex of her thighs.

Amy drew in a whimpering breath.

If his weight hadn't anchored her to the bench, she would have flown out of her body, she was sure of it. She turned her head to press a kiss into his hair. "Fox . . ." She lifted her hips, wriggled against him.

Fox groaned. "Amy." His forehead bumped against hers.

Hazily, she gazed into his eyes. "Oh Fox, this is . . ."

"We can't!" His voiced sounded strained. "We can't possibly, Amy. Not here. I'm not that far gone that I would take you here and now." He shook his head. Sweat dripped from his temples, ran down the sides of his face. Yet as if he couldn't help himself, he brushed his thumb over those curls once more. Her hips bucked.

With a tormented sound that might have been a half-smothered curse, he hastily drew his hand from underneath her skirts and rubbed it against his breeches before he cupped her face in both of his hands. "We can't," he muttered. "Really, we can't, sweetheart."

They couldn't? Very slowly the passionate haze cleared from Amy's brain.

His thumbs rubbed over her cheekbones. "I don't know what is the matter with me. I've never wanted to let things go this far, you must believe me."

It was an effort to make her thoughts work properly. "But didn't you promise to ravish me?" she asked, perplexed.

"Don't use that word, I beg you!" he moaned, as if she had just ripped his heart out. "When I said . . . I meant *kissing*. I swear I meant . . ." He leaned closer to nuzzle her cheek and temple. "Ahhh, I can't get enough of you. Kissing you has a worse effect on me than the strongest rum." A shudder tore through his body.

Instinctively, Amy put her hand over the back of his neck. "Fox . . ."

"We have to stop!" he cut in, his voice almost desperate. Yet at the same time, his gaze lowered and he stared at the rise and fall of her flushed breasts like a man hypnotized. With a tortured groan he closed his eyes. "We have to stop," he repeated as if to convince himself.

The tips of Amy's breasts ached as they rubbed against the material of her stays, while the rest of her body tingled in the most uncomfortable fashion. She was certain her condition would not improve if they stopped. "Why can't we—" But before she could finish the sentence, Fox's hand closed over her mouth, hard.

"Don't tempt me, I beg you!" He jumped up and drew her to her feet. "Your . . . your dress. You had better fasten it." His fingers trembled as he touched the fine material. The next moment, though, he snatched his hand back as if he had been scorched.

With her body still in turmoil, Amy felt more helpless and vulnerable than ever before in her life. Love and passion gnawed at her like wild beasts and threatened to tear her apart. She wanted to be angry with him; however, she knew he was merely behaving honorably, as became a gentleman. "Fox—"

He rubbed his forehead. "We should go. If we stay . . . I don't know what I'll do if we stay. And I can't dishonor you in such a way." He gave a self-demeaning laugh. "Lord, if my brother knew what I've *already* done to you, he would throw a fit! Responsible Richard. Heck, he would *kill* me!"

Amy wanted to remind him that she had promised to tell nothing to the earl. But she bit her lip and remained silent, because he was right, of course: to indulge in such pleasures not sanctified by wedding vows was madness. *Think of the consequences*, flickered through her mind. *Nothing is certain in this world. And if you let him ravish you now, it might spell your ruin later on.* . . . Yet what she felt for him was ever more spiraling out of control, until it seemed to devour her alive.

A shiver coursed through her. "What is this between us?" she whispered.

Their eyes met. In his she saw the same confusion and alarm she felt herself.

After a moment or two, Fox shook his head. "I don't know." He gestured toward the door. "We should go." His eyes pleaded with her to be strong, to resist the lure of passion.

Finally, she nodded and, with unsteady hands, started to fasten her dress and pelisse, while Fox slipped into his coat.

They left the Temple of the Muses in subdued silence. On their way back to the house, they walked apart as if afraid of the merest touch. Amy's body still burned with the sensations his caresses had invoked until she thought she would go mad with them. They tortured her even as they stepped through the entrance door, and when she went back to her room and rang for her maid to help her change into a tea dress. Her nails digging into her palms, Amy tried to stand still while Rosie arranged the folds of the dress to perfection. *Your nerves are simply over-sensitized. If you look at it in the clear light of the day* . . .

She sank down on the stool so the maid could do her hair. *You burn because he has touched you; that is all. When he doesn't*—Her heart clenched. How could she bear to be bereft of his touch? She twisted and kneaded her fingers in her lap.

Full of apprehension, she went to the South Drawing Room, where the dowager countess sat and played cards with Admiral Reitz, where Isabella was busy with some embroidery and Lady Rawdon was immersed in a conversation with Fox, who had changed into beige trousers and blue frock coat over a gray-and-blue striped waistcoat.

Amy's breath caught.

Fox looked magnificent.

In a daze, she sank down on one of the sofas. No, not next to him, even though she wanted to. But he had been right: it was madness. For she didn't only burn when he touched her. Even now, every inch of her body was on fire for him.

The admiral looked up and gave her a kind smile. "Did you enjoy your turn around the park, Miss Bourne?"

"Yes," she murmured. "Exceedingly."

The dowager countess gave her a sharp look. "Are you feeling all right, Miss Bourne?"

"She has probably caught the flu with all that running around in the vaporous air." Isabella didn't bother to spare her a glance, but concentrated on her thread and needle instead to form those tiny, tiny stitches of which her mother was so proud.

"Perhaps we ought to send for the apothecary," Lady Rawdon suggested, her voice worried.

Amy's eyes met Fox's and their gazes held. For a moment it was as if they were both transported back to the Temple of Muses, as if she could still feel his hands on her body, his mouth on her lips.

His eyes darkened and a muscle jumped in his cheek. "I can assure you, Bella, that Miss Bourne is perfectly fine," he said, without breaking eye contact with Amy. "Are you not, Miss Bourne?"

She swallowed hard. "Oh, perfectly," she finally managed, and looked away. If only she had brought her book with her! Then she could have pretended to engross herself in *The Horrible Histories*. Her hands twisted in the material of her skirt.

Don't think of Fox. Don't think of the searing heat of his mouth . . .

Amy gulped. What was the last episode she had read? Something about a Lady Sigrun who had been abducted by a Scottish monster. Yes, exactly. Lady Sigrun . . .

A footman entered the room and went to Lady Rawdon to whisper something into her ear. The countess visibly paled and abruptly stood. "If you will excuse me? It would seem that—" She swallowed. "It would seem that my son Richard had a nasty fall on the stairs."

Amy blinked. Abruptly her mind cleared and all tortorous, improper thoughts vanished from her head as if they had never been. Young Dick, who liked climbing things? And a fall on the stairs, of all places? She shook her head.

The next hour they spent in agonized waiting. Fox went to fetch his brother from the estate, while Lady Rawdon and the dowager countess sat with little Richard. The admiral, Isabella, and Amy remained behind in the drawing room in uncomfortable silence.

When the apothecary finally arrived, he was able to calm all worries: except for a slight concussion and a sprained ankle, Baron Bradenell had suffered no serious harm.

Later in the day Fox and Amy visited the small patient and found him lounging grumpily in his bed. Amy stayed behind and watched how Fox took a box with battered tin soldiers from a wooden chest underneath the window. The shock about Dick's accident had helped her passion abate. She still yearned for Fox, but her hunger was no longer a gnawing ache in her flesh and bones. She had tamed it. Content, Amy looked on as both man and boy were soon immersed in their play and forming battle lines on Dick's blanket. Just when Amy wanted to go and join them, the door opened and Pip slipped inside the room.

Fox threw a look over his shoulder and flashed his nephew a grin. "Well, Pip. Have you run away from the nursery maid again?"

"Mmhm."

"Then come and join us." Fox winked. "We won't betray you to the nursery maid, will we, Dickie?"

Young Richard nodded. "You can have some of Uncle Stapleton's soldiers."

Yet Pip remained at the door, his back pressed against the wood. "Hm."

Amy assumed it was because Fox's attention was focused more on Dick and the tin soldiers than on Pip that he didn't react to his nephew's uncharacteristic hemming and hawing. She fully turned to the small boy. "What is it, Pip?" she asked quietly, while behind her the blanket was transformed into the grounds around Waterloo.

Pip threw a look at his uncle and brother, then looked back at her, indecision written plainly on his face.

"Won't you come, Pip?" Dick asked, aligning his canons in order to smite a company of Fox's soldiers.

"Hm."

"Pip?" Amy prompted. His strange behavior caused a twinge of uneasiness in the pit of her stomach. Slowly, she went over to him. "What is it?"

He regarded her with earnest dark eyes. Then he took a deep breath and blurted, "I've found something."

She raised her brows. "You did?"

"Where Dick slipped." The muscles of his throat moved as he swallowed hard. "On the stairs."

"Oh."

He reached into his coat and drew forth a wrinkled brown object, only slightly smaller than Amy's fist. He presented it to her on his flat hand. "This."

She stared, then frowned. "It looks like a folk charm. The heart of some animal pierced with nails and thorns.

Chapter Nine

Gasping, Amy staggered back. This was magic. Real magic.

"Is something the matter?" Fox asked from behind her.

She fought for control and managed to make her voice sound almost cheerful. "No, everything is all right."

Pip had his head cocked to one side and eyed her curiously. She gripped his arm.

"Show me where you found it," she whispered fiercely. More loudly, she added, "Pip and I will step in front of the door for a moment. We will be right back."

"Boom!" Dick crowed. "I got your left flank, Uncle Stapleton!"

"Come." Amy opened the door and steered Pip outside. "Now, show me."

He threw her another strange look before he finally trotted to the staircase in the tower that led to the schoolroom and the nursery. Halfway between the first and second floor he squatted down and pointed to a loose brick in the whitewashed wall. He glanced up. "It's difficult to discern."

Nearly impossible to discern, she would say, for the brick had been chosen well: near the bottom of one step, shadowed by the step above. Abruptly Amy sank down to sit on the stairs, her knees suddenly feeling as weak and wobbly as syllabub.

It was impossible to tell how long the charm had been

hidden here. She drew the brick out and fingered the small enclosure behind it. "How did you find it?" she whispered.

"I thought it strange that Dick fell. I thought he must have slipped, and that's why I looked. You said it's a folk charm?" Pip's voice rose and echoed eerily within the stone staircase. "What sort of charm?"

Amy answered automatically, reciting what she had learned about this particular form of folk superstition. "A heart, pierced with nails and thorns, placed in a chimney to cause harm to the people living in the house."

"To cause harm?"

"Yes." Only normally it didn't work, of course. Because normally there was no magic added.

But this . . .

Amy felt sick.

Above them a door was opened. "Is that you, Master Philip?" the voice of the nursery maid was to be heard. "I expect you to come back immediately!"

Pip looked at Amy, and weakly she nodded. "Go. But wait! Give me that thing first."

He watched as she wrapped it in her handkerchief.

"Master Philip!"

"Coming!" he hollered, but still he hesitated. "It's"—he searched her face—"it's more than a simple country charm, isn't it?"

Amy swallowed. "Yes. Yes, it is." She took a deep breath. "But you don't need to worry. I will get rid of it."

"*Master Philip!*"

Again, the boy cocked his head to the side and eyed her from head to toe. "Promise?"

"I promise."

He nodded, and finally dashed up the stairs.

Amy sat on the edge of her bed and watched numbly how the flames in the fireplace consumed the charm. The stench of burned flesh filled the room, and the nails stuck into the heart glowed an eerie orange.

Real magic.

Dark magic.

And there was nothing she could do.

Amy shuddered. Where had the heart come from? Who would wish the Stapleton family harm? Thoughts whirled in her head and chased one another like frightened rabbits. Fear crept into her bones. Whatever should she do now—without magic and without any hope of regaining it anytime soon?

She forced herself to breathe deeply and coughed at the horrible smell.

Calm yourself. You have already destroyed the charm. Still, the horrible fear she felt could not be subdued. It tightened her throat and transformed her blood into ice. It did not matter that she told herself no real harm had come to young Baron Bradenell, except for a sprained ankle. Whatever purpose the pierced heart had served, it had not achieved it.

Her breath escaped on a sigh. No, the foul magic had not achieved its goal. Amy closed her eyes.

And yet . . . and yet . . . and yet . . . The force of the evil had been terrifying. In the safe world of Three Elms she had never encountered anything like this before.

She rubbed her hands against her thighs as if this might erase the stain of dark magic from her soul. Now she finally understood why her uncle had been so adamant that none of them, neither she nor her cousins, dabbled in blood spells and the like, and why he was so irate when he found her reading books that were kept in a special locked part of the library at Three Elms. Over and over again he had told Amy and her cousins how easily the misuse of magic could corrupt a person, had shown them the miniature of a long-ago friend, a smiling blond youth, who had found too great a fondness for the powers he could exert over others. Eventually he had turned his back on all that was decent. Uncle Bourne had tried to stop him, but all in vain. Through blood magic the other's powers had risen to indescribable heights and Uncle Bourne had been lucky to escape with his life. Only now that Amy had touched real evil herself could she fully comprehend the horror and helplessness her uncle must have felt.

Amy didn't know how long she had sat on her bed, thoroughly shaken, when a soft knock sounded on the door. Rosie, her maid, entered and curtsied. "Good evening, Miss Bourne. Lady Rawdon sent me to tell you that dinner will be served in three quarters of an hour's time." She coughed. "Sh-shall I help you change? Eww, what's that smell? Is the chimney blocked?" She went over to the fireplace to investigate.

"A dead mouse perhaps," Amy said quickly. "Fallen into the fire. These things happen."

"Indeed, miss. I will air the room while you're at dinner."

Amy gave her a wan smile. "Thank you, Rosie."

What if it had been something other than a modified country charm? What if she had not been able to destroy it? Desperately, Amy tried to suppress the trembling of her hands while the maid helped her to prepare for dinner.

Since Amy had already chosen her evening dress that morning so that it could be ironed, she now only had to change. Rosie adjusted the fall of the white muslin over the pink satin slip and drew the pink sash tightly around Amy's waist, before she held it in place with a pin in the front. In the back she tied it in a neat bow, which she deftly secured with more pins.

Afterwards Amy sat down on the stool in front of the mirror so Rosie could do her hair. "I have thought to do it in the French style this evening, if this is all right with you, miss?"

"Perfectly," Amy murmured, for what did it really matter which hairstyle she wore?

"I have ordered some sweet peas from the greenhouse. They will look lovely with your dress." Rosie arranged the back of Amy's hair into a tuft, which she adorned with a coronet of delicate sweet pea blossoms in shades of pink.

Judging from Fox's dumbfounded expression when Amy entered the South Drawing Room some time later, it was certainly a most pleasing arrangement. A smile blossomed on his face as he came toward her. "You're looking exquisite," he whispered to her. He inhaled. "Hmmm, and sweet smelling, too."

Even though she had attempted to don a cheerful mask before she went downstairs, something must have given her away because Fox's smile quite suddenly dimmed. "What is it, my dear?" he asked, pressing her hand. "Tell me. It's not . . ." He peered into her face and dropped his voice. "Is it because of what happened at the Temple of the Muses?"

At his tender, worried tone, tears sprang into her eyes. Sniffing, she shook her head. "No, no, it's not that," she choked out. "Young Dick could have been seriously injured and—"

The soft brush of Fox's fingers against her lips stopped the flow of words. "Ah, but nothing has happened to him except for a sprained ankle. You've seen it for yourself." He lifted her hand and bestowed a gentle kiss on her knuckles. "This is merely the delayed reaction to a shock. Truly, there is no need to worry," he murmured huskily.

But there is! she wanted to yell.

Behind them the dowager countess cleared her throat. "Sebastian."

Fox's lips twitched. "Do you hear that? We're being called to order." Under the eagle-eyed stare of his mother, he led Amy to one of the sofas. Amusement registered on the faces of the others. Surely they had taken their brief exchange for lovers' play. Amy bit her lip. If only they knew!

As if he had felt the dark turn of her thoughts, Fox touched her shoulder. "Everything is fine." His whisper stirred the fine hair curling around her ear, while his scent enveloped her in the warmth of bergamot.

Amy took a deep breath. Perhaps he was right. Perhaps her worries were nothing more than delayed reaction—not to the shock of Dick's fall, but to shock of the evil charm. However, now that it was destroyed, it could no longer wreak any damage.

At dinner, Fox sat next to her, and while the conversation moved around them, while they ate and drank, he found ample opportunity to touch her hand or arm and to let his knee brush hers as if to reassure her with his body that yes, indeed, everything was fine once more. When he took wine with her, raising his glass and gazing at her, the glow of his bluish-gray eyes and the warmth of his regard were sufficient to dispel her last lingering worries. With her mind now at rest, she basked in his affection. Each small touch thrilled her and brought her secret delight. It seemed a continuation of what they had started in the Temple of the Muses that morning, and just like then, her hunger for him blazed to life. What a fool she had been to have thought it tamed!

When Fox laid his hand on her thigh, she looked up at him and found the same hunger burning in his eyes—and the sight of it sealed her fate.

She wasn't aware of having made a conscious decision; she only knew of the hum of the blood in her veins, of the heavy pulse that had started deep inside her. Her skin felt painfully thin, and she absorbed the smallest of his movements next to her with a painful intensity. Each little touch, each accidental brush of elbows now became a sweet torment. Despite the food she was eating, she felt starved.

Amy never knew how she made it through dinner, nor through tea and coffee in the drawing room afterwards. At the earliest possible moment, she excused herself.

Fox took a step forward. "Allow me to escort you to your room."

"With pleasure." No, she couldn't have helped smiling, even had she wanted to.

So she said her good nights before she put her hand on his arm and let him lead her out of the room. They walked in silence down the corridors and up the stairs, yet the air throbbed between them. At her door she turned her back against the wood and lifted her eyes to his.

For a heartbeat or two, they only gazed at each other.

Finally, he reached up to cup her cheek in his hand. "You're so beautiful." His voice sounded as tormented as she felt.

Amy laid her hand against his chest and felt his heart beating, hard and fast. Her own pulse quickened. Fire licked along her veins and she moistened her lips. "Come to me later," she said.

All at once his expression sobered. He searched her face.

"Come to my room later," she repeated. She thought of the pleasure they had shared in the Temple of the Muses— his hands on her breasts, her bare thighs. The flames flared up, burnt her inside out. Compared to this scorching desire, the reasons why they should not indulge in pleasure seemed trivial. If she could not have him—tonight—she would die; she was sure of it.

"Amy—"

"Don't say no." Her voice quavered. She took a step forward and leaned into his body. Her hands curved around his waist. "I wouldn't be able to bear it," she whispered. Shivering, she pressed closer against him, his warmth; she felt his muscles bunch. "I need you." A sob caught in her throat as her feelings for him rolled over her like a tidal wave. "I need you, I need you, I need—"

Strong fingers lifted her chin and his mouth closed over hers in a hard, intense kiss which made her bones melt.

"Yes. I will come," he said against her lips, while his hands feverishly followed the shape of her body from shoulder to hips. His hardness swelled against her belly and caused her insides to flutter with mingled apprehension and delight. "*Soon.*" And then Fox strode down the corridor.

Dazed, Amy opened the door and stepped into her room. Leaning back against the door, she closed her eyes. Her whole body tingled and sang and felt more alive than ever before. A delighted laugh gurgled in her throat and the next moment she danced and whirled around while joy exploded inside her like a thousand soap bubbles.

Eventually she rang for Rosie so the maid could help her undress and get ready for the night. When all hooks, pins, buttons, and laces were finally undone, Amy sat down on the stool and let the girl brush out her hair. The gentle motions of the brush and the crackle of the fire melted together into a hypnotizing melody. Amy twiddled the discarded sweet pea blossom in her fingers, while she eyed herself critically in the mirror.

Her nightdress was thick and rather plain, and for a moment she wished she had bought one of the sheer, gauzelike chemises she had seen in London. To wear one of those would have been daring, to be sure, but she suspected Fox's face would have been worth it. A rosy glow warmed her cheeks. Was this forward creature truly her? How could she sit here so calmly when she was prepared to take the ultimate step and lose her innocence within the span of this night?

And yet, as she looked at her shining eyes and glossy lips, she was once more overcome by the memory of the heavenly delight she had found in Fox's arms that afternoon. Her passion for him burned inside her like a white-hot flame that cauterized all doubts and worries.

All would be fine.

More than fine.

He would take her to heaven tonight, she was sure of it.

After Rosie had dressed Amy's hair in a tight plait for the night, she took a step back. "Will this be all, miss?"

"Yes." Amy smiled at her in the mirror. "Thank you, Rosie. If you could just give me my shawl—no, not the beige one. The red." She felt her cheeks flush even more, but hoped the maid wouldn't notice in the mellow candlelight. "I have got a fancy to read a little in bed," she added hastily, "and the red is the warmer shawl." Not to speak of lending her simple nightdress an exotic, alluring touch.

Rosie went to fetch the shawl, which she proceeded to drape around Amy's shoulders, before she picked up Amy's discarded clothes to brush them out and put them away.

When she was finished, she curtsied.

"Good night, Rosie," Amy said.

"Good night, Miss Bourne." With the softest click the door closed behind the maid.

For a moment Amy sat as if frozen in the silence of her room. Then, with a deep sigh, she stood and slowly walked over to the bed, where the blankets and the quilt had been turned down earlier by the maid. She eyed the white wrought-iron bed as if she were seeing it for the first time. She tried to imagine it filled with Fox's large form.

A delicate shudder tore through her.

She climbed into her bed and leaned back against the headpiece, a pillow in her back.

When would he come? What if he had changed his mind? What if common sense had won once more?

She twisted the corner of the quilt between her hands.

But he had promised, hadn't he? No, no, this time love would triumph.

Time seemed to pass endlessly slowly. Amy strained her ears so she wouldn't miss even the smallest sound. Still, when the knock at her door finally came, it made her start violently. Her voice trembled as she called out to enter.

She saw the door open, and then *he* slipped into the room, resplendent in a dark green banyan. In helpless admiration, her gaze roamed his body. Underneath the coat he was in shirtsleeves, which she saw when the heavy material fell open to reveal a flash of white. Her candle flickered and sparked a glint of fire in his hair.

"Amy," he breathed.

Their gazes met and clung.

With a soft click, the bolt at the door slid close, shutting them into the room together. His lips curved.

"Amy," he repeated.

She remembered how he had whispered her name against her skin, and unfettered, her breasts swelled. Amy held out her hand to him.

With a few large steps he was across the room and at her side. His palm slid against hers. Their fingers twined.

"Lovely, adorable Amelia." His gaze fell on the book that lay on her nightstand. "Still *The Horrible Histories*?"

She nodded, moistened her lips. "I find my reading time rather curtailed."

"Do you?" he murmured, while his thumb caressed the pulse point at her wrist in delicate little circles. But still she was sure he felt her pulse speed up. "I wonder why."

Amy aimed at keeping her voice as calm as his. "I have a fondness for walks in the gardens."

"Do you?"

Oh, yes. She had to bite her lip to hold back a moan.

He must have noticed something, because the smile that hovered around his mouth widened. "Do you indeed?" His eyes gleamed. "Is there any place you are particularly fond of?"

"The Temple of the Muses," she whispered. Truly, she liked that he could tease even now, but oh, how much more she would prefer that he start the ravishing!

"Ahhh, a most fetching place indeed." He leaned forward as if to kiss her.

Yes yes yes! Her lips opened.

But at the last moment, he turned his head away. "Perhaps you would like to read something to me now?"

"Now?" she squeaked. Why didn't he kiss her, for heaven's sake?

"Yes. Now." With his free hand he reached for the book and handed it to her. Again he leaned forward, and this time his mouth nearly brushed her ear. The puffs of breath against her skin made her shiver.

"Read me . . . read me your favorite scene so far."

"My favorite—"

"Yes."

Amy tried to clear her befuddled mind. Gracious, he was only touching her hand so far, but already she felt overheated with desire. "The . . ." She licked her lips. "The episode when Markander saves fair Alexandie from the horrible lindworm."

"Read it." Each word was a caress. "Read it to me." He drew back, his gaze intense. "Please." His hand slipped from hers. "Please." His voice wound around her like dark velvet.

How could she deny him then? Even though she would have preferred if he had just kissed her. She fumbled a little with the pages until she had found the correct one. "N-noble Markander, like a bold and daring hero, then entered the valley where the dragon had his abode," Amy began haltingly, "who no sooner had sight of him, but his leathern throat sent forth a sound more terrible than thunder."

The mattress dipped as Fox put one knee onto it.

"The size of this fell dragon was fearful to behold, for . . ." Her voice trailed away as she felt Fox reaching for her plait.

"Go on," he said softly.

Amy gulped. "For . . . for, from his shoulders to his tail the length was fifty feet, the glittering scales upon his body were as bright as silver, but harder than brass—"

"Impressive." With his fingertips he drew her shawl aside.

"Fox, what are you—"

He threw her a look from under half-lowered lashes. "Go on reading." One tug and the bow at the neck of her nightdress slid open. "What about the dragon? Tell me about the dragon, Amy."

"His belly was the color of gold . . ." She glanced at him, but his eyes remained impassive and told her nothing at all. Well, *fine*, if he wanted her to read . . . Had she not already established only a few short hours ago what a beastly man he was? Frustrated, she continued in a more forceful voice than before: "His belly was the color of gold and larger than a ton. Thus weltered he from his hideous den, and so fiercely assailed the gallant Markander with his burning wings, that at the first encounter—"

The end of her plait was trickled across the soft skin at the base of her throat. Amy drew in a sharp breath.

"Yes?" Fox's concentration was focused on the plait he used like a brush on her body—with much success, since all of her skin had started to prickle and tingle.

"Do you wish to drive me deranged?" she demanded crossly. Only, the whole effect was marred by the tremble in her voice.

His teeth flashed white. "Perhaps. Read on."

When she wouldn't immediately comply, the hand holding her plait stilled. Wordless he gazed at her. The message was clear: no reading, no tingles.

She bit her lip and let her eyes plead with him.

Instead of an answer, he shrugged out of his banyan. "The dragon, Amy."

"Oh, all right," she finally growled, defeated. "Thus weltered he from his hideous den, dadadah dadah"—she waved her free hand around—"and assailed the gallant Markander, dadah, that at the first encounter he had almost felled him to the ground."

With a gentle tug, the blankets and the quilt were thrown back. But no, this time, she would *not* acknowledge him! Whatever dastardly deed he might be doing, she would remain stoically calm and composed.

"But the knight, nimbly recovering himself," she breezed on, "gave the dragon such a thrust with his spear that it shivered into a thousand pieces!"

A large, warm hand slid up from her ankle to her knee.

Calm and composed, she told herself.

"Upon which," she continued coolly, "the furious dragon smote him so violently with his venomous tail that then, indeed, he brought both man and horse to the ground, and sorely bruised two of Markander's ribs in the fall—"

"Poor fellow," she heard Fox murmur.

No, no, she would not take any note of him. "But he, stepping backwards, chanced to get under an orange tree . . ." Two fingers marched over her ribs, and the rest of the sentence ended in a fit of giggles. Yet not to be bested so easily, she twisted away and strove for composure "Which had that rare virtue in it that no venomous creature durst come within the compass of its branches," she read on loudly, "and here valiant Markander rested himself, till he had . . ." She gasped. The tickling fingers were back. Drat! "Had recovered . . . uh . . . his former . . . ah, no! . . . strength . . . ha . . ."

"Good for him," Fox said, and then his mouth was on hers, and one of his hands cupped her breast, and the book fell from her nerveless fingers, utterly and completely forgotten.

When his thumb grazed her hardened nipple, Amy finally understood why Fox had made her wait so long for his touch, had prolonged the anticipation, for now she burned. The slightest caress made her moan out loud, the gentlest kiss whimper in desperation. She ran her hands over his body, down his back and up again, helped him pull his shirt over his head. Her lips raced over the freckles covering his skin, specks of cinnamon dust.

She hardly noticed when her nightdress disappeared, but gave herself completely to the flame that burned higher and higher inside her. And Fox certainly knew how to fan the fire.

He whispered endearments against her sweat-slickened skin, and trailed kisses, which made her cry out in delight, across her breast and belly. By the time he finally shucked his trousers, her arousal had reached fever pitch, so when he slowly moved up the bed on his hands and knees, she opened her legs wide in invitation. The breath caught in her throat as she watched how the light of the candle danced over his skin and made his coppery body hair gleam. Sparks of fire on arms, chest, belly and thighs—she ran her hands up over his biceps, clasped his shoulders. "*Fox*."

"Slowly." His voice was hoarse. His arms, which held his weight above her, trembled with his effort to retain his control.

But control was something Amy didn't want. Lacing her hands behind his neck, she drew him down, down, and with a deep groan Fox followed her lead. The sharp sting as he slid inside her made Amy gasp, but the pain was fleeting and soon forgotten as they moved together. He rocked them slowly at first, allowing her to get used to the feeling of his flesh inside her, filling her with his heartbeat. Yet as her breaths shortened and turned to whimpers, his thrusts quickened and became more powerful. His forearms under her shoulders, he cuddled her close, melded their bodies together until she thought she would drown in his heat and his scent. Bergamot and musky sweat mingled with the sounds of their lovemaking, his gruff breaths against her ear. Whimpering, Amy dug her nails into his skin, felt the sting of teeth at her shoulder while passion burnt away all barriers between their bodies. Arms and legs tangled and then . . .

And then the flames consumed them both.

Arching her back, Amy cried out, felt Fox's release explode hotly inside her.

It was exquisite. Utter and pure joy. The sensations fizzed inside her head like the most potent sparkling wine. Amy gasped and laughed and muffled the sound against Fox's shoulder. She felt wild and beautiful and utterly, utterly greedy.

"Again," she demanded, while still trying to catch her breath afterward. She drew her legs up and around his waist, loving the feeling of his hard, lean body against her. With legs and arms she hugged him tight. "Again! Again! Again!" she begged.

And she laughed with unadulterated joy.

Despite the bliss she had experienced, dark dreams troubled Amy's sleep that night, and when she woke, her heart thudded in her ears. Hammered an angry staccato against her breastbone.

Amy sat up. Darkness enfolded her like a shroud. Her breath hitched in her throat.

But slowly, very slowly, her eyes adjusted to the night. Silver moonlight fell through the window, and one by one, the black bulk of various pieces of furniture emerged from the darkness.

Her heartbeat calmed. She took a deep breath.

How silly to be frightened by faceless, nameless dreams like a small child!

She turned her head, and her gaze fell on the man sleeping beside her, his long limbs and lean flanks hidden beneath the blankets.

Her lips curved.

Even in the dim light of the moon, it seemed to her that his hair had a distinct carroty tinge.

She reached out her hand to tousle his hair, gently, so as not to wake him—and froze.

. . . a carroty tinge . . .

This time, nothing diverted her from the memory rising up from the depths of her mind. Slowly, oh so slowly, an invisible fist squeezed the air from her lungs.

Better Fox than Carrot. Or Fish. For he is as cold as a fish, that one.

Amy gasped.

She pressed her fists against her mouth, bit into her knuckles so she wouldn't scream. She had not liked him. Neither had she loved him. In fact, she had thought him an arrogant bore.

Numb with that realization, she sank back against the pillows. Icy coldness ran through her veins as she listened to the soft sounds Fox made in his sleep.

She had not liked him.

And yet . . .

She stared up at the dark ceiling.

What had happened?

He murmured, lost in dreams, moved, and his hand landed on her belly. Amy looked at it as if it were a giant spider, a poisonous snake, a monster to eat up her soul.

When had it started? Once again, thoughts raced in her head. Memories replayed. Image after image, frozen in time, whirled through her mind. Memories of sights and sounds, of city lights and elm tree whisperings. An endless stream of faces, the mouths growing larger and larger. They talked—loudly, insistently, all at the same time—until her head buzzed with the ghostly sounds of her memories.

Her breath caught.

And there, at the core of everything else, it was. Brilliant and crystal clear: the point of no return.

She had not liked him at the ball when she had danced the waltz with him for the first time. She had not liked him either when she had driven to Lady Worthington's musicale in the Bentham carriage. But afterwards—

Oh, afterwards, she had loved him. Madly. Deeply.

"Do you think there is something wrong with this punch?" she heard her own voice say.

And she remembered.

Remembered.

Yes, she had loved him then. Utterly and completely.

In the velvety darkness she lay naked beside her fiancé, and her blood ran cold. For it had all been an illusion. Only an illusion, even if her heart now bled.

An illusion.

Wicked. Magical.

And she herself more powerless and helpless than a kitten.

She might have made a sound like a frightened child at night, for he woke. "Amy?" His voice was still fogged with sleep. "What is it, sweeting?" The hand that searched for hers was warm. His fingers curled around hers and shared his heat.

When he rolled up on one elbow, the moonlight turned his fair skin into cold ashes, the cinnamon spots of his freckles indiscernible. But Amy already knew their pattern by heart. Even after only one time, she knew every detail of his body. Remembered each hair, each blemish of his skin.

Magical—the images and sensations imprinted on her mind forevermore.

"What is it?" His voice whispered, making the fine hair on her body stand up.

Dear God, what have I done? Her senses had been dazzled by a mere illusion, and now she was indeed ravished. And ruined. For how could she marry him?

Tears welled up in her eyes.

Her hand snaked around his neck and drew his head down. "Nothing," she whispered. "Nothing . . ."

His mouth, so hot on hers, kindled fire in an instant, even now.

Yet, it was only an illusion, it had to be; and Amy squeezed her eyes shut.

"Nothing," she murmured against his lips.

Chapter Ten

Amy woke to a cold, gray morning and an empty space beside her in the bed. For a moment she lay absolutely still as the memory of what had happened, of what she had learned the night before, flooded back. With a groan she clapped her hands in front of her face.

What have I done? she thought again.

She had shared her body with somebody to whom she was not married, with somebody whom she probably didn't even like, and who would never have slept with her if it had not been for some sort of love potion. For, of course, there must have been a potion in that punch. Looking back, she now saw how completely it had changed her behavior. Dear heaven, how careless and forward she had been with Fox! The liberties she had granted him! And last night she had even taken the ultimate step: she had shared her innocence.

Something occurred to her, and she hastily scrambled out of bed and threw back the blankets. Anxiously she inspected the covers.

No blood!

Her shoulders sagged with relief.

Thank God, there was no blood. For how would she have explained this to the maid? Something they had never thought of last night, of course. And what was more . . .

Suddenly feeling faint, Amy sank down on the side of the bed and put a trembling hand on her stomach.

They hadn't thought about pregnancy, either.

Fear gripped Amy. Her eyes stung, and she felt as if she were about to be sick. She was ruined. She had slept with a man to whom she was not married, and their engagement was based on a mere illusion. All the affection she felt for him conjured up by the love potion. Yet even this knowledge, even the memories of his odious behavior at the ball and at the beginning of Lady Worthington's musicale, did not diminish this false regard.

What a mess! What an utter, horrid mess!

And of course, she could never tell him. He wouldn't believe her anyway, not in a thousand years. Not Mr. Sebastian Stapleton, who had lectured her on the importance of rational thought and the dangers of flights of fancy. No, he wouldn't believe her.

A shiver ran through her body.

Her *naked* body.

Oh, sweet heavens . . .

Again, Amy clasped her hands in front of her eyes and fought against her tears. *Whatever shall I do now?* She had never felt more alone or afraid.

She had to take several deep breaths before she managed to regain her composure. With a sigh she wiped the wetness from her cheeks—drowning herself in her tears would not help her now.

She sniffed, then went over to the washstand. She splashed some of yesterday's water into her face, dried herself with the towel, and straightened to look in the mirror. Except for a small bruise at the side of one breast, hair that was tousled more than usual, and lips that were slightly puffy, her body remained unchanged.

Almost disbelieving, Amy looked herself up and down. But no, her arms and shoulders were still rounded, her breasts still full, her hips still generous, and her skin still rosy and smooth. No scarlet mark of guilt anywhere.

Not even on the bed linen.

A nervous giggle escaped her. At least she had been

blessed with a hymen that broke without much fuss. Thank heavens for small mercies!

She smoothed her hair and donned her crumpled night-dress before she rang for her maid.

By the time Amy reached the breakfast parlor, her mood was subdued once more. The luminous colors of the room seemed jarring today, the exotic birds on the walls garish. She shook her head.

The earl, the countess, and Admiral Reitz were already present and talked animatedly about the cultivation of apples. The admiral, Lady Rawdon explained to Amy as she joined them at the table, had chosen to buy a house with an apple tree in its back garden.

"A Kerry Pippin," the admiral said.

Lord Rawdon chuckled. "And now he falls out of his apple tree on a regular basis."

"Easy enough for you to say, Rawdon." The admiral pointed his knife at the earl. "After all, you let your *gardeners* fall out of your trees."

Lord Rawdon barked a laugh. "Too true. You see, Miss Bourne"—he turned to Amy—"my head gardener is currently trying to cultivate a new breed, the Rawdon Gold, he would call it. So far, though, he hasn't had any luck with his endeavors."

The door opened, and Fox entered the room. An apple puff fell from Amy's nerveless fingers. With her heart thundering in her ears, she watched him swagger toward her. His mouth curved into a smile.

"Good morning."

As if from a distance, Amy heard the others wishing him a good morn. Her own voice, however, seemed paralyzed. Her tongue stuck to the roof of her mouth. And then he stood before her, and the warm scent of bergamot sneaked out to envelop her.

Amy swallowed hard.

At that, his smile widened. "Good morning, Miss Bourne,"

he said, his voice a soft rumble. He leaned forward and bussed her cheek.

Amy's eyes fell closed. For a precious moment the heat and scent of him surrounded her like a warm blanket. But the sound of a hand slapping on cloth broke the spell.

"Sebastian Stapleton, will you please stop this canoodling in my breakfast parlor?" The countess might sound amused, but the steel in her voice was unmistakable.

Amy's eyes snapped open. Her cheeks flamed.

Unperturbed, Fox winked at her, then strolled whistling to the sideboard to choose his breakfast.

Lady Rawdon leaned close to Amy. "Don't let my brother-in-law embarrass you, my dear," she said quietly. "He is a veritable rascal, that one." Her eyes twinkled merrily. "It's never too early to take him in hand."

Amy managed a wan smile. Oh, among other things, she had indeed taken him in hand last night—though in a much more literal sense than the countess could ever imagine. Her shoulders slumped.

And how much delight she had felt when he had groaned and his body had shuddered under her ministrations! At that moment she had felt like the most powerful woman in all of Britain.

Even without her magic.

She sighed.

This morning, by contrast, she felt like the least powerful woman in all of Europe.

Lady Rawdon threw her a worried glance. "Are you feeling all right, Miss Bourne?"

"Oh yes, yes," she murmured.

"You look indeed somewhat under the weather," the admiral remarked. "You should take care not to catch a chill in the humid climate of Norfolk!"

The entrance of Isabella Bentham distracted Amy, and so she only murmured something noncommittally and watched her walk to the sideboard. Amy frowned. It had been Mr. Bentham who had given them the fateful punch. Surely he must have known about its contents. He had put the potion in their glasses himself, most likely!

Amy turned her attention to her half-eaten apple puff. Her frown deepened. Why had Fox felt it necessary to invite Isabella, too, to Rawdon Park? Had this really been his idea, or perhaps Mr. Bentham's? Her stomach turned as she realized that it could well have been Isabella who had brought that evil charm, which Pip had found on the stairs, to Rawdon Park.

Yet the question remained: Why?

Lost in thought, she barely registered the rest of the breakfast conversation. Only when Lady Rawdon touched her arm and whispered, "Sebastian has asked you a question, dear. Take pity on the poor man," did she look up sharply.

Fox was observing her closely. A sharp worry line had appeared between his eyebrows.

"Are you feeling all right?" His tone was gentle.

It was the second time someone had asked her the question today. All at once, Amy felt the desperate urge to scream and rant. *No! Nothing is all right! NOTHING!* But of course, she didn't. They would only have thought her raving mad.

"I am . . . fine."

The lines of worry on his face smoothened. His eyes brightened. "Then, would you like to start on our walk around the gardens?" A boyish, endearing smile lifted his lips and broke Amy's heart.

She blinked against the sudden sting of tears. "I think . . ." Her voice failed her.

"Amy?"

Oh, how she hated to see the worry return to his face!

She took a deep breath and, under the cover of the tablecloth, dug her nails into her palms in the hope that the physical pain would divert her from the pain in her heart. "I am sorry. Not today." She managed a small smile. "I feel a little . . . tired this morning."

Tenderness lit his face up like a lantern. The corners of his eyes crinkled. "I see."

Desperately, Amy tried to swallow the lump in her throat. This was awful.

"Perhaps you would like to rest in the drawing room?" Fox suggested eagerly. He turned his head toward the sideboard. "Ramtop, has the fire in the South Drawing Room already been lit?"

"Of course, Mr. Stapleton," the butler replied.

"Good, good." Fox focused his attention on Amy again. "Would you like to read? Shall one of the footmen go and fetch your book?" Not waiting for her reply, he turned to the sideboard once more. "Ramtop, please have somebody bring—what was the title again?—*The Horrible Histories of the Rhine*?"

Amy nodded faintly.

"Please have somebody bring those horrible histories from Miss Bourne's room to the drawing room."

"Yes, sir."

"And perhaps a pot of fresh tea?" Lady Rawdon added. She turned to pat Amy's hand. "Let Sebastian make you comfortable in the drawing room, my dear. Afterwards he can take a stroll with the earl and the admiral. Perhaps they could even go and shoot some bird or other for our dinner table. Miss Bentham, would you also like to—"

Isabella's lip curled. "I have got some letters to write," she said.

"Oh. Oh well, if that is the case . . ." The countess gave Amy's hand a last pat. "I shall join you in the drawing room presently. Now off you go. You *are* looking a trifle wan this morning. Sebastian?"

But of course, he wouldn't have needed the prompt. He was already up and around the table to help her stand and then offer her his arm to escort her to the drawing room. Never had the way to the back wing of the house seemed longer to Amy! To walk beside him, almost close enough for their shoulders to brush, and to know . . . to *know* . . .

It was torture.

Just inside the drawing room, Fox finally let her go. Amy bit her lip, then made herself ask lightly, "I've been meaning to ask you this for ages—was it your idea to invite Isabella to Rawdon Park?"

"Miss Bentham?" The question clearly puzzled him. "No, Mr. Bentham suggested it to make you feel not so alone among strangers." He searched her face. "Are you sure you are all right?"

"Oh yes, yes. I'm merely a little bit tired." Again, Amy forced her lips to curve into a smile. And again that tender expression that made her want to cry suffused his face.

"I see." He trailed his forefinger down her cheek. "I wasn't . . ." He hesitated, frowned. "I wasn't too rough, was I?"

Too rough? Last evening she had been sure he would carry her to heaven—and he had done it. It was not his fault that she had been cast into hell only a few hours later. "Oh no. Not at all," she whispered. As she looked up at him, his face swam out of focus. "I am so sorry."

"Oh sweetheart, sweetheart." He touched her chin, then his hand curved to cup her jaw. "Don't take this so hard. It is only a walk in the garden, isn't it?"

Amy averted her face.

"Isn't it?" This time, his voice was more insistent. He tried to peer into her face.

Miserably, she nodded. For how could she have told him? How could she have told him of the magic? The potion? The evil charm? He would never have believed her!

His thumb rubbed over her chin. "Sweetheart," he murmured, just before his mouth brushed over her lips in a sweet, tender kiss. "Take a little rest, and don't worry about the walk." A last caress down her cheek, and then he was gone.

Amy sank down onto one of the sofas. Desperately trying to control the urge to cry, she closed her eyes and clasped her hand over her mouth. If only . . . if only she had never attempted the spell that had turned Three Elms cobalt blue!

She drew in a shuddering breath and quickly let her hand fall to her side, when a footman entered and brought her book. Shortly afterwards the butler himself followed, with a tray and biscuits. "Will this be all, Miss Bourne?" he asked.

She nodded a thank-you, and he left the room. She was alone.

Amy didn't know how long she sat and stared into empty space, while she turned the whole situation over in her mind and desperately tried to find a solution. This was how the dowager countess found her some time later.

"My dear child." Lady Rawdon walked across the room and sat down next to her on the sofa. "I have heard you are feeling unwell this morning?" She glanced at the empty and obviously unused teacup and the plate with biscuits. "Perhaps you need something more restoring. Shall I order a cup of hot chocolate for you? Cocoa is supposed to work wonders for the constitution." Lady Rawdon made to rise, but Amy quickly put her hand on the woman's arm.

"This won't be necessary, I assure you. I have been thinking . . ." She bit her lip.

Lady Rawdon's kind brown eyes rested warmly on her. "Yes?"

"I understand that Miss Bentham accompanied me to Rawdon Park so I wouldn't feel lonely. But how could I ever feel lonely here when you all have been so kind to me?"

"Oh, my dear." The dowager countess took Amy's hands and squeezed them. "You must know that we all love you exceedingly well."

Oh yes, she knew. She had felt it. And it only made this whole situation so much worse. For she must harden her heart against this affection as well. She could not afford to grow any closer to the Stapletons: in the end, they were nothing but strangers who must never learn about her secrets, her magic. Even though it tore her heart apart, she had to concede there was no future for her and Fox. They were too different. Why, they had *detested* each other! And surely he would come to loathe her again once the effects of the potion wore off. Or once she could obtain an antidote. Uncle Bourne would certainly know one. And so, before long, she would return to Three Elms, and in time would become the spinster aunt of her cousins' children. No, she could not afford to grow any closer to the Stapleton family.

"I have thought," Amy continued, forcing her voice to remain strong: this was not the time for tears. "It would be so unkind to keep Miss Bentham from her family during the Christmas season. And now that it has started to snow . . ."

"It would be better if she returned to London soon." Lady Rawdon finished her sentence. "You are quite right. It would be wrong to keep Miss Bentham from her family any longer. Who knows what kind of winter we will get this year! If I think back to 1814—" She shuddered. "I will talk to her today, so that if she so wishes, we can prepare for her departure before there is more snow."

And thus, one potential danger would be removed from Rawdon Park. Amy breathed a sigh of relief.

The rest of the day passed uneventfully. The men stayed out shooting, so the countess made sure they were sent a hamper with rolls and cold meat for their luncheon. In the afternoon, Amy sat awhile with little Dick before she joined the other ladies in the drawing room for a game of cards. She was relieved to find Isabella absent and to hear her tormenting the fortepiano in the music room with something that again sounded vaguely like Beethoven. Conversing with Isabella was difficult at the best of times; with Amy now harboring suspicions as to Isabella's motive for staying at Rawdon Park, any sort of conversation with her would only have been stilted, if not downright disastrous.

And so the women played until the men returned and it was time to get ready for dinner. Throughout the meal, Amy kept her eyes trained on her plate so that she didn't have to look at Fox across the table. But later, when she excused herself at the earliest possible moment, she could not prevent him from offering to accompany her to her room once more.

"Naturally, we will be waiting for you to come downstairs again, Sebastian," the countess pointed out wryly, which caused everybody to chuckle.

But Fox only shrugged and held out his arm to Amy. How could she possibly reject him while everybody else obliquely watched with gentle amusement? It would have been too cruel to say no to his offer and embarrass him in front of his friends and family.

No, she couldn't do this to him. Yet the sight of the hesitant smile he gave her when she nodded cut her deeper than any knife. Oh, how she wished she could simply run away from it all!

A bittersweet moment came when she slipped her hand into the familiar place in the crook of his elbow, when her wrist rubbed against the inside of his arm. She didn't want to remember how she had run her hands over his naked arms the night before, how she had reveled in the hard strength of his muscles; yet, unbidden, the memories rose to taunt her.

"You were very quiet today," he finally said as they walked up the stairs. "Tell me, please . . ." He stopped and turned toward her, anxiously searching her face. "Have I offended you in any way?"

"No, of course not."

"Then what—" He shook his head. "Your eyes are overbright with unshed tears." With a gentle finger, he brushed the tears away when they finally overflowed. With a groan, he drew her into a tight hug.

Closing her eyes, Amy hid her face against his chest and listened to his heart hammering against her ear. She buried her front teeth into her lower lip to hold back her sobs while he rocked her back and forth. A kiss fell on her hair.

"What is it, my sweet?" he whispered. "Can't you tell me?"

Never. Because which man in his right mind would believe her?

She pulled back. "I am sorry." She dashed her hand across her eyes before she turned, and continued walking up the stairs. He fell in step beside her. "I am . . ." she tried. "Oh, Fox, we got so carried away last night."

His eyes crinkled at the corners. "That we certainly did."

"We shouldn't have."

"No?" His face fell.

They turned into the corridor that led to her room.

"Then, you didn't enjoy—"

"You know I did," she cut in quickly. She had enjoyed it so much that, even now, she wished she could simply drag him into her room and let him have his wicked way with her until she forgot everything but the scent and taste of him, the weight of his body on hers. "But it is unseemly," she continued. "Think of it: under your brother's roof! What if your family finds out about this? Didn't you tell me yourself how irate the earl would be?"

His brows drew together. "I—"

Of course, as the love potion had apparently lowered all their inhibitions and done away with all sense of propriety, he might no longer care what his family thought. Hadn't they both considered it more sensible to stop their love play yesterday morning? Then, only a few short hours later, that had all been forgotten in face of overwhelming passion.

Amy grimaced. "And what if I should become, you know, with child?"

"Oh."

They had reached the door to her room. She stopped and turned, her hand on the latch.

"I have not thought of this," he admitted, a little shamefaced. The next moment, though, his eyes lit up again. "I will think of something." He reached for her hand and flashed her a grin. "There are ways . . ."

Oh heavens! She stared up at him in dismay.

"Oh, there's no need to look so worried." His smile became tender as he pushed a loose tendril of hair behind her ear. "It's nothing that will hurt, I swear." He put his hand on the doorframe above her and leaned closer. "What about tonight?"

"Tonight?" It came out as a squeak.

"I could just hold you in my arms. Or we could—"

"No," she said quickly. She had a fine idea of what else they could do. After all, she had already caressed him quite intimately. Doing it again, with a love potion still raging through his system? "No. The temptation would be too great."

"Would it?" His hand slipped from the doorframe to curve around the side of her throat. His fingers slid into her hair and massaged her neck, while his thumb brushed over her lower lip.

With devastating effect.

Amy sucked in a breath.

"You are so sweet," he murmured. "Sweeter than a ripened peach." His head descended.

Yet she couldn't possibly let him kiss her. "Good night." It came out as another undignified squeak, but she was beyond caring. She fumbled with the latch, pushed the door open, and stumbled into her room.

"Amy . . ."

Hastily, she slammed the door shut behind her and slid the bolt home. Her heart hammering, she stood stock still and listened as he heaved a big sigh and finally walked away.

Amy closed her eyes.

In the following days she learned to avoid him, or at least learned to avoid being alone with him. Ruthlessly she suppressed the pain she felt about missing those morning walks with him in the park. And just as ruthlessly she suppressed any remorse at Fox's bewilderment over her thorough—if subtle—rejection. She could not afford to dwell on it if she wanted to get through the day.

She often sat with young Baron Bradenell, but after three days of lying in bed, he was allowed to get up again and limp through the house on crutches. The children now frequently spent the whole afternoon in the drawing room, where Admiral Reitz regaled the boys with stories of maneuvers on the high seas, and they quizzed him about the manner of living onboard a ship, the regulations, the work, the clambering around high up in the sails. Afterwards Pip would hurry to fetch their tattered copy of the Navy List, and then he and Dick would huddle close together on one of the sofas and pore over the list to find out the names of all the ships the admiral had commanded during his long career. Of course, they had already marked all the names, but they seemed to take much delight in listing them all again and asking him endless questions about each and every ship.

More snow fell, and all three children impatiently awaited the day when the lake would be frozen and the ice thick enough for skating. At the same time, they greatly lamented the fact that the boys' tutor had not yet returned, for it seemed he was the one who had taken them onto the ice in the past. But it seemed that Mr. Ford was snowed in up in Scotland, and would not be able to return for a several more weeks. When this news reached them, the children's expressions were so woebegone that Amy finally promised them she would go with them in the tutor's stead.

"You can skate? On the *ice*?" Open-mouthed, Pip gaped at her.

"Spiffing!" Dick exclaimed, while Annie simply beamed at Amy in silent adoration. The stone skipping had indeed been a great and long-lasting success.

Abruptly, Amy's cheerful mood vanished. It would have been better not to encourage the children's affections.

A moment later Fox sat down next to her on the sofa and

nonchalantly leaned back. From the corner of her eye she watched him brushing his hands over the front of his coat as if to remove invisible specks of dust—a betraying little gesture, which revealed his offhand manner as a mere facade.

She could have wept as she realized how well she could read him. Or at least, read that part of him that was befuddled by the dratted potion and hence besotted with love. Of the real Fox—the cool, aloof man about Town—she had caught only glimpses and didn't know him at all.

He leaned closer until his breath caressed her cheek. "I see you have utterly charmed my niece and nephews, Miss Bourne," he murmured, his voice deep enough to send delightful ripples through her body.

Amy bit her lip. *It's an illusion*, she fiercely told herself. *Only an illusion. Remember? You called him Mr. Carrothead to yourself. If it weren't for the magic, he would only give you one of these haughty stares.*

His warm hand slipped into hers and gently squeezed her fingers. "Don't you want to work your charm on their uncle, too?" Amy stared at their hands, at his large fingers, which easily engulfed hers. *But a charm is already working on you*, she thought miserably. *And I haven't the slightest idea when it will wear off or how to shake you out of it right now. I don't even know how to cleanse myself of its influence. And I no longer know what is real and what is not.* If only there were a possibility to contact her family!

Fox turned her hand, cupped the back of it, and drew his thumb in fiery circles over her palm, skin gliding on skin without even the flimsy protection of gloves. Despite herself, her breathing quickened.

She didn't need to look at him to know that his mouth curved into the small smile she so liked. His hand drew back, his fingers spread wide, inviting her to twine her fingers with his.

She should have resisted the temptation. Yet her stomach was hollow with longing and worry, and she missed the closeness they had shared, and so, in the safety of the drawing room, where enough people were present that nothing else could happen, she allowed herself to brush her hand against his until their fingers were firmly entwined, palm pressed against palm.

For a short moment Amy closed her eyes and allowed herself to forget everything but this: his warmth and strength and the love that poured from him.

But as she looked up again, she caught Isabella watching them, her mouth curled into a sneer, and abruptly all feeling of remembered bliss fled. A sliver of ice touched Amy's heart.

She was certain that Isabella knew about the charm and the potion. Yet what purpose did the magic serve? To what end had it been planted? And what sort of man was Bentham to embroil the niece of a friend in such an intrigue?

She must warn her uncle. Indeed, the fact that she had not received any sort of reaction to her engagement from Aunt and Uncle Bourne should have alerted her much earlier. What if Bentham had never sent a letter to them to inform them about the engagement in the first place?

Amy tried to remember whether anything about the upcoming nuptials had been put into the papers. But she had spent the days and weeks after Fox's proposal in such a state of bliss she wouldn't have noticed even if the Thames had suddenly changed its course, and so she couldn't be sure.

That evening she therefore tried to pen another letter to her family in her room. Yet as before, the ink melted away and left the paper creamy white and pure. Tears of frustration burning in her eyes, she laid her head on the table.

She was alone, all alone, and there was nobody in whom she could confide.

She was never more happy than when Isabella finally left Rawdon Park at the end of the week. As they all stood on the front stairs and waved at the carriage that would take the young woman home to London, Amy couldn't help the sigh of relief that escaped her.

Whatever putrid influence the young Miss Bentham had brought to Rawdon Park, it was gone now, and with luck all danger to the Stapleton family was removed as well.

Amy threw a last look at the carriage before it disappeared behind a group of trees. "Good riddance," she murmured. *And never come back again!*

Chapter Eleven

The weeks passed and there was still no news from Amy's family. Several times she had now tried to write letters to them, but it was all in vain: her uncle's spell was still firmly in place. If the Ladies Rawdon ever wondered why she received no notes or mail, they never commented on it, even though Amy now spent more time with them in an attempt to avoid Fox as much as possible. Fortunately, the winter weather presented her with a perfect excuse to stay inside.

November brought ever more snow, and the temperatures steadily dropped. Soon an icy crust covered the lake and began to thicken, much to the children's delight. The gardeners now daily checked the ice to see if it would carry weight. And then, one day, it did.

Mist had risen that morning and wrapped the world in clogging white. When it receded sluggishly, reluctantly, toward midday, it revealed trees and bushes white frosted, looking as if they had been transformed into fragile confections. Young Baron Bradenell, his ankle all healed, climbed onto the window seat in the library where Amy had settled with *The Horrible Histories* in hand. For a moment or two he stared critically out of the window, before he turned around to announce to the world, "It's perfect for skating!"

"Hm," Amy said, for just then the Wicked Sorceress Jewellyn had bonked her wand on Maid Maiken's head and dragged her off to drink the virgin's blood to be granted everlasting youth. Who would save the fair maiden from a most gruesome death? Only one man . . .

A thud. "You *said* you would go skating with us." Baron Bradenell's voice reflected lordly impatience.

The brave Gilldan!

Amy looked up.

Dick had jumped from the window seat and now stood, arms akimbo and his head thrown back so the cowlick over his forehead appeared even more pronounced than usual. "You promised!"

She suppressed the urge to smile. Instead she raised her eyebrows and asked, her voice tinged with slight incredulity, "Did I?"

He gasped, clearly outraged. "You did!"

"Hm. If you say so." She turned her attention back to her book and pretended to read on.

For a moment silenced reigned, then a step sounded on the wooden floor. A small hand tugged at her sleeve. "But you promised! You did!"

Indeed she had. *Take them skating, only this once*, a tiny voice whispered in her mind. *What harm can come of it?* And so, with a laugh, Amy snapped her book shut. "If I did, then I guess I must keep my promise, mustn't I?"

Realization dawned. "Oh," Dick muttered, "you pulled my leg."

"And a real lordly leg it is." Teasingly, she tugged on his cowlick. "So, where is your entourage, my lord?"

His face lit up. He leaned back. "Downstairs." His arms flailed about with his eagerness. "They're already waiting downstairs. With the runners." He gave her a mischievous grin.

"All bundled up against the nip of the frost?" She tapped on his nose. "You, my Lord Bradenell, should learn to be less sure of yourself. It's unbecoming in a man when he deals with a lady."

He made a face.

Putting her book aside, she rose. "Besides, I'll need to change first. Surely you can't expect me to let myself be dragged onto the ice in all my finery?" She grinned. "So run and tell your brother and sister to wait outside so they won't stew in their own juices." Lightly, she clapped his shoulder to send him off.

Half an hour later, the small skating party frolicked along the white-dusted paths in the park, their faces glowing beneath woolen caps, their breaths little clouds of white. Annie's mitten-covered hand rested securely in Amy's while they traveled through a wintry world that had been robbed of all color. Against the dull, gray sky, the trees seemed to be transformed into pale, still ghosts.

"It's spooky," Annie whispered.

Amy attempted to shake her own uneasiness off. "It's winter." Then, more cheerful: "Look, your brothers are rather *un*-spooked indeed."

At this moment Dick broke into howls of delight, as he had just managed to hit one of the statues straight in the face with a snowball. The stony face disappeared behind a crust of snow, which the boys apparently thought endlessly amusing. Not even Pip could contain his giggles.

Amy looked down at Annie and arched her brow. "Boys."

The little girl joined the giggling and started to skip along the path.

Soon they reached the lake. Glittering like a diamond it lay before them, the ice thick and white. The boys already sat on one of the stone benches and wrestled with the runners, which they strapped under their boots. Pip looked up and gave Amy one of his wide, gap-toothed smiles.

"See? The gardeners have removed the snow this morning."

"Perfect." Amy swung a squealing Annie up in the air and sat her down on the bench. "Hold still, sweetheart," she instructed the child while she fastened the set of smaller runners under Annie's boots. "So you had it all planned?" she said to the boys.

"Because you promised," Richard reminded her.

"I did, I did. Wait!" She checked woolen caps, mittens, scarves, and bootlaces. "All righty, off you go."

Shrieking and laughing, the children dashed off onto the lake. Amy hastened to strap her own runners on, adjusted her scarf, and flew after them. Exhilarated, she laughed as the cold air prickled on her skin and her runners glided smoothly over the ice. Oh, it was indeed wonderful! Flying couldn't be better than this!

Yet the next moment, her steps faltered for—oh, how she would have wanted to share this experience with Fox, to have him by her side . . .

She shivered a little.

During the day she tried to be reasonable and stayed away from him as much she could so she wouldn't be tempted to blurt out secrets that had better remained hidden. And during the night . . . He would come to her in her dreams, torture her body with the memory of the passion they had shared, of the sweet pleasure of sweat-slickened flesh sliding against her, inside her.

And each night she would awake, gasping, her body burning with unfulfilled longings.

Then she would stare into the darkness and wonder whether the love potion still continued to work on her. Were the dreams only the aftereffects of a spell?

Amy sighed. She didn't know. Her emotions were all tangled: she didn't even know whether she could trust the affection she still felt for him. When she thought of the happy, blissful days when they had been so close, she could have wept. It was only the aftereffects of the potion; they would vanish in time, she tried to tell herself. *Think of how boorish you thought him at the beginning of your acquaintance!* But nothing quelled the longings of her heart.

A small body bumped against her legs. With a surprised "Uff," Amy sat down on her behind, hard. Giggling, Annie straddled her legs.

Ah yes, little girls—the best thing to expel dark thoughts.

Amy made a suitably dark and horrible face. "You little devil," she growled. "Wait till I get you!"

With another loud shriek, Annie scrambled to her feet and dashed away. Amy followed hard on her heels, but made sure Annie always remained in the lead.

The boys gave up chasing each other and came over to circle around Amy and their sister. "Did you fall?" Pip asked.

"No," Amy said.

"Yessssss!" Annie squealed.

All in all, Amy mused, it was a good thing they were skating at the far end of the lake, well away from the house. That way, the others would still be able to enjoy their peace and quiet in the drawing room over there.

"I did not!" she huffed.

"Ha! You did!" Dick crowed. "I saw you! You sat down on your butt!"

Amy made a grab for him. "Really, Lord Bradenell, what a terribly impolite word!"

He stuck out his tongue and, grinning, skittered away.

"Oh! Oh!" Annie shouted and pointed. "Fish! B i i i i g fish!" She flung her arms wide, lost her balance and fell.

Amy slid toward her and put her back on her feet. "Hurt, sweetheart?"

"Big fish!" The little girl wriggled away. Her eyes shone with excitement. "Oooh, so big!"

"Yes! There!" Pip spun around. "Wow! That's a big one indeed!"

"Must be a carp." Dick gave his expert opinion with all the earnestness that became an older brother.

"Where?" Amy turned. She just caught a glimpse of a large shadow briefly brushing up against the ice before it disappeared again into the darkness below. She frowned. "Gosh, that's not a carp. No, it must be"—she waited a moment, then whirled around to make a snatch at the nearest child—"a whale!"

Laughing, the children fled from her.

"A whale! A whale!" Annie shouted.

"Ha!" Dick shook his head. "A whale would never fit into our lake! A whale is way bigger than the lake!"

Pip flashed Amy a grin over his shoulder. "You don't know much about whales!"

"Pah!" Amy snorted.

As if it knew they were talking about it, the large fish brushed against the ice once more. It appeared to have swum in a circle and was now drawing closer to the children.

"Whoo!" Annie's eyes glowed with excitement. The shadow was almost underneath them. "Big fish! Look, Amy, look! B i i i i g!"

It bumped against the ice.

Pip laughed. "And definitely not a wha—"

With a screeching sound, the ice under him cracked and plunged him into the water. His shrill scream was cut short as his head went under.

"Pip!" Richard's horrified shout echoed across the lake. Annie burst into tears.

Coughing and spluttering, Pip reappeared, his face white with cold and fright. His arms flailed wildly.

"Pip!" Dick leaned forward and made as if to dash to his brother. Amy could only just grab the back of his coat.

"No! Richard, no!" He fought against her, his little boy's fists already hard. "No! Get your sister off the ice!" She shook him. "Get Annie off the ice!"

From the corner of her eyes, she saw the dark shadow of the fish under the ice. A moment later, Pip screamed even louder than before. "Help! It's dragging me down! It's—"

Only then did Amy see how the ice had broken. Not in sharp cracks and pieces, but with smooth lines. Unnaturally smooth. As if it had been cut with a knife—or with magic. She felt her face go numb with shock. "Oh my God." Roughly, she shoved the two children toward the bank. "Get Annie off the ice, now!"

When Richard finally obeyed, she flung herself onto her

belly and crawled toward the hole. Pip still hung on to the edges of the ice for dear life.

"You have to stay still, Pip." His lips, she saw with worry, were already tinged with blue.

"It's dragging me down," he whispered, his eyes wide with fear.

No, this was not a fish at all. Yet she was helpless. Would more ice break if she tried to pull Pip out? Oh dear God, if only . . . "Give me your hands." She tried to keep her voice calm, even though panic clutched at her heart. "I will not let you go down." She risked a glance over her shoulder. Richard and Annie had just reached safe land. *Good.* She focused her attention back on their brother and gripped those hands hard. "When you feel it coming, kick at it, Pip. Can you do that?"

His teeth had started to chatter, but he managed a small nod.

"Good. And now let us get you out of there." Carefully she pulled him toward her and, crawling backwards, managed to get his elbows to rest on the ice.

"It's coming again," he whispered.

"Kick at it, hard," Amy said firmly.

Pip started struggling, his breath coming in agonized puffs. Amy gritted her teeth and held on tight. "Kick it, Pip! Kick it!" She thought of the metal runners on his feet—twin weights dragging him down, but on the other hand fearsome weapons as well. She watched the water whirl as the small boy pumped his legs. The hateful dark body pressed up against the ice, vanished again. "Harder, Pip!"

Then, finally, bubbles rose, and the stink of rotten eggs, which made both of them cough. But the dark shadow, Amy saw with relief, swam away.

Her lips lifted. "Well done, my boy, and now let us get you out of there." She risked a glance over her shoulder and hollered, "Dick! Run to the house and get help!"

His boots crunched on the snow, then the sound of his steps receded into the distance.

Amy gripped Pip's hands, then his elbows, hauling him toward her until she could slip her hands into his armpits. He kicked and struggled, and together they somehow managed to haul him fully onto the ice. Gasping, they lay side by side. The ice creaked ominously underneath them, but held; for all around the hole it was still thick and strong, not yet touched by whatever evil lurked in the depths of the lake. But who knew for how much longer?

"Come," she gasped, and crawled away from the hole, dragging the boy with her.

Their runners scraped across the ice, an angry, screeching sound that made Amy's hair stand on end. She scrambled to her feet and, with her arm around his waist, managed to pull Pip upright. "Come!" She took most of his weight and, stumbling and skidding, they slid toward the bank.

Some distance away, Annie sat on the stone bench, her little face blotchy with tears as she watched them, wide-eyed. And then her shrill little girl's scream: "The fish! The fish!"

"Damn!" Amy swore. The beast was coming back. The kick had been only a feeble distraction after all. "Damn!" The words of a protection spell whispered through her mind, but she could not speak them. Her tongue remained paralyzed. "Damn!" Tears burned in her eyes. Pip's fearful whimpers nearly broke her heart.

She drew him tighter against her body. "Faster, sweeting. We have to go faster."

It was awkward. Pip could hardly keep himself upright, and she feared they would lose their balance any moment. And then she felt it: the bumps of a large body beneath them. The fish that wasn't a fish had caught up.

"No!" Amy yelled. "No! Go away, you beast! Leave us alone!"

They had almost reached the shore, almost—

Another bump made the ice tremble. A dry sound came as it cracked.

"No!"

Amy summoned all her remaining strength and propelled Pip towards the bank, then flung herself after him just as the sound of splashing water arose behind her. She came to rest with her face lying in the snow, her feet dangling in the water. Annie knelt beside her and tugged at her brother's hair, tears streaming down her face.

Amy shook herself and came up on her hands and knees. Bright red dropped into the snow. She shook her head to clear her brain before she turned to Pip. The boy was unconscious, his skin almost as white as the snow.

Quickly, she unfastened the clasps around her boots, then those around Pip's, and left the runners lying in the snow. She dragged him up the small slope toward the stone bench, where she sat him down. She sank down next to him and her arm went around him to hug him against the feeble warmth of her body. He seemed colder than a block of ice. "Pip, sweetheart, you have to wake up."

"Is he dead?" Annie sobbed.

"No, no." Amy reached out her free hand and drew the little girl close. "Hush, sweetie. Everything will be all right," she whispered. But as she looked out over the lake, where now two black holes gaped in the ice, she knew that nothing would be all right. Evil had invaded Rawdon Park and she didn't have the means to hold it at bay. And so, all she did was sit on the bench and hug the frozen boy and the sobbing little girl close to her body, while her wet feet went slowly numb.

It seemed half an eternity before she finally heard shouts on the path. The grooms and the stable hands reached them first, bringing blankets smelling of horse and hay. One was wrapped immediately around Pip and he was carried off. Annie was bundled in another, and a third came to rest around Amy's shoulders. At this point everything had become an indistinct blur to her.

"Miss Bourne."

Swaying she stood, the blanket clutched between numb

fingers. She was aware of a hand touching her shoulder, a worried face hovering next to her. One of the footmen.

"I . . ."

She thought she could hear the earl's voice farther ahead, where the groom carried Pip. Dick's boyish tones mingled with those of the admiral, and then—

"Amy!"

Fox.

Her breath escaped in a sob.

"Dear God, Amy!" He hauled her into his arms, and her hands slipped around his waist, held tight to his big, solid body. She pressed her cheek against his chest where she could hear the rapid beating of his heart. Large hands stroked frantically over her back.

"Amy . . ."

Her eyes fell closed.

"Amy . . ." She felt herself lifted in strong arms. "Dear God, your poor face!"

"Hmm?" Her head sank against a shoulder, her nose buried against his warm neck where she could inhale the familiar scent of bergamot. With a sigh, she snuggled closer and allowed the world to fade away.

Fox deposited her into Rosie's and the housekeeper's care, who clucked over her, helped her change her clothes, and fed her some hot broth. Amy sat at the window, bundled into a woolen blanket—this one smelled neither of horses nor of hay—blinked drowsily and felt like an overlarge chick. She didn't know how much time had passed when a knock sounded on the door. Mrs. Dibbler went to answer it and had a whispered conversation with whoever stood outside. Finally she came back to Amy. "Miss Bourne, Master Philip is asking for you. The apothecary has seen him and wants to give him a mild sedative, but the poor child won't settle down."

Amy blinked. "I'll come." When she stood, the blanket slid from her shoulders. "Thank you, Mrs. Dibbler." The housekeeper held the door open for her, and outside she found the earl's valet himself waiting.

"If you'll come this way, miss."

He led her into the wing where the family's apartments were located, and to the boys' room. The countess sat on the bed and held Pip's hand, while the earl stood a little aside and conversed with a burly, grey-haired man.

"My lord, my lady," the valet said, "Miss Bourne is here."

Lady Rawdon rose and, with a small cry, hurried across the room to hug Amy hard. "Thank you for saving my son's life." When she drew back, her eyes were filled with tears. "He's been asking for you. He seems to think a monster lives in the lake."

"Oh dear," Amy said weakly.

The countess sniffled and quickly dashed a hand across her eyes. "We told him there are no monsters, but he got so distressed. And we thought talking to you might alleviate his fears. I am sorry we have to inconvenience you again—"

"Not at all," Amy cut in. She put her hand on the other woman's arm. "I'll speak to him." She went to the big bed where Pip's small, white face anxiously peeked up at her. A wave of tenderness swamped her. How fragile he seemed!

"How are you, sweetie?" she asked and sat down on the edge of the bed.

"Better," he croaked.

With a gentle hand, she brushed his hair out of his face. "But you don't want to sleep?"

He shook his head. His voice dropped to a whisper. "They say the monster is not real."

"I know." For how could they accept that something that only existed in nightmares had stepped into their world?

"But it is." His eyes glittered feverishly.

Amy cupped his cheek in her hand and stroked her thumb over his skin. "Yes," she murmured, low enough that only he could hear. "Yes, it is." And leaning forward: "You mustn't worry. I will keep you safe."

He searched her face. "How?"

"I'll find a way."

"Promise?"

"I swear," she said. *On my life.* "Will you now take your medicine?"

He nodded, and his eyes closed. His hand felt around until his fingers closed over hers. "I'm glad you're here," he mumbled.

And yet, without my magic, I'm not much help. Her eyes burning, she kissed his forehead. "Sleep well, sweetheart." Quickly, she stood. After she had taken a deep breath, she turned. "You can now give him the medicine," she said brightly to the man who must be the apothecary.

When she stepped away from the bed, the earl came to her and accompanied her to the door. For once, his face was creased with worry. "Thank you for what you did today." He threw a look back at the bed. "The gardeners checked the ice this morning and it all seemed safe."

Suddenly, Amy didn't only feel bone-tired, but also very badly wanted to cry. Instead she forced herself to say, gaily almost, "That's what the boys said. It would appear that ice can be deceptive. Perhaps it would be best if everybody stayed off the lake for now." *Oh yes, stay away until I can find a way to kill the evil lurking within.*

"No more skating adventures," Lord Rawdon agreed, while his valet opened the door. "But now you should rest, too, my dear."

In a daze, Amy made it back to her room. Twice within an hour, Rosie helped her out of her clothes. Clad only in her chemise she climbed into the bed. "Leave the candle burning," Amy murmured.

"Yes, Miss Bourne."

A rustle of clothes, then the door clicked shut.

Wearily, Amy closed her eyes. How should she fight against the darkness that had crept into Rawdon Park? What could be done without magic? Without the means to contact her family? In this, she feared, she was all alone.

All alone, with no magic.

Despite the warmth of the blankets and the heavy quilt, Amy shivered.

All alone . . .

The door opened.

"Who—?" She half turned.

"Shush," Fox murmured. His hand stroked over her hair. "Shush."

She heard the rustle of clothes, then the blankets were lifted and Fox's warm body slipped in beside her.

"What—"

"Shush." He took her into his arms, drew her back against his chest. Softly, he kissed her shoulder. "I need to hold you tonight. Just hold you. Nothing more." His fingers stroked down her arm. "Relax, love, I'm here. I'm here now." He pressed another kiss onto her hair.

And despite herself, she snuggled back against him. She was too tired to fight this, the pull of the potion, the magic that had distorted their relationship. She no longer cared whether this was real or not, she knew only that he offered her his arms, his body as a safe haven from the world. For just one night she needed to hold on to this illusion. For just one night she needed the shelter of his arms.

Even though she knew it was only that: an illusion.

Chapter Twelve

The soft sound of the door latch was what woke her in the darkness of the early hours of the morning. Her candle had long burned down, and the bed beside her was empty. Yet even though Fox had left to sneak back to his room, his warmth and scent still clung to the linen. Amy turned and buried her nose in the pillow where his head had rested. She inhaled deeply. Bergamot and Fox. Instantly, her nipples hardened, and heat pooled low in her belly. Even now, her body craved his. Even now . . .

She sighed.

It wasn't just her body. Her heart, too, hungered for him. She yearned to be near him . . . to talk to him . . . to touch him . . . to kiss him. But how could she trust her own feelings when she no longer knew what was real and what was not?

She did know, though, that the danger for the Stapleton family was very real, indeed. And they didn't suspect a thing.

Oh, how could she keep them safe? Despite her attempts to fight her fondness for the Stapletons, she had come to love them all and couldn't bear the thought that something might happen to one of them. However, if she told them the truth, they would probably think she had taken leave of her senses. And worse, she might lose Fox.

Fox? Her heart contracted as she realized she wasn't

ready for that, no matter what the truth of her emotions. Nevertheless, she had to do something against the evil powers at work in Rawdon Park, or else somebody would end up dead. First of all, she would need to find out exactly what kind of magic she was dealing with.

Determined, she sat up and swung her legs over the edge of the bed to rummage for the tinderbox. When she had lit a new candle, she went over to the fireplace, where the fire burned low. She stirred up the embers, put a new log onto the grate, and soon the fire was flickering merrily. She donned her wraparound stays, a simple dress, and her thick boots and left her room.

It was eerily silent in the hallways—and dark, for it was still too early for the servants to light the candles. Her lone candle threw trembling shadows on the walls as Amy crept down into the entrance hall. She got her pelisse, scarf, and muff from the cloak room and stepped outside.

The grayish light of predawn, reflected by the snow, allowed her to walk down the path to the gardens without a lantern. Indeed, she preferred the shadowy dimness. This way, her early-morning foray into the park might remain undetected.

She walked down the same path they had taken the afternoon before. The statues at which the boys had thrown snowballs looked down on her with worried faces. Yet Amy trudged on, the crisp morning air like a thousand needles on her skin. Finally, the lake lay before her, a wide, pale expanse of ice.

Carefully she stepped down the small slope to the edge of the water, where she crouched down. Even though a thin layer of ice already covered the hole nearest to the shore, she could see the way ice had initially broken in smooth, not craggy lines. A small breeze blew some stray tendrils of hair across her face. Amy tugged them behind her ear. Intently she stared out across the lake and listened. And then she closed her eyes and opened her mind—and nearly staggered under the weight of evil that bombarded her.

Gasping, she opened her eyes. This was powerful magic. It must have festered here for some weeks and would continue grow if nothing were done.

Fear gripped her at the throat. What could she do? She was powerless, helpless . . .

"Think," she muttered fiercely. *"Think."*

She couldn't speak any spells, that was true, but surely there was another way to deal with this. Surely she knew enough of magic to fight, didn't she? She rubbed her hand over her chin and winced when she touched the place where a stone had scraped her face yesterday afternoon.

"Drat!"

But then her eyes widened. "Oh!" Yes, she couldn't speak any spells, but there *was* another way to cast magic: with blood. It was difficult, dangerous, and not something a nice young girl should do or even know of as her uncle had often enough told her. However, it produced powerful magic. Almost certainly powerful enough to deal with whatever had decided to take residence in Rawdon Park.

Amy jumped up.

Yes, a protection spell, enforced by blood. But how to start it?

She frowned. In one of the forbidden books in the library of Three Elms she had read stories so old that nobody could tell anymore whether they were fact or fantasy—stories of kings of yore who had entered a union with the land to ensure a fruitful reign. If she did something similar, if she could adapt such a ritual, she would be able to use this melding with the land as the basis for a protection spell, to let the land protect the people who lived on it.

Her heart beat faster.

Hadn't she always loved to experiment with spells? This was her chance to prove to herself she could do better than turn a manor house blue. She would need to be careful, would need to use all her skills and knowledge. And most importantly: she needed to find the perfect place to put it all in motion.

She made it back to the house and to her room undetected. Even though the candles were now lit, it was still too early to ring for either Rosie or a tray with breakfast. Impatiently she walked up and down her room, which suddenly seemed much too small, the walls closing in on her. Her gaze fell on the book on her nightstand. With a sigh, she reached for it and plopped down on her chair. After all, it simply would not do if she wore a hole in the carpet.

She flipped the book open, smoothed down the pages, and read. Yet even though Chapter XIII was certainly a most interesting episode—Kassian, Gidonius, and Martinus ventured off to the Perilous Orchard, where they ate from the Forbidden Cherries—she could hardly concentrate on the text. Again and again her thoughts wandered off to contemplate the task that lay before her. When the nymphs, the fair Ladies of the Orchard, lulled Gidonius and Martinus into an unnatural sleep with their magical song, she could not help thinking about the spell she had to weave with her blood alone. Yes, dangerous it would be, more dangerous even than venturing into the Perilous Orchard. She would mesh with the land, body and soul, and form a union that could only be broken by her death.

Amy shuddered a little and quickly read on about how the nymphs buried Gidonius and Martinus under cherry blossoms. But when worthy Kassian turned out to be a young woman and thus not affected by the song of the nymphs, Amy was reminded of the charade she herself was forced to play.

She rubbed her fingers over her forehead. How she hated to keep the truth from Fox, about the magic, their relationship . . . and how she longed to regain their closeness of those happy weeks when the world had been a place of sunshine and bliss. No matter how often she reminded herself what a bore he had been when they had first met, she couldn't help feeling drawn to him now, to the tender lover, the playful man and kind friend. But, of course, she couldn't give in to those longings.

She closed her eyes. Perhaps her love for him was real. After loving him for so long under the influence of the potion, who could tell if what she felt for him now was only the aftereffects, or true affection? Amy felt as if she were closed into the Labyrinth, where somewhere the horrible Minotaur was lying in wait for her.

With a sound of disgust Amy closed the book. She did not care about how Catrina would proceed to save her two fellow knights. For of course, she would save them. But would Amy manage to save the Stapleton family?

Unable to stand another second of sitting still, she jumped up and took up her prowl about the room once more. Finally, *finally*, it was late enough for her to ring for her maid. She felt too tense to have breakfast in the breakfast parlor with all of the others, and so had a tray sent up to her room. She nibbled on the buttered toast, took a bite from the apple puff—and then she simply couldn't endure to stay closed into her room a moment longer.

She went to the South Drawing Room, which was wonderfully empty at this time of the day, but still, the fire already had been lit and lent the room a cozy warmth. Amy went straight to the large, high windows that looked out over the green and offered an unhindered view of the lake. Mesmerized, she stared at it.

Amy didn't know how much time had passed when the door behind her opened. "Ah, there you are," Fox said.

She looked over her shoulder.

He was wearing a dark green frock coat with a pistachio-colored vest over the same buff breeches he had muddied that first time in the pineapple-crowned pavilion. A lump formed in her throat, and quickly she turned back to the window. Behind her she could hear his steps—the soft creaks of the floorboards and the muffled sounds when he was walking across the carpet.

"I've been thinking," she began.

Warmth behind her, then an arm slipped around her waist, hugged her against his body. "Yes?"

Her eyes fell closed as he nuzzled the side of her jaw. The warm scent of bergamot enveloped her. It tickled in her nostrils, reminding her of shared kisses and of sweaty, sultry hours spent in his arms.

Only illusions.

Her stomach felt hollow. Yet she resisted the desperate urge to run away from him, to hide from the attraction and affection she still felt, God help her. Instead, she turned and subtly put some distance between them. "Are there any old monuments to be found in the vicinity?" Gazing up at him, she forced herself to smile. "You know, stone circles and such?"

He chuckled. "Have you had enough of Roman ruins and the sculptures in Richard's gardens?"

She had not managed to fully evade him, and now his hand rested warm and large on her waist. Even through the heavy cotton of her stays Amy could feel the subtle pressure of his fingers. She licked her lips.

"I am fancying something more primeval," she answered. "I have heard that some of these stone monuments are awe inspiring."

A rueful smile curved his mouth. "I am afraid I must disappoint you. We have nothing as spectacular to offer as the Salisbury Plain."

Amy held her breath. Whatever should she do now?

"But"—his smile deepened—"there is indeed a small circle not very far from Rawdon Park. Though it's nothing but a heap of old stones, of course."

A wave of relief washed through her. It weakened her knees enough that she let him draw her back to his side. He kissed her temple. "Would you like me to show it to you?" he murmured against her skin.

"Yes. Oh, yes."

He pulled back a little, his eyes suddenly worried as they scanned her face. "But we will have to wait a few days to make sure you haven't caught a chill."

Impatience made her want to cry out, but she bit her objections back and forced herself to remain calm. It would not do to appear overly eager, since it would only rouse his suspicions. She aimed at a cajoling, teasing tone. "Perhaps we shall wait until this afternoon, then?"

Amusement softened his eyes, and he touched a tender finger to the graze on her chin. "We shall see. How are you feeling this morning?"

His voice caressed her like warm syrup, and lead filled her stomach. She swallowed, hard. "Very well." Yet another lie.

"I'm glad." He touched his forehead against hers. "I'm sorry I had to leave you this morning. I would have wished to hold you in my arms all through the night until sunrise." Emotion and passion lent his voice a raspy edge. "But soon I'll be able to see the first rays of the sun kiss your skin," he murmured. "Marriage will become me very well indeed."

If he had taken a knife and sliced her veins wide open, it would not have hurt more. His face swam out of focus.

"Oh sweetheart." He leaned down to kiss the corner of her mouth. "We will be so happy together," he crooned against her cheek.

Her tears overflowed.

More snow fell that afternoon and kept them from going to the stone circle after all. Pip, as it turned out, was not suffering from any worse aftereffects of his dunking in ice water than a slight sneeze. The family was relieved, yet the feeling of dread would not leave Amy. Who knew what else lay in store for them all? What other spells had been planted in Rawdon Park? And so there was another reason why she could not possibly tell any of them the truth: should this somehow jolt Fox's memory and perhaps even break the potion's hold on him, and should she be sent from Rawdon as a result, who would protect the Stapletons? Even if she had lost her own magic, she knew at least of the seriousness of the threat hanging over the family. By contrast, Fox, with his firm belief in common sense, would most likely consider the notion of a magical threat quite ludicrous.

After the morning mists had lifted the next day, the sun shone from a brilliant blue sky and turned the layers of snow that covered the land into sparkling diamonds. And since Amy neither coughed nor sniffled, she managed to talk Fox into showing her the stone circle that day. Indeed, given that this was going to be their first joint outing in weeks, he seemed more than happy to oblige her. He ordered the light sleigh to be brought to the front of the house after their luncheon and, huddled in furs, the two of them set off. With a faint crunching sound the runners glided over the snow. The coldness bit into Amy's skin, yet as she cast a glance at Fox, who handled the reins with easy confidence, she suspected his face was glowing with more than simply the cold.

He caught her eye and flashed her a smile. "A most wonderful day, is it not?"

"Yes, indeed."

"If it weren't for the snow, we would have been able to walk. It is not all that far from the estate."

"Isn't it?"

"No, three quarters of an hour perhaps. A rather leisurely walk, wouldn't you say?"

Perhaps not so leisurely if she took it in the middle of the night.

He threw her another look, but this time the inner glow he radiated was slightly dimmed. "Are you sure you are all right? Perhaps we should turn around—"

"Oh no!" she hastily cut in. But she couldn't meet his gaze as she lied to him. "I am absolutely fine."

As they left the carefully groomed grounds of Rawdon Park, the vast flatness of the land struck Amy anew. It stretched endlessly before them, a brilliant glare of white against the giant dome of the sky.

"Rather overwhelming, isn't it?" Fox remarked. "Deucedly *empty* when you're used to life in Town."

This was the land she was going to join with. Amy swallowed. It was an overwhelming thought indeed!

They passed a newly ploughed field. In the sunlight the ridges of black soil gleamed like the flanks of a powerful animal.

"The only excitement to be had in these parts," Fox continued, "is the butter market in Downham Market." He wrinkled his nose. "If you can call this excitement. Of course, one could always climb on the tower of St. Edmund's Church and hope to catch a glimpse of Ely Cathedral."

Amy thought that certainly was impressive, given that Ely lay several miles away on the road to Cambridge.

The chill and the wind made her eyes water. She blinked and caught Fox darting a glance at her. "Have I already told you how beautiful you are?" His voice was husky with emotion. "Utterly bewitching." Suddenly the corners of his mouth curled. "More bewitching in fact that Keats's 'Belle Dame sans Merci—'

> 'I saw a lady in the meads,
> Full beautiful—a faery's child,
> Her hair was long, her—'

Drat. I've forgotten the rest."

Amy's breath caught. He had read Keat's "Belle Dame"? The same man who had lectured her on the dangers of flights of fancy? She had to clear her throat several times before she finally could ask, "Didn't you tell me that you don't hold Keats in high esteem?"

He shrugged and his cheeks turned a shade redder than could be accounted to the cold. "Since you like those new poets, I thought I might give them another try."

And of all poems he had chosen "La Belle Dame sans Merci," with which she had teased him all these weeks ago and which he had so clearly hated. This time it was not only the wind that made tears spring to her eyes. Amy turned her face away so he wouldn't see her inner turmoil.

Fortunately, they reached their destination soon thereafter: seven bulky stones rose on a small hill, a precious spot of dry land back when the Fens had not yet been drained and the stones were surrounded by watery moors and marshland.

Fox lifted Amy from the sleigh. With a frown he looked down to where the hem of her dress and pelisse dragged through the snow. "You are sure that—"

"Yes," she said, without averting her gaze from the stones, which wore white caps of snow. "I want to look at them."

She plodded onward, not caring about her clothes or about the coldness that clawed at her limbs. Behind her, Fox sighed, then started to follow.

On top of the hill, Amy drew off her right glove and reverently laid her hand against one of the stones. Closing her eyes, she took a few deep breaths and felt the place. A prickling, a . . .

"Do you like it?"

Her eyes snapped open, and she snatched back her hand. For a moment, the tingling in her fingers remained. Oh yes, even though the stones were nowhere near as big as those of Stonehenge, this was still a powerful place. A site where old magic slept deep in the earth and only waited to be awoken once more.

Amy turned to look at Fox. This time she didn't have to force her smile. "It is wonderful."

"Shall we . . . um . . ." He made a vague movement with his hand. "Step inside?" He stared past Amy. "Or perhaps we shouldn't? Look at how pristine the snow looks inside. We would destroy all that perfection."

"No." She slipped past him through the gap in the stones. "I don't think they would mind." She walked to the center of the small circle, where she slowly turned around. All around them lay flat land; the trees of Rawdon Park were barely discernible in the distance.

All alone they were in the white landscape, the sky overhead sapphire blue with the sun shining down on their heads.

Mine, Amy thought. *I will make this all mine.* Once bound to the land, she would forever feel a yearning for it. To the end of her days she would long to return here. And, strangely, that thought did not frighten her. It was good land, and she felt old strength running through it.

Amy threw her arms wide and raised her face to the sun. With closed eyes, she whirled around and around, faster and faster, until her hat fell into the snow and her hair tumbled loose. She laughed with the joy of it all.

Yes, this was good land. It would be no hardship to be bound to it—

The laughter died.

Slowly, she came to a halt, opened her eyes.

The question was if she would survive the binding. If the land would accept her.

"You are the most beautiful woman I have ever met," Fox said softly behind her.

She turned.

He still stood between the gap in the stones where she had left him and gazed at her as if spellbound.

Which he was.

Amy swallowed.

"I love you so much," he whispered, his voice raw.

She walked back to him. He watched her, keeping his eyes firmly trained on her as if she were an apparition that could disappear at any moment. The uncertainty and vulnerability that were reflected on his face tore at her heart. She stopped in front of him and, standing so near, she could feel the tremor that passed through his body.

"What is it?" she asked quietly.

His Adam's apple moved convulsively. "I've just remembered . . ." His voice trailed away and he stared across the circle.

Amy searched his face. His eyes were curiously blank and even bleaker than the flat, white winter Fens. "What?" Apprehension made the word into a mere breath of a sound.

He blinked several times. Very slowly he reached out his hand and laid it against the nearest stone. "They're dead," he muttered tonelessly. Then he shook himself like a wet dog and turned to her with a wry smile. "You must think me a lunatic." Becoming aware that he was still touching the stone, he let his hand drop to his side. "I used to come here as a small boy and pretend I could . . . *hear* . . . the stones. Can you imagine?" He gave a little laugh. "A lunatic indeed."

"No, not at all." Amy choked, her eyes stinging. "What happened?"

He glanced at her, then shrugged, clearly aiming at an offhand manner. "I was stupid enough to tell the old earl one day. I thought—heck, I thought he would be pleased, take it as a sign that I belong here just like . . ." He didn't finish the sentence.

"Oh, Fox." Amy thought her heart would surely break.

"All he gave me was a sound whipping." He snorted. "And I was told never to indulge in such flights of fancy again. I haven't, you know." He looked down at her, his face reflecting the bewilderment of the little boy who had desperately wanted to belong.

Something hot and wet trailed down Amy's cheek. "I know you haven't."

"And now the stones are cold and dead," he said, his voice flat. "It was never but a figment of boyish imagination. But when I saw you dance just now—" His hand trembled as he raised it to her face. "—it almost seemed real after all." The leather of his glove glided over her skin before he cupped the side of her face. "I *love* you."

Something inside Amy gave way. With a little sob she slung her hand around his neck, rose on tiptoe, and drew his head down until her lips brushed against his. And then the world fell away. Nothing existed anymore but this one man.

With a small groan he pulled her closer, subtly turning her until her back rested against a stone. His body blocked the coldness as he deepened their kiss.

After a small eternity, or perhaps after no time at all, he lifted his head. One hand leaning against the stone above her head, he regarded her. After a while his lips curved, and he drew his finger over her eyebrows, nose and mouth, as carefully as if he were touching rarest china.

Amy watched him with heavy-lidded eyes. Her blood sang in her veins, a wild song that made her forget all caution and care.

"I have got something for you." His breath formed white clouds in the cold air.

She wetted her lips. "Show me," she whispered.

He took her hand and bestowed a moist, lingering kiss onto her palm before reaching into his coat and drawing out a small sponge and a flacon. Both of them he dropped into the hollow of her hand.

"What are these?"

The sparkle of mischief she so adored, which she had so missed, lit up his eyes. He leaned closer and skimmed his mouth over her ear. "Were you not afraid of getting with child, my love? With these you will need have no fear." The air escaped her in a high, breathy sound of surprise, and his teeth closed in a gentle bite on her earlobe. "Will you let me show you how?" He drew in a deep breath. "Tonight?" The word shivered against her skin.

For a moment Amy stood rock still. She remembered all the reasons why she should resist him—he didn't know

Chapter Thirteen

Thus, he came to her during the night, slipped into her bed, and as their bodies entwined and became one, all secrets and words slipped away. They were replaced by the language of skin gliding over skin, of hearts straining to beat as one, of the smell and taste of sweat sweeter than dew.

How to describe an act of perfect bliss and harmony? When passion became a dark wave that drew them under, and tenderness so overwhelmingly sweet it could reduce a grown man to tears? In his arms Amy found a freedom of body and mind beyond anything she had ever experienced before.

And yet, while she lay shuddering beside him, his face buried against her breasts, one of his arms slung over her belly and hip, while one of her hands stroked his heaving shoulders, she was filled with the bittersweet knowledge of the transience of it all. Built on foundations more fragile than thinnest glass, such bliss could not and would not last. She could not build her hopes on what he had experienced more than two decades ago. As a child he might have believed in magic, but the man, the real Sebastian Stapleton, did not. And who could fault him?

On their third night together Amy slid away from him as soon as she was certain he was asleep. The scrape of the flint made him grumble in protest and nestle his face deeper into the pillow; the next moment though, his breaths turned into soft snores once more.

Amy's throat closed on a wave of tenderness. Who would have thought it: At night the fox became a baby bear.

She blinked against the sudden sting in her eyes. With a determined shake of her head, she turned away. She moved around the room and dressed as quickly and quietly as possible to the flickering light of the candle. From her chest of drawers, she took the small knife she had found in the weapons collection of Rawdon Park and thrust it into one of the pockets underneath her dress.

At the door she threw a last look at Fox. In the soft light his hair seemed darker than usual. Heavily tousled, it stuck up on all sides, and she remembered how she had run her hands through it not yet an hour ago. The blankets had slipped down to reveal the smattering of freckles across his shoulders, a sprinkle of cinnamon dust. She had teased him about them, had traced invisible lines between them and had called them his map of stars.

For a short moment she wondered whether she would see him again, but quickly she brushed the thought aside. It was time to go.

Noiselessly she slipped out of the room into the hallway and wandered the corridors of Rawdon Park in stockinged feet, her boots in one hand, the candle in the other. The pale light of the full moon fell through the tall windows of the stairway hall as she padded downstairs. In the entrance hall she donned her boots before she fetched her scarf, muff, and pelisse from the cloakroom. There she also found a cap lined with thick fur, which she took as well. It would keep her warmer than any of her own winter hats.

Outside, the air was crystal clear and so cold it stung her lungs. Amy adjusted her scarf to cover the lower half of her face and then strode away from the house. After she had left the grounds of Rawdon Park, she took a shortcut through the fields, where the snow crunched under her feet. The moon made the landscape gleam in an eerie light, and it seemed to her as if she had entered a realm of the Otherworld. She only hoped she would not fall into a ditch filled with ice.

Finally she saw the short, bulky forms of the standing stones rising as dark shadows against the sky. She quickened her steps until she marched up the little hill. Just outside the circle, she stopped to catch her breath. Uncertainty made her falter. She listened to the harsh sounds of her breaths and the dull thuds of her blood in her ears. Would her plan really work?

She brushed her hand against her side and felt the length of her knife dig against her hip.

Madness!

She thought of her parents, her father who had attempted to save her mother's life and whom the all-too-powerful magic had only brought death.

But then she thought of Fox, lying naked and vulnerable in her bed, not knowing of the danger that threatened his family. She thought of the children, of Pip breaking through the ice. She thought of Lord and Lady Rawdon and the dowager countess, who all had welcomed her so warmly into their midst. And in the end, her thoughts returned to Fox once more, the raw sound of his voice as he had sworn his love to her at this place three days ago. "*I love you so much.*"

Amy took a few deep breaths and let her fear and uncertainty ebb away with the air she exhaled. Not only did the Stapletons need her protection, but she would also never forgive herself should anything happen to one of them. She brushed the cap from her head and let the muff fall into the snow. Afterwards, she drew off her gloves and laid her hands against the icy stone to each side of her. She opened her mind and let the peace of the circle fill her being.

With a small sigh, she shrugged out of her pelisse, loosened the lacings of her dress and drew it over her head, took off her petticoats, her stays, her chemise, boots, and stockings until she stood naked and shivering. Goosebumps covered her whole body and her nipples hardened. Like a ravaging beast, the cold clawed at her body.

Amy clenched her teeth and tried to suppress the shivers. She reached for her pockets and drew out the knife, which she clenched tightly in her hand. Slowly she proceeded into the middle of the circle, where she had trodden down the snow three days before. She laid her head back and looked up to the moon, standing pale and round above her: Luna the White, who sailed across night-darkened skies. "Help me," she whispered.

Smoothly Amy drew the knife from the sheath. Now it began.

She had thought this ritual through a hundred times. She had pondered on each step she would need to take, on each word that would need to be spoken, and on each drop of blood she would shed into the snow. For the sake of the Stapletons she could not afford to fail.

She closed her eyes and reached out her mind for the stones once more. *Standing still and silent in a circle of power, a circle to bind the power, a circle to awaken the power, power of darkness and light—*

The blade of the knife bit into her palm.

Amy hissed with the pain.

She opened her eyes.

Blood ran down her fingers and dropped darkly onto the snow.

The shivers increased.

Grinding her teeth together, Amy started to cut a seven-pointed star into the snow. Each stone was a point, at each stone a drop of blood.

When she was finished she returned to the center of the star and the circle, dipped her finger into her own blood and drew a crescent moon on the center of her chest. This done, she slowly lay back into the snow and flung her arms wide, a willing sacrifice to spark the hunger of the land.

Immediately the coldness embraced her, numbed her body, and she gasped.

The icy cold was more than she thought she could bear. Yet in order to be reborn as one with the land, she needed to die first, if only in ritual. Renewed dread clogged her throat. She wanted to flee, rush back to the warm house, to the lover waiting in her bed. But she was the only one who could keep the people of Rawdon Park safe. She had to go through with the ritual.

For long moments, Amy stared up at the moon, before she closed her eyes.

Circle of power . . .

I am here . . .

A thousand needles piercing her skin, the pain so intense that tears trickled from below her closed lids. Defenseless, she lay in the snow. While the stones looked on, the breath froze in her lungs, the cold ate up her insides.

She bit her lip until she tasted blood.

I am here. Hear me, Old Mother Moon, you Elders of Stone, I am here. Please accept my sacrifice.

Amy sobbed.

She arched her throat. "I am here." A small moan only, but in the earth deep below her she could feel a stirring.

Another sob. She whimpered with pain and fear.

"I AM HERE!" she cried.

And then something roared toward her and through her and exploded in the stones all around. Her high, wailing scream was cut abruptly short.

When Amy came to her senses, she was lying in a tight ball in the middle of the stone circle, still naked, but now filled with a curious warmth.

She blinked. The snow around her had in part melted away, and the star she had drawn had vanished.

Slowly she sat up, her limbs heavy and weak like those of a newborn lamb. In a daze, she stared at her hand, where the cut of the knife had closed and was no more than an angry red scratch. Then, finally, it dawned on her: She had survived the ritual. With tears in her eyes, she looked up to the moon.

"Thank you," she whispered. "Thank you, thank you, thank you."

The moon, which ruled the bodies of all women and appeared as the symbol of goddesses all around the world, smiled a little and sailed on toward the horizon.

Giving herself a mental shake, Amy stumbled to her feet. She gazed at the stones around her, and as she now opened her mind, she could feel a deep humming inside them. She smiled.

Oh yes, she had been successful. All would be well: no more harm would come to Rawdon Park. She laughed with the joy of it all.

Before she left the circle, she once more touched the two stones where she had entered it. "Thank you." And then she stepped outside and hastily donned her clothes.

All the way back to the house, a soft glow warmed her body from the inside out and robbed the cold of its bite. Still, when she finally slipped back into her room, she felt bone weary. She fumbled with her clothes and hid them in her chest of drawers before she crawled back into bed.

Fox stirred. Sleepily, he looked over his shoulder. "Where have you been?" he mumbled.

"Shh." She burrowed against his body, and willingly he turned to enfold her in his arms.

He pressed a kiss onto her forehead. "You haven't been rambling around the house, have you?" He gave a contented sigh as he nestled his face into the curve of her shoulder.

"I couldn't sleep," she whispered.

He raised his head. "So you *have* been rambling around the house?" he said, fully awake now. He snorted. "You must be daft, sweetheart. You could've caught your death in these cold hallways." He bussed her cheek. "Don't do it again."

"No," she breathed. "I won't." She slung her arm around his waist and hugged him tightly against her body. "I won't."

Over the next few days Amy set about perfecting her spell by pricking her finger repeatedly and drawing small signs against evil in strategic places throughout the house. She drew the same signs on the forehead of the children, who now, after she had displayed her skill at skipping stones, not to speak of her having saved Pip, firmly believed there was nothing she could not do. For the lake she made a small sachet filled with salt and cleansing herbs, and let a few drops of blood fall onto the mixture before she broke a hole in the ice and threw the sachet into the water. She watched dark bubbles rise to the surface, and hoped the spell would work.

In the depth of the night, when Fox lay lost in dreams beside her, she drew the sign against evil on his forehead, too. She kissed his cheek, then put her chin onto his shoulder. Despite the fact that he was fast asleep, he immediately adjusted his position to fit her against his body. With a sigh, Amy laid her head on his chest and drank in his scent and warmth.

Thus she had done all she could to ensure the safety of the Stapletons, but still, the niggling worry deep inside her would not vanish. Not only was she painfully conscious that she was living on borrowed time, but as the days passed, she also found it increasingly difficult not to confide in Fox. She hated lying to him, yet what would happen if she *did* tell him? For even knowing what she did, she could not bear the thought of losing him.

Chapter Fourteen

Ten days after Amy had been to the circle, a special punch ceremony was held at Rawdon Park as a foretaste of the Christmas festivities that were soon to follow. In the late afternoon, when darkness had fallen around the house, the whole family assembled at a table in the drawing room. Admiral Reitz, it appeared, would act as the Master of Ceremonies. The children skipped from one foot to the other with excitement. "*Feuerzangenbowle, Feuerzangenbowle*," Dick and Pip chanted, while Annie chirped in between, "Fir-ang-bowl, fir-ang-bowl."

"The admiral has spent many a Christmas at Rawdon Park," the dowager countess explained to Amy. "And each year he delights us with a *Feuerzangenbowle*. He picked up the recipe when staying with an acquaintance in Frankfurt years ago, did you not, Admiral?"

"Indeed, I did." He gave Amy a smile. "It is a special punch that is served in the winter months. Very popular with the students, too, or so I have heard."

The door opened and Ramtop, the butler, appeared, carrying an enormous pot filled with fragrant, steaming red wine. Two footmen followed him with trays, one of which held glasses, the other a ladle, a bottle, a white cone, and what looked like a pair of tongs. The pot was put on a wooden plate in front of the admiral, and the trays set down on the table. Afterwards the footmen bowed and left the room, while the butler brought a candle and a fidibus.

"So," the admiral said.

Dick gripped the edge of the table and leaned forward. "Do we start? Do we start now?"

Annie sidled up to Amy and gripped her hand. "Fir-ang-bowl." She beamed up at her.

"For those among you who have never seen a *Feuerzangenbowle*"—Admiral Reitz made a bow in Amy's direction—"what we need for it is this: dry red wine boiled with orange slices, sticks of cinnamon, and cloves. A pair of tongs"—he picked up the item from the tray—"long enough to be laid across the top of the pot, and a sugarloaf." He took the white cone and wedged it into the tongs before he put them onto the pot. "And then, the most important ingredient: rum." He held up the bottle to the children's excited ahhs and ohhs.

Annie clapped. "And now? And now? And now?"

The admiral threw the little girl a smile, which made her giggle. "We dim the lights." He nodded at Ramtop, who proceeded to walk around the room and extinguish all candles except for the one still burning on the table.

"And now?" Annie reached for Amy's hand again, tugged at her fingers. "And now?"

"We dash some rum over the sugar, like this . . ."

"And now?"

"We *light* the sugar!" the two boys crowed in unison.

"Exactly." Admiral Reitz chuckled a little as he reached for the rolled paper and lit it on the candle.

"Ooooooh!" Annie breathed and snuggled closer to Amy's side. Wide-eyed, the girl watched as the admiral set the sugar on fire.

Sizzling, the orange flame sprang from the fidibus to the rum-soaked sugar and turned a light blue. Wherever it touched the surface of the white cone, the sugar became brown until thick drops trickled through the brackets of the tongs.

"Lovely," the dowager countess said.

"The alcohol will burn away and the liquid sugar will drop into the wine," the admiral explained while he was critically watching the flame.

"A bit more rum, eh, Admiral?" Lord Rawdon suggested as the flame started to burn lower and lower.

As if on cue, his sons jumped up and down. "Yes! More rum!"

"Yes, definitely more rum." Smiling, the admiral poured a liberal dose over the sugarloaf. Immediately the blue flame shot up high. Just in time he jerked his head back. Dick and Pip chortled with delight.

"You nearly set your mustache on fire, Admiral Reitz!" Dick cried.

His brother giggled. "Or your eyebrows." His giggles intensified as the admiral waggled his brows at him.

"You have to be fast for this." He proceeded to show them, and poured more rum over the sugar.

This time the fire snaked into the neck of the bottle and struck a small flame there. Annie squealed. Yet, unperturbed and expertly, the admiral blew out the fire in the bottle.

From the corner of her eye, Amy saw Fox stepping behind her. "Well, Miss Bourne," he murmured. His hand briefly touched her arm. "Are you enjoying yourself?"

She smiled up at him.

He searched her face, then lifted his hand to draw a tendril of her hair back behind her ear. "Oh yes, you are." His eyes, which were black in the dim light, crinkled.

As it so often did, his tenderness and affection gave her a pang. Her cheerfulness dimmed. Quickly she averted her face so he would not worry about her. She slipped her free hand through his arm and, thus cuddled up to him, watched the rest of the sugar melt.

How could she go on lying to him and keeping him in ignorance of what had happened to them? It seemed selfish despite the possibility that the truth might drive him away. For how could she expect him to accept the existence of magic when the real Fox so adamantly believed in rational thought?

Amy sighed. In the past ten days there had been no further incidents, no further sign that evil was still at work in Rawdon Park. Everybody had been astonished when the ice on the lake suddenly thawed and the gardeners found a most ugly creature on the banks—half fish, half worm, rather dead and giving off a most dreadful odor. With satisfaction Amy had heard that it had been burned straightaway. She was now fairly confident that the threat to the Stapletons had been removed—but still, she could not in good conscience keep quiet any longer. She had reached a decision: she needed to talk to her aunt and uncle, and she would put a plan into motion today.

She swallowed, then glanced up at Fox. Nervousness made her stomach cramp. How would he react when he learned the truth? What would happen when the spell of the potion was broken?

She bit her lip and worried.

When the last of the sugar had melted and dripped into the wine, Ramtop lit the candles again while Admiral Reitz put a spoon into each tumbler and proceeded to hand out the hot punch. A footman brought hot chocolate for the children.

The admiral filled the last tumbler for himself. "So—" He looked up and smiled. "Before we drink, let me say a few words. Once again, it has been a delight staying with you, my friends. This year it has been a particular joy to get to know Miss Bourne, who will soon be part of the Stapleton family." Everybody smiled, but Amy's heart sank. "And—who knows? Next year there might be yet another addition to the family circle come Christmas." He gave Amy and Fox a broad wink, to the general amusement of the Stapletons, who all broke into hearty chuckles.

Fox laughed. "Aww, Admiral . . ."

The earl raised his glass to his brother. "We would certainly be delighted about any new addition to the family."

Annie looked up from her chocolate. "Which?"

"Shh." The dowager countess put her hand on her granddaughter's shoulder. "This is going to be a surprise." She smiled.

Amy grabbed Fox's arm. *Don't let me be sick. Please, don't let me be sick.* Her fingers dug into his muscles.

Surprised, he looked down. "Amy?" Worry laced his voice.

Luckily, the admiral chose that moment to continue. "And thus I would like to thank you for your hospitality, and here is to all the wonderful changes that will await this family in the coming year. Cheers."

"Cheers!" The drawing rang with joyful voices; only Amy felt as if her insides had turned to stone.

Hastily she took a sip of the fruity, spicy punch and closed her eyes as it exploded into warmth in her stomach. Would this torment never end?

Eventually, everyone strolled across the room to take seats on the sofas. Amy chose a spot next to Fox and circled the mouth of her glass with her fingers, trying to gather her composure. The voices around her merged into a buzzing noise, which reverberated in her head.

She took a few deep breaths.

Entwining his fingers with hers, Fox leaned toward her. "Are you feeling all right?" he whispered.

Desperately, she tried to swallow the lump in her throat. "Oh . . . yes."

He lowered his head to peer into her face. "Are you sure?"

"Absolutely." Amy finally managed a tight smile. She allowed herself a last look at this face, at the earnest blue-gray eyes framed by pale lashes, at the sweet sprinkle of freckles across his nose. Then she squeezed his fingers, and, "I have thought . . ." She turned toward the earl. "I need your advice in a certain matter, my lord."

Fox's brother raised his brows in silent inquiry.

"You see ... when our engagement was announced, I asked Mr. Bentham, who acted as my temporary guardian, as you know, to send a letter to my uncle in Warwickshire."

"Yes?" The earl took a swallow of his punch.

Fox's thumb rubbed over the back of her hand. He would never know how much it cost her to force out the next few words. "But because it all happened so *fast*—" Again, everybody chuckled, making it doubly difficult for her to continue. But ruthlessly overriding her own pain, she went on, "I worry that he might have forgotten. So I was wondering whether you would be so kind . . . Or perhaps Mr. Stapleton should . . ."

"What an excellent idea!" Lady Rawdon's eyes sparkled. "We will let Richard write a letter; the official Rawdon seal looks wonderfully splendid I've always thought."

"Ha!" Fox growled. "He will tell the Bournes the most dastardly things about me—"

His sister-in-law clucked her tongue. "Fiddle-faddle. He will write only the nicest possible things. Won't you, Richard?" She threw her husband a sharp look. *"Richard?"*

"Oh yes," Lord Rawdon hurried to say. "You will only need to give me the address, Miss Bourne."

"It's . . ." Amy faltered. One last chance to change her mind. But, no. "It's Three Elms, near Warwick," she said, her voice surprisingly firm.

"Wonderful." The countess beamed at her. "You will write the letter first thing tomorrow morning, won't you, Richard?"

And so they had passed the point of no return.

Numbly Amy sat, while Lady Rawdon detailed exactly what her husband ought to put in the letter, before the conversation eventually moved to another topic. Admiral Reitz entertained the round with the adventures of his travels in Scotland, how one bellwether or other had taken a fancy to his canary yellow curricle and led the whole sheep herd after said curricle. And the faster the admiral had driven, the faster the sheep trotted until they dashed after the carriage at full gallop.

Amy blinked.

The story was certainly bizarre enough to fit her state of mind. Indeed, she mused inconsequentially, she probably wouldn't have been surprised if the admiral's sheep had suddenly sprouted wings. Or perhaps his horse could have been the one to sprout wings. Like Pegasus.

She frowned.

There was a commotion in the hallway. The next moment the door was flung open, and the butler stumbled into the room, his face paper white. "M-My lord . . ."

He was thrust aside by a young, blond man, exquisitely groomed. Just inside the room, the stranger stopped. "Ahh," he said, and a smile that sent shivers down Amy's spine curled his lips. Heavens, she knew this man! She had seen his face before, she was sure of it—

The men rose. "What—" Lord Rawdon began, but uniformed men were already swarming past the blond stranger, and the light of the candles flickered over the blades of their swords.

As if from a distance, Amy heard the gasps of the people around her, while her heart was hammering against her ribs. *This shouldn't be happening!* she screamed inside. *I secured the house with protection spells! I used my blood!*

But within moments they were surrounded by blinking steel and herded together at one end of the drawing room. Annie started to cry.

"Shh." The dowager countess quickly drew the little girl to her side to muffle the sobs against her dress. Lady Rawdon slung her arms around the two boys.

"What is the meaning of this?" Lord Rawdon thundered.

With a bang, the glass in the windows exploded and flew out into the snow. Wind swept through the drawing room, making the candles flicker madly. The breaths of the people around Amy quickened, became white clouds in the sudden cold, and she could hear the children weep.

Evil, she sensed.

"Ahh, my dear Rawdon." A musical, lilting female voice.

On the arm of another man in uniform, a tall woman entered the room. A dark green dress swirled around her, trimmed with fur on hem and sleeves. Lady Rawdon inhaled sharply. Fox's breath hissed through his nose.

Amy shot a glance at the earl, whose face had frozen into an inscrutable mask. As she watched, a muscle jumped in his cheek.

The woman smiled. "And so we meet again." She turned to the blond man at the door. "Have the servants been rounded up in the servants' quarters?"

He bowed. "Yes, my lady."

"Perfect." Once more she focused her attention on the group of people her men were keeping covered. Yet with a clap of her hands, they stepped back and formed something like a guard of honor.

Her smile deepened. A dark eyebrow arched. "Don't you want to greet me, my lord?"

The earl took a step forward, his face flushed with anger. His mouth opened—

"Do what she says, Richard," Lady Rawdon hissed from behind him. "For heaven's sake, do it!"

Another trilling laugh filled the room, an eerie counterpart to the wind that whistled around the empty window frames. "So, the hussy whom you took as your countess has brains? Well done, Rawdon. Well done."

Lord Rawdon's color heightened, and a vein pulsed across his forehead. "Welcome to Rawdon Park, Lady Margaret," he forced out.

Mockingly, the woman tut-tutted. "Temper, temper, dear Rawdon." She turned her head a little to the side, as if to look at the blond man. "A chair!"

"Immediately, my lady." At a snap of his fingers, an

armchair slithered across the floor and came to stand behind Lady Margaret. Gracefully, she sank down upon it and smiled at the horrified expressions of the people who faced her. It was clear they had never seen such magic.

Amy's eyebrows rose. It would seem she had found the source of the evil that had invaded Rawdon Park. For surely the Stapletons would not attract the attention of more than one dark wizard.

"What do you want?" the earl growled.

"What do I want?" Lady Margaret repeated and looked him up and down. "What could I possibly want?" She let her gaze glide over the Stapletons. "Did I not tell you when you left me that you would regret your rash decision?"

Lord Rawdon snorted. "That was *ten years* ago, Margaret."

Her eyes widened. "Exactly. Exactly ten years. To the day." She raised her hand to her temple. "I never forget anything, Rawdon."

A cold shiver slithered down Amy's spine.

"Gracious!" Fox muttered. "That woman is mad."

His brother took another step forward. "So, you've waited ten years," he sneered. "And for what?"

"Why, revenge, of course. And how much sweeter it will taste after all this time!" She sent him a serene smile. "I will shatter your life, piece by piece. Nobody leaves me, Rawdon." Her expression shifted, became thin and pinched with anger. "*Nobody*. You were mine." The tip of her tongue showed as she moistened her lips. "Mine. Body and soul." She let her gaze travel suggestively over his body, undressed him with her eyes. Abruptly she looked away, at Lady Rawdon. "How do you like it, my lady"—a mocking pause, during which her lips curved—"that I had him before you? That I made him feel things you would never be able to make him feel?"

From the admiral came a smothered sound. Yet Amy didn't dare look around and chance a glance at either the earl or the countess. A quiver ran through Fox's body beside her, making her stomach clench. He would not do anything rash, would he? Surely he saw how dangerous those people were?

"Do you know," Lady Margaret continued, "that I could reduce him to a thing that was barely human? Oh, how he would beg for me to touch him, to release him—"

"You!" Fox exploded. "How dare you—" He made as if to rush forward.

"Sebastian!"

"Fox!"

Lord Rawdon's and Amy's cries mingled and each of them grabbed one of his elbows.

Lady Margaret threw her head back and laughed. "The Fox. The unruly, spirited younger brother." Her gaze sharpened on Amy. "And our cuckoo child."

Immediately Fox shifted so that his body was in front of Amy's. "Leave her alone!" he snarled.

"Priceless!" Lady Margaret chuckled, then turned to the man Amy had come to think of as the woman's pet sorcerer. "Splendid work, truly splendid work."

He smiled thinly and bowed. "My lady's pleasure is mine. Even though there are other advantages to this arrangement." His eyes shifted and came to rest on Amy. "By a splendid stroke of fate I have made an old friend's little brat our cuckoo child. Too bad, is it not, Miss Bourne, that you obviously haven't inherited the talents of your virtuous uncle."

Amy's breath caught. Now she finally knew where she had seen him before: he was Uncle Bourne's friend who had turned bad—and who hadn't seemed to age a day since the miniature was painted.

Her face shining with delight, Lady Margaret clapped. "This is going to be vastly entertaining!" She gave the blond man a nod before she turned back to Lord Rawdon. "Look at your brother: So great is his love that he would die for the lady of his heart—would you not, Mr. Stapleton?"

Amy's blood ran cold. The blond man had started to

march toward them, an unholy amusement glinting in his eyes.

"Fox," she whispered, and tried to pull him back, yet he would not budge an inch.

"Such great love, you would give your life," the blond man taunted as he drew nearer.

"Margaret!" the earl barked. "What is this? What do you want from my brother?"

Amy dug her fingers into Fox's arm. "Fox," she whispered.

Inexorably, the Lady Margaret's minion came toward them. "It must be true love then, mustn't it? True, everlasting love?"

Dimly, Amy was aware of people shifting nervously around her, but she only had eyes for that hateful man whose lips now lifted in a cruel smile. He stopped so close to Fox that they stood almost nose to nose. He cocked his head to the side. "True love?" His gaze caressed Fox's face as if they were lovers.

Amy heard Fox's sharp breath. Then, his voice, clearly, steadily, and with a mocking lilt of his own, "Oh yes."

She bit her lip.

"Then let me tell you a secret, Mr. Stapleton." The blond man leaned closer, so his mouth almost brushed against Fox's ear.

Amy clenched her free hand into a fist. "It was a potion," she blurted.

Both heads—carroty red and blond—snapped around.

Fox frowned. "What—?"

The blond man's eyes narrowed for a short moment, then amusement flickered across his face. "What a bright little cuckoo child we have chosen." He turned to Fox. "Oh yes, Mr. Stapleton, a potion. A love potion—for you and her. And she knew. A cuckoo planted in the midst of your family to bring you all down. Such a wicked little bird, the cuckoo, and you've brought her to Rawdon Park. Aren't you proud of yourself?" Each word was formed with obvious pleasure. "That's what your true love is." Metal glinted in his hand. "A hoax."

Fox drew in a sharp breath, and in the first moment Amy's brain refused to comprehend what had happened. She heard the shocked cries of the people around her, the words the blond man murmured into Fox's ear, "That's what you're dying for: a hoax." Then the man turned and walked back to his mistress, while Fox sagged to the ground, dragging Amy with him, a dagger visibly protruding from his shoulder.

The admiral was at her side in an instant, and the earl, both supporting Fox. He gasped for breath. A dark spot formed on his blue coat.

Lady Margaret laughed.

"Fox," Amy whispered. She clutched at his arm, his head, his shoulder. "No."

He looked up at her, his eyes wide with shock. His lips trembled. "A . . . hoax?"

"Fox," she repeated. She fumbled with the knot in his neck cloth, his waistcoat, the fastening of his shirt. "No. Oh, no no no." He couldn't die. Couldn't . . . if she had her magic back—if only she had her magic back!

"Miss Bourne."

With a sob she clutched at the dagger, pulled, drew it out of his flesh.

"Miss Bourne!"

Fox gasped, spasmed against her lap. More blood bubbled up.

"No," she said. "No no no!" Frantically her hands slid over his skin and got sticky with blood. She found the wound, pressed against it to stem the flow. If only she had her magic back, if only—

Fox stared at her, his eyes almost black. "You . . . knew?"

"Miss Bourne!"

Amy pushed against the barrier in her mind, pushed and pushed until the blood roared in her ears and stars flickered in front of her eyes. Under her fingers she felt Fox's pulse weaken. Desperation sliced through her. "NOOOO!"

And something inside her gave way.

Power rushed through her, the power of the stones, of the earth. Her whole body prickled with it. She pressed her hands against Fox's wound and, staring into his eyes, felt his skin warm. Saw the shock as the flow of blood stopped. His chest lifted with a deep breath.

"Yes." She blinked her tears away. He was safe.

Safe.

"Oh my!" Lady Margaret exclaimed. "Who would have thought how much excitement the chit would provide?"

The buzzing inside Amy's ears stopped. She reached for the bloody dagger where it lay on the ground and slowly stood. Anger burned inside her, such an intense anger as she had never known. It heightened the power that still coursed through her, until it filled her to the brim and crackled along her skin. Dimly she heard the soft *plings* as her hairpins fell to the ground and her hair unraveled.

She turned toward the woman and the uniformed men at the far end of the drawing room, all of them laughing.

"*You,*" Amy breathed.

Lady Margaret chuckled. "Look at the cuckoo child— isn't she delightful?" She gave Amy a cruel smirk. "Quite an impressive demonstration, my dear. But leave it be, child. It will only hurt you more in the end. You cannot compete with his magic." She patted the arm of the sorcerer who stood beside her. "Leave it be."

Power gathered inside Amy, tickled in the tips of her fingers. "*You.*" She took a step forward.

Lady Margaret's laughter stopped. She waved her hand at the men with the swords. "Keep her away."

Two of them raised their weapons. Stepping toward Amy, they crossed their swords in front of her. Unperturbed, she continued to stare at the duo across the room. Another step. Steel pressed against her dress. She took a deep breath, raised her arms and let the magic loose.

The strength of it flung the two men in front of her aside. Her hips gently swaying from side to side, Amy walked forward. She felt the magic rushing alongside her, heard the tinkling of glass as fragments and splinters outside in the snow realigned and were sucked back into the window frames. But Amy never once took her eyes from the two people across the room.

"You. What a nice little plan you hatched out there. A nice little potion that you had us given, then some nice little attacks on the children, first on the heir, then on the spare—but all in vain," she hissed.

Lady's Margaret's sorcerer took a step toward her. "You are but a child. You will not prevail." He raised his hand. "Your uncle wasn't able to withstand my powers, and neither will you."

Amy's lips curved. She turned the dagger in her hand until the point cut into her skin and her blood ran over the blade. "Won't I?" she said mildly. "You will not work your evil at Rawdon any longer." In her hand, the dagger began to glow.

The sorcerer threw his head back and laughed. "You silly child! You cannot harm me, my magic has taken root at Rawdon Park in ways you cannot imagine."

The dagger flew through the air, described a fiery arc. The sorcerer was still laughing when it hit his heart.

Chaos broke loose all around. Somewhere, magic shattered. Lady Margaret screamed at her men to kill Amy. Amy swayed. Magic still pounded through her, rushed into her and was amplified by the powers of the earth; and in the end, it was simply too much. The magic raged out of control. Lady Margaret and her men never stood a chance. It slithered and wound around them, cut through skin and choked the life out of them. It left them lying on the ground with contorted faces and bulging eyes.

Dizziness overwhelmed Amy. Her mind was raw with the powers that were coursing through her; her senses reeled from the events that had unfolded. Black spots danced in front of her eyes. Desperately, she tried to catch her breath. She was aware of people milling about her, somebody touching her shoulder. Distorted words that didn't make any sense. But she had kept them safe. Yes, she had kept the Stapletons safe . . . Amy gasped. If only she could get her air back! The floor rolled and rose to meet her. The last thing she saw before darkness engulfed her was Fox walking out of the room, his shoulders rigid.

Witch, witch, witch, she heard.

And then she knew nothing more.

Chapter Fifteen

Fox sat hunched forward on his bed, his hands buried in his hair. Surely it must all be a dream, a horrible nightmare, and if only he could manage to wake up, all would be as before and he would be head over heels in love with an adorable little bit of a woman . . .

A witch, a sorceress.

He groaned.

No, no, it couldn't be. He had held her in his arms, had lost himself in the sweetness of her body. . . .

All a lie!

And she had known it! Damn it, she had known it all along, had laughed about him most likely, about the poor fool who had danced attendance to her, so besotted he no longer knew left from right and whose emotional outpourings must have amused her to no end.

A love potion? It seemed so fantastic. How could it possibly be real? But how else to explain his infatuation with the brassy, impertinent chit? For now he remembered it all. Their conversations at the ball and at the Worthington musicale. Her lack of style and accomplishment. How could he have forgotten all of that?

And oh, the things he had seen her do today! Not just the killing of those people, which had been bad enough, but broken glass, shattered into a million pieces, repairing itself and being sucked back into the window frames.

Fox shuddered.

It was unnatural. *She* was unnatural. Perhaps she had even put a spell on him as well. For wasn't this what Lady Margaret's man had implied when he had called her a cuckoo child, planted at Rawdon Park? And Fox himself had brought her here and had thus endangered his whole family.

Heavens!

He jumped up and pulled the bell rope hard enough that the thing nearly came off. Impatiently he marched up and down the room until finally the door opened. "Thur?" Hobbes asked.

"Pack my things. I'll spend the night at the Crown in Downham Market, and from there we will return to London tomorrow."

Hobbes gaped at him. "Thur?"

"My *things.*" Fox threw up his arms. "Heavens, that can't be so difficult, can it?"

"Now, thur?"

Fox gritted his teeth. "Yes, indeed." The family was fine, none was hurt, and Richard was currently dealing with the magistrate, who had been called to Rawdon Park. There was nothing more for Fox to do here.

"And M-mith Bourne?"

"To hell with Miss Bourne!" Fox roared, loud enough to make Hobbes jump. Who cared due to which twisted logic she had eventually turned on those of her like? Sorceress, witch—she had been in this all along, had practiced her wiles on him.

Again, he shuddered. To imagine he had even bedded the wench! It was vile, unnatural! He would go mad if he stayed here an hour longer.

So: "My things," he repeated. *"Now!"*

"Ath you wish, thur." After a last dubious look, followed by a shake of his head, Hobbes disappeared into the dressing room.

Fox heaved a sigh of relief. Yes, this was for the best: He would leave for Downham Market straight away and take the coach to Cambridge tomorrow morning, and from there return to London. Once home, he would settle back into his old life, and in no time at all, the past few weeks would indeed seem like a dream to him. Something that had never happened, had never been real.

Without his volition, his hand crept to his shoulder and rubbed at the lingering soreness. As he became aware of what he was doing, Fox shuddered. As quickly as if he had burned himself, he let his arm fall to his side. In a few weeks' time this would all be but a bad dream. Only a dream.

Having his bones rattled in a stagecoach for hours on end did nothing to improve Fox's temper. He left it to Hobbes to air his rooms at Albany and went out to his club in order to get drunk and perhaps lose some money at the gambling tables. Only nothing came of the gambling, because he met Drew and Cy and was obliged to tell them the whole sorry story. At least, though, he could get well and truly sloshed while telling it so their horrified faces swam nicely out of focus. Afterwards, the Right Honorable Lord Stafford took his elbow and dragged him away from the joys and consolation of port and brandy. He marched Fox up cold St. James's Street and back to Albany—deuced fellow! But fortunately Fox fell half asleep just as they crossed Piccadilly, so he completely missed entering Albany anyway.

He was rudely shaken awake the next day. "What do you think you are doing?" his brother roared into his ear—loud enough to make Fox fall out of his bed.

"For Christ's sake! Are you mad?" Rubbing his behind, upon which he'd landed, Fox picked himself up. A glance at his brother's face made him grimace. Richard's whole head had taken on a mottled color, and a dark vein pulsed across his forehead.

"Mad? If anybody is mad, it is you, Sebastian! What were you thinking, running away like that?"

Fox staggered to the door and peered into the hallway. "Hobbes!" he hollered. "Bring me some coffee, will you?"

"Thur?" The old man shuffled into sight and looked nervously from Fox to Richard and back.

"Coffee."

"Yeth, thur."

With the flat of his hand, Richard banged the door shut. "Listen to me," he growled. "You will pack your things and go back to Rawdon Park with me."

With a sigh, Fox turned and wandered over to the washstand. "No, I will do no such thing," he said calmly, knowing full well that his calmness would enrage Richard even further. He pulled his rumpled, sweaty shirt over his head—Lawk! he smelled like a pig—and let it drop onto the floor, before he began to wash himself with the icy-cold water, which Hobbes must have prepared for him the evening before. From the corner of his eye, he shot a glance at his brother. Richard looked ready to throttle him.

Fox raised an eyebrow. *My, my*, he thought with malicious glee. The unflappable, dignified Lord Rawdon was throwing a temper tantrum.

Glaring at him, Richard put his hands on his hips. "Does it not interest you at all that Miss Bourne has taken ill and—"

"No." Fox splashed some water into his face. "Not at all." Yet this time, it was more difficult to force his voice to remain calm. How he had loved her! His heart clenched. What a bloody fool he had been—and still was, to bemoan the loss.

"You've got an obligation to her!"

"No." Fox reached for the towel and rubbed his face dry. Straightening, he turned to Richard. "Did you not hear what was said in your drawing room the last time we were all assembled there?" He bared his teeth. "It was all a lie. A *lie*." He managed to keep the bitterness out of his voice, if not his soul.

His brother took a deep breath. "You're still engaged to marry her."

For a moment, all was silent in the room. Silent enough for Fox to hear somebody clumping down the stairs and the crunch of carriage wheels at a distance in the streets. Then he threw back his head and laughed.

"You, Lord Rawdon, must be mad!" Abruptly he sobered. "Marry a sorceress? Who lied to me for goodness knows how long? Who probably was in this whole plot from the very beginning?" he hissed. "I don't think so. Heavens, I don't even *like* the chit!" Lawk, how much her lilting, mocking voice had grated on his nerves, and how she must have laughed at him these past weeks!

Richard's eyes nearly bulged out of the sockets. "How can you be such a cold-blooded bastard?" he roared. "How could she have been in any plot? She saved your bloody life!"

"Is that so?" Fox's voice was arctic.

"Yes, it bloody well is!"

Fox turned his back to him and continued his morning ablutions. "Tut-tut, big brother, the language you're using." He could hear Richard taking a few deep breaths.

"Look," the earl said, his voice rigidly controlled, "if you don't care for the girl . . ." Another deep breath.

Fox clenched his jaw. To hear Richard talk, one would have thought she was a fragile little flower! What rubbish!

There was a knock on the door. Since his brother wasn't making any move to open it, Fox strode forward while Richard continued, "But you cannot possibly break the engagement without bringing dishonor to our family name."

Fox snorted. "You must be out of your mind!" he snarled

over his shoulder. "To marry a *witch?* You have seen the things she is capable of! How can you be so matter of fact about this?" He flung the door open.

"Your c-coffee, thur." The tray Hobbes held out swayed gently back and forth.

"I'm not matter of fact about this!" the earl shouted, for once in his life forgetting that it didn't do to speak rashly in front of the servants. "But she saved your life!"

"So?" Fox shrugged with exaggerated nonchalance. "Perhaps she only didn't want to lose the foolish fellow who had become her sex poppet." He stepped back to let the old butler pass. "Thank you, Hobbes. Put it on the nightstand. And afterwards you can show my brother out."

But Richard had already brushed past and, with enough force to make the windows rattle, banged the front door shut behind him.

In the following days Fox spent more and more time at his club, and once or twice even at one of the more disreputable gaming hells of London. He drank a lot, lost an indecent amount of money, won some of it back . . . and all of the time felt his heart bleed dry.

It had all been a lie. Each look, each touch, each word they had spoken—all deuced lies. The most complete bliss he had felt in all his life: a bloody delusion.

One evening after a week or more—Fox had long lost track of the passing days—Drew cornered him in the club and dragged him home to Albany, where he poured impossible amounts of coffee down Fox's throat while Hobbes clucked around them like a worried mother hen.

"Really, Foxy," Drew said in reproachful tones, "it can't go on like this."

"Like what?" Irritated, Fox waved Hobbes aside when the butler would have poured him some more coffee. "Heavens, will you both stop it! Now I need to have a piss." He marched into the bedroom to relieve himself in the water closet in the dressing room. Slamming the door, he scowled at the stylish water closet as he already felt the effects of the coffee kicking in. The whisky he had drunk this evening had cost a small fortune—money down the drain. How extraordinarily wonderful.

The door was thrust open and Drew strode in. "Really, Foxy, has nobody ever told you that running away is hardly constructive for discussions?"

Hobbes's wizened face appeared behind the other. The butler nodded earnestly.

Fox ground his teeth, and indicated the used water-closet. "Does *that* look as if I fobbed you off?" he growled.

His friend continued as if he hadn't spoken: "Rawdon told us that—"

"I don't care one fig what my brother told you." Fox decided it would be better to button himself up again, since Drew seemed hell-bent on having this little conversation right now no matter what.

For the moment, he gave Fox his best sad little puppy-dog face. "Oh, Foxy, you don't really mean that!" His expression brightened. "Is it true that Miss Bourne saved your life with some . . . uh . . . magical healing powers? How very curious!"

"Fantastic," he grunted. The mere mentioning of her name was like a dart to his heart. "Are you done?" It was just his bad luck to have a friend who was suffering from childish enthusiams and who thus no doubt found the notion of devilish magic vastly intriguing.

A line appeared between the other's brows. "Won't you at least inquire about her health? Rawdon said—"

"*Andrew,*" Fox warned.

"—that she is in ill health."

"How ill can she be?" He snorted. "She is a sorceress! A witch! She will be chirping merry by now." Fox rubbed his temple. He really didn't want to talk about this. About her.

Especially not about her.

All lies and flummery.

And the deuced thing was, the pain became less bearable the more time passed. If this should continue he would soon howl at the moon over a broken heart like a dog. Broken heart? Bosh!

He roused himself. "Chirping merry, indeed. As will I be soon." Chirping merry, oh yes, he knew what it would take to achieve such. "Bring me my hat and my coat, Hobbes, will you?"

Drew's expression turned weary. "Whatever are you going to do?"

"What do you think?" Chin up, Fox strolled into the study to retrieve his gloves and take his coat and hat from Hobbes. "It's still early enough to catch a nice little bird at Madame Suzette's."

Hobbes's eyes widened. "B-but, thur!" The butler sounded genuinely shocked.

Fox raised a brow. "Perhaps that sultry doxy of the Italian hue, eh, Drew?" Oh yes, all lush curves, soft flesh . . .

. . . golden hair and pansy blue eyes . . .

He groaned. No no no! Why could he not stop thinking of her? He must be still under that horrid spell! But it was time to exorcize her, once and for all.

Drew gripped his arm. "Shouldn't you take your responsibility to Miss Bourne more seriously? After all, you're engaged to marry her!"

"The hell I am." With a brusque movement, Fox freed his arm. "I tell you something, Drew: If you're so worried about her, why don't you marry the chit yourself?"

Somewhere at the back of his mind, Fox knew full well that he was behaving abominably. But he didn't care. All he knew was that he had to get away from their reproachful looks, escape to a place where nobody knew her name and couldn't torment him with it. He would go insane if he stayed—mad with grief over something that had been only a stack of lies.

What an utter ninny he was!

"And for now—adieu. You can see yourself out, Drew, can't you?" And Fox whirled and left his rooms, to disappear into the cold London night.

Chapter Sixteen

The heavy knocks cracked his skull open, surely they did. Groaning and swearing, Fox opened one eye. Like lightning, sunlight splintered his retinas. A flood of oaths streamed over his lips. A flood of coarseness, of vileness, the worst curses he could think of.

His muscles sore, he rolled off the armchair where he had apparently spent the night, and tripped to the front door. The knocks had not ceased; if anything, they had increased in volume.

"What the devil?" He jerked the door open.

"Good morning." His friend Cyril, disgustingly neat and stylish, regarded him with faint interest.

Fox rubbed his hands over his face. "Whaddya want?"

Cyril raised an eyebrow. "Where's Hobbes?"

"He left," Fox growled. Eleven years the old man had been in his employ, and now he had left because of Fox's supposed cold-hearted desertion of a lovely young woman. Truly, the whole world had turned into a madhouse! "Look, what do you want here, Cy?"

"Talk." The other pushed past him into the apartment. "What else? God, what has happened to this place? Has somebody broken in and trashed it?"

Fox slammed the door shut—and immediately wished he hadn't. Grimacing, he rubbed his aching head. "Talk?" He followed his friend into the study. "What kind of nonsense is this? Drew has already been here to 'talk.' Days ago. The same day my bloody butler left, actually. What are you doing?"

"Letting in some fresh air." Cyril turned away from the window he had flung wide open. "This place reeks like the worst kind of distillery. And no wonder..." With distaste he surveyed the array of empty bottles that littered the room. "God, Fox, what have you been doing to yourself?"

Fox leaned against the doorframe and shrugged. If only it weren't so deucedly bright in the room. "What all wealthy young bucks do around town: drinking, whoring, and gaming. What else?" He gave another shrug and tried to stick to a nonchalant pose, even though a brownie with a large drum seemed to have taken residence inside his skull. "Close the shutters, will you?"

His friend stared at him. "No, actually, I won't."

"Great! Wonderful! Do whatever you please!" Fox threw up his hands, then trudged into the room and slumped down on the armchair he had abandoned earlier.

"Drinking, whoring, and gaming?" Cy echoed. "When only a few weeks ago you swore never-ending love to—"

No, he simply couldn't let his friend say the name. "It was a lie!" Terrible pain sliced Fox's chest, cut his heart to ribbons. Heavens, why did Cyril have to bring this up, when Fox tried so hard to forget? He shuddered. "All a blasted lie!"

Unperturbed by this outburst, Cy looked at him with perfect calmness. "Was it?" he asked.

This was certainly more than any man should tolerate. "Yes! Goddamn it, yes, it was a lie!" Fox roared. His fingers clenched into fists, and he had to suppress the terrible urge to bash them into Cyril's face. "And she knew it. She knew it all along; otherwise how could she have told me before—"

All at once the rage ebbed away and left only the ashes of despair behind. Like a rag doll, Fox sank forward and, with a groan, buried his face in his hands. His fingers dug into flesh and bone, the skin surprisingly intact despite the raw pain that filled him. "You want to hear a funny thing? Hilarious, really," he said, his voice muffled against his palms so it sounded like a stranger's even to his own ears. "Despite everything, she is still in my blood and I can't get her out. Not that I haven't tried. Oh, how I've tried!" He pressed the ridges of his palms into his eye sockets. "To drown her in alcohol, forget her over the thrill of the card table or in the bed of another woman. And all I succeeded in doing"—he gave a harsh laugh—"was to make myself the laughingstock of all the larks in London." Wearily, he looked up. He felt battered, even though he hadn't taken a physical beating. "The Fox has lost his edge."

Cyril's gaze was still perfectly calm. He stood, seemingly relaxed, his arms crossed in front of his chest. "And so we talk."

Fox shook his head. How tired he felt! "What is there to talk about?"

"Oh, there's plenty to talk about. For example, why you while away your time here in London instead of being at the side of—"

"She is a witch," Fox said sharply. No, he really wouldn't be able to bear hearing her name.

"You feel sorry for yourself." And still Cy's voice remained calm, hatefully calm.

"It was all a lie," Fox forced out between gritted teeth. Blast it! Why didn't they understand? Hadn't they heard a word of what he had told them after his return? He had been under the influence of a bloody love potion—still was, as far as he could tell—and she had known it. She had known it and had said nothing. Not one word. And worse: the things he had seen her do. It was unnatural—like his obsession with her. All unnatural.

"You are engaged to marry her," Cyril pointed out in that same hatefully composed tone.

"The hell I am! She is a goddamned witch!" Blood throbbed in Fox's temple.

"She is still your fiancée."

It was too much. Fox jumped up like an irate bull with the matador's spear in his side. "Blast it all, Cyril! Haven't you heard a word of what I said? She is a bloody witch! You don't know what she is capable of! She was in this plot to destroy my family from the very beginning!"

His friend just arched his brow. "Was she? Perhaps *that* was a lie. Have you thought about that?"

Mute, Fox shook his head. For even if what Cyril suggested should be the case, she had still lied to him, had kept him caught up in an illusion so he could make an utter fool of himself.

"I heard she saved your life," his friend continued relentlessly. "At least that's what your brother claimed when he came to London after you. Are you saying he didn't tell the truth?"

Fox clenched his jaw so hard his teeth hurt. "He did," he growled. "But that doesn't change anything! She is—"

"Still your fiancée, the woman you claimed to love."

"It wasn't real!" Fox tore at his hair. "Don't you understand? None of it was real! It was all that bloody love potion, all sorcery!" he spat.

"And she is dying," Cy added calmly. "Is that real enough for you?"

Fox stared at him. He opened his mouth, yet no sound emerged. Only his breath whistled softly in and out of his lungs.

Cyril regarded him with something like compassion. "You didn't know that, did you?"

"No," Fox said. All at once he felt lightheaded. The blood buzzed in his ears like a swarm of angry bees.

"It's all over town: the beautiful Miss Amelia Bourne wasting away from an unknown ailment. The mourning cards have already been written, or so I've heard."

Fox swayed.

The beautiful Miss Amelia Bourne wasting away from an unknown ailment . . .

The beautiful Miss Amelia Bourne wasting away . . .

The beautiful Miss Amelia Bourne . . .

Amy.

His Amy.

Small, plump Amy with the impish smile and the pansy blue eyes. Eyes that turned to midnight blue when she came apart in his arms, when they moved skin to skin, when her smallness became so great it encompassed him, enveloped him, let him drown in her arms, in her sighs, her scent, the words of love she whispered into his ear.

His Amy.

Dying.

"See?" Cyril said softly. "*That's* what we needed to talk about."

He rode like a man possessed. He ate up mile after mile, changed horses, and let the pounding of hooves fill out his whole being. Mud flew up to cover his boots and trousers and, merciless, the wind bit into his exposed skin. Yet he neither cared nor noticed. For him, the world had narrowed to the strip of muddy brown ahead of him, to the movements of strong equine muscles beneath him, and to the fear, the all-encompassing fear that he might be too late.

> *Oh what can ail thee, wretched wight,*
> *Alone and palely loitering?*

His eyes burned, yet if he shed tears the wind whipped them away.

> *I met a lady in the meads,*
> *Full beautiful—a faery's child.*
> *Her hair was long, her foot was light,*
> *And her eyes were . . .*

Pansy blue, midnight blue, the color of the quiet ocean, the color of the sky on a sunny summer day.

Fox could no longer deny what was in his heart and what he had taken such pains to bury underneath his bitterness and anger. What did it matter now whether his feelings for her had been induced by a love potion or not? The truth was, he could not imagine a world without Amy, without her sweet smile and teasing voice.

He rode like a man haunted by the seven hounds of hell, like a man racing against death.

Wintry twilight fell all too soon and turned the sunny brilliance of snow to ashes, the whistle of the wind to Herne's hounds yapping at his heels. They chased him across the land where canals bisected snow-dusted meadows and fields, chased him past ruins of once-proud castles and over old battlefields, until finally he came to the valley filled with bare elm trees. In their midst huddled a sturdy manor, the windows blazing golden in the gray wintry afternoon.

The land of elm trees where men worked in the belly of the earth, and where in secluded valleys magic was wrought. But that no longer frightened him. The only thing he dreaded now was the bony step of the Grim Reaper, out to steal his heart's delight.

And this is why I sojourn here,
Alone and palely loitering . . .

His heart thudded once, twice, as he stared at the cozy house before him: Three Elms, where Amy had been brought, according to Cyril. He took a deep breath, then urged his horse on, up the drive to the front steps of the house. When he slid out of the saddle, his knees buckled with exhaustion, but gripping the saddle and gritting his teeth, he forced himself upright. Another deep breath, then he clumped up the stairs to the entrance door. He reached for the heavy, lion-headed knocker and let it fall back against the dark wooden door.

A few moments later it was opened by a pinch-faced butler,

and a blast of warm air hit Fox. "Good afternoon"—the barest of hesitations as he looked Fox, with his muddy clothes and wind-chafed face, up and down—"sir."

Fox blinked. The warm air made him dizzy, and he had to lean his hand against the doorframe to prevent himself from falling flat on his face at the man's feet. He ran his tongue across his cracked lips. "I am . . ." He blinked again.

The man eyed him quizzically. "I am afraid the family is not receiving at this time, sir," he said politely.

Fox shook his head. "Miss Bourne . . . Amy," he croaked. "I need to see her."

The man's expression closed up. "This, sir, is impossible. Perhaps you ought better retire to the inn in the village below."

He made as if to close the door, but with a last burst of strength, Fox's hand shot out to keep it open. "I am . . ." His voice cracked. He shook his head, tried again. "Stapleton. Sebastian . . . Stapleton. Her . . . betrothed."

The other's lips compressed. For a moment he regarded Fox silently, then seemed to come to a decision. "In that case, sir," he said in frigid tones, "you had better come in." He opened the door wider and stepped aside to let Fox pass. "I will tell one of the footmen to make sure that your horse is looked after. Fred! Your coat and hat, sir?" He took both, as well as Fox's grimy gloves, then indicated one of the chairs standing in the entrance hall. "If you wish to wait there . . ."

Not in some salon or drawing room. But Fox didn't care, didn't care at all. If only they let him see Amy. . . .

He sank down onto one of the indicated chairs, while the butler quietly conversed with a liveried young man for a few moments. The latter then went outside and the former upstairs. Fox rubbed an unsteady hand across his cheek. After the cold and wind had numbed him, his skin now burned as if devoured by the flames of hell. And, sweet heavens, surely he would be in hell if he were too late.

He swallowed.

Suddenly there was a loud bang somewhere in the house, the sound of raised voices; then, on the stairs, hurried footsteps. Somebody came hurtling down the steps. And farther up: "Flann! Stop it!"

More footsteps, the high-pitched voice of a young boy, "No! I will get that bastard, that—"

"*Flann!*"

Inexorably the sound of footsteps came nearer, and then a young boy hurled himself from the stairs into the entrance hall. With curly, black hair, eyes flashing, and his face dark with fury, he came to a skittering halt in front of Fox. "You!" His small chest heaved, his eyes narrowed.

"*Flann!*"

The boy took a step toward Fox. "You, it's *you*! How dare you show your face here? I'll—" He raised his hand, murmured something Fox didn't catch, and suddenly, there was a ball of blue light growing in the boy's palm.

"*Flann!*"

An unholy light glowed in the boy's eyes, Fox saw with detached interest. Were they blue like that glowing sphere?

Fox blinked.

"No! Flann, no!" A dark-haired young man raced across the entrance hall and, with a curse, tackled the boy. The ball of light dissolved into lightning, which shot toward the ceiling and left a dark, scorched spot in the gleaming wood.

Stupefied, Fox could only sit and gape at the blackened spot. Dimly, he was aware that the young man shook Flann.

"Are you out of your mind?"

"It's him!" the boy yelled hysterically. "He's got no right to be here!"

"*Enough!*" a new voice bellowed. The man who stepped down the last few stairs was a good few inches shorter than Fox, but with his weather-beaten face and the gray, short-cropped hair, he looked as if he could easily have commanded whole regiments. He strode across the hall, followed by the now anxious-looking butler and a horde of more black-haired boys and young men.

"Devlin," he continued more quietly, "bring Flann to his room and see that he stays there."

"But—" Flann started to protest.

"No. I don't want to hear it."

"He's got no right, he—"

"This is quite enough, Flann. Devlin, bring your brother upstairs." While young Flann was dragged away, the older man turned his attention to Fox. "Bourne. You're Stapleton?" His voice was sharp.

Belatedly, Fox remembered he should maybe stand, and stumbled to his feet. "I'm here to see Amy."

At that, the younger boys started to mutter—until their father raised his hand. Abruptly, they fell silent.

"Please," Fox said. "I didn't know . . ." Another bout of dizziness assaulted him. What if they didn't let him see her? Desperately, he repeated, "I'm here to see Amy."

Her uncle only stared at him. With disgust, Fox thought.

"Please." He would beg, he would even go down on his knees if necessary. If only they let—

"It might help," one of the young men offered.

After another while, Bourne finally nodded his head. "Very well," he said. "Surely nothing else has helped so far."

Such immense relief flooded Fox that he felt lightheaded with it. Yet in the next moment, the meaning of the man's words sunk fully in. *Nothing else has helped so far.*

His voice hoarse, Fox asked, "Does that mean . . . ?"

"Come and see for yourself." Bourne turned back to the stairs. Fox followed him. The man's various sons followed Fox. To wait for a chance to throw another ball of lightning at him?

Nonetheless, Fox stumbled on.

Up the stairs. Down a hallway. Beyond a door. Two women were there. They looked up when the door was opened, but Fox took no notice of them. He only had eyes for the motionless figure which lay in the half-tester bed. So still. He lurched forwards.

"Amy?" he whispered.

Her skin was porcelain white and so translucent that he could see the fine web of blue veins beneath. The blood roared in his ears. Almost imperceptibly, her chest lifted with shallow breaths. Not dead, no, not dead yet, but . . . He reached for her hand. Cold and lifeless, it lay in his.

"Amy?"

There was no answer.

"She can no longer hear you," said a woman he took to be her aunt.

Once again, Fox's knees buckled; he didn't have any strength left to keep himself upright. He sank down beside her bed, lowered his forehead onto the white linen, and cried.

Chapter Seventeen

It was a long time until he composed himself. When he had cried all the tears he had and Amy's hand still remained cold and lifeless in his, her uncle led him to the study and pressed a glass of brandy into his hand. "Drink," he said roughly.

Fox wiped the sleeve of his frock coat across his face. Shortly it crossed his mind that he must look a fright with his dirty clothes and his now no-doubt-blotchy face, but just as quickly, the thought was swept away by the memory of Amy, his Amy, lying on that bed. Dying.

He downed the brandy.

"Is there nothing that can be done?" he asked hoarsely.

The other spread his hands in a helpless gesture. "Nothing. If we knew what was wrong with her, perhaps. But we don't. At first we thought she was simply drained of energy. It would have been logical: after all, she not only had to thrust through the spell I put on her—and it was a powerful one . . ." He grimaced, as if now feeling sorry about how powerful he had made his spell. A moment later he shook his head and continued, "No, she also had to break that other fellow's guard. But if she had simply drained her energy, she would have either died straight away or would have improved by now. Instead . . ." He had to clear his throat. "The opposite is the case: her condition has only worsened." Mr. Bourne gave Fox a sad smile. "If I'm not mistaken, the housekeeper has had a room prepared and a change of clothes brought for you. So, why don't you take advantage of those. Afterwards you can sit with Amy, if you like."

Sit with her. Only sit with her, because nothing could be done. *Nothing.* Once more Fox felt his eyes burn, and all he could manage was a nod.

A few minutes later he found himself in a cozy guest-room, where two jugs of warm water and somebody else's clothes were awaiting him. Numbly, he went through the motions of undressing and sponging himself down. He had just put on the fresh trousers and shirt when there was a knock on the door.

His heart clenched. Amy? Had she taken a turn to the worse? Had she—?

But no, no! His heart wouldn't hear such tidings.

Quickly, he was across the room and pulled the door open. Two of Amy's cousins stared back at him. Dimly he recognized one of them as Devlin, the young man who had saved him from the blue ball of lightning earlier on.

"We've come to talk," Devlin said. Both young men must have been in their twenties, a few years younger than Fox himself.

"Now?"

"Yes." They brushed past him.

Warily, he closed the door. "What is it, then?"

They exchanged a look. "The matter is this," Devlin Bourne began. "We've been thinking, Coll and I." He glanced at his brother, who promptly took over.

"Lord Rawdon told father about the weeks prior to that attack on all of you. How Amy suddenly seemed to be more subdued and no longer went for walks in the gardens with you."

Both young men looked at Fox expectantly. He slowly nodded: Yes, he well remembered the misery and confusion of these weeks. In the end he had put her behavior down to attempting to fight against the passion raging between them. And once he'd obtained that sponge, all had seemed well—hadn't it?

"The earl also told father about that strange incident on the lake," Colin Bourne continued. "About the boy breaking through thick ice and the strange creature that was found on the shore a few days later."

"We must assume this was another magical attack," his brother cut in. "So even though our father wouldn't want to hear of this, we think if Amy knew something was wrong and if she was desperate enough to keep your family safe . . . well . . ."

The brothers exchanged another look, while Devlin's last sentence echoed ominously in Fox's head. *Desperate enough to keep your family safe* . . . His blood ran cold. How horribly he had misjudged her. He felt as if he were about to be sick. He had horribly, horribly misjudged her.

Devlin swallowed hard, then turned to Fox and blurted out: "We think she might have used blood magic."

"Blood magic." Fox blinked.

"Yes," they said in unison, and with equal expressions of distaste.

Fox stared at them. Had they been talking Chinese, he could not have been more astounded. Or perplexed. "So . . ." He frowned. "Why don't you tell your father?

"Good Lord, no!" Colin Bourne exclaimed. "He would never accept that Amy knew anything of such matters. It's not something that a gently bred young lady would do—or even know about!"

Devlin nodded. "It's like her walking down St. James's Street—in her *underwear*."

Fox managed a weak "Oh." In his experience, gently bred young ladies normally didn't know about either magic or *blood* magic, whatever that was supposed to be.

Colin rubbed his neck. "But Amy always loved rummaging around in the library and reading these old tomes. Goodness knows what she found there! Blood magic is mostly used for"—he hesitated a moment—"*darker* purposes. It drains a person, so a knowledgeable magician would be careful not to use his own blood."

"Oh," Fox said again. His knees felt decidedly weak. It all sounded so fantastical. Absurd. Surely not something that might happen here in England.

Devlin cleared his throat. "We think Amy might have used her own blood for a protection spell."

"Her own . . ." Fox had to sit down. Heavens, what had she done? Suddenly a memory sprang up in his mind, brilliantly clear. The day after Pip had almost drowned in the lake—by magic, according to the two young Bournes.

"*I was wondering,*" Amy had said. They had been in the drawing room, and she had been standing at one of the windows that looked out over the lake.

He had gone to her, slipped his arm around her waist. "*Yes?*"

"*Are there any old monuments to be found in the vicinity?*" She had looked up at him, her eyes very blue. "*You know, stone circles and such?*"

Fox gasped. He had thought it an idle question at the time, but now . . . Wasn't it said that the Celtic druids had performed their pagan rituals in these circles and henges?

He licked his lips, cleared his throat. "She asked me . . ." Cleared his throat again. "Asked me whether I knew of a stone circle in the vicinity."

"Stone circle?" both of them echoed—and turned an identical shade of sickly gray.

"Dear heavens!" Colin Bourne sank down on a chair and, elbows leaning on his knees, rubbed his hands across his face.

Devlin stared down at his brother's bent head. "Do you think she really did . . ." His voice trailed away. If possible, he lost even more color.

"Of course she did!" Colin snapped, lifting his head. "It all makes a horrible kind of sense now, doesn't it?"

His brother's breath escaped in a sharp hiss.

Uncomprehendingly, Fox looked from one to the other.

Apprehension made the fine hair at his neck tingle. "What does?"

Yet they didn't pay him any attention.

"She joined with the land." Devlin swayed on his feet.

"Joined with the land?" Fox echoed. What the devil were they talking about? This all sounded as if taken straight out of a shilling romance where brave knights fought against dragons, ogres and whatever other kinds of monsters they could find.

"Of course she did," the other young Bourne said urgently. "If she then used her blood for a protection spell—"

"It would make for the most powerful protections of all," Devlin finished. A moment later, though, he shook his head. "It doesn't make sense, Coll. Why then could that other fellow invade Rawdon Park? Capture them all? Why hasn't she *recovered* by now?"

Brooding, they gazed into space.

Fox's patience snapped. "What? What is it? And what do you mean, 'she joined with the land'? How do you join with the land? *What did she do?*"

And then, finally, they told him the most fantastic tale. How a person could bind himself to the land; how the kings in ancient times had done it in order to cement their power, and how they could just as well have dropped dead during the ceremony itself. Amy obviously hadn't dropped dead, but apparently it had backfired on her. And on top of it, the whole magic thing hadn't even worked properly.

Fox groaned. "Do you think she was delusional?"

"Delusional?" Colin Bourne raised a brow.

Fox swallowed. It was a terrible thought, really. Terrible enough to make his voice hoarse. "That she went and did such a thing, even though she must have known of the danger." He shook his head. "It must have been that wretched love potion," he muttered and shuddered.

The two young men stared at him as if he were the one who was delusional. "What has the love potion to do with it?" Devlin asked.

"What? What? *Everything*!" Prowling up and down the room, Fox ran his hands through his hair. "If she hadn't been under the influence of that dastardly potion, surely she would never have risked her life in such a manner!"

"Oh," Colin said in the strangest tone. "That's it, then."

"Yes, *yes*!" Fox's hands tightened into fists. He gritted his teeth. "I'm going to kill—"

Unexpectedly, Colin shook his head. "She must have already known about the potion then."

"So?"

"When found out, these things lose most of their power." He gave Fox a sad little smile. "So, when my cousin risked her life for your family, she acted not under the influence of a love potion."

Dumbfounded, Fox ogled them. But that would mean . . .

"Perhaps that other chap was simply too powerful for her," Devlin suggested. "After all, he had already done that thing with the lake, given you the potion—"

Fox frowned. "Actually—no." He forced his mind back to the issue at hand.

"No?"

"I'd never seen him before."

"Never?"

Fox shook his head. "I'm sure I would have remembered had he given me something to drink."

"But then, how—"

"That day . . . when Lady Margaret and those men came to Rawdon Park . . ." Fox gnawed on his lip, tried to remember. *Think, Foxy, think.* "Amy said . . ."

He closed his eyes and pictured the scene: his own shock after he felt the wound in his shoulder close, the edges of flesh merging . . . Amy walking away from him, her hair loose . . . Why was her hair loose? It moved as if in the wind—oh yes, and then he had felt it, too, the gust of air that swept through the drawing room. His skin tingled with it. Or perhaps with the sight of the pieces of glass lying scattered outside the empty window frames, trembling and then flying up—white clouds of smashed glass—eventually forming perfect panes once more—and Amy said—

"'What a nice little plan you hatched out there. A nice little potion that you had us given, then some nice little attacks on the children, first on the heir, then on the spare—'"

"Both children broke through the ice?" Colin Bourne cut in, leaning forward.

Fox opened his eyes. "No, only Philip, the younger one."

"Have there been any other incidents?" the other pressed.

"No, no, not at all. Well, Richard fell down the stairs a few weeks before, but—"

Colin Bourne jumped up. "He fell down the stairs?"

With a wave of his hand, Fox brushed it aside. "Don't all little boys at one time or another? Now look here, about this potion, she said he had it given to us. It wasn't him, though."

Devlin glanced from Fox to his brother and back again. "So who was it?"

Colin opened his mouth, then shut it again. "Hmm . . ." He cocked his head to the side. "When did you, you know, fall in love with Amy?"

"Well, I suppose . . . it must have been . . ." Fox pursed his lips. "The Worthington musicale. Yes, I believe that must have been it. I remember now: Drew asked me to go and to keep Amy company. I wasn't keen on the thought, but after the musicale . . ." He shrugged. "I was in love."

"Then you must have drunk something there." Both brothers looked at him expectantly.

"Well . . . just punch. It tasted a little bit funny, if I remember correctly, but what would you expect at a Worthington musicale?" Again he shrugged. "They couldn't have put it into the punch, could they? Else all of the guests would have been affected. Besides, Amy's guardian himself gave us the glasses."

"Mr. Bentham?"

"Indeed. His daughter accompanied Amy to Rawdon Park. Now, come to think of it, they weren't fast friends, which made it a bit odd. And Amy herself asked my brother to send Miss Bentham home after a week or two. Actually—"

"It was right after your nephew had fallen down the stairs." Colin Bourne finished the sentence for him.

"Bentham, father's *friend*?" Devlin swore.

His brother nodded. "And there was more than one attack. These things never happen in twos, but in threes, so there must be one trap left. Which might just be the thing that is slowly killing Amy right now."

The three men stared at one another. Anger flashed in their eyes, darkened their faces. Their hands clenched into fists.

"Bentham!" Fox spat. "I'll ride to London and wring his traitorous neck!"

An unpleasant smile played around Devlin's lips. "Oh yes, we will all ride to London tomorrow and pay this smart chap a little visit."

In the end it was Amy's uncle who rode to London with Fox, for his sons had told him about their worries after all. Grimly he had listened to them; then he had questioned Fox about what exactly Amy had said and done. Finally, he strode into Amy's room to examine her once more. "Hell and damnation," he swore when he returned.

His wife followed on his heels, her expression murderous. "Your friend Bentham, you said? The same Bentham to whom *you* sent our niece? The same Bentham who was supposed to introduce her into society?"

"Mary." He raised his arms. "I—"

"Don't you 'Mary' me! You sent her into a family who were unscrupulous enough to embroil her in some dastardly intrigue!"

"I have known Bentham since our days at university. He always seemed an honorable man."

"An honorable man!" She snorted. "That's what they said about Brutus, too."

Bourne sighed and ran a weary hand through his hair. "I know. Believe me, I know. And I deeply regret—" He took a deep breath. "We will see to Bentham. And we will get the truth out of his daughter. As to Amy . . ." He looked over his wife's shoulder at the door to her room, and his expression turned bleak.

Fox's heart thudded once, twice. "Will you be able to save her?" he pressed, his voice hoarse. "Now that you know?" God, if only he had come earlier. If only he hadn't let his damnable pride dictate his actions.

If only . . .

If only I had loved her more.

Fox squeezed his eyes tightly shut. He felt like crying again. Howling. A shudder ran through his body. He should have known she would never be capable of the devilry and betrayal of which he had accused her. He should have listened to what his heart had been telling him.

"We will need to bring her to Rawdon Park, won't we?" Colin Bourne said.

Fox's eyes shot open. "Rawdon Park?" he gasped. "Surely you jest! The journey could kill her!"

Arms akimbo, Mrs. Bourne answered briskly, "Then we have to make sure that it doesn't." The next moment, though, her cool facade cracked and her expression registered terrible worry and fear. "If we don't take her, she will die anyway. But if she joined with the land, the land itself might heal her. We have to hope." She swallowed. Tears welled in her eyes. "And pray," she added on a whisper.

Thus, a little time later, Bourne and Fox were on the road to London. They kept to the turnpike, which had been cleared of snow, and changed the horses every hour.

"I would have thought that sorcerers used other means

of travel," Fox commented. Looking over to Bourne, he wondered what exactly the man was capable of. After all, he had witnessed what the niece could do and had seen one of the sons handle a ball of blue fire.

But the other only snorted. "Flying carpets and such?" He shook his head and his expression was grim. "Nay. Though God knows how much I would wish for one!"

They fell quiet once more, and indeed most of the trip they spent in silence, giving Fox enough time for regrets and bitter self-recriminations. Why, oh why hadn't he come earlier? Why hadn't he listened to his brother? To Drew? Even his man, Hobbes, had been able to perceive where Fox had gone wrong. Only Fox himself hadn't seen it. Instead he had stubbornly clung to his pride and nursed the feeling of having been wronged. Not only because she had kept things from him; no, mostly because she was *other*.

Arrogant, arrogant fool!

With a pang he remembered their first afternoon at Rawdon Park, when he had told her the truth about his birth. She hadn't held it against him. Instead, she had been loving and understanding. And he? He had promised to love her forever—whatever might happen.

How quick he had been to discard his vow! Yes, they had both been under the influence of that blasted potion, but that hadn't stopped her from risking her life to keep his family safe. What an utter heel he had been!

Fox groaned.

O what can ail thee, wretched wight,
So haggard and so woe-begone?

Dusk had already fallen when they reached the outskirts of London. They left the horses at the stables in the City and took a hackney into Town. Their progress was slow, for High Holborn was crammed with carts and carriages— indeed, half of London appeared to be out on the streets that evening. Fox clenched his hands into fists. "Damn those fools! Hey, driver!" He opened the window and leaned outside. "Can't you drive faster?" Frustrated he sank back onto the seat. "Can't you do something?" he asked Bourne.

But the older man only raised his brow. "Make them disappear into thin air? Nay." His eyes narrowed. "But on second thought, there might be something . . ." He closed his eyes for a moment. An expression of intense concentration appeared on his face as he muttered a few words. The air inside the hackney started to tingle. And then, with an audible *puff*, the tingles were gone. "So," Bourne said in satisfied tones and opened his eyes. "That should do the trick."

Whatever magic he had wrought made the coach pick up speed. In no time at all they had reached Oxford Street and, after that, Holles Street and Cavendish Square. Fox climbed out of the hackney after Bourne. "Wait for us," he told the driver, before he followed the other to the front door of the Benthams' house.

As Bourne looked up at the facade of the building, his face darkened. A muscle jumped in his jaw. "I trusted you. I *trusted* you!" he hissed. "And look how you've repaid my friendship." He made an abrupt movement with his hand, and the front door sprang open. Grimly he went inside, followed closely by Fox.

A footman came running. "Sirs, what—"

"Bring us to your master," Bourne growled. Now that they had finally reached their destination, his anger seemed to burst forth. The footman goggled at their crumpled clothes, before he belatedly remembered his training.

"If you would wait in the hall, sirs," he said, businesslike. "Mr. Bentham is keeping company, but I can inquire whether he will be free to see you."

"How fortunate that he is in. Then you can take us with you straightaway."

"Er, no, sir, I'm afraid I must insist, sir—" His words ended on a squeak as Bourne had grabbed the unfortunate footman by the collar.

"Take. Us. To. Your. Master. Now!" He released the footman, and whatever the servant had seen in Bourne's eyes was enough to make him hastily comply.

They were led to the dining room, where, as it turned out, the Benthams were giving a dinner for Lord Munthorpe. At their entrance, all color leached from Bentham's face. He scrambled to his feet, crumpled his napkin between his fingers, and made an attempt at a smile. "B-Bourne. And Stapleton." One of his hands rose and fumbled with his necktie as if it had suddenly become too tight. "W-What a surprise."

His wife, by contrast, looking them up and down, wrinkled her nose. "How . . . unconventional."

Bourne didn't spare her a glance, but kept his eyes trained on his erstwhile friend. "Spare me the playacting. Did you do it or not?"

Mrs. Bentham trilled a laugh. "Why, my dear Mr. Bourne. From the way you talk, one could be led to assume you've come straight from Bedlam!" She batted her lashes. "You talk in riddles."

"Like an oracle, indeed!" her daughter chimed in. "How is dear Amelia, Mr. Bourne?"

For the first time, Bourne looked at Miss Bentham, his expression thunderous enough to make her shrink back on her seat. "My niece," he forced out between gritted teeth, "is *dying*. So tell me, Bentham"—his attention swiveled back to the father—"why did you do it?"

"Do what?" Bentham still held on to his bluster. "I am of course very sorry that Amelia is poorly, but I fail to see—"

"Bosh!" Fox's patience snapped. He stepped up to the table and slapped his hands flat on the surface. "You helped Lady Margaret to take revenge on my brother, and Amy was the pawn you used—and sacrificed."

"I—"

"It was you who gave us the potion, was it not?"

"Potion?" Munthorpe, who had been following the exchange with a flabbergasted expression, spluttered, "What potion?"

Fox glanced at him, at dear old Munty, so fond of his sheep. Suddenly he felt pity for him, because of all the women of London, Munthorpe had developed an affection for a vicious little viper. "A love potion," he said more calmly—and when Munthorpe's eyes widened with disbelief: "Yes, I know. It's hardly believable, but I assure you it's true."

Isabella Bentham burst out laughing. "Oh, this is delicious, is it not, my lord? Truly, Mr. Stapleton, we are so very sorry to hear about dear Amy, but it seems that the grief must have befuddled your brains."

Yet Munthorpe didn't join in her laughter. "A . . . a love potion?" He frowned. "Whatever for?"

"Indeed," Bentham choked out, his face now flushed with color. Bourne still stared at him as a basilisk would at a rabbit. "This is a m-most fa-fantastical tale! Ha ha!" Surreptitiously he tugged at his cravat. "Love potions! 'Tis preposterous!"

"Why did you do it?" Bourne repeated. "You must have run into debts—but with that Lady Margaret of all persons?" His eyes narrowed. "Back at university, there were rumours that you gambled more than was healthy . . ."

Beads of sweat glistened on Bentham's forehead. Weakly he sank back onto his chair. His wife threw him a disgusted look and stood, brimming with determination.

"Really, gentlemen, this is a most unusual way to talk in another's house. To come here and throw about ludicrous accusations—no, this will not do. We must ask you to leave now. Gregory!" she called to the footman in the hallway. "Please escort these two gentlemen to the door!"

The next moment, the door to the dining room banged shut, apparently with no help from anyone, making the people around the table start violently. With a yelp, Mrs. Bentham fell back on her chair.

Bourne didn't even blink an eye. "I don't think so," he said. "It appears we both should have listened more carefully to the rumors at university."

The door handle rattled as somebody outside tried to

open the door in vain. And as realization dawned in Bentham's eyes, his face turned a sickly gray. "So he was right," he muttered. "You are of the same ilk. Sorcerer, warlock."

Bourne's gaze sharpened. "What are you talking about?"

"He knew you! Lady Margaret's man, he knew you!" Bentham gave a hysterical laugh. "To imagine: the virtuous Bourne—a sorcerer!" Giggling, he twisted the napkin between his fingers.

Bourne threw a questioning glance at Fox.

"He is right," Fox said slowly, only now remembering those strange bits of conversation in the drawing room of Rawdon Park. "It would seem that Lady Margaret's sorcerer knew you. Young, blond-haired fellow? He appeared delighted that he had been given the chance to take revenge on you."

"Samuel Lovell . . ." Losing some of his color, Bourne shook his head. "He doesn't seem possible. And Amy killed him you say?"

"She killed—" Bentham choked out. "Lord, what sort of girl is your niece? To imagine she lived under our roof all this time!"

"A killeress," Miss Bentham breathed. "How awful!" She grabbed Lord Munthorpe's arm.

"You!" Bourne turned on Bentham. "You used my niece to infiltrate Lord Rawdon's family, didn't you? So a few nice magical toys could be planted on Rawdon's estate."

"On Rawdon's estate?" Munthorpe echoed, getting more confused by the second. "Miss Bourne did . . . ? And killed . . . ? But . . . but . . ."

"Oh, my niece didn't know anything about those charms. That potion had made her so besotted with Stapleton, she couldn't think straight; otherwise she might have noticed earlier that something was amiss and that his family was in danger."

"Really, Mr. Bourne," Mrs. Bentham rallied once more. "Do you see how you contradict yourself? First you accuse my poor husband of using your niece, as you put it, and then you go on to say that she couldn't possibly have done whatever ghastly things you are talking about. Even though she *has* killed some poor man, apparently."

Fox shook his head. Drew had been right all along to avoid this woman at all costs. "Ah," he said, "but Amy did not travel to Rawdon Park alone, did she? Your daughter accompanied her."

Munthorpe gaped. "You mean to suggest . . ." Very slowly he turned his head to look at the object of his devotion. "What exactly have you done?" he whispered.

"Nothing!" Isabella Bentham snapped and tossed her head back. "I did nothing wrong."

Munthorpe regarded her as if he had never seen her before. "Your friend is *dying*. Does this not affect you?"

Sullenly, she shrugged. "She has never been my friend," she scoffed. "And you heard what they said. What she did."

"My niece is dying because she tried to protect the Stapletons from the evil charms *you* have planted at Rawdon Park!" Bourne hissed.

"I see," Munthorpe said slowly. "I see." His face haggard, he stood. "I believe it is best if I now leave."

"Oh, but you can't!" Miss Bentham raised her eyes to his. "Not in the middle of dinner."

"Shush, my dear," her mother tried to appease her. "After all, these two gentlemen have managed to ruin the evening anyway. But there will be other dinners, other—"

"Now, this is where you are wrong." With jerky movements Munthorpe smoothed nonexistent wrinkles in his suit. "I am afraid I will not return to this house."

"What!" Mrs. Bentham cried. "How can you? When you are practically engaged to my daughter?"

Munthorpe's jaw hardened. "I am not yet engaged to her—which I consider fortunate indeed, for I now believe we would not have suited at all."

"Not suited?" Isabella Bentham screeched. "How dare you? If you walk off now, the whole of London will believe you the most dishonorable of men!"

"Then I choose to be dishonorable," he answered, his back already turned on her. "Stapleton. Bourne." He nodded at them. "I am very sorry about Miss Bourne's affliction. If there's anything I can do—"

Fox shook his head. "I'm afraid there isn't. But thank you."

"I am very sorry to hear it." Munthorpe inclined his head once more, then walked out of the room with brisk strides. For him, the door yielded easily.

Mrs. Bentham shot to her feet. "You! *You*! This is all your fault!" She glowered at Fox and Bourne. "How dare you walk in here and—"

"How dare *you*?" Bourne hissed, leaning forward. "How dare you use my niece in your foul play? How dare you sit here, so self-righteous after you've brought death to Rawdon Park?"

Her mouth opened and closed like a stranded fish's.

"W-What do you want?" Bentham asked wearily. "I had no choice, if you must know. They threatened me, I—"

"Be quiet!" Bourne thundered. "Save your pitiful excuses. I want to know what your daughter carried to Rawdon's estate. There was something for the stairs, something for the lake—and what else?"

Bentham muttered something unintelligible.

"What?"

"A plant," he muttered.

"A plant?" Bourne's face turned ashen. "Oh dear God," he whispered.

Fox's stomach gave a lurch. He didn't know what bothered Amy's uncle about this, but whatever it was, it was bad. When he thought of Amy, lying pale and still in her bed, then looked at the sullen faces of the Bentham family before him, he felt an overpowering urge to throttle the lot of them. "And what exactly did you do with it?" he barked at Isabella Bentham.

She shot him a spiteful glance. "Why should I tell you?"

"She was to plant it in the garden," Bentham said quickly. "Now look here, Bourne, I am really sorry about—"

"Where in the garden?" Bourne growled.

Bentham cleared his throat. "Um. Isabella, dear?"

But the girl only shrugged.

Bentham's lips trembled, then lifted into a grimace of a smile. "T-Tell them, my dear."

"Doesn't one corner of green look like any other?"

Bourne took a deep breath. "Very well." He turned toward Fox. "I believe our job here is done."

Yet before they had reached the door, Bentham spoke up one last time—rather unwisely. "I am profoundly sorry, my dear chap. I can assure you we had the greatest affection for little Amelia, and it truly pains me that—But who could have foreseen it? I had no choice in the matter, my hands were bound, I—"

Bourne stopped. "Do not exert yourself, Bentham." His eyes glittering, he looked over his shoulder in a manner that made a cold shiver slither down Fox's spine. Darkness seemed to assemble in the corners of the room. "I see you've drunk wine tonight? I hope you've enjoyed it. For from now on, all wine you drink will be bitter and all food you eat will turn to dust. Your fortune will run through your fingers like water, faster than you can count the days. I curse this house for seven-score years. All that you've gained through your greed will crumble and wither." He gave Bentham a terrible smile. "Good evening, my friend."

And with that, he and Fox finally left.

They took the hackney to Albany next. They paid the driver on Piccadilly Street and entered Albany from the front, through the mansion itself, then down the steps to the Rope Walk at the back of the house. Yet for once the sight of the lit windows to the left and right failed to lift Fox's heart. In silence they walked to his block and up the stairs. Just as he had inserted the key into the door of his apartment, it was flung open with flourish.

"G-good evening, thur," Hobbes said.

Dumbfounded, Fox stared at him, then blinked once, twice—for surely he must be seeing ghosts.

"W-Won't you come in, thur?" The old man stepped aside. "Shall I thend for thomething to eat?"

"But . . . but . . ." Fox spluttered, "you were gone!"

The old man eyed him. "Yeth, thur," he said mildly. "But tho were you, were you not? In Warwickshire, I believe?" He looked past his employer to Amy's uncle.

Still flabbergasted, Fox showed Bourne into hallway of the apartment, where Hobbes took their coats and hats. "But how did you know?" Fox asked, relief swamping him. Thank heavens Hobbes was back! He had missed the old chap, with his peculiar ways.

"L-Lord Thtafford wath kind enough to inform m-me of your de-departure, thur."

"Ah," Fox said. And, more feelingly, "That devil!"

Chapter Eighteen

They spent the night at Fox's rooms in Albany. Fox had insisted that Bourne should take the bed while he slept in one of the leather armchairs in his study. The next morning they were on the road again, only this time their destination was the Fen District. A steady drizzle of snow slowed them down that day, and thus it was late in the evening before they finally reached Rawdon Park.

"Sebastian!" his sister-in-law greeted him on the stairs. She tugged at his shoulder to make him lean down so she could press a kiss on his icy cold cheek. "We received a message from Warwickshire last night," she whispered. "Poor Amy! It's dreadful!"

He nodded and stepped back. "Mirabella, may I present Miss Bourne's uncle. Mr. Bourne, Lady Rawdon."

"We have already met, Sebastian," Bella said softly. "When Mr. Bourne came to collect Amy."

Fox gripped the banister so hard that his knuckles shone white through his skin. He felt an utter heel.

Bourne cleared his throat. "My lady, I hope you will forgive this intrusion, I—"

"Oh, Mr. Bourne, think nothing of it!" she stopped him, laying an impulsive hand on his arm. "We were all truly sorry to hear dear Amy has not improved at all, and we will do our utmost to help you find a cure for her." She looked from one man to the other. "Do you know what ails her? Is it . . ." Her voice faltered a little. "Magical?" she finally whispered.

"I am afraid it is, my lady," Bourne answered gravely.

"Oh."

"It is worse than that," Fox added in a grim voice. "It is here in Rawdon Park. They hid something else."

Confusion registered on her face. Her fine, black brows drew together. "Something else?"

"It was not just the lake, Bella."

"Oh, my goodness." Her hand covered her mouth. "And who—?"

Once more, anger boiled up inside Fox. He gritted his teeth. "Isabella Bentham," he growled.

"Ha!" Bella exclaimed. "I *knew* there was something wrong with that girl! That little snake!" She shook her head, then touched Fox's arm. "You must tell us all about it over dinner. And what needs to be done to help Amelia." She glanced at Bourne. "But for now, there will be rooms prepared for you and hot baths. I'll tell my husband's valet to go and see what can be done about a change of dry clothes for you, Mr. Bourne."

Amy's uncle bowed his head. "Thank you, my lady. I am most obliged."

"Not at all, Mr. Bourne, not at all." She gave him a sad smile. "It is we who are deeply indebted to you. Without your niece . . . Who knows what would have happened if Amy had not been here."

Yes, they all had known it, seen it, except for Fox. Once more regret and self-recriminations sliced him deep. *Dear God*, he prayed, *don't let it be too late.*

When they were finally warm and dry again, Fox and Bourne told the family and Admiral Reitz over dinner what they had learned about the cause of Amy's illness.

"And you believe that if this plant is destroyed, Miss Bourne will recuperate?" Richard asked.

Amy's uncle hesitated with the answer, and all at once Fox remembered Bourne's reaction when Bentham told him of the plant: plain and unadulterated shock. Fox's stomach tightened. Suddenly the meal on the plate before him lost all its appeal.

"I don't know," Bourne finally said. "I just don't know."

Fox reached for his glass of wine and took a deep gulp. Was it not better to know the whole truth? "It is worse, is it not?" he finally asked, his voice hoarse. "Because it is a plant."

Once again, Amy's uncle hesitated before he formed a reply. "Plants thrust their roots deep into the earth. And if they have grown from seeds of evil . . ." He shrugged, clearly uncomfortable. "They saturate the earth with that same evil." His expression turned solemn. "This plant will have had plenty of time for its roots to grow thick and deep."

The dowager countess leaned forward. "So you are saying there is a chance that destroying the plant will not help Amelia."

No! Fox stared at his plate. A deep humming filled his ears. Surely everything could not have been in vain in the end? Surely not.

He was aware that his mother's eyes flickered toward him, but he could not look up. His fingers curled around the edge of the table, crumbling the heavy damask of the cream-colored tablecloth. Through the buzzing in his ears, he heard Bourne clear his throat.

"This is indeed a possibility."

"And what will you do if . . ." Bella's voice trailed away.

There was a sound very much like a sob. Whether it had come from himself or somebody else, Fox didn't know. All he cared about was this terrible, terrible pain blossoming in his chest, such a great pain that eventually it would engulf his whole body. And he knew, knew without a shadow of a doubt, that if Amy died, a part of himself would, too.

> *I see a lily on thy brow*
> *With anguish moist and fever dew,*

And on thy cheek a fading rose
Fast withereth too.

"Well," the admiral's resolute voice cut into his reverie, "let us cross this bridge when we get to it. For now we should concentrate on finding that plant. Perhaps your footmen and gardeners will help with the search, Rawdon?"

When they parted for the night, they were all hopeful—all except for Fox. Misery weighed him down, and even worse, the overpowering feeling of guilt. If only he had come earlier to Amy's family. If only he had not been so proud, so pig-headed, so determined to cloak himself in self-righteousness. How he loathed himself!

Miserable, he stared at his reflection in the dark window. As if this were a mirror of his soul, his mind's eye conjured up another face for him: sweet and round cheeked, a mischievous smile playing around the lips. The teasing glint in the pansy blue eyes challenged him, heart and mind. It had done so from the first. But arrogant fool that he was, he had been affronted by it and had sought the less complicated joys to be found with Madame Suzette's girls.

Shallow cad.

He closed his eyes. It seemed to him he could hear her laughter, her rich, full chuckles—cheeky and naughty when they had stood in the British Museum and looked at the naked glory of the Elgin Marbles; and later so full of delight as she had hugged him to her for the first time, during those first precious moments of their engagement. And even more delight, sweaty and sultry delight, when she had first lain beneath him with his flesh embedded deep inside her—so deep that the boundaries between their bodies had blurred until their hearts had beaten as one. He remembered the shiny ecstasy on her face and the half-smothered laugh of discovery she had snorted against his shoulder afterwards. *"Again,"* she had demanded, and bit lightly into his sweaty flesh. *"Again!"* she had laughed, still breathless.

"Again! Again! Again!" And she had hugged him wildly, exuberantly, with arms and legs, had pressed him into her softness, while bubbling over with joy and delight.

Suddenly Fox knew that he would not be able to spend this night in his cold and empty bed. He opened his eyes and reached for his robe. He slipped into it, took the candle, and left his room. Down the long corridors he went until he reached that door he knew so well. He pushed it open. The light of his candle flickered over the interior of the Rose Guestroom.

Of course, the bed linens had been changed since they had last lain there together. None of her sweet, fresh scent remained. Lily of the valley. But still, he could imagine, could he not? Could remember and hope.

He lit the candelabra which stood on the chest of drawers. As the mellow light filled the dark corners of the room, he started to rummage in the drawers, the closet, the writing desk. If he could find . . . Perhaps there was something left of hers, something wedged into a tight corner and thus missed when they had packed her things. "Anything," he whispered. "Oh please . . ."

A knock sounded on the door.

Frowning, Fox went to open it.

"I knew I would find you here." His mother stood on the threshold, smiling sadly. "May I come in?"

After a moment he gave a silent nod, then stepped aside to let her in. A soft, misty smile curved her lips. "The last time I saw you clad only in your robe, you were still a small boy." With a small sigh, the dowager countess brushed past him. "Sometimes it seems as if it were only yesterday that I brought my fox cub home to live among the hounds. But then I turn and you're already a man grown . . ." She stepped to the window and peered out at the dark and silent gardens. When she turned, he thought he saw tears glittering in her eyes. "A stubborn, complicated man, perhaps, but one dearly loved by his family. You know that, don't you, Sebastian?" She looked at him intently.

Fox swallowed. "How did you know that you would find me here?"

She sat down on the chair at the window and scanned the room. "Oh, my dear . . . Was this not Amelia's room?" Her gaze came to rest on him.

"Yes." All at once, all strength seeped out of him. He sank down on the bed and leaned forward to bury his face in his hands. "Yes." Muffled against his palms, his voice sounded choked. His cheeks and hands became wet.

"And this is where you spent the night with her, is it not?" Sybilla asked gently.

Surprise cut through his misery. He looked up, not caring that thereby he revealed his ravaged face to her. "How do you—? Has Richard—?"

Another soft, sad smile. "No, not Richard. One of the upstairs maids saw you slipping out of her room. She went to the housekeeper, and Mrs. Dibbler decided to come and see me about the matter rather than Mirabella." A note of soft reproach entered her voice. "It was a naughty, irresponsible thing to do, Sebastian. But we came to the conclusion that I would not berate you about it since the two of you were already engaged—and so obviously in love with each other."

Fox felt his face crumple. He sucked in a breath. "She truly loved me, Mama," he choked out. "Despite the potion, even after she had found out . . . she still loved me. Truly and deeply." He sucked in another breath, feeling battered and bruised and more desperate than ever before in his life.

"And yet you stayed away for so long," Sybilla said.

"I didn't know . . ." He ran an unsteady hand through his hair. "I didn't know it was all real in spite of everything. I didn't know that I—" His voice broke.

She shook her head at him. "Stubborn and complicated. And much too proud for his own good."

A vise constricted around his heart, squeezed all breath from his lungs. And then it burst out of him, with all glibness and sophistication erased as if they had never been. "I love her, Mama. With all my heart and all my soul, I love her. If she . . . if something happens to her . . ." He tried to draw breath, to keep a lid on his emotions after all. Yet the sobs already rose from his chest and wracked his body. "I wouldn't be able to bear it," he forced out.

"Oh, my dear boy." His tears obscured the expression on his mother's face, but he saw her open her arms wide. "Come here."

And then he was on his knees before her, his head buried in her lap. He felt her stroking his hair. "Hush now, hush," she whispered to him. "Have a little faith in your love."

"I didn't know . . ." He raised his head. Desperation sliced his heart into a thousand ribbons. "Before, . . . I didn't know."

"Hush." His mother wiped the tears from his cheeks. "But now you know, don't you? So have faith in your love, my son."

He shook his head. "But—"

She cupped his face between her hands and looked at him intently. "Amelia had faith enough in her love to believe it would keep us all safe. Now it is your turn."

Faith? How should that help against the evil that threatened her life? "But—"

"No buts." The dowager countess gave him a wry smile. "Don't you think, Sebastian, that in a world where a girl can heal a wound in her lover's flesh with the touch of her hand, anything might be possible?"

He stared at her, speechless.

She chuckled a little, then pressed a kiss onto his forehead. "So have faith, my son. Have faith in your love." And with that she rose and left him alone in his beloved's room.

Chapter Nineteen

The wind blew icy cold the next morning when Richard assembled his men in the forecourt: gardeners, footmen, stablehands—Rawdon Park's small army. But would they be enough? Fox's heart tightened painfully.

His brother, though, seemed to know no such worries. Hands on his hips, Richard stood on the front steps and listened as Bourne detailed what exactly they were looking for.

Yet what they knew was pitifully little: a plant that looked out of the ordinary, probably prospering even in winter, or perhaps it might appear blackened and dead. The estate workers looked at each other and scratched their heads. Wouldn't they have noticed anything out of the ordinary before?

"It has most likely been planted in a hidden corner of the estate," Bourne continued, his voice controlled and easily carrying across the forecourt.

Would they recognize it even under all the snow? the head gardener inquired.

Oh yes, they would. Bourne was sure. "When you see it, you will know it for what it is."

It sounded ominous enough to make Fox shiver.

He looked back over his shoulder into the entrance hall, where his mother stood with Mirabella. Sybilla gave him a smile. *Have a little faith*, he half-heard her voice whisper.

But it was difficult to have faith when it all seemed like a wild goose chase.

Just as they were about to split in twos and depart for the gardens, Dickie and Pip came clumping down the main stairs. "Wait!" Dick hollered. "Wait!"

Their mother reached out and grabbed the cuffs of the boys' thick coats. "And what do you think you are doing?"

Her oldest tried to wriggle free. "Helping search!"

More noisy steps on the stairs announced the arrival of the tutor, who apparently had managed to escape the wilderness of Scotland. Breathless, he halted in front of Bella. "I apologize, my lady. Shall I escort the young masters back upstairs?"

Dick stared at him like a belligerent terrier. "We won't go!" he growled.

His brother tried a different tack. "We know the gardens so well. And we're small: we can look under the bushes."

Frowning, Richard turned. "You will go back upstairs pronto, young men."

"But—"

"Now!" Richard hollered, loud enough to make everybody from the potboy to his countess jump. Round eyed, his sons gaped at him.

And no wonder, since the Earl of Rawdon was not known as one who raised his voice. It was then that it dawned on Fox that his brother might be as worried and as nervous as himself. His solid, well-grounded brother was seriously rattled and not nearly as calm and confident as he wanted others to believe. It was indeed a most surprising revelation.

It was something Fox still pondered when he walked down one of the paths of the pleasure garden with Bourne a little time later. Thick blankets of snow covered the flower beds and lay on the bare hedges. Dubious, Fox cast a glance around. "Are you *sure* we will find that plant under all this snow?"

The older man gnawed on his lip. "I am," he finally said. "I have to be."

But you aren't, Fox thought despairingly. *And you don't know whether it will be enough to save Amy after all.* His eyes pricked, but he rapidly blinked against the sting of tears. He took a deep breath. *For now, focus on doing what you can.* They needed to find that plant.

At midday they returned to the house to warm themselves and drink steaming cups of hot tea and the soup Cook had prepared for them. Only, Fox stole away without having eaten and slipped back outside. He went to the lake and bleakly stared across its expanse. Their search this morning had been fruitless. Would they *ever* find the plant? To find a single plant on grounds the size of Rawdon Park was akin to finding the proverbial needle in the haystack. Oh, why hadn't Isabella Bentham been more forthcoming? His throat closed, and he swallowed convulsively.

God, what was he doing here, standing around like a ninny? He must search for the plant! And so, frantic, he dashed off to continue the search alone while the wind chafed his cheeks.

Three quarters of an hour later, the others joined him again. His brother came over and clasped his shoulder. "You look dreadful. What were you thinking? Going all alone out here again?"

With barely veiled impatience, Fox shook his hand off. "I need to find that thing."

This time, Richard gripped both of his shoulders and wrenched him around. His kind brown eyes searched Fox's face. "You should have at least eaten. Mother worries about you."

Fox snorted. "Would you eat if it were Bella?" He shook his head, not liking how his brother's gaze sharpened.

"The last time we spoke about this you were very angry."

"The last time we spoke about this, I was fool," Fox hissed. "A stupid, arrogant fool."

Richard regarded him a moment longer, then pressed his shoulders. "Good. I'm glad you saw the light. And Sebastian . . ." His hand curved around Fox's jaw. "We will all do our utmost to find that plant. You know that, don't you?"

With a hollow laugh, Fox dropped his head and rubbed his hands over his face. "But you've heard what Bourne said: it might not be enough in the end." And with that, Fox stalked off to continue his search.

In the evening, when they finally returned to the house, they learned that the carriages with the rest of the Bourne family had arrived. Amy had been carried upstairs to her old room, where Mirabella was sitting with her, and Fox, still in his muddy boots, raced up the stairs.

When he saw Amy, lying still and pale in the bed where they had last shared a night of joyful passion, his knees buckled. He sank down beside the bed and warily touched the back of her hand. "She looks worse than before," he said hoarsely, not looking at his sister-in-law.

"Have you found anything?" Bella's voice was soft.

Wordless, he shook his head. His gaze roamed Amy's face, traced each blue line that was visible through the skin.

"Would you like to sit with her after you've changed?"

Again he shook his head. Her hair had lost its luster and straggled down over her shoulders. Carefully, he took a strand and rubbed it between his thumb and forefinger.

"Sebastian—"

It seemed only yesterday that he had buried his face in her hair, while his body had still been buried deep inside hers.

"I'm not going to leave her," he said.

"Sebastian—"

"No." He shrugged out of his damp frock coat and put it over the back of a chair.

Bella sighed. "You're adamant, are you not?" She handed him a book. "Here. I've been reading this to her. She's never had the chance to finish it." She stood, straightening her skirts. "Shall I send a tray to you?"

Once more, he shook his head.

Lightly, she laid a hand on his shoulder. "But you have to eat, Sebastian. Starving yourself to death won't help Amy."

She leaned forward and kissed his temple. "I will send a tray."

Quietly, she closed the door behind her.

For a moment Fox sat very still. The light of the candles flickered over the walls, kept the darkness at bay, which was waiting outside the windows like a great beast.

He turned the book between his hands. Dark red leather, soft and smooth like silk. The flash of gilt letters and ornaments. He rubbed his thumb over the inscription on the spine: *Histories of the Rhine*.

He flicked the book open. The frontispiece showed a strapping young man in the dark robe of a scholar, a fat book raised high over his head. In front of him crouched what looked like a cross between Cerberus and a sheep. "Worthy Markander and the three-headed monster poodle," the description read. And on the title page,

THE HORRIBLE HISTORIES
OF THE RHINE
Being the True Story
of Seven Brave Knights
of Mayence
& what Befell them

A few colorful threads, interwoven into a narrow ribbon, marked page 271. Fox remembered how he had watched Amy knotting that same ribbon all those weeks ago. How deftly her fingers had worked: he had been transfixed.

If only he could transport them back to that day! The world had seemed perfect then, their love indestructible. Had she already known then?

But no; no, that had been long before Dickie's fall on the stairs, before her behavior had so markedly changed. She wouldn't have suspected anything either. How often had he seen her and Mirabella giggling over the pages of the book. It had lain on the nightstand when he had come to her room that first night and she had read to him the episode of the battle between the ghastly lindworm and worthy Markander.

With the flat of his hand Fox smoothed down the pages of the book.

"Heim Heinrik's words so abashed the fair maiden," he began to read out loud, his voice rough, "that she went with all the speed from the tower and told the giant, how a knight of Mayence remained at the gate, who had sworn to suffice his hunger in despite of his will . . ."

For the next few hours, Fox read to Amy how brave Heim Heinrik saved the girl-princess Idonia from the clutches of the evil giant and how he continued to win the heart of Queen Cristiana. But too soon, Heim Heinrik had to leave his beloved again: "This letter was very welcome to Queen Cristiana, who now began to set such high esteem on Heim Heinrik, that she judged him worthy of the empire of the world. And now, he being the sole monarch of her heart, she could not but breathe forth some sighs to think upon his absence; but then considering upon what an honorable account he was engaged, she could not but applaud his undertaking: yet to give him some clear demonstration of her affection to him, upon his marching away, she went in her chariot to speak to him, whom she found at the head of his troops, and kindly bade him farewell and bestowed upon him a scarf of her own with these words: *Let me request you to wear this scarf for my sake, that by looking on the same, I may not be altogether out of your remembrance.*"

By now Fox's voice was hoarse. He had to clear his throat, before he could croak, "End of Part II of *The Horrible Histories of the Rhine.*"

He looked up.

Amy lay as still and pale as before.

With a deep sigh, he put the book aside and took up her hand. "If you were held captive by the most horrible giants or the most dreadful of lindworms, I would lay siege to their castles and lairs and not budge until I held you safe in my arms." Softly, he kissed her palm, then pressed her hand against his cheek. "But what can I do against this? How can I help you now?" He closed his eyes and nestled his face into her hand, trying to pretend that it lay not limp and lifeless and cold, so cold against his skin, but warm and vibrant.

After a while, he opened his eyes and placed her hand back on the bed. When he glanced around the room, he noticed for the first time that the candles had burned down and that somebody had left a tray with food on the desk. He stood and rubbed a hand over the stubble on his cheek, then went over and ate a bit of bread and a slice of Mrs. Ogg's venison cake, which he washed down with the wine Mirabella had had sent up—thank heavens not the ginger beer Richard was so partial to!

Fox yawned. He took off his boots, shucked his waistcoat and trousers, and went back to the bed. Clad in his drawers and shirt, he slipped underneath the covers beside Amy. With one arm protectively curved around her, he dozed.

He was up again early the next morning, before any hint of light showed on the horizon. He left a maid sitting with Amy and went to his room to change. By the time he went downstairs, it was still dark and he had to ring for the butler to get a hastily assembled breakfast served. He had just finished it, when his brother stumbled into the room. Richard had obviously dressed in a hurry and was not yet quite awake.

"Sebastian . . ." Richard blinked. "Whatever are you doing?"

Impatient, Fox threw a glance out of the window. "The plant. I need—"

"Heavens! It's not even light outside. You can't want to bump around in the dark, Sebastian."

Richard was right, of course. Fox narrowed his eyes. Not

even the tiniest band of gray showed on the horizon. And so he was forced to wait—wait until dawn finally broke, wait until everybody else had had breakfast. Like a caged tiger, he walked up and down the window front of the breakfast parlor.

That day, as bad luck would have it, it took the sun a long time to banish the shadows of the night. Clouds were hanging low, and when the men finally assembled in the front yard once more, thick wet snowflakes fell and clung to their clothes. On their skin the flakes immediately melted to splotches of icy-cold water.

This morning, it was the younger Bourne boys who protested when they had to stay behind. Yet their father was just as adamant as Richard had been with his own sons the day before, so they went back inside with long faces.

The men spread throughout the park and gardens. The fat flakes quickly dampened their coats. Coldness seeped into their bones while they searched empty flower beds, while they looked under hedges and checked the undergrowth in the park. Faster and faster the snowflakes fell, until they resembled a gray, cold veil, behind which the world disappeared.

Fox lost all sense of time as he stomped through the snow side by side with the admiral. They had searched the walled gardens, had lifted forcing pots and opened the lids of the forcing frames. They had sneezed at the concentrated stench of manure that greeted them. But the only thing they had found were ripening strawberries. They had marched through the glass houses, walked along neat rows of peach trees and beneath cucumbers and fat melons as round and full as small green moons.

It was long past midday when they reached one of the utmost corners of the park and entered a small grove, which hid the outer wall surrounding the park from view. Cutting coldness bit at Fox's skin, making him shiver. They would not find the plant.

Snowflakes whirled around him as he stood staring into thin air. "We won't find it." A shudder ran through his body.

"What?" The admiral half turned toward him. "My dear young friend, don't tell me that you will give up now."

"We won't find it," Fox repeated. Despair slowly knotted his insides. "We won't." He shook his head. "We won't, we won't, we won't."

"Nonsense," the admiral said firmly. "Look here." And then, in a very different tone, "Oh . . . oh my. Look here, Sebastian. Look!" Snow and gravel crunched underneath his boots as he strode forward. "Sebastian!"

And Fox looked. Stared. Could hardly believe his eyes.

With a cry he stumbled after the admiral: a small distance away, the snow had melted away from blackened earth. They followed the stripes of black until they reached the wall. And there they found their quarry, nestling between two withered bushes: black with a glistening dark ball at its top, the plant had unfurled thick, meaty leaves that slithered close to the earth. One of them covered the rotting remains of a robin's wing; the stalk of another had curled around a long-dead mouse. The stench of death and decay saturated the air.

"Heavens!" The admiral's exclamation ended on a cough.

The plant quivered. The leaves rustled across the earth, shifted and revealed the scattered bones of another small mammal. The men took a step back.

"It knows that we are here," Fox murmured, pressing the sleeve of his coat against his nose.

Keeping his gaze trained on the plant, the admiral reached for the gun he was carrying and fired a shot into the air—the sign they had agreed on. The central stem of the plant bent toward them, the black ball at the top moving from side to side like an evil eye.

It hissed.

"Heavens!" Sweat beaded on the admiral's forehead. With his thumb and forefinger he rubbed his mustache. "I daresay I've never seen anything quite like it."

Fox nodded slowly. Transfixed he stared at the plant, gazed at the blackened earth all around it, and followed the curving stripes of black that snaked out toward trees and bushes in the vicinity. Some of the smaller bushes were already covered with dark slime and had withered and died. Black pustules had broken out on the trunk of a nearby oak tree.

"What—" Breathless, two of the gardeners arrived. Their eyes widened as they caught sight of the plant; then the stench hit their noses. They started coughing and wheezing. "Gracious!"

The admiral gave another shot.

From all sides, men came toward them. Richard arrived with his head gardener, who appeared about to burst into tears when he caught sight of the damaged oak tree. He made as if to step toward it, yet Richard grabbed the back of his coat.

"You want to stay away from that, Mr. Chapman. At least until Mr. Bourne says it is all right."

Bourne finally came in the company of one of the footmen, closely followed by his two eldest sons. All three of them paled at the sight of the plant.

Fox's heart sank. He moistened his lips. "How bad is it?"

The men all fell silent as they awaited Bourne's answer, yet he seemed scarcely able to form words. After two starts, he finally managed, "It's worse than I thought. Much worse." He shuddered.

"But will you be able to get rid of it, sir?" Chapman asked eagerly.

Another shudder ran through Bourne. "It won't be easy. Impossible most likely." He swallowed, hard. "What you see here is only the damage that thing has wreaked on the surface. But the roots . . . oh, the roots will have spread so much further. It . . ." His voice broke.

"It has poisoned the land," Colin Bourne supplied softly. "And because Amy has joined herself with the land . . ." His face spasmed. For a moment, his control seemed to slip. After a shuddering breath, he added, "It's no wonder that she is ailing. It has poisoned her, too."

Richard frowned. "Why would they have wanted to poison the land?"

Bourne gave a hollow laugh. "A mere side effect, my lord. From what I understand, the two other attacks were directed at your children? Then look what this thing does." He pointed to the bones and the ripped-off, rotting wing of the bird. "Now it is only small animals, but imagine how tall the plant would have grown in spring . . ."

Fox had never seen his brother go as pale as he did when the full meaning of Bourne's words sank in. A murmur of shock rippled through the men around them.

Richard swayed, his face ashen. "They . . . she . . ."

The admiral's hand shot out to steady him. "Easy, my friend. Easy."

"Yes," Bourne said quietly. "Oh yes. That is what they wanted to happen."

"Which would be . . . ?" a female voice sounded from the back of the crowd.

They turned. The men stepped aside to let the countess and Mrs. Bourne pass. "What is—," the latter began, then caught sight of the plant. She drew in a sharp breath, before her face tightened. "Those bastards!" She shook her head.

"It will be difficult to kill." Her husband's voice sounded tired. "Look at how it sways from side to side as if it understands each word we're saying."

"How awful," Bella whispered. She stepped to Richard's side and slipped her arm around his.

Mrs. Bourne, however, straightened. "No matter if it does or doesn't understand, it won't help the nasty little bugger," she growled. She threw her husband a pointed look. "You dashed away so fast, you forgot to take *anything* with you. How fortunate that at least one of us kept their wits about them."

Apparently, Fox thought in a daze, Mrs. Bourne still hadn't forgiven her husband for sending their niece to live with the Benthams.

"Mary—," Bourne began, only to have his wife cut in, "I have brought books." Her tone and the look on her face were triumphant.

"You have . . ."

"Yes." And she started ticking off her fingers, *"The Red Book of Chulmleigh, The Black Book of Caernarfon, The Writings of Rhodri the Great*—doesn't he cover plants as well?— and, of course, *The Revelations of Domangart of Alba."*

As Bourne's shoulders sagged with relief, her expression softened. "I thought they might prove useful," she added more gently.

"Thank goodness." Obviously not caring about the audience, Bourne wrapped one arm around his wife's shoulders and drew her into a tight embrace. "Thank goodness that I have the cleverest wife in all the world." His voice sounded choked.

Their sons gaped at them. "B-but Mama," Devlin Bourne stuttered. "Those are . . . apart from *The Writings of Rhodri the Great*, those are . . ." As he seemed too astounded to continue, his brother finished the sentence: "Those are all books from the forbidden part of the library!"

"Of course," their mother said with perfect calm. "All books on dark spells and blood magic and old, better-forgotten rituals. How else shall we understand what we are dealing with?" She pressed a kiss on her husband's face, then took a step back. With her hands demurely clasped in front of her, she looked again the proper lady. Nobody who saw her now would have guessed that only moments before, her eyes had been burning with fury.

Fox blinked. The transformation was indeed astonishing.

A memory flashed into his mind of the way Amy had looked when she had broken through the spell of Lady Margaret's sorcerer. She had been frantic when the dagger had pierced his shoulder and his blood had run through her fingers. He remembered the warmth of her touch on his skin, the heat that had flowed from her hands into his shoulder. It hadn't fully registered with him, though; he had only had eyes for the love that softened her face as she stroked his cheek. But then, as she had turned away—oh, how her expression had changed! Her eyes had glowed with murderous fury when she had confronted their tormentors.

Her fierceness had left him staggered. For then he had known she would kill to protect him. And she had.

His chest expanded on a deep, agonized breath. Guilt stabbed him anew and it hurt worse than the wizard's dagger. What a fool he had been! Such a bloody, bloody fool!

Meanwhile Mrs. Bourne proposed that they all go back to the house in order to read up on evil plants before they attempted to kill this particular specimen the next day.

"Tomorrow?" Mr. Chapman asked. "Shouldn't we whack it with a spade first?" His gaze flicked from the plant to the old oak tree and back again.

"My dear man"—Mrs. Bourne gave him a kind but somewhat pitying look—"in cases such as this, when magic is involved, it is always best to not take any chances. Especially when it might not only cost you a perfectly good spade, but also your arm." She sniffed. "Look at that little creeper. So full of evil."

They all stared at the plant, whose central stalk continued to move from side to side. Perhaps it did indeed know they were planning its destruction, because its leaves slithered to-and-fro, scattering the remains of the small animals buried underneath even more.

"No," Mrs. Bourne said decisively. "Today we are going to plan our counterspell, and tomorrow at first dawn we will kill that thing."

So they returned to the house, cold, wet and exhausted from their long search, but in a far happier mood than they had been that morning. For the very first time Fox allowed himself to hope.

When he sat with Amy in the evening, her cool hand resting between his palms, he thought of how easily the Bournes had included his family in the planning of the spell—as if they had taken it for granted that they would and could all work together whether they had magical abilities or not. The Bournes had even called in Mr. Chapman to advise them on how best to kill regular weeds. At this point, the admiral had scribbled down notes as well—no doubt, come next spring he would attack the moss growing on his apple trees with strong lime water.

"It's most curious, is it not?" Sybilla later remarked to Fox. "How much care and effort putting together such a spell takes. Why, it's almost like composing a song."

It seemed his family had easily accepted the existence of magic. *But it goes against all common sense and rational thought!* something inside Fox clamored even now.

He looked down at where he had laced his fingers with Amy's.

He was a man not given to superstition or flights of fancy, one who didn't believe in fairy tales. And yet . . .

His thumb smoothed over the back of Amy's small hand where her skin was as soft as eiderdown. Being with her had reminded him of a time when he believed that stones could hum. Vividly, he remembered how her dancing in the stone circle had filled him with wonder. Anything seemed possible with her at his side.

Fox leaned forward and brushed his mouth over her cheek. "Don't leave me now, sweetheart," he murmured. "I would be lost without you, and the world would be such an empty place."

It occurred to him that if it hadn't been for the potion he would be sitting in his club right now, or spending an evening at Madame Suzette's, slaking his lust in a meaningless encounter. What a shallow fellow he had been! He would have never pursued Amy, would have never made the effort to see beyond his annoyance and value her for the sweet, witty person she was. She might not fulfill the ideal of the polished, stylish debutante, but she was courageous and resourceful, kindhearted and talented in ways he had never imagined.

If it hadn't been for the potion, he would have continued his merry but empty bachelorhood or, perhaps, would have eventually relented and married a society debutante after all. They would have had a sparkling, sophisticated society marriage—and everybody knew what *that* meant! Fox grimaced. He would have never known the bliss he had found in Amy's arms, would have never known that closeness of body and soul he had experienced with her.

Yes, they were different—a man who put rational thought above all else, a woman who lived a fairy tale. The potion had pulled those superficial barriers down and had thus allowed them to find each other after all.

With a sigh, Fox laid his head next to Amy's on the pillow and his closed his eyes.

Please, you must come back to me.

The next morning they all assembled around the magical plant once more. Mr. Chapman brought a large, sturdy sickle, which he had sharpened the evening before, and his assistants carried water cans and buckets filled with concentrated lime water. Colin Bourne held two pouches of salt—one large, one small. It had been Mrs. Bourne's idea to scratch Amy's skin and mix a few drops of her blood into the salt to increase the powers of the spell she and her husband were about to invoke.

Richard leaned over to whisper into Fox's ear. "How curious. I always thought such things would require the full moon."

Fox shrugged. "Apparently not. Lady Margaret and her minions didn't require the full moon, either, did they?" He watched how Bourne took the sickle and the smaller bag of salt. Mrs. Bourne, armed with a can of lime water and the larger bag, positioned herself near the plant, and gave her husband a nod.

Taking a deep breath, Bourne turned. "And here it begins. If you would all take a step back, my lord, my ladies, gentlemen."

With measured steps he then circled the plant, dropping grains of salt onto the earth. His lips moved as he murmured under his breath, but the words remained unintelligible. Carefully, he drew a circle around the plant, his wife and himself, and when the last few grains of salt touched the earth to complete it, the round began to shimmer with blue light.

Hissing, the plant shot forward as if to snap at Bourne. Yet he stood out of its reach and, unperturbed, lifted the sickle slowly with both hands. Rays of the winter sun caught and sparkled on the gray steel, and it seemed as if a gleaming star was lodged at the tip of the blade. The next moment, the sickle swung downward in a graceful, deadly arc. Yet instead of chopping off the main stalk, Bourne cut deep into the earth in order to hit the main root..

A high-pitched wail made them all start. Faster than lightning, the main stalk shot forward and the black ball at its top unfurled to sink a row of sharp thorns into Bourne's arm. He grunted with pain. Still, his free arm never wavered, and he drew the sickle out of the ground with one hand. The tip of the blade had blackened.

Dark red liquid oozed up from the wound in the earth, and Mrs. Bourne quickly aimed a gush of lime water at it. Already the plant seemed to weaken; the stalk sagged; the leaves' rustling decreased.

While his wife steadily poured the water on the plant, Bourne raised the sickle once more, and this time he did cut through the main stalk. Another wail was abruptly cut off. The black ball fell away from Bourne's arm. Although blood tripped from his wound to the earth, the hiss of the sickle swinging from side to side and cutting into leaves and roots never faltered. With each blow the blade turned blacker and blacker until, with a screech, the metal burst and splintered like dry wood.

In unison the group of spectators gasped.

The can of lime water spent, Mrs. Bourne put it aside and opened the bag of salt. Murmuring a spell under her breath, she sprinkled it liberally over the dying remains of the plant to stamp out all life. Under the influence of the salt and her spell, the dark leaves and roots withered away and turned into black slime that lay thick and oily on the earth. With a graceful wave of her hand, Mrs. Bourne brought her spell to an end. She looked at her husband, a small smile hovering around her mouth. "Done," she said.

With the tip of his boot, Bourne smudged the line of salt that described the border of the magic circle, and immediately the blue light expired. With a deep sigh he stepped out. "Well, now." With the back of his hand he wiped his forehead. "The roots need to be dug up and burned together with all the earth. Afterwards, the whole area must be purified."

"What about Amy?" Fox pressed. "Will this help her?"

Bourne lifted his shoulders, then grimaced in pain. "That remains to be seen." He glanced at the now useless handle of the sickle in his hand, and frowned as if he had only now become aware that the tool had broken. With a shrug he threw it away.

Mrs. Bourne went to her husband and, putting her hand on his shoulder, inspected his arm. "This wound needs to be cleaned and looked after. You should have chopped off that nasty little thing at the top first, after all."

"And have its blood splatter everywhere?" Bourne asked wryly.

She wrinkled her nose. "No, you're right. It would have ruined everybody's coats. And these things are usually terribly difficult to remove from fabric. That would have been aggravating indeed." She turned her attention back on the remains of the plant and on the surrounding area. "I am afraid the bushes are beyond saving, Mr. Chapman," she addressed the head gardener. "And that poor old oak tree probably needs to be cut down as well. Everything else ought to be rubbed down with lime water and then we'll have to wait and see how this turns out."

The group scattered: the gardeners went back to their work, while the Bournes, the Stapletons and the admiral returned to the house. Pip and Dick bubbled over with excitement about what they had witnessed, and asked the young Bournes a thousand questions.

When they finally reached the house, a miracle awaited them: A maid came running, and called out breathlessly, "It's Miss Bourne! She woke up! Indeed, she did! Right half an hour ago, she suddenly opened her eyes and sat up straight in her bed."

Richard, Bella, and Fox hurried upstairs after the Bournes. The sight that greeted them in the Rose Bedroom made Fox fall weak against the doorframe: The maid who was sitting with Amy was just giving her a sip of water. As they entered, Amy's head turned slowly, ever so slowly. She caught sight of her aunt and uncle, and a hint of a smile flickered across her face. And then she saw him.

Fox swallowed hard. "Amy," he whispered. The next moment he was across the room and down on his knees next to the bed. Tears spilled past his cheeks as he took her hand and lowered his head over it in order to press a kiss onto her knuckles. "I am sorry. I am so sorry," burst out of him. And overpowered by his feeling of unworthiness, he couldn't meet her eye.

Something touched his cheek. Amy's finger, trailing over his skin in a feather-light caress.

He raised his head and stared at her. His heart drummed so loudly against his ribs, he thought she must surely hear it. Desperately he searched her pansy blue eyes, which had lost their usual brightness and looked wan and tired. What he saw there humbled him—and gave him hope.

"Hello, Fox," she murmured, and her lips curved into a soft, little smile. "It is so lovely to see you again."

Chapter Twenty

Even though she had wakened, Amy did not further improve. She remained weak and listless, and slept almost all day. Fox sat nearby most of the time, anxiously looking over her, counting every breath she took when she slept, softly talking to her in the few precious moments when she was awake. "I was such a fool," he said to her one afternoon. "Such a proud, arrogant—"

"Hush." She put a weak finger against his lips and the corner of her eyes crinkled. "You thought I would suddenly sprout a beaked nose, grow a wart or two and start cackling in the most frightful fashion like a veritable fairy tale witch."

"Amy—" He threw her a helpless look.

"Hush," she repeated, her hand stroking across his cheek. "I understand."

He captured her hand and pressed a kiss into her palm. She watched him, her eyes over-large in her small, thin face. "I couldn't tell you," she whispered. "It was awful . . ." Her eyes fell close. "When I knew and you didn't. But you wouldn't have believed me. Do you remember your lecture about common sense and rational thought when we first danced the waltz?"

"That man was a pompous ass," he growled.

She gave a little laugh and blinked up at him. "How could I have asked you to believe in potions and evil magic?" she asked, serious once more. "And if by chance you had, what if it had broken the spell wrought by the potion and I had been sent back home? There would have been nobody to protect you all."

Leaning forward, Fox buried his face in her hair. "You did so much for my family." Desperation at his own shortcomings sliced his heart. "I should have trusted you. I should have loved you better."

Her breathing deepened. When he lifted his head, she had already fallen asleep again.

Most of the time Amy was too weak to talk, and so he took her book and read to her. He read to her how Alexandie, now worthy Markander's wife, was abducted by the horrible Green Man, a wild, dark creature living in the depths of the forest, and how he struck Markander with a deep, unnatural sleep. His voice faltered as he came to this passage, but her hand slipped into his and her fingers weakly squeezed so that he would continue. Thus, he read on: how Martinus and Gidonius set out to free fair Alexandie, and how Martinus slayed the Green Man with the mighty, magical sword he had received from the King of Swedes, Ikerad. And Fox could not help remembering the sickle Amy's uncle had used to kill the plant outside in the garden. It seemed fantastical, as if the characters of a book had stepped out of their story and into the real world. But would the story end happily in real life, too?

The longer Fox sat at Amy's bedside, the more he doubted it. No, she did not improve. Day after day he watched her closely, eager to catch the smallest improvement. So far, he had detected none.

And worse: Amy's family seemed doubtful, too, in regard to her recovery.

One evening, they all met in the South Drawing Room. "It hasn't helped her, has it?" Richard asked. "The gardeners have dug up all the roots of that plant, have burned both them and all the soiled earth, but it hasn't helped."

Bourne sighed. "No, it hasn't helped." His voice sounded

utterly weary. "We have given her additional healing potions and conventional medicine, but none of these have helped, either. The poison has saturated the land far beyond the reach of the roots of the plant . . ." His voice trailed away.

Fox clamped his eyes tightly shut and bit his lower lip. He wanted to rant and rave against fate, wanted to weep and cry.

For a moment they all sat in silence.

"Surely there must be something," Bella began hesitantly. "Is there anything that can be done?"

Again silence reigned, a silence which rang horribly loud in Fox's ears. His eyes snapped open. He sprang up from his seat. "There must be something!"

"There might be."

All eyes turned to Colin Bourne, who exchanged a glance with his brother Devlin.

"Well . . ." Devlin licked his lips. "We have talked about this, and . . . well . . ."

One of the younger boys fidgeted on his seat, then leaned forward, excitement making his eyes sparkle. Fox recognized him as the one who had wanted to throw blue lightning at him. "We should try to heal the land," the boy blurted, "not Amy!"

"Heal the land?" His father frowned.

"It might be worth a try," Colin argued. "So far we have only tried to heal Amy and it hasn't helped her. You said it yourself, it's the land that is poisoned."

"But, dear"—Mrs. Bourne clasped the arm of her husband—"how could we . . . ? We would need . . ."

Devlin rubbed his neck. "Granted, it isn't ideal. It's neither Beltane nor midsummer." He shrugged. "But still, it might work."

His mother narrowed her eyes. "You really mean . . ." Abruptly, her head swiveled around, and she stared at Fox. "*He* would have to . . ."

Her intense gaze made Fox uncomfortable. "What is it?"

"He is so not ideal," Flann of the blue light muttered. The next moment though, his expression and tone lightened. "What about sacrificing him? 'The Holly King must die' and all that?"

Devlin reached out and slapped the back of his younger brother's head. "You're crackers! The next thing you'd know is Amy coming after you with a knife!"

What a relief! Fox didn't quite know whether to laugh or to cry.

"No, we were speaking, of course, of . . ." Devlin cleared his throat, looked at Colin.

The older brother gave a small grimace. "The Great Wedding," he finally said.

As one, all members of the Bourne family turned to gaze at Fox.

"Er . . ." What was he supposed to say? "A wedding? How will a wedding help her? I will wed her, of course, if it will help." Fox winced at his own awkward phrasing. "I'll wed her in any case," he hastened to add.

This, however, didn't have the expected effect. Instead, young Flann glowered at him. "He *is* a dunderhead," he muttered darkly.

"Shut up!" Devlin clipped him again.

"*Ouch!*"

"For heaven's sake, will you two stop!" Mrs. Bourne snapped at her sons. "We're not speaking of a conventional wedding," she said, turning back to Fox, "but of a Great Wedding. Domangart of Alba describes the ritual in detail. It's the . . . the . . ." She made a vague movement with her hand. "The union of the Lord and the Lady." She gave him an expectant look.

Fox blinked. "Who?"

"Oh, dear." She sighed. "I'm not explaining this properly." And, prodding her husband: "Tell him."

"Well . . ." Bourne gave every appearance of a man who

felt extremely uncomfortable in his skin. "In that ritual Amy performed, she became the Lady of the Land—in a manner of speaking, that is. Now, we believe the land might be healed if she had a companion."

"You," Colin cut in, looking at Fox.

Richard leaned forward. "I don't understand. How?"

"You mentioned Beltane and midsummer earlier on," the dowager countess chimed in. Her brows rose. "Surely you don't mean . . . ?"

Bourne gave her a small, apologetic smile. "I'm afraid we do."

"By intercourse?" Her brows rose even higher. "Heavens."

A strangled sound came from the direction where the admiral sat. "I *say*!"

"What?" A strange ringing filled Fox's ears. Surely he couldn't have heard right. Wildly, he looked from his mother to the Bournes.

"You have to become the Stag King," Mrs. Bourne said softly.

Nodding, her husband reached for her hand. "The Horned God."

"On midwinter night," his eldest added.

Dumbfounded, Fox sank back in his seat. Good gracious! They had all taken leave of their senses.

In the end, though, there was little Fox wouldn't try in order to help Amy. And so he sat down with Bourne and his wife and let them explain it to him again and again: what he would have to do, to say, how the heck he supposed to become—what?—the Stag King. "Do I have to wear antlers?" he asked suspiciously. He imagined himself clad in furs, the head of a stag balancing on his head as if he were one of the primitive people who had lived in these regions thousands of years ago. Heavens, that would be as bad as taking part in a mummers' play!

"No, no." Leaning forward, Mrs. Bourne reached for his hands and gripped them tightly. "But you'll have to *believe* you are."

"So it's all make-believe?"

She smiled a little. "*Belief*. A lot of it depends on believing. In here." With two fingers she tapped against his temple, then laid them on his heart. "And in here."

He might have been able to do this as a boy, when he had still believed in humming stones, but now? And yet the life of the woman he loved depended on his taking part in some pagan, magical ritual. The mere thought was sufficient to make him break into cold sweat.

"Amy will also be there to help you," Bourne added.

"But she's weakened." Fox frowned. "Surely she can't—"

Bourne shook his head. "The stones will amplify her power"—he raised his brow—"if you manage to waken them. And remember, the . . . well, intercourse will be unlike any other you've known before. It will be ritual."

And that is supposed to mean what? Fox wondered darkly. Really, it all sounded most fantastical, and it was still difficult for him to take in.

"But still, you will be careful, won't you?" A worried note had entered Mrs. Bourne's voice. "Considering that it will be Amy's first—"

Fox couldn't help himself: He blushed. The tips of his ears positively burned.

Taken aback, Mrs. Bourne looked him up and down. "Oh," she said. "I *see*." Her eyes narrowed dangerously. "You are a veritable rascal, young man. You would have deserted her, even though you already had—"

"Yes. I know," Fox said, deeply ashamed of himself.

She sniffed. "Well, then—"

Her husband cut in, his tone deceptively mild, "You'd better see to it that you do right by her this time." He arched his brow.

"Of course." Fox did not avert his eyes from Bourne's,

even though the man probably thought about throwing a ball of blue fire at Fox, or worse.

Oh yes, he planned to do right by Amy this time.

He'd become the deuced Stag King.

Chapter Twenty-one

December 21 dawned bright and clear. Fox sat on the bed beside Amy, her head bedded on his thigh while she slept, and watched how the sky turned from darkest gray to brilliant blue. Somewhere out in the park, a robin heralded the new day.

How fitting, Fox thought. *Today the Holly King must die and make way for King Robin.* He grimaced. What a relief that the Bournes had not gone with young Flann's idea of a royal sacrifice, with Fox standing in for the Holly King. Though . . .

He looked down to where Amy's cheek, no longer plump and rounded, rested against his thigh. With the back of his finger, he gently stroked her pale skin. A wave of tenderness clenched his heart and he leaned down to press a kiss against her forehead. If it truly had been the only way, he would have played the Holly King, too.

He drew a hand through her hair, which had lost all its former luster. Amy made a small sound and turned her head a little.

"Fox?" she murmured, her eyes still tightly closed.

"Shh, I'm here, sweetheart." He slung an arm around her shoulder. "Go back to sleep." He petted her head, her shoulder, then leaned down and nestled his nose against her temple. "Sleep," he whispered.

Later in the morning he rode to the stone circle together

with Bourne and his two eldest sons. They cleaned the inner round of snow, and Bourne marked the four cardinal points with fat, sturdy candles, which he placed inside terra-cotta pots. Afterwards they stuck seven torches into the snow at the outside of the stones.

"So," Bourne said, "we're finished here. Colin and Devlin will return with blankets and furs later on."

Fox nodded.

"And now . . ." Bourne blew onto his hands. "Now we only have to tell Amy."

"She won't like it," Colin predicted.

She didn't.

"It's preposterous," Amy whispered agitatedly. She looked at her aunt.

"It might be the only way to heal both you and the land," Mrs. Bourne said gently.

Amy sniffed. "Preposterous!" Slowly, and with such great effort Fox could have wept for her, she turned her head to glare at her uncle. "It is not the right time of the year!"

"What do you propose? To wait until midsummer?" Bourne shook his head. "No, my dear, we have to do it now before your condition worsens once more."

Two spots of red appeared on her cheeks, and she continued to glare at him. "What about the dangers?" she croaked.

"Dangers?"

"To *him*." She flicked her eyes to Fox. "It's too dangerous!"

After what she had done for him and his family? Fox inhaled sharply.

"He knows of the dangers," Bourne said, his voice even.

"No." Amy's jaw clenched. "I won't have . . . anything . . . to do with it."

"Yes. Yes, you will." With two long steps, Fox was at her side. He raised a knee onto the bed and leaned down to press the side of his head against hers. "You *will*," he said fiercely, his mouth against her ear. "It's your only chance, love. And I couldn't bear . . ." He swallowed hard. "I couldn't bear to lose you," he added hoarsely. He raised his head to look at her and didn't bother to hide the tears in his eyes. "You must."

Her eyes flashed, and for a moment, she looked like the old Amy. "No. It's too dangerous."

He gave her a crooked smile. "After what you have already done? Surely not!" He rested his forehead against hers. "Please," he whispered. "Say yes. Let me do this for you."

She searched his face. No doubt they both thought of that famous lecture of his on common sense, rational thought and whatnot.

"Are you sure?" she asked softly.

"I have never been surer of anything in my life."

For a moment longer she resisted, but then her eyes softened. Slowly, very slowly, she lifted her arm and laid a trembling hand against his cheek.

"All right."

The rest of the day dragged on; hours became small eternities. Once more Fox sat on the bed next to Amy and watched her sleeping. His fingers drummed against his thigh. Tonight was the night that would decide her fate. Tonight was the night.

With a silent oath he reached for the book on the nightstand. Better to lose himself in the adventures of the seven knights from Mayence than to crack up from tension.

He read on when a maid came to light more candles, and he still read when Mirabella knocked to ask whether he would like tray to be brought up with his dinner. But Fox shook his head. Dinner! Gracious, he wouldn't have been able to eat anything right now!

And so he read on, and forced his wary mind to concentrate on *The Horrible Histories of the Rhine*, read on and on until the letters seemed to dance in front of his eyes. He read how the seven knights killed the seven dastardly giants, how valiant Catrina, formerly known as Kassian, rode to a necromancer's castle to save the beautiful Maid Gellna from a horrible fate.

The valiant knightess, when her enemy came unto her, struck him so terrible a blow upon the visor of his helmet, that with the fury thereof she made sparkles of fire to issue out with great abundance, and forced him to bow his head unto his breast. The necromancer returned her his salutation, and struck her such a blow upon the helmet that—

"Sebastian?"

Fox looked up.

His brother stood in the door. "It is time," Richard said.

Fox glanced at the window—the light of the candles reflected in the glass, and beyond stretched a sea of darkness. The longest night of the year had well begun.

Fox put the book aside and stood. He cast a last lingering look down at Amy, rubbed his thumb across her pale cheek, before he took a deep breath and strode out of the room. Mrs. Bourne and Mirabella waited in the hallway and, after he had stepped through the door, entered the room to prepare Amy. Richard meanwhile took him to his rooms to keep him company while he changed clothes. Hobbes had already laid out a selection of warm woolly garments and now agitatedly flitted around Fox. When he was finally finished, he stood back and looked Fox up and down. "Well," he croaked, "I b-believe that w-will do, thur."

"Thank you, Hobbes," Fox murmured.

The old man eyed him worriedly. "Thtay thafe, thur."

There were, Fox noticed with numb surprise, tears welling up in the old chap's eyes. "I will."

"G-good luck, thur."

Fox gave him a last nod before he left the room to go downstairs with Richard. On the stairs, however, Fox abruptly stopped and turned to his brother. "I have never asked you: Do you mind?"

Richard's brows puckered. "Mind what?" he asked in perplexed tones.

Feeling his face grow warm, Fox shrugged and looked away. "Mind that I will now belong to Rawdon Park." When his statement was met with total silence, he eventually returned his gaze to his brother. Richard stared at him as if he had suddenly sprouted a second head.

"What exactly are you talking about, Sebastian?" The earl made a sharp movement with his hand. "Why should I mind this? You have always belonged to Rawdon Park."

His mind suddenly empty, Fox could only ogle his brother.

As realization dawned, Richard's expression shifted to anger. "Oh Lord! It's father. Don't tell me you listened to all that bosh." His fingers closed around Fox's shoulders like a vise. "How could you? Is this why—?" He broke off and shook his head.

"He always made it clear I was the unwanted bastard," Fox said, still in a daze.

Letting go of his shoulders, Richard sank down on the stairs and rubbed his hands over his face. "Heavens." When he looked up again, his features were curiously haggard and he seemed to have aged ten years. "I will only say this once, so you better listen carefully. If anybody was a bastard, it was the old earl." He snorted. "Do you remember that dog I had when I was a boy of twelve? He made me drown her puppies."

"But . . . but . . ." Fox spluttered. "You love the land just like he did. He always took you on tours around the estate."

Richard gave him the strangest look. "I love the land, yes. But if I had had a choice—I would have preferred to explore it with my younger brother."

"Oh." His knees weak, Fox sank down on the stairs next to him. "Do you know that when I was a small boy I could hear the stones in that circle?" he said somewhat incoherently.

His brother grunted.

"I could actually *hear* them," Fox repeated dreamily. "When I told father, he called me a heathenish brat and thrashed me within an inch of my life. And now I can hear them no longer." He turned to Richard. "I am not sure whether I can awaken the stones tonight, whether I can play my part in that . . . ritual. What shall I do when I can't do it, when the stones remain dead?" He shuddered.

Richard exhaled in a long sigh. Reaching out, he grabbed the back of Fox's neck and bumped their foreheads together. "Sebastian Stapleton, I will not stand you talking such fudge," he said hoarsely. With a strangled laugh, he pulled them both to their feet. "After we have survived being attacked by different charms and spells, not to speak of Margaret's wizard, and after we have witnessed the killing of a magical plant . . . an old pagan ritual should be a piece of cake, don't you think?"

Fox managed a feeble smile. Without the tremor in his voice, Richard might have almost been convincing. Yet his brother was far from certain about the outcome of this night. *It can't be helped*, Fox thought. *I have to see it through.* "I—"

Richard gave him a small push. "Of course you will manage. I won't accept anything else." Fox heard him swallow. "I won't stand to lose you, you know. And now go. *Go.*"

Together they walked down into the entrance hall, where, their family as well as Amy's had assembled to take their leave of the couple. Fox endured it all silently. Despite Richard's assurances, he felt unworthy, inadequate to perform the magic that they needed. If it went wrong tonight, he could kill them both. Heavens, he should have let them sacrifice him as the Holly King after all! A strange numbness of the senses stole over him. He felt like an automaton, going through the motions yet not being fully there.

The dowager countess was the last in line. She kissed his cheek and whispered, "Remember, my dear: have a little faith." With an encouraging smile she sent him outside.

Fox swung himself up into the saddle of his horse. To his left and right Richard and Bourne did the same. Footmen stepped up to them and gave them torches, while Colin Bourne approached Fox's horse. He carried Amy, who was only semiconscious and was all bundled up in a blanket. Fox took her from him and, wrapping an arm around her, settled her securely in front of him. And then they were on their way into the darkness.

The snow reflected the flickering light of the torches, so it seemed they were traveling within a golden halo.

A curious feeling befell Fox as he rode in silence along the indistinguishable lanes and pathways: The night and the snow made all signs of civilization vanish, and if they should by chance step through a ripple in time back a thousand years, surely they would never notice. Had the priests of old felt like this? The Celtic druids—had they followed the same paths as these horses did now? If they had, they had surely never experienced such insecurity as he did.

Fox's breath formed white clouds in front of his face. In his arms, Amy stirred.

He pressed her a little tighter against his body and kissed her temple. If this were all true, if an old power were still running through this land, if Amy knew how to awaken it—would it be enough? What if he failed in his part? And what if he didn't—He would have to allow the magic to take control of him, do with him whatever it wanted. A sliver of ice ran down his spine.

A short while later, they reached the hill where the standing stones rose black against the sky. Richard and Bourne slid to the ground and lit the torches along the outside of the stones. The fire lent the ancient rock a soft, reddish tint, made the shadows in the inner circle lengthen and tremble until it resembled a darkened cave.

The womb of the Earth Mother, Fox thought, and shivered.

Bourne doused his torch in the snow, then came forward to take Amy so Fox could finally dismount. The crunching sound of the snow under his boots seemed unnaturally loud. Fox drew a steadying breath and became aware that Richard was watching him closely and with worry.

Fox cleared his throat. "It is all right. We will . . . manage." But would they? Would they really? Would he?

He drew in another deep breath.

Richard nodded. His lips lifted a little. "Good luck." With his free arm, he drew Fox into a tight embrace. "Good luck, little brother," he murmured against Fox's ear, his voice hoarse.

"It is time," Bourne said.

A shudder tore through Richard's frame, made the breath catch in his throat with the strangest sound—a sob? "Good luck," he said again, then stepped back to make a place for Amy's uncle.

Bourne pressed a kiss onto Amy's forehead. "Be blessed, my child," he whispered. Strain had etched deep lines in his face, but his voice as he addressed Fox was steady. "I entrust her into your care." He passed the precious bundle in his arms to Fox. And after a moment of hesitation, "The Goddess keep you both safe."

Fox inclined his head. A month ago he would have considered this blasphemy, but not now. For this was the night of the old powers, of the old gods. Perhaps they had truly slipped through the web of time into the pagan past of this country, when Christianity still belonged to a distant future, when the Lady of the Light ruled the land with the Stag King as her consort and beloved. He certainly hoped so. It would make his task so much easier.

Richard passed his torch to Bourne before the two men mounted their horses, so he had one hand free to reach for the reins of Fox's horse and lead it away with them. For long moments Fox looked after them, watching how that flickering globe of light became smaller and smaller.

"Fox?"

He looked down. Heavy-lidded pansy blue eyes blinked up at him.

"Are we—?"

"We are at the stones," he said.

She regarded him solemnly. "Are you sure this is what you want?" she whispered.

"I am sure."

She bit her lip. "Even though it's . . . dangerous? And can never be reversed?"

"Hush." He leaned down to brush her mouth with his. "We will be in this together," he murmured against her lips. "I am very sure."

Her eyes fell close. "So be it."

"Yes. *Yes*." Gripping her a little bit higher against his chest, he straightened. "So be it."

For a moment he closed his eyes to breathe deeply and let the cold winter air flow through him. With each breath, the tension inside him ebbed away, and as he opened his eyes once more, a strange calmness had settled on him.

And so it begins . . .

With measured steps he walked toward the stones and then stepped through the circle of light into the darkness within. It was not bleak or utterly black, but a shifting, living thing, created from shadows and flickers of light.

As his eyes adjusted to the dimness, Fox could discern the thick bed of furs and blankets that had been prepared for them—and the four pots with candles at the cardinal points that waited to be lit.

Once more panic gripped him, chased all the confidence away. "The candles! We've got nothing to light the candles!"

"Hush." Cold, trembling fingers found his mouth. "Hush," Amy repeated weakly. "Put me down on the blankets. Don't worry about the candles."

"But—"

"Hush. My head has to face east."

Trembling and shivering, he put her down as she directed. Why, oh why had he not thought of the candles? He should have brought a tinder box, should have . . .

"Hush," she murmured again, as if she could hear his

thoughts. Her fingers stroked from his mouth down to his chin, and further down his throat. He reached up to undo the scarf he was wearing, so that her fingers could trail unhindered over his skin, all the way to the hollow of his throat, where she pressed a little until his blood pulsed against the tips of her fingers.

"Close your eyes," she murmured. "Imagine the circle of light that surrounds us, closes us in. A perfect, unbroken circle of light."

His brows furrowed a little, but it was an easy thing to do, what with the round of torches complementing the circle of stones. He could easily imagine the flames of the torches fusing together until they formed a golden red band.

"Perfect and unbroken," he whispered.

"Yes." There was a smile in her voice. "Now go and invoke the powers of the East."

That he could do, too. The Bournes had told him all about this, had made him memorize the words. He opened his eyes, rose and walked past Amy to the outer boundary of their circle.

"You powers of the East . . ." Awkwardly he cleared his throat. No, this didn't feel right. He turned. "Amy?"

"Do it joyfully." Her whisper came out of the dimness. "Imagine . . . the lark that rises over the fields . . . in the morning. This is where . . . everything begins. . . ." Her voice trailed away.

Joyfully? Fox grimaced. How was he supposed to be joyful?

Imagine the lark . . .

He closed his eyes, breathed deeply. And from the deepest recesses of his mind sprang a memory: how he and Richard had stolen outside one morning in spring when they had been hardly older than his nephews were now. Frost had covered the ground, had crunched underneath their boots as they trotted through the gardens and the park all the way to the outer wall, where they slipped through a small door. Richard had reached for his hand and had urged him to walk faster until they had reached the wide field. There they had waited, had watched the sky turn from gray to pink, had listened to nature awakening all around them—the hustling and bustling of small animals, the still feeble chirps of birds. And then the sun had risen over the horizon, a fiery ball, and had filled their boyish hearts with elation. And beside them a lark had risen high into the sky and had sung, brilliantly, joyfully, and Fox had felt as if he could fly himself. Laughing, he had flung his arms around his brother . . .

A laugh bubbled up in his throat. Fox flung his arms wide. "Hail thee, you powers of the East!" His voice was strong and sure, was reflected and increased in intensity by the stones around them. "Hail to the winds, the small breezes, and the birds that ride them weightlessly! Hail thee, Aurora, Goddess of the Morning, of rebirth and all beginnings. Be with us tonight!"

"*Yes,*" Amy whispered behind him. He felt a small push between his shoulder blades, and when he looked down, a flame grew at the wick of the candle. It had worked! Oh, thank goodness, it was working!

"And now on to the South," Amy murmured, and with wonder in his heart, he stepped to the next terra-cotta pot.

"Hail thee, you powers of the South, where fire burns hotly. Hail to Vesta, Goddess Guardian of the Fire. Guard us tonight."

Again he felt Amy's power like a push against his back, and the next moment a flame rose from the candle at his feet.

"And to the West."

Another few steps. His skin started to prickle. "Hail thee, you powers of the West. Hail to the waters, the rivers and the oceans, which bring forth new life. Hail to Aphrodite! Let us swim in your waters tonight in order to be reborn."

The candle flamed.

"And to the North." Amy's voice was almost inaudible.

Three more steps. "Hail thee, you powers of the North. Hail thee, Goddess of the Earth, great Demeter! Guard us in your womb tonight!"

He braced himself for the push. It seemed feebler this time, but still the candle was lit.

"And now . . . back to the East . . . to complete the circle," Amy breathed.

And thus he went to where he had started.

"Seal it . . . seal it with a kiss."

Closing his eyes, he leaned forward, pressed his mouth against the rock. Cool and smooth it touched his lips—the kiss of the Earth Goddess, the Lady of the Land.

Slowly, he turned. Amy lay spread before him in a web of light and shadow. Her skin was as white as the snow itself. As white as marble, as the blossoms of lily of the valley. For a moment, fear for her closed his throat. But this was not the time for fear.

Have a little faith. He heard the voice of his mother in his mind.

He stepped around Amy until he stood at her feet. Her eyes had been closed, but now she opened them, two dark, shimmering pools in her pale face. She watched him as he slipped out of his coat, his jacket, his waistcoat. Watched him as he pulled the shirttails out of his trousers, opened the fastenings at his throat and wrists, and pulled the shirt over his head. The coldness bit at his skin, but he hardly noticed, for he only had eyes for Amy. The Lady of the Land.

The discarded shirt fluttered down onto the pile of clothes behind him. He bent and retrieved a small jackknife from the pocket of his coat. He let it spring open. Keeping his gaze trained on Amy, he raised the knife and drew the blade along his thumb. The skin slid open, blood welled up.

Imagine . . .

Blood to blood.

Very slowly, he drew his bloody thumb across his forehead.

Look, the Stag King is here.

He walked toward Amy, his steps in time with the heavy beating of his heart. Right before her he bent down, sank to his knees, straddled her. "My lady," he whispered. "Your consort has arrived."

"Yes," she breathed. With visible effort she took the knife from him and cut into her own thumb. Her arm trembled as she lifted it toward Fox's face. He leaned down.

With a touch as light as a feather, she drew her thumb across his forehead, mixing her blood with his. Warmth seeped from her finger and flowed through him. With a heavy sigh, she let her arm fall to her side. Her eyes closed.

Fox swallowed hard. She was so weak. How was he supposed to . . . ? Dear God, he couldn't. Surely, he couldn't!

Her lips moved. "Kiss . . . me . . ."

Taking a deep breath, he leaned forward, braced his weight on his hands next to her head, and touched his lips to hers. They were cold. As cold as the stone he had kissed. A sob caught in his throat.

Desperately he opened his mouth over hers and, once started, he couldn't seem to stop. He gave her feverish, fervent kisses, felt his passion for her rise in him. *My love, my love, my love.*

"Yes," Amy whispered.

He drew back.

Her eyes were still closed, but the ghost of a smile played around her lips. "Look . . . look at the stones."

He looked—and the breath caught in his throat. He stared, slack jawed.

The stones glowed. They did not only reflect the firelight, they glowed from within.

"Undress . . . me," Amy said softly.

His gaze snapped back to her face. "But the cold—"

Her smile deepened. "Don't you . . . feel it?" Her eyes opened: deepest blue, as deep as the ocean. As deep as the sky. Deep enough to drown in forever. "Feel it . . ." They drifted shut again.

And only then did he become aware that the air inside

the circle had warmed. It hummed with faint, deep vibrations.

"Undress me. . . . Undress . . . the Lady of the Land."

Fox looked down at her. She seemed so delicate, so horribly frail.

Have faith in your love.

He sank back on his haunches and, with hands that shook, drew aside the blankets that were wrapped around her to unbutton her long gray coat. Underneath, she wore a white dress.

The virgin sacrifice.

Yet she was no longer a virgin, as he should well know.

Gently he turned her around so he could undo the lacings of her dress and stays. He rolled her onto her back and with infinite care removed her boots, dress, petticoats, and stays until she lay before him clad only in a thin chemise.

He bent to capture her mouth with his and kissed her deeply, while his hands stroked over her body, reacquainting themselves with her flesh. The tips of his fingers tingled. How he had missed her.

He drew his mouth over her soft cheek, down the vulnerable line of her throat, and kissed the curve of her shoulder. Deeply, he inhaled her scent. It was different than before, had been affected by the weeks of illness, yet he would still have recognized it as hers among a thousand others.

His hand cupped one of her breasts, and his lips closed over the tip. He remembered this, too. Oh, how he remembered.

The memory of what they had shared cramped his stomach and made him groan. Sweat beaded on his forehead as he suckled her nipple, felt it harden against his tongue.

The softest whimper. A small hand coming to rest on his head, trembling like a small bird. Fox looked up. Her throat was stretched taut, her lips slightly opened.

"Mmmm."

He caressed her throat with a long lick, then kissed her

briefly before he focused his attention on her other breast. He fondled and suckled it until the nipple, now as hard as its twin, pressed against the wet material of her chemise.

He sat back. In a long, sweeping caress he drew his hands from her breasts to her waist and rested them on her stomach.

Amy sighed. A rosy hue had appeared on her pale cheeks.

Slowly Fox stood and unfastened his trousers. He stepped out of them and kicked them away. For a moment he stood silent and gazed down at Amy.

Imagine . . .

You are the Stag King.

The line of blood they had drawn across his forehead pulsed faintly.

Imagine . . .

His back proudly straightened. His erection hardened, pulsed in time with the mark on his forehead. Could he really see the shimmering form of a stag just beyond the stones? *Believe it.*

The humming around him increased.

He lowered himself over Amy. "Look, beloved, your consort is here, your champion and lover," he whispered into her ear. "He's here to serve you, to pay homage to the Lady of the Land."

His fingers fisted on the neckline of her chemise. The muscles in his arm bulged, and then he ripped the flimsy material apart.

A distant, civilized part in him was appalled at his actions. Never before had Sebastian Stapleton, suave, cool man about Town, ripped a lady's chemise. But the thought was fleeting, and was easily pushed away. He had never before lain naked in a circle of glowing stones, either. And never before had he felt so wild and powerful.

Skin rubbed over naked skin. Soft breasts pressed against his chest; his penis twitched against her belly. Fox groaned. "Are you ready to receive me, my lady?"

She was. He slipped between her thighs and inside her, easily, all the way until his hip met hers. He hissed with pleasure. Her eyes shot open; her fingers twined with his, clutched, while her body arched like a bow. Warmth flowed between them, a powerful stream from her body into his.

And the stones . . .

The stones shone like beacons in the night.

"Stay," Amy whispered when he would have moved. "Stay. You must send out the power."

"How—"

"Look."

The shimmering stag pranced beyond their circle of light.

Far away, that civilized part of him quaked with fright, protested against the evidence of his eyes. But—

Have a little faith in your love.

And the wildness inside him easily overran all fear and disbelief.

Amy sighed. "Send it out." Her eyes closed. Her hips moved against his. "Let me . . . ride on it."

Fox looked at the stag. It was beautiful and terrible, bigger than any stag he had ever seen. The antlers loomed wide and massive.

Go, he told it silently. *Run wherever she wishes you to go.* He shut his eyes, moved inside his beloved with long, measured strokes. *Go.*

"Yesss." Her breaths turned to little gasps. "Yes."

And even though his eyes were still closed, he could see the stag running, leaping across the night-darkened country. First to the north . . .

"Across the wash . . . into the wold . . . to the stones at the river . . ." Amy gasped.

Another beacon of light was lit far away from them.

The stag raced farther.

"On to the moors . . . to the long stone on the heath . . ."

A moan shuddered through her as another stone blazed up in the night. From there, she sent the stag south, to burrows and henges, and with each new light her movements became more frantic. She writhed against Fox, rotated her hips, threw her head from side to side.

Fox gritted his teeth. The breath rattled in his chest, but he somehow understood that his strokes must remain even, to anchor her and to drive the stag on. Sweat ran down his temple, slickened his body. Specks of light danced around them, flickered against his closed eyelids.

On and on the stag ran, all the way to the Salisbury Plain, the spiritual heart of Britannia. And then the great stones themselves blazed up the night with a mighty roar.

Amy's half-smothered shriek echoed from the stones, making Fox tremble with the effort to hold back. Her legs rose to grip his hips. The heels of her naked feet dug into his thighs. "Now, bring it home . . ." she cried. "Ohhhh!"

He opened his eyes to look down at her. Heavy-lidded pansy blue irises met his gaze. Shining with passion. Indeed, her whole body was radiant, glowing a healthy pink.

"Bring it home." Smiled and pushed against him. "Bring it home, beloved." She licked her lips.

And he did. On and on he drove their stag; faster and faster he pumped into her, slapped against the cradle of her hips. Her sighs and moans drove him wild. His muscles quivered with the strain to hold back.

. . . on and on . . .

He gasped.

. . . on and on . . .

Her nails bit into the back of his hands.

. . . on and on . . .

Fiery circles appeared in front of his eyes. He thought his heart would burst. Amy whimpered, shuddered, but not yet—no, not yet . . .

. . . on and on . . .

And then the stag was there, appeared out of the darkness like a gleaming meteor. Amy's triumphant laugh turned into a whimper. Her body shuddered, and his—dear God, his was in flames. Surely it was too much, too—

With a powerful leap, the stag jumped into their circle—and around them the world exploded into light.

Amy's high-pitched scream of delight mingled with Fox's roar as he reared back. Power pulsed up from her core, surged through his body. A stream of brilliant, pure light shot high into the sky at the same time as his seed pumped into her body.

... *on and on* ...

And then ...

Nothing.

Epilogue

Birdsong woke them, the sweet tones of a red-breasted robin, which eyed them curiously as they lay huddled among the furs and blankets in a tight tangle of arms and legs. Fox blinked, muttered an oath as a ray of sunlight pierced his eyes.

Beside him, Amy giggled. Sleepily she rubbed her nose against his cheek. "Good morning, grumpy." A puff of air grazed his flesh as she yawned.

His eyes shot open. His heart beating hard and fast, he turned his head to look at her. "Are you . . . ?"

Her sweet face crunched tight as she wrinkled her nose at him. "Fit as a fiddle." Her eyes twinkled. "And sore in places I didn't know existed!"

With a deep, relieved laugh, he hugged her to him and kissed the crown of her head. For a moment they lay quietly.

"I am sorry," he finally said, his voice fierce, his heart heavy. "I am sorry I was such a muttonhead and didn't understand."

For a heartbeat or two she was quiet. He listened to her breaths, which suddenly turned into a chuckle. "I think I might forgive you. You're the only man who has ever made snowdrops and crocuses bloom for me in December."

Frowning, he drew back a little so that he could look at her. "What?"

"Look around you, Fox." She trailed a hand over his cheek. Her lips curved. "Look what we wrought last night." She exerted gentle pressure until he turned his head.

What he saw made his eyes widen. "How—"

"Magic," she said with obvious and intense satisfaction. She stretched out an arm, wriggled her hand. "Oh yes, it's all back."

Around them the delicate green stems of snowdrops mingled with sturdy crocuses, white mixed with yellow, lilac, and blue.

Suddenly, she chuckled. "To imagine that the man who gave me a lecture on the importance of rational thought drove a ghost stag across the country—oh, it's too delicious!" She smothered her merriment against his chest.

Fox blinked. He took in a deep breath. Well, he supposed he'd better get used to it all, since it seemed he would be married to a modern-day witch after all. Grinning, he lay back and slipped an arm around her shoulder. "So tell me, now that I've joined with the Lady of the Land . . ."

She blushed a little.

He raised his brows. "You can't be *shy*?"

Fascinated, he watched her cheeks darken. "Can't I?" With a smile, she reached out to draw his head close.

Their kiss went on a bit longer than she might have planned, since he simply couldn't let her go so fast. The feeling of having her safe in his arms once more was just too delightful. He deepened the kiss until she moaned and shivered.

Grinning, he released her—and earned a thump onto his shoulder. "Cocky chap." Then she smiled and stroked his shoulder. "You were a magnificent Stag King." She tugged at a lock of his hair. "Despite being such a cocky fellow."

He inclined his head. "I am glad to hear it. I aim to serve my lady." He kissed her hand. "Now tell me: Since we're now joined with this land, I suppose we should stay close to it, should we not? I know a small, snug house nearby where we could settle down."

Her eyes widened. "You, the slick man about Town? Settle down in the country?"

"Oh yes." He blinked up at the sky, which arched wide and blue above them. It had almost the same color as Amy's eyes. Indeed, upon closer inspection, it turned out to be a rather nice sky. He supposed he could get used to the Fenland fog as well. He might just spent foggy days in bed with his wife. Now, there was a cheerful prospect if he'd ever heard one! He was already looking forward to foggy days.

"A small house?" Amy prodded. "With a cat? And dogs?"

He grimaced. "If you like."

She laughed. "And a child or two?"

A child . . . ? *Their* child. Suddenly choked up, he leaned his forehead against hers. "Or three or four?" he asked softly.

"Cocky, redheaded girls with fierce temperaments?" she whispered.

"Small boys with golden curls and magic inside them." His hand stroked over her hip.

"Little boys with golden curls?" She resolved into giggles. "Oh no! Their cousins will tease the poor mites to no end!"

Fox shrugged. "They can always turn them into frogs."

She kissed him. "You learn fast." The sentence ended on a gasp as his hand closed around her breast.

"I move fast, too." He grinned and stroke his thumb over her nipple. And for the next few moments neither of them spoke while they made love among the snowdrops and crocuses to the song of the robin.

Afterwards they dressed, whispering and chuckling. It amused her to no end when he stared at her ripped chemise in dismay. He took his revenge by slowly kissing his way up her back while he laced her stays and dress, and all her wriggling and moaning did not help her. By the time they were both dressed and bundled up in their coats, they were grinning like a pair of fools.

Fox bent to pick a purple crocus, which he tucked behind

her ear. "Shall we go?" He held out his hand, watched her eyes widen.

"On foot?"

"Well . . . somehow we forgot to talk about this part of the plan."

Another laugh gurgled in her throat—a sound he would never grow tired of hearing. She took his hand. "Then by all means, let's go—and hope somebody remembers about us."

They stepped through the circle of stones. For a moment, Fox stopped. He touched one of the stones, then leaned in to press a kiss onto the cool rock. *Thank you. Thank you for bringing her back to me.*

He remembered how he had stood here as a small boy, awed by the power of the stones. For a little while he had lost the belief in miracles and wonders, but thanks to Amy he had found it again.

With a smile he turned back to her and led her down the hill. "I am sure somebody will remember about us. Did you know your whole family is here? We will all celebrate Christmas together, I suppose."

"Ah." She wrigg led her nose. "So when will I have time to finally finish those *Horrible Histories of the Rhine*? I really want to know what happens to Markander after Martinus has slayed that horrible Green Man."

"Well . . ." He twined his fingers with hers. "They go to wise Ulrika, of course. And she gives a special cake to Gidonius. And when they drop a crumb of this cake into Markander's mouth, he wakes and—"

"They live happily ever after," Amy sighed just as happily.

"Er . . . no. I think they might all die in the end."

"Die?" She snorted.

"Those books always end with the death of the heroes. Just think of *The Seven Champions of Christendom*."

"Bah." Grumbling, she stomped on. "Stupid book!"

"But they might die in an interesting way," he offered. "Like . . . um . . ."

"A mountain drops onto them!" She laughed.

"Exactly."

"So let's find out."

"Yes. Let's."

And together they walked on into the reborn world, while behind them the robin heralded a new morn.

Phantom

Every night at midnight Dax could start to feel the change. The curse that made him less human as the Phantom inside struggled to take over, reminding him that he was never safe. Nor were the ones he loved.

As a girl, Robyn had pledged herself to him. But that was a lifetime ago. Now she was a woman. Beautiful. Pure. Every time she was near—her soft skin, her delicate scent—the Phantom wanted to claim her, to bring her body to the greatest heights of pleasure. Then steal her soul. Dax couldn't allow that to happen. Deep down, he knew her love could save him. If the Phantom didn't get her first.

Lindsay Randall

AVAILABLE JUNE 2008

ISBN 13: 978-0-505-52765-3

ENCHANTING THE LADY

In a world where magic ruled everything, Felicity Seymour couldn't perform even the simplest spell. If she didn't pass her testing, she'd lose her duchy—and any hope of marriage. But one man didn't seem to mind her lack of dowry: a darkly delicious baronet who had managed to scare away the rest of London's Society misses.

Sir Terence Blackwell knew the enchanting woman before him wasn't entirely without magic. Not only could she completely disarm him with her gorgeous lavender eyes and frank candor, but his were-lion senses could smell a dark power on her—the same kind of relic-magic that had killed his brother. Was she using it herself, or was it being used against her?

One needed a husband, and the other needed answers. But only together could they find the strongest magic of all: true

KATHRYNE KENNEDY

ISBN 13: 978-0-505-52750-9

CHRISTINE FEEHAN

Savannah Dubrinski was a mistress of illusion, a world-famous magician capable of mesmerizing millions. But there was one—Gregori, the Dark One—who held her in terrifying thrall. With a dark magic all his own, Gregori—the implacable hunter, the legendary healer, the most powerful of Carpathian males—whispered in Savannah's mind that he was her destiny. That she had been born to save his immortal soul. And now, here in New Orleans, the hour had finally come to claim her. To make her completely his. In a ritual as old as time . . . and as inescapable as eternity.

DARK MAGIC

ISBN 13: 978-0-8439-6056-3

To order a book or to request a catalog call:
1-800-481-9191
This book is also available at your local bookstore, or you can check out our Web site **www.dorchesterpub.com** where you can look up your favorite authors, read excerpts, or glance at our discussion forum to see what people have to say about your favorite books.